ACT TWO

Written by Aleš Kot
Drawn by Danijel Žeželj
Colored by Jordie Bellaire
Lettered by Aditya Bidikar
Design by Tom Muller
Production by Ryan Brewer

CHAPTER SEVEN:
GUTS

"But revolutions usually begin by terrorism."

—Kathy Acker, *Empire of the Senseless*

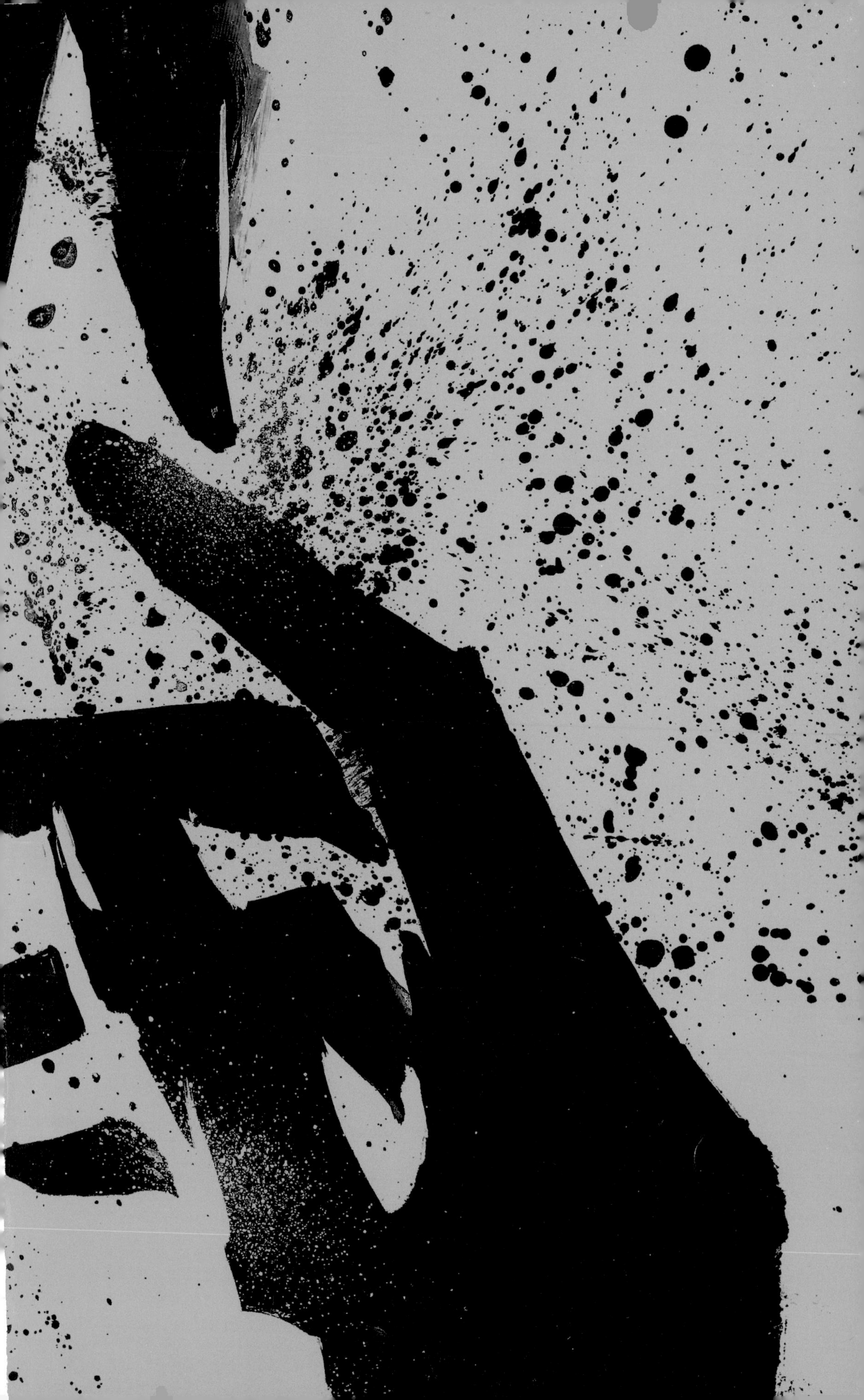

DAYS OF HATE

OF

HATE

Days of Hate, Act 2 — Originally published as Days of Hate #7–12

SEVEN
WEEKS
LATER.

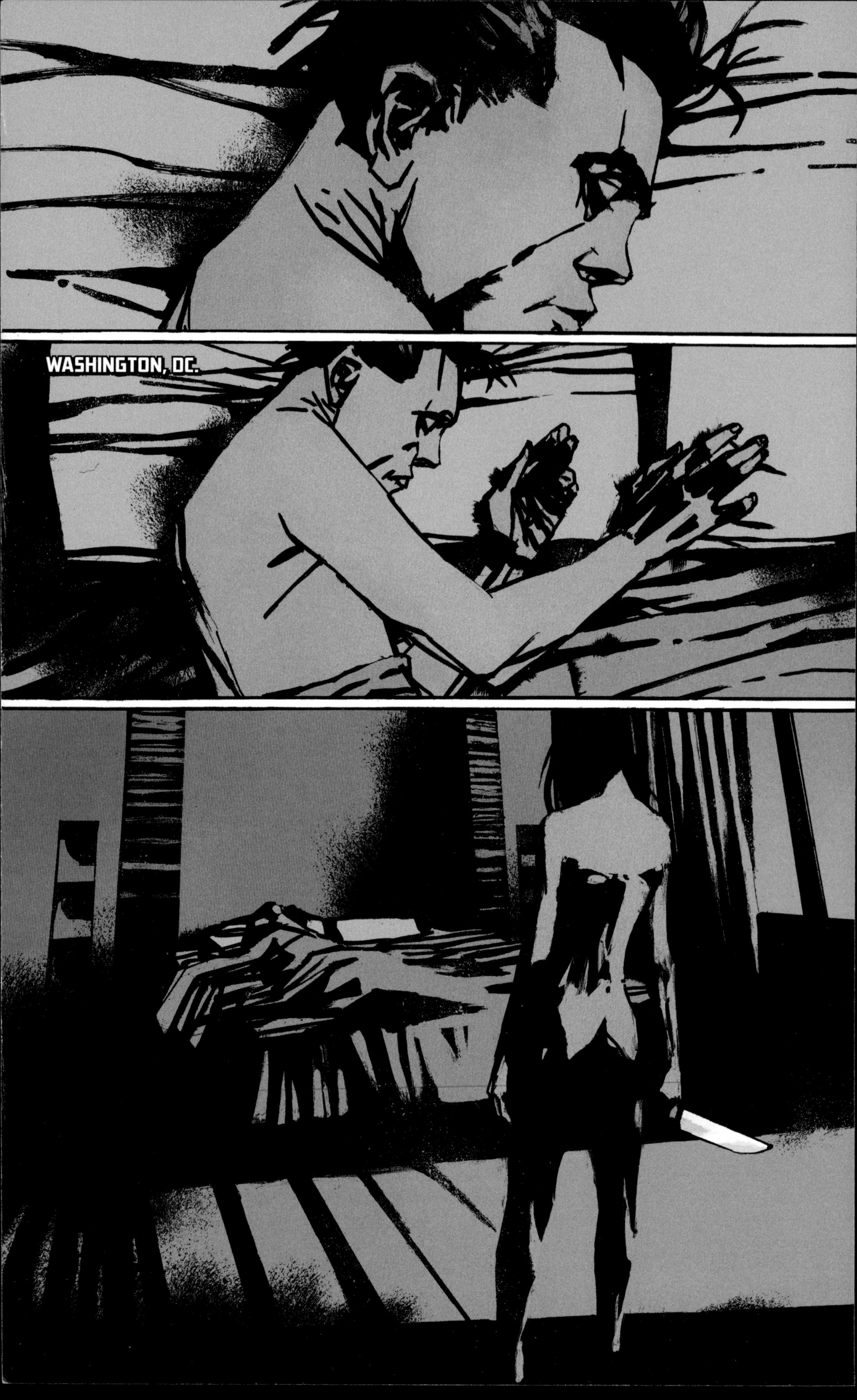
WASHINGTON, DC.

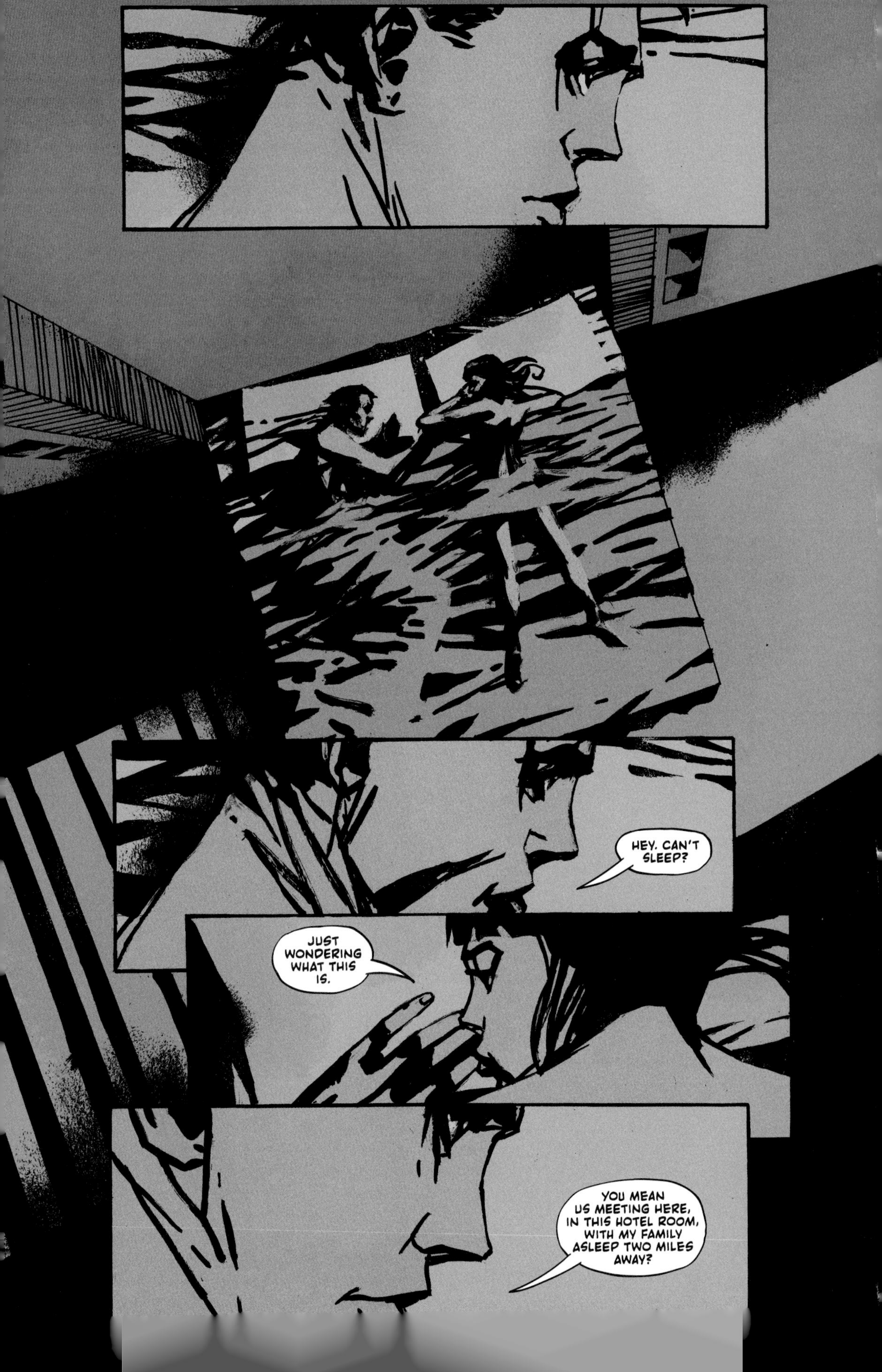
HEY. CAN'T SLEEP?
JUST WONDERING WHAT THIS IS.
YOU MEAN US MEETING HERE, IN THIS HOTEL ROOM, WITH MY FAMILY ASLEEP TWO MILES AWAY?

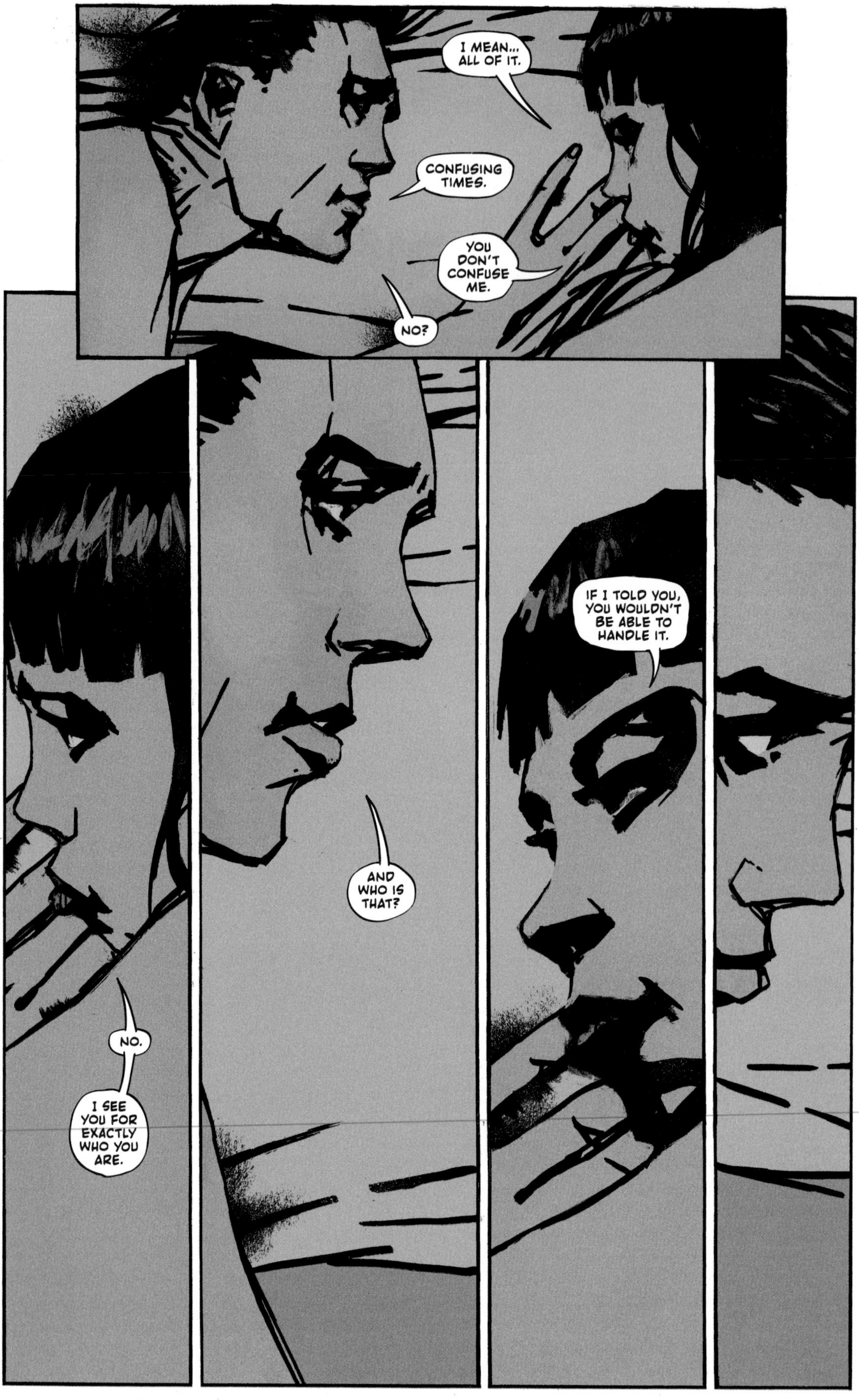
I MEAN... ALL OF IT.
CONFUSING TIMES.
YOU DON'T CONFUSE ME.
NO?
NO.
I SEE YOU FOR EXACTLY WHO YOU ARE.
AND WHO IS THAT?
IF I TOLD YOU, YOU WOULDN'T BE ABLE TO HANDLE IT.

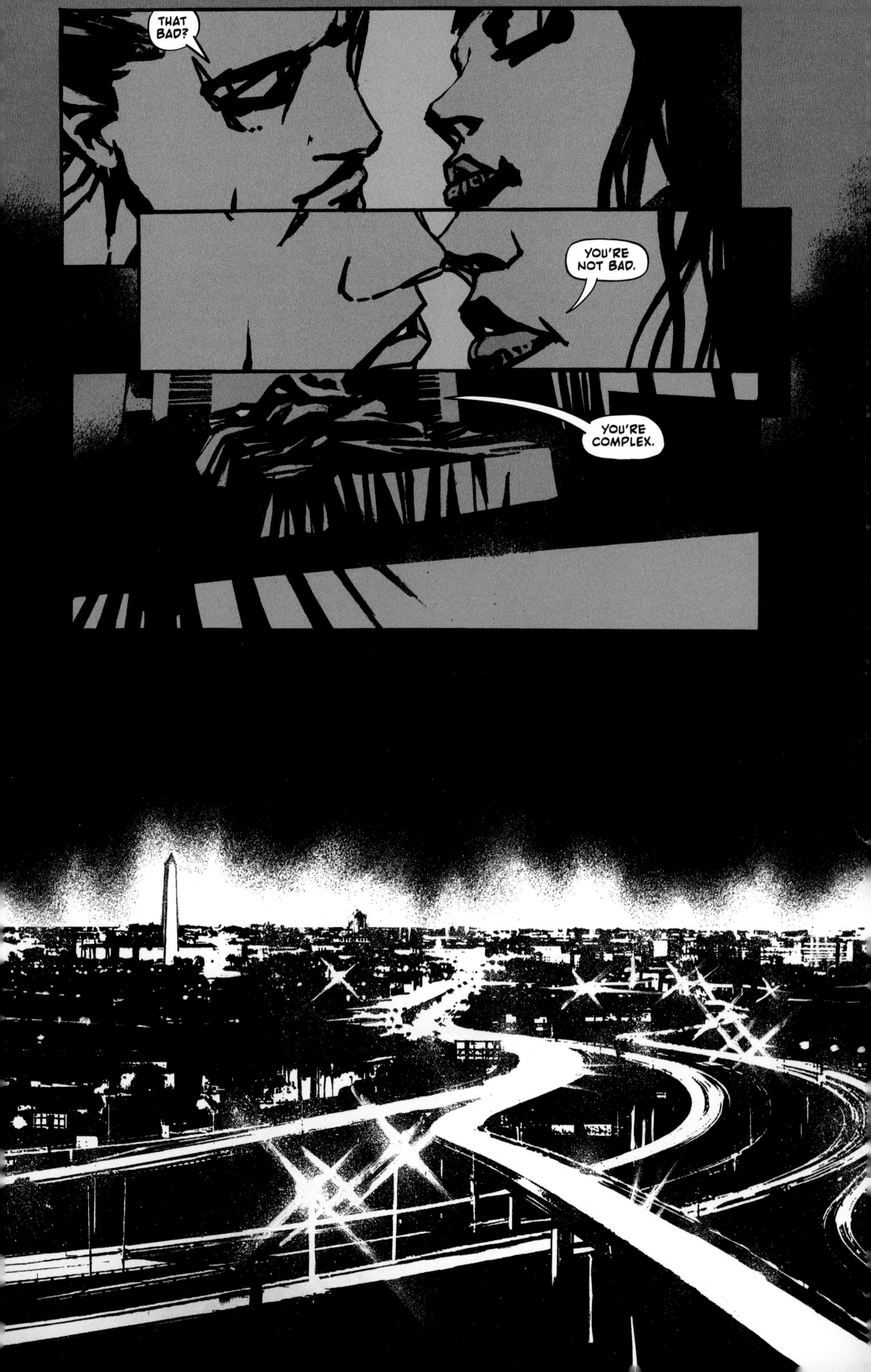
THAT BAD?
YOU'RE NOT BAD.
YOU'RE COMPLEX.

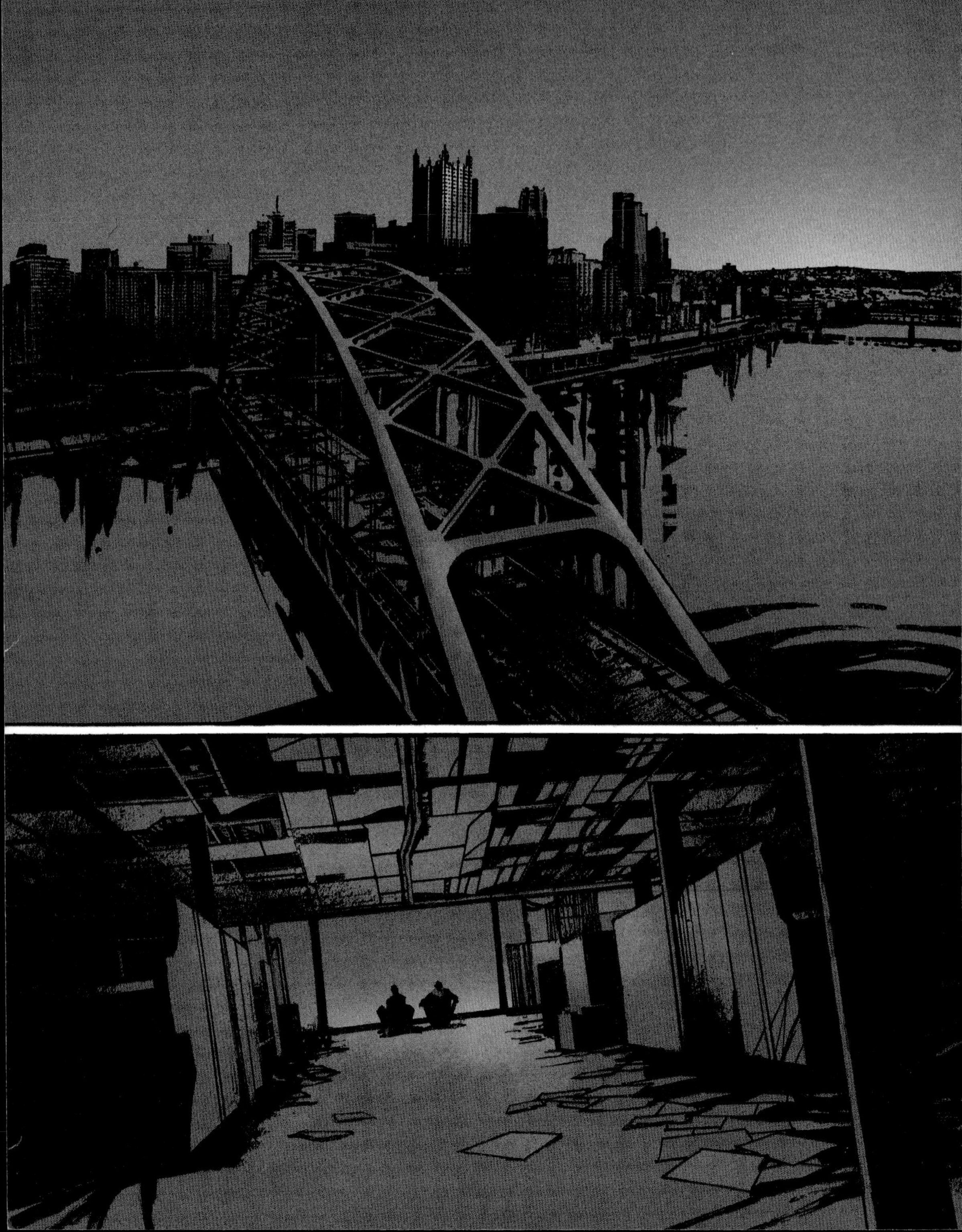

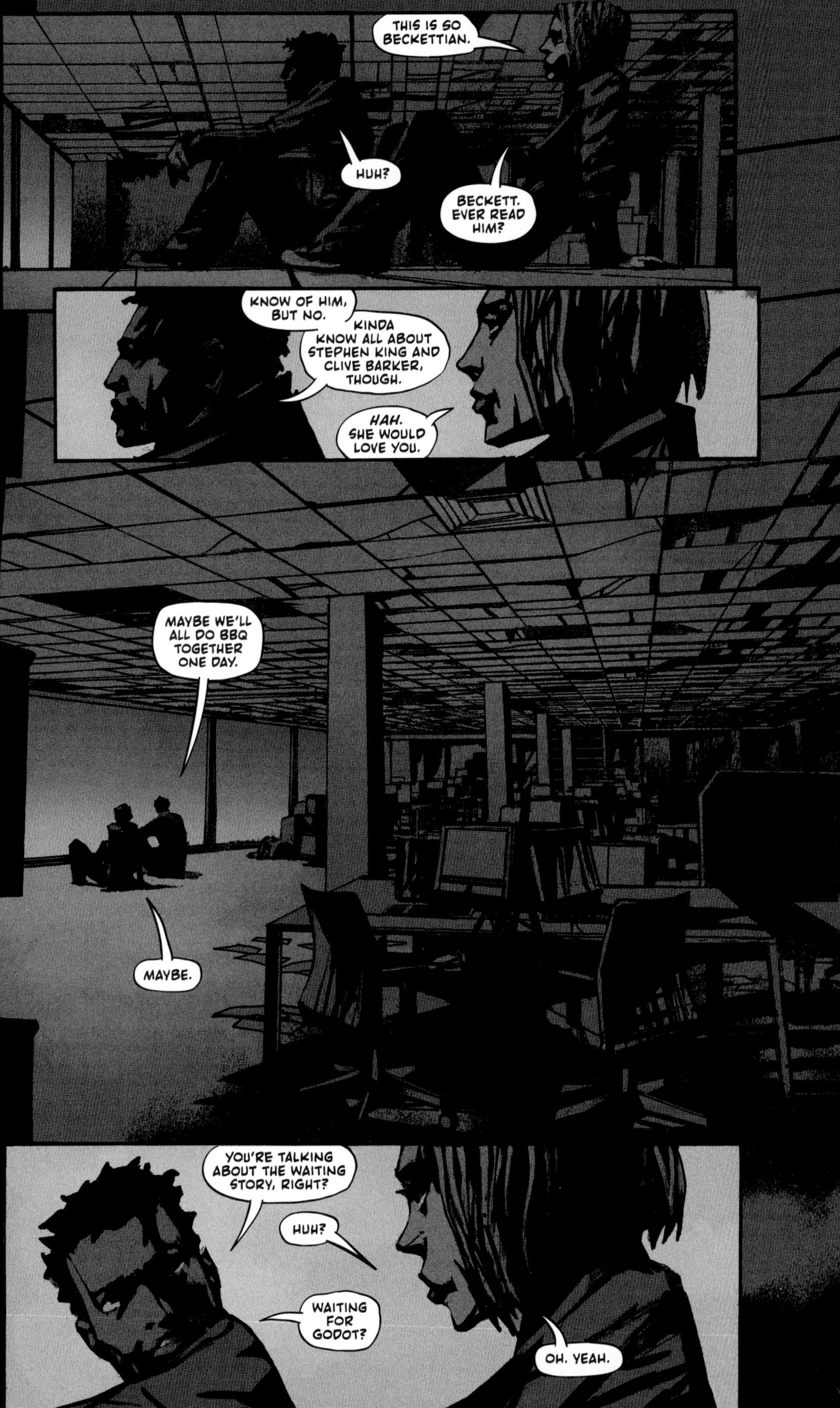
THIS IS SO BECKETTIAN.
HUH?
BECKETT. EVER READ HIM?
KNOW OF HIM, BUT NO.
KINDA KNOW ALL ABOUT STEPHEN KING AND CLIVE BARKER, THOUGH.
HAH. SHE WOULD LOVE YOU.
MAYBE WE'LL ALL DO BBQ TOGETHER ONE DAY.
MAYBE.
YOU'RE TALKING ABOUT THE WAITING STORY, RIGHT?
HUH?
WAITING FOR GODOT?
OH. YEAH.

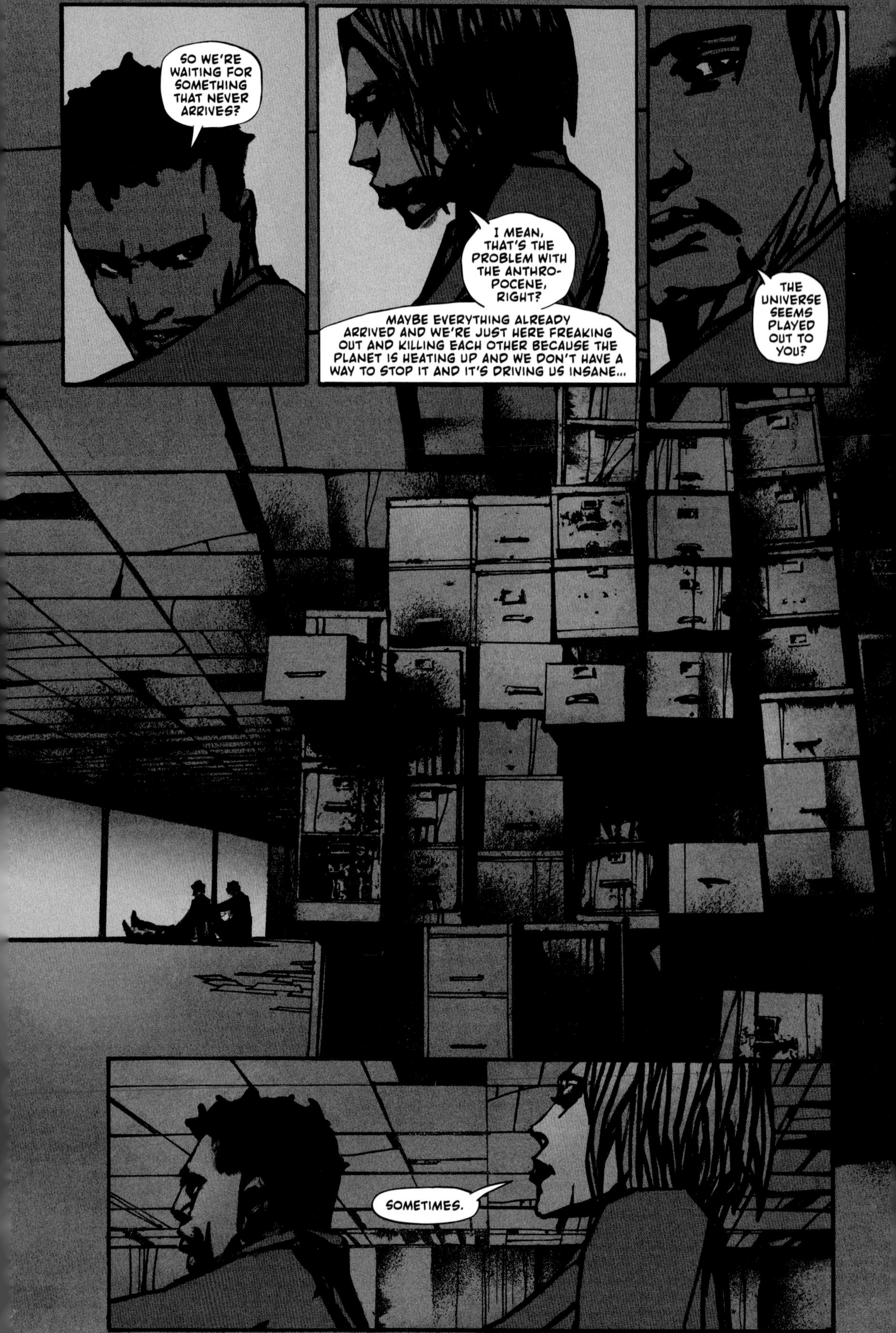
SO WE'RE WAITING FOR SOMETHING THAT NEVER ARRIVES?
I MEAN, THAT'S THE PROBLEM WITH THE ANTHRO-POCENE, RIGHT?
MAYBE EVERYTHING ALREADY ARRIVED AND WE'RE JUST HERE FREAKING OUT AND KILLING EACH OTHER BECAUSE THE PLANET IS HEATING UP AND WE DON'T HAVE A WAY TO STOP IT AND IT'S DRIVING US INSANE...
THE UNIVERSE SEEMS PLAYED OUT TO YOU?
SOMETIMES.

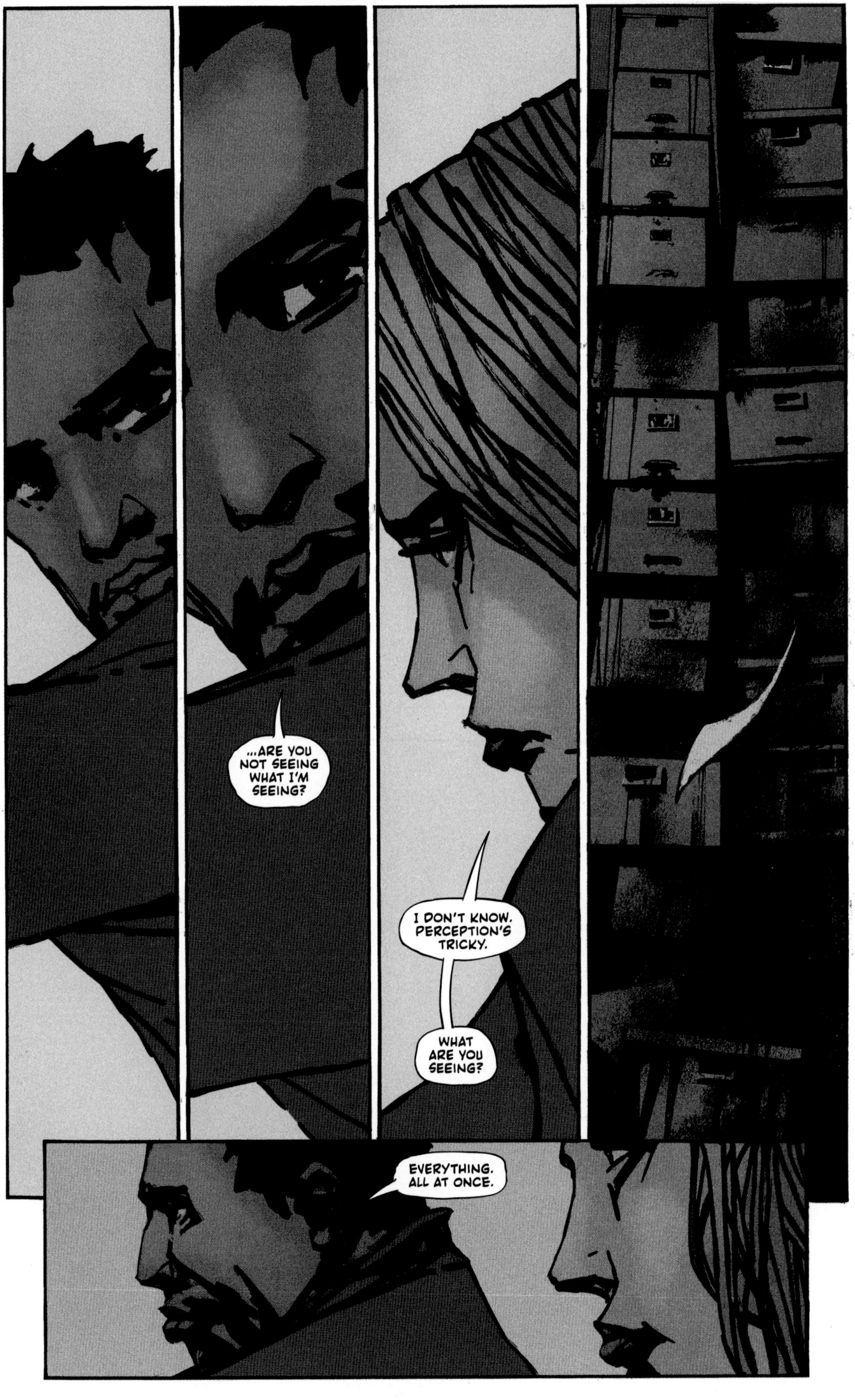
...ARE YOU NOT SEEING WHAT I'M SEEING?
I DON'T KNOW. PERCEPTION'S TRICKY.
WHAT ARE YOU SEEING?
EVERYTHING. ALL AT ONCE.

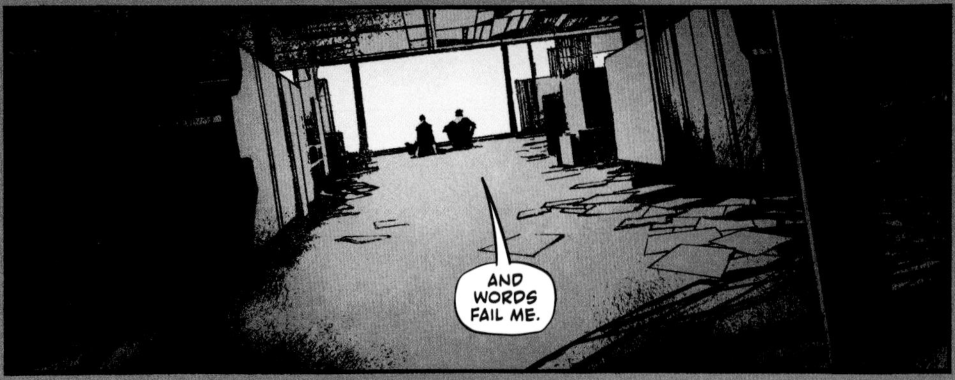
AND WORDS FAIL ME.

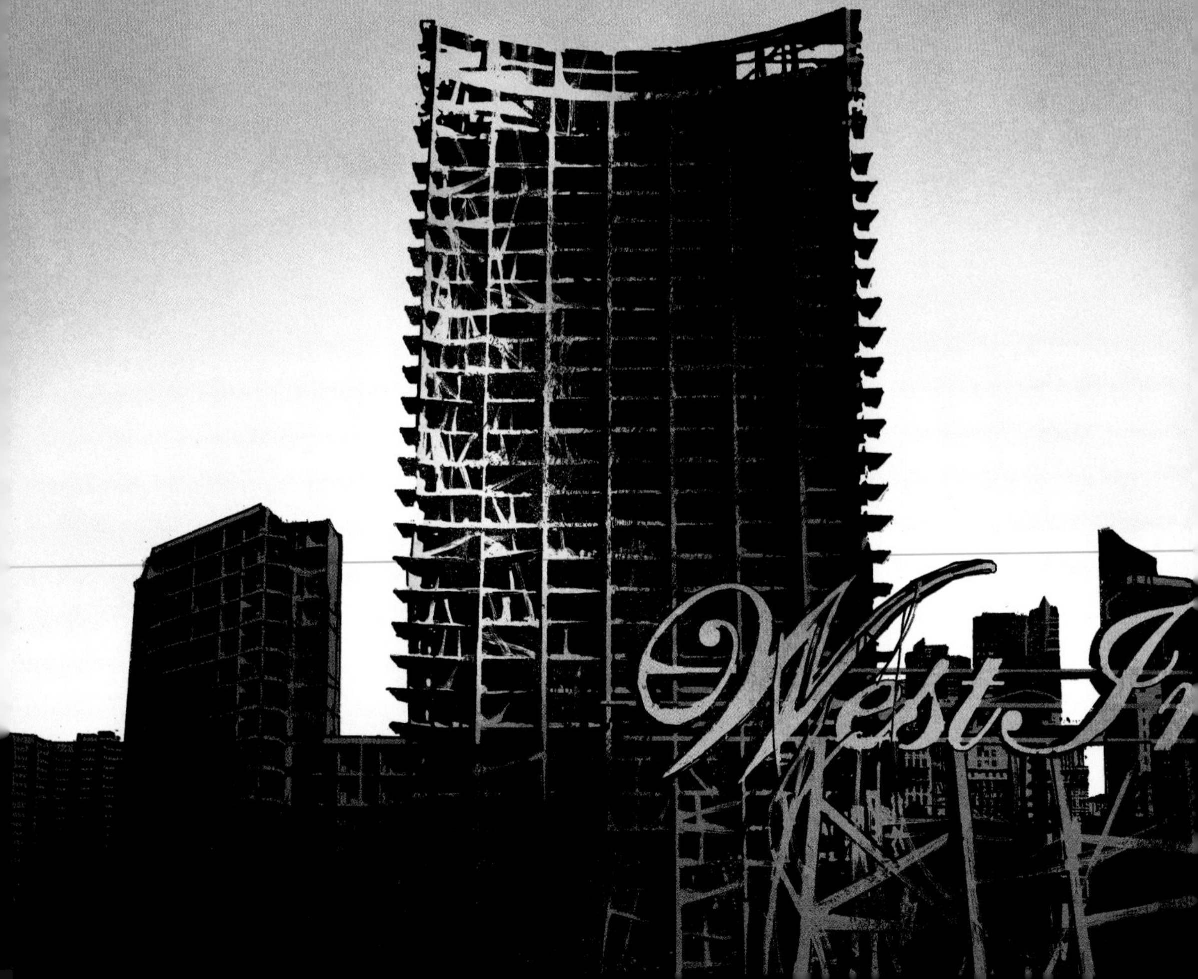

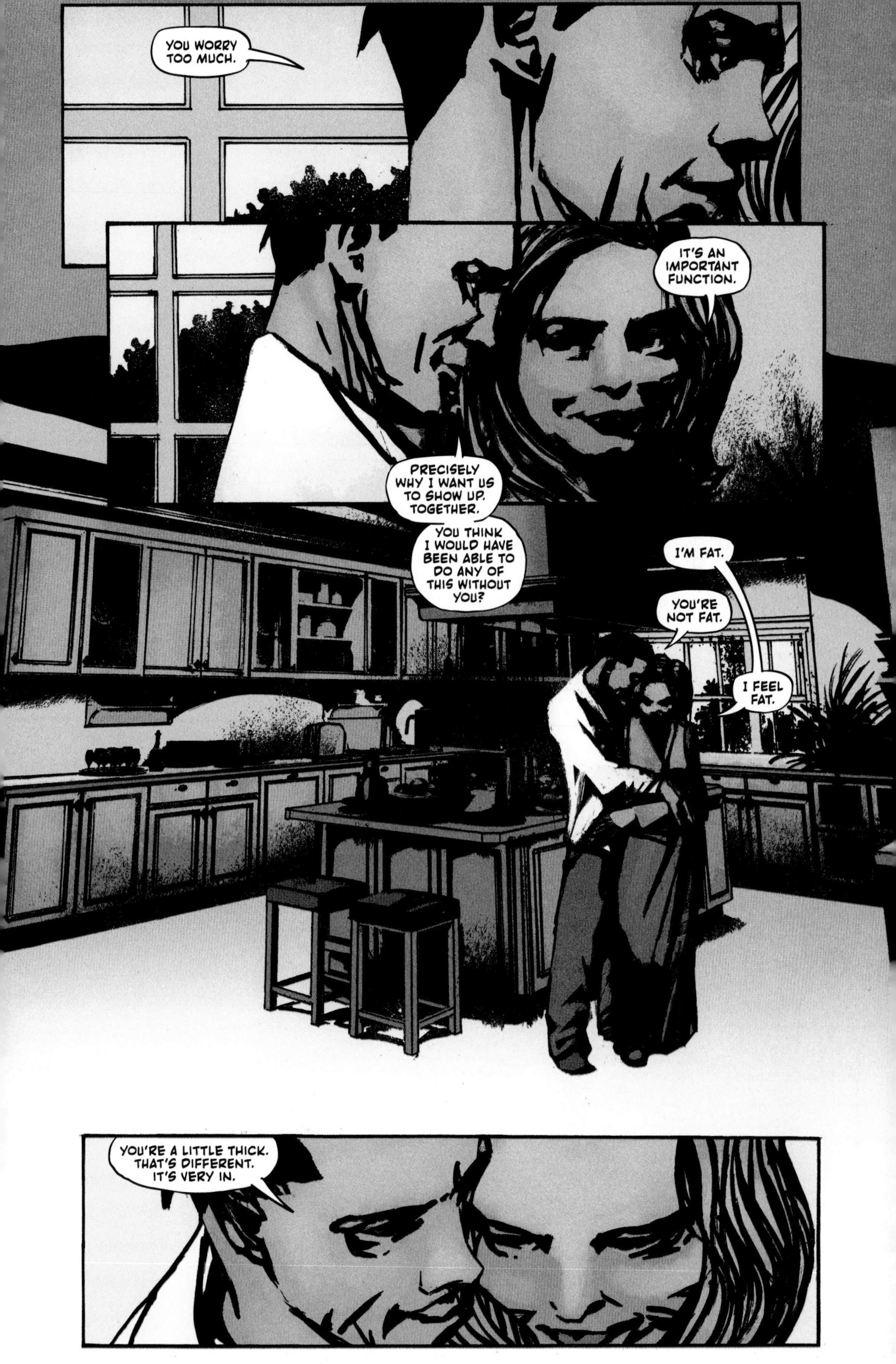
YOU WORRY TOO MUCH.
IT'S AN IMPORTANT FUNCTION.
PRECISELY WHY I WANT US TO SHOW UP. TOGETHER.
YOU THINK I WOULD HAVE BEEN ABLE TO DO ANY OF THIS WITHOUT YOU?
I'M FAT.
YOU'RE NOT FAT.
I FEEL FAT.
YOU'RE A LITTLE THICK. THAT'S DIFFERENT. IT'S VERY IN.

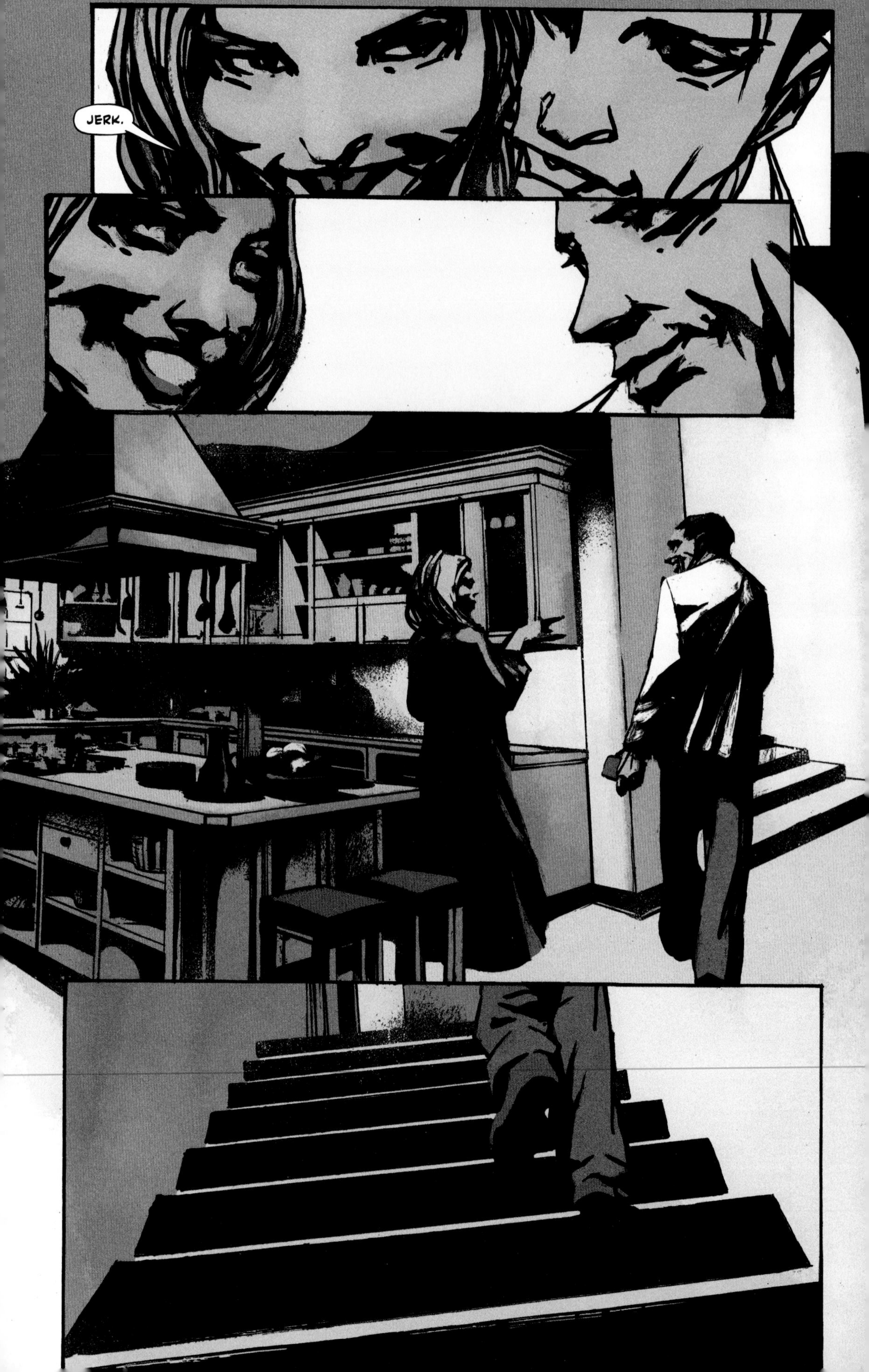
JERK.

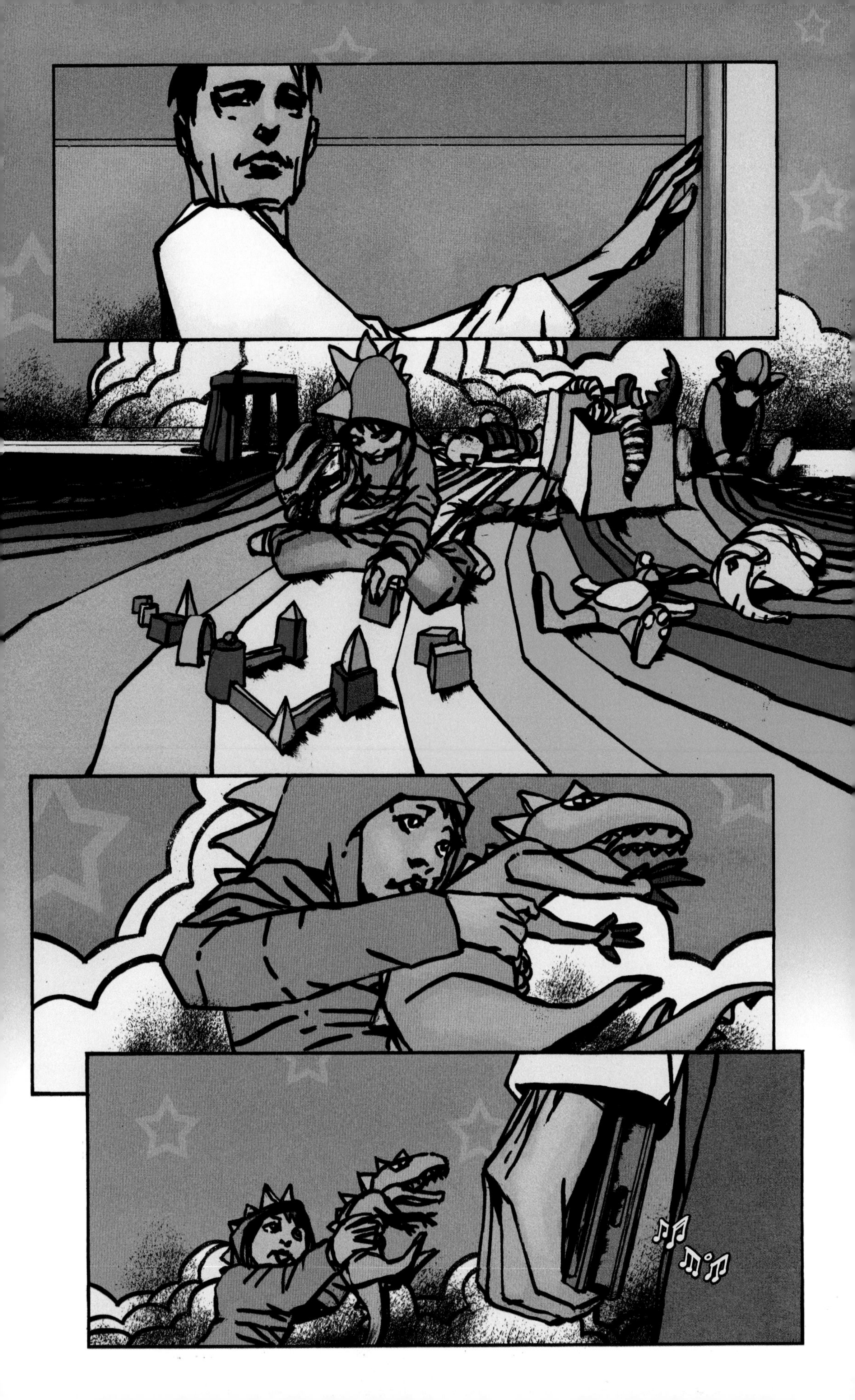

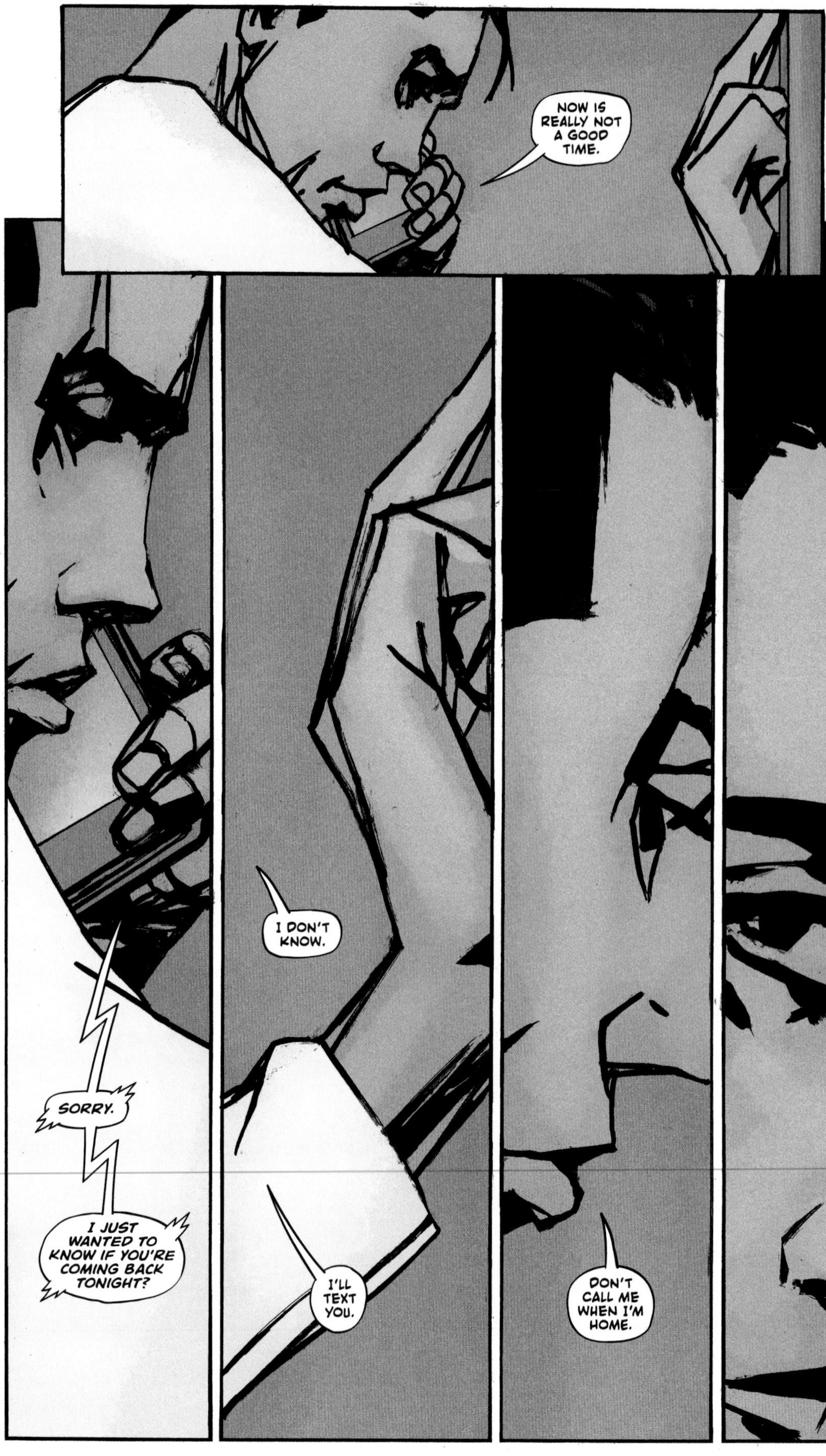
NOW IS REALLY NOT A GOOD TIME.
SORRY.
I JUST WANTED TO KNOW IF YOU'RE COMING BACK TONIGHT?
I DON'T KNOW.
I'LL TEXT YOU.
DON'T CALL ME WHEN I'M HOME.

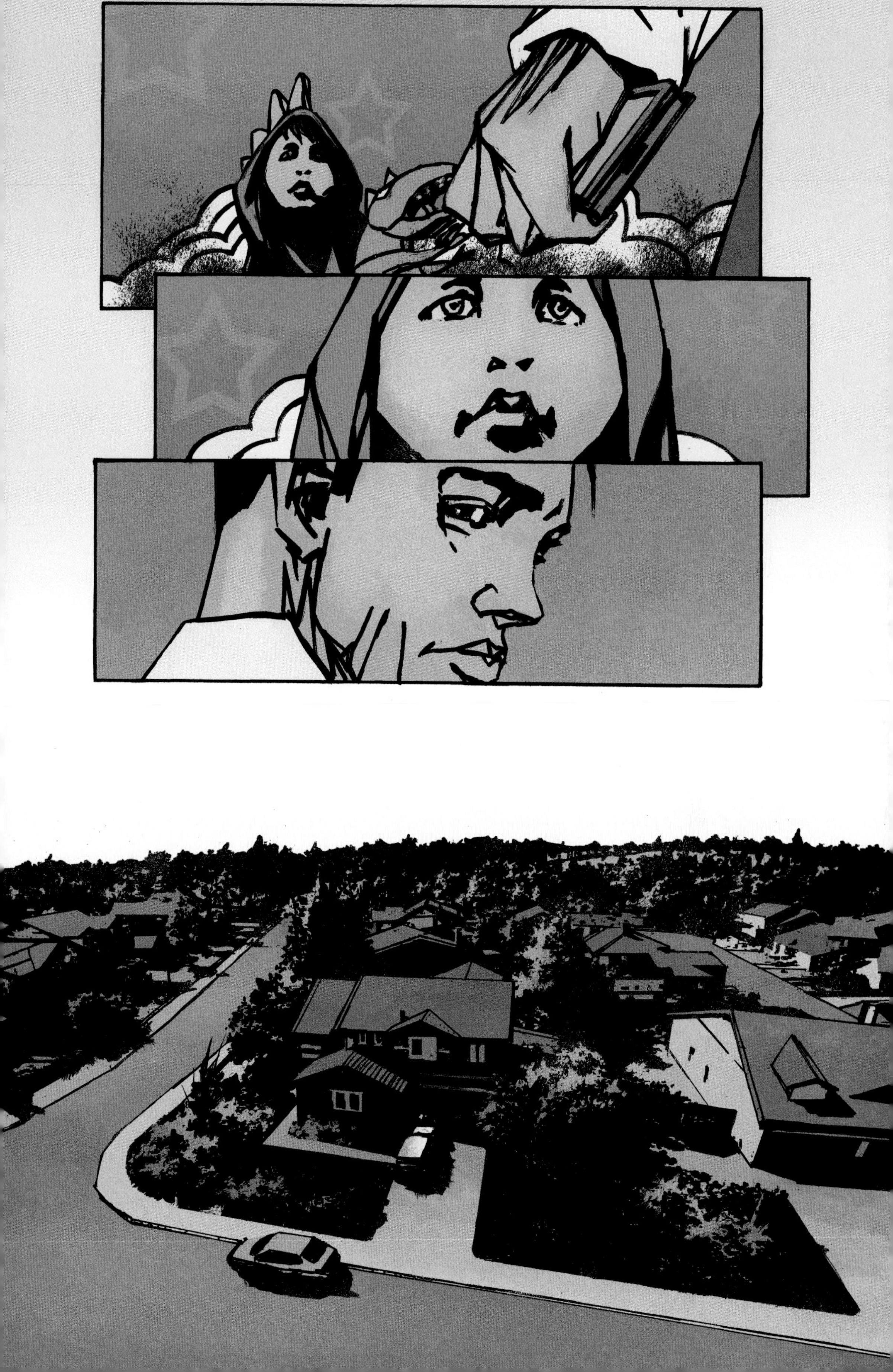

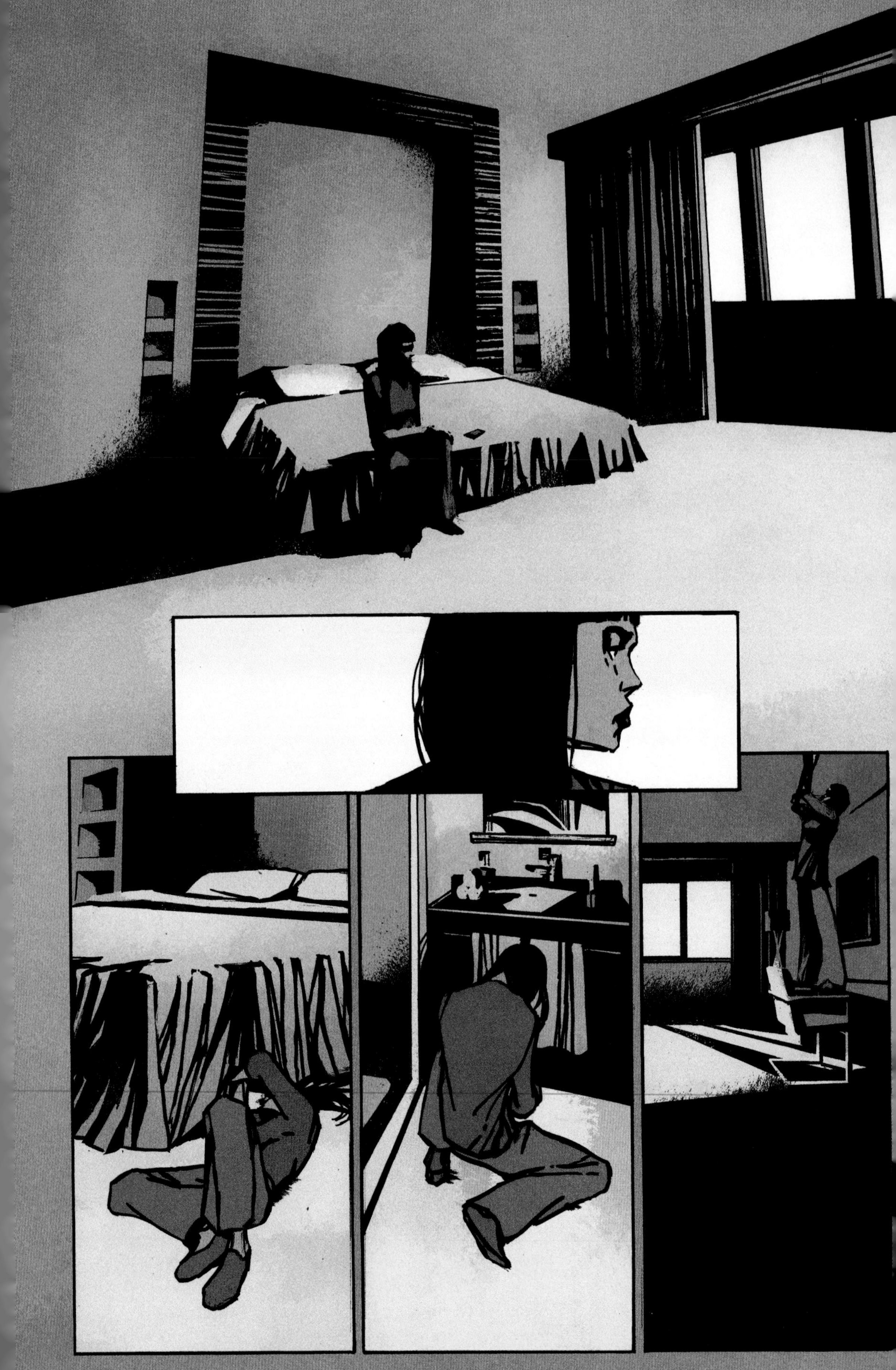

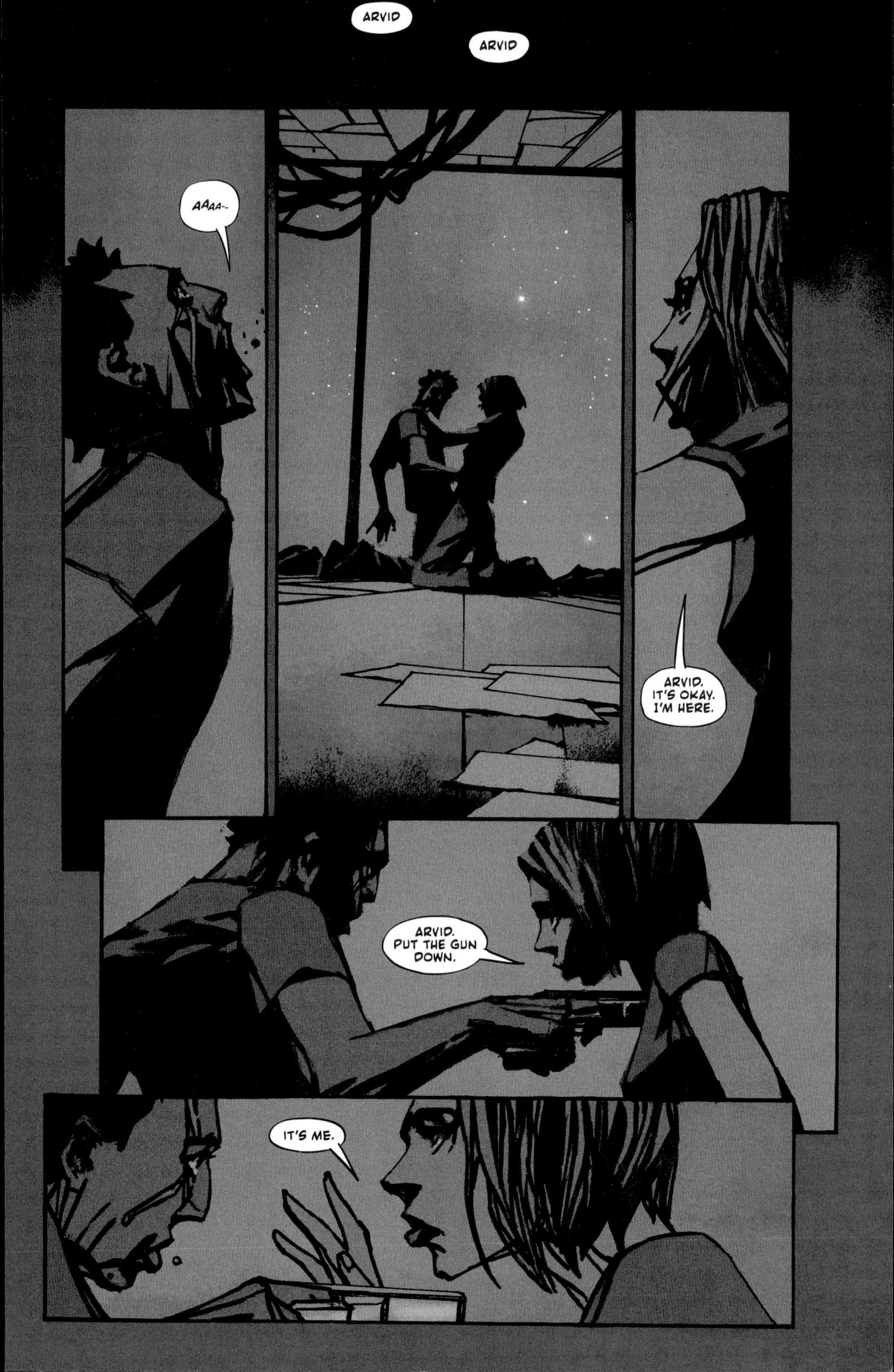
ARVID
ARVID
AAAA--
ARVID. IT'S OKAY. I'M HERE.
ARVID. PUT THE GUN DOWN.
IT'S ME.

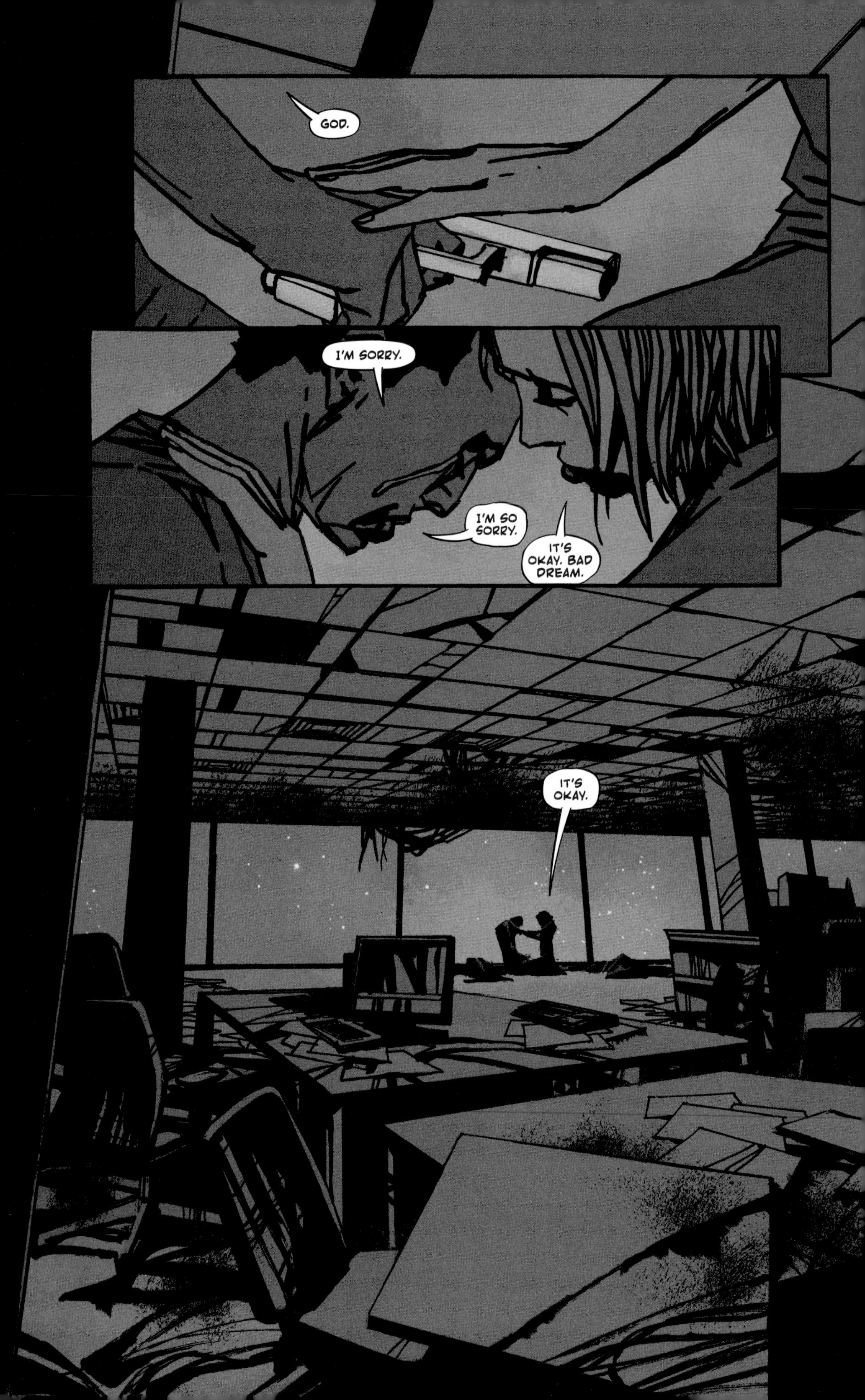
GOD.
I'M SORRY.
I'M SO SORRY.
IT'S OKAY. BAD DREAM.
IT'S OKAY.

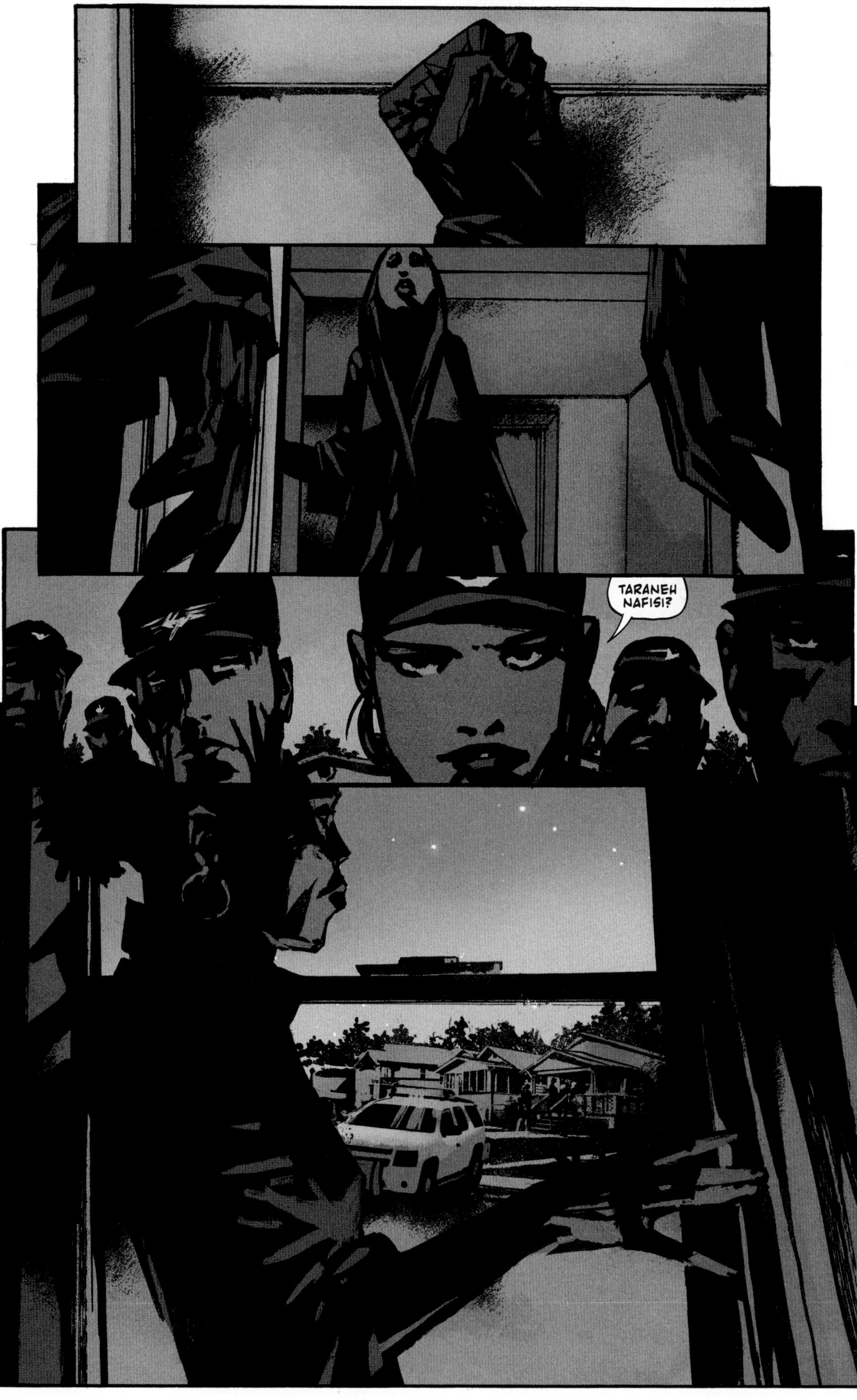
TARANEH NAFISI?

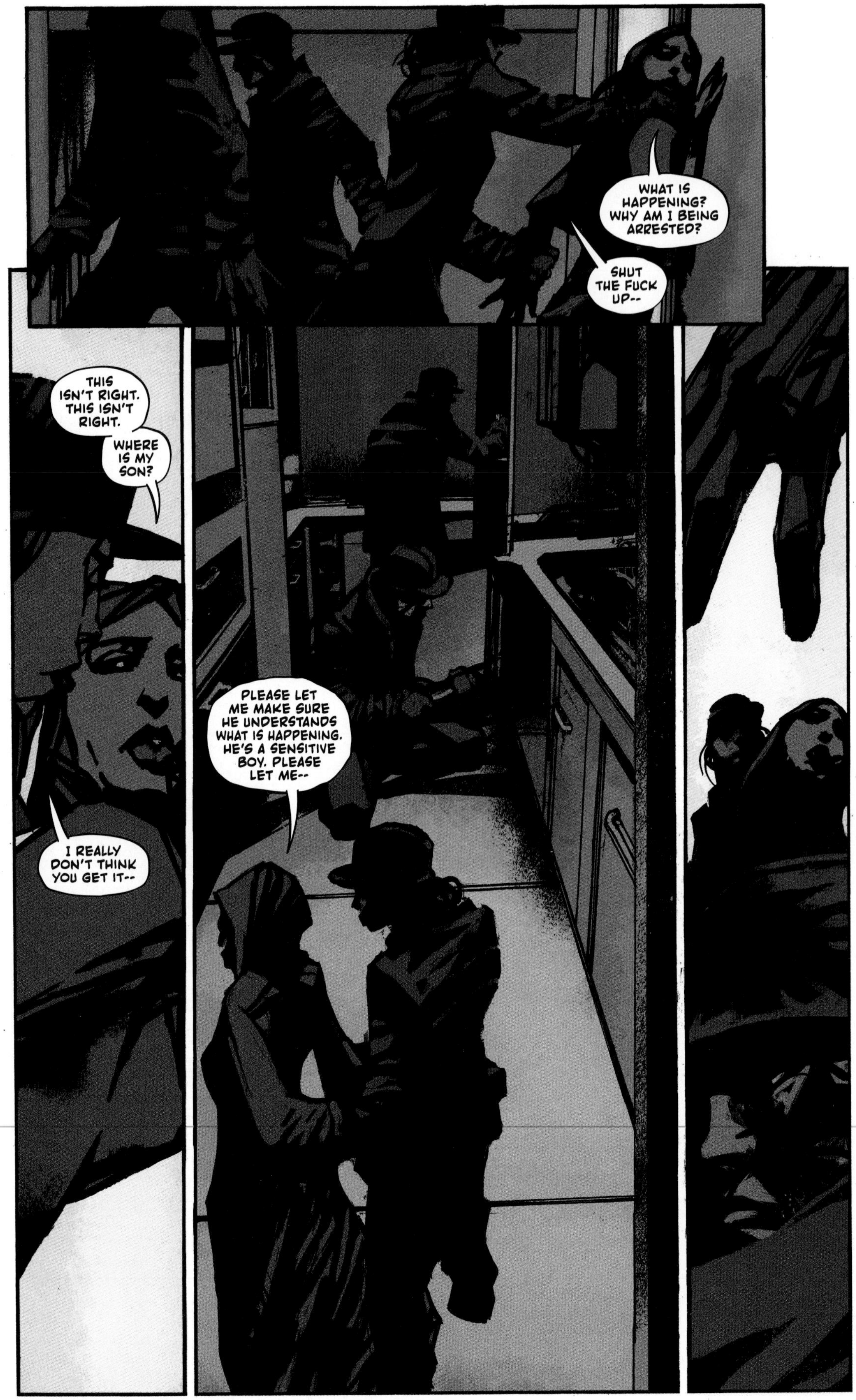
WHAT IS HAPPENING? WHY AM I BEING ARRESTED?
SHUT THE FUCK UP--
THIS ISN'T RIGHT. THIS ISN'T RIGHT.
WHERE IS MY SON?
I REALLY DON'T THINK YOU GET IT--
PLEASE LET ME MAKE SURE HE UNDERSTANDS WHAT IS HAPPENING. HE'S A SENSITIVE BOY. PLEASE LET ME--

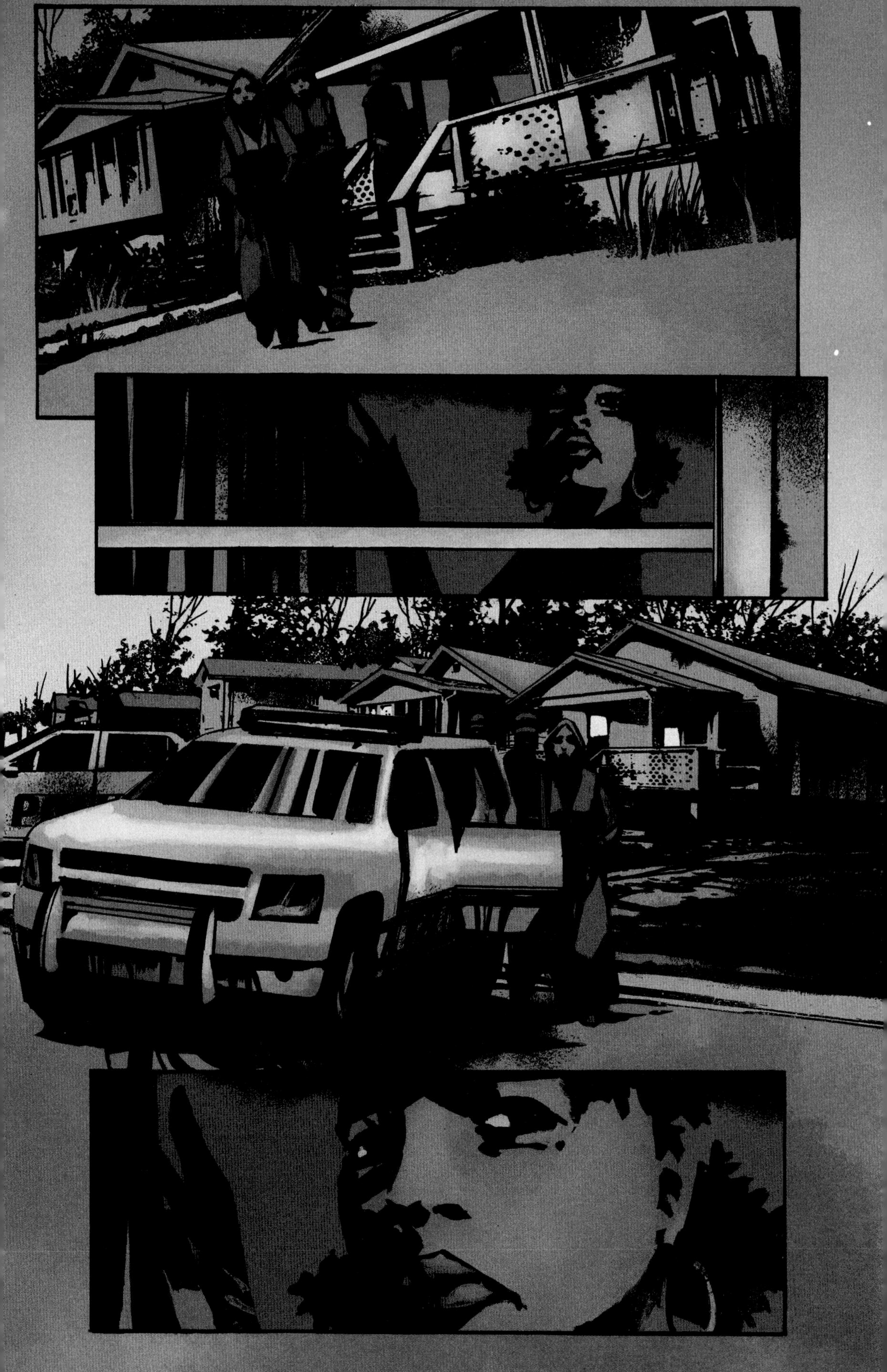

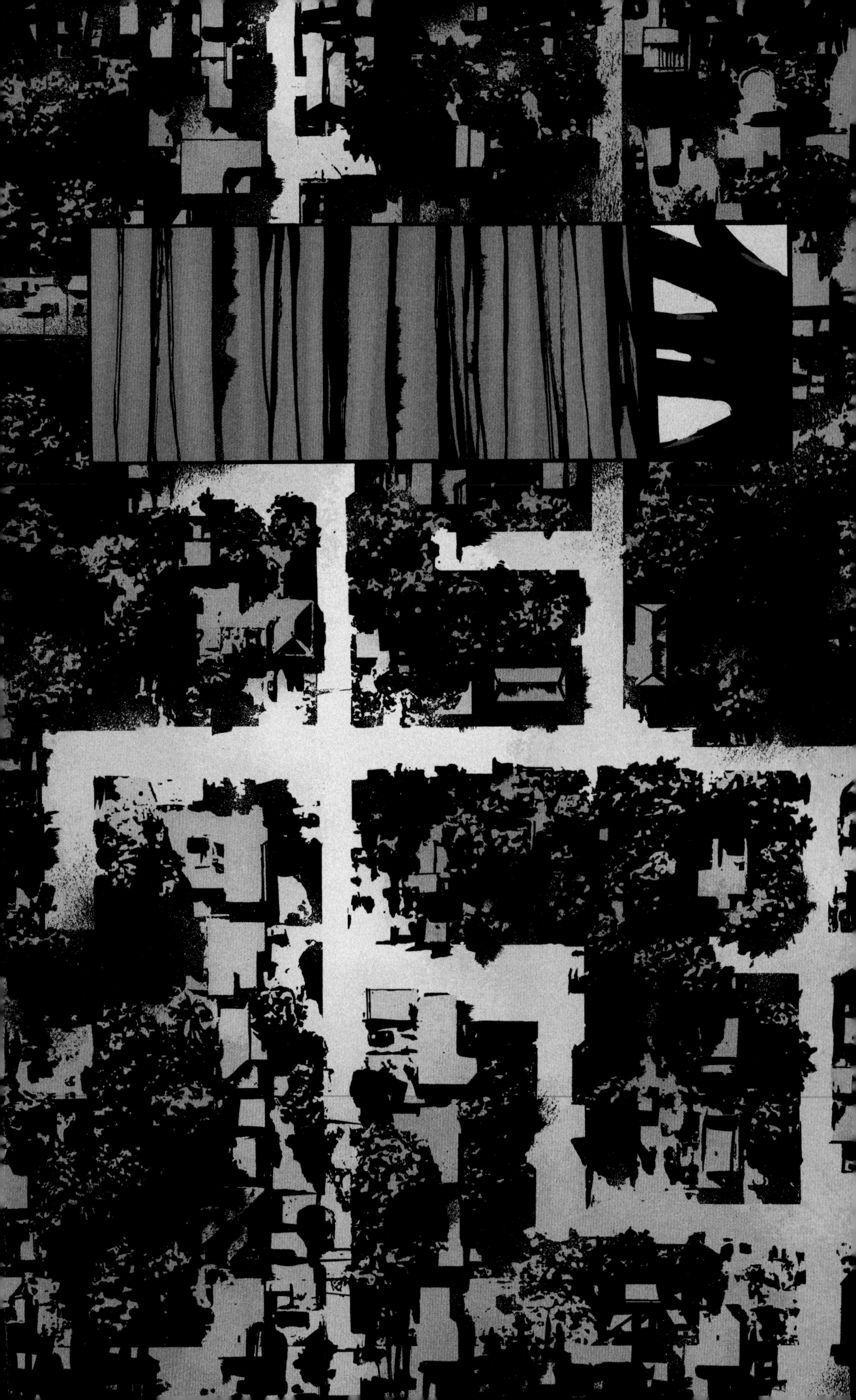

CHAPTER EIGHT:
PURITY

I waved to my neighbour
My neighbour waved to me
But my neighbour
Is my enemy
I kept waving my arms
Till I could not see

"Fifteen Feet of Pure White Snow"
—Nick Cave and the Bad Seeds

"One of my teachers at Columbia was
Joseph Brodsky...and he said 'look,' he
said, 'you Americans, you are so naïve. You
think evil is going to come into your houses
wearing big black boots. It doesn't come
like that. Look at the language. It begins in
the language."

—Marie Howe

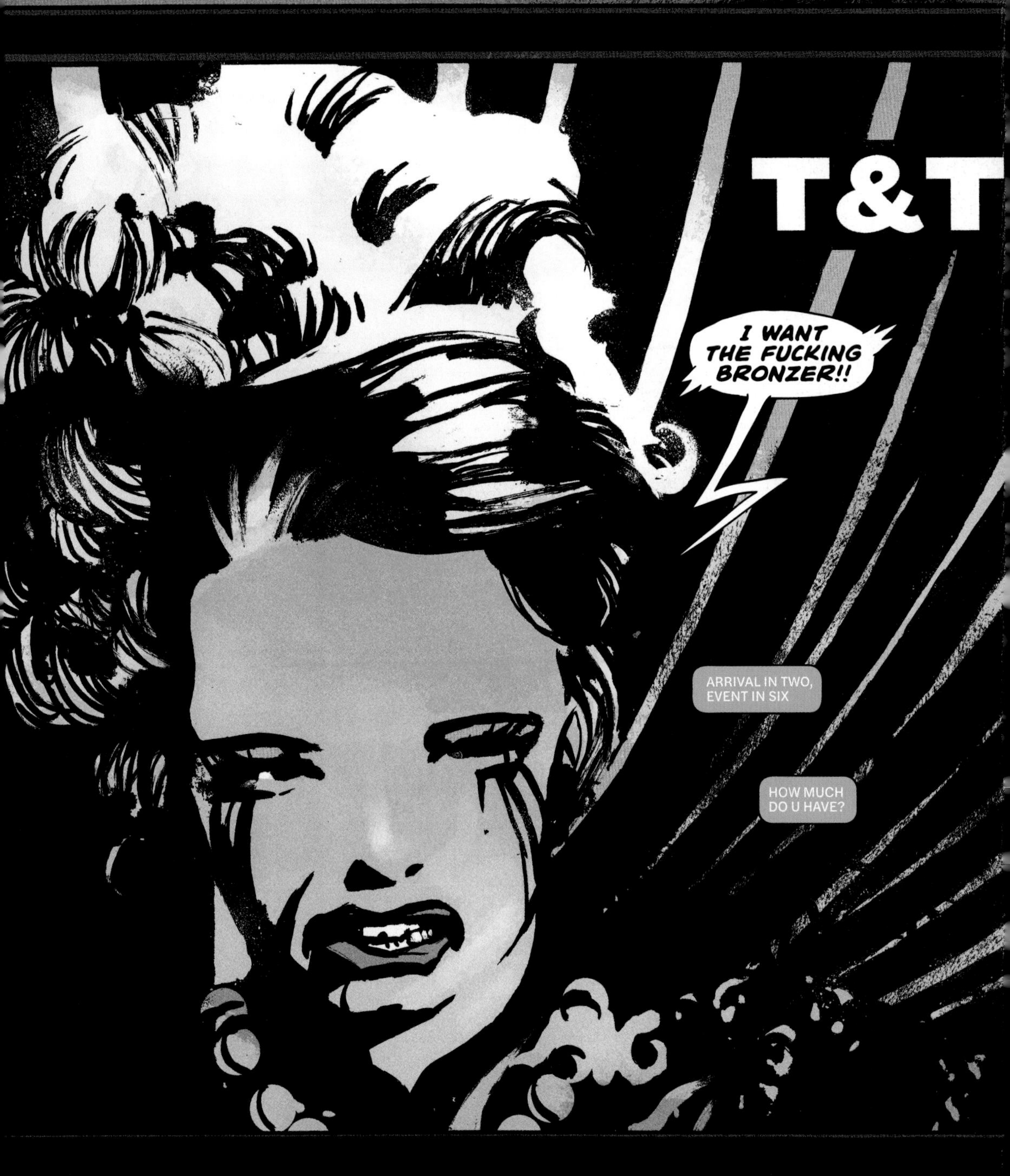
T&T
I WANT THE FUCKING BRONZER!!
ARRIVAL IN TWO, EVENT IN SIX
HOW MUCH DO U HAVE?

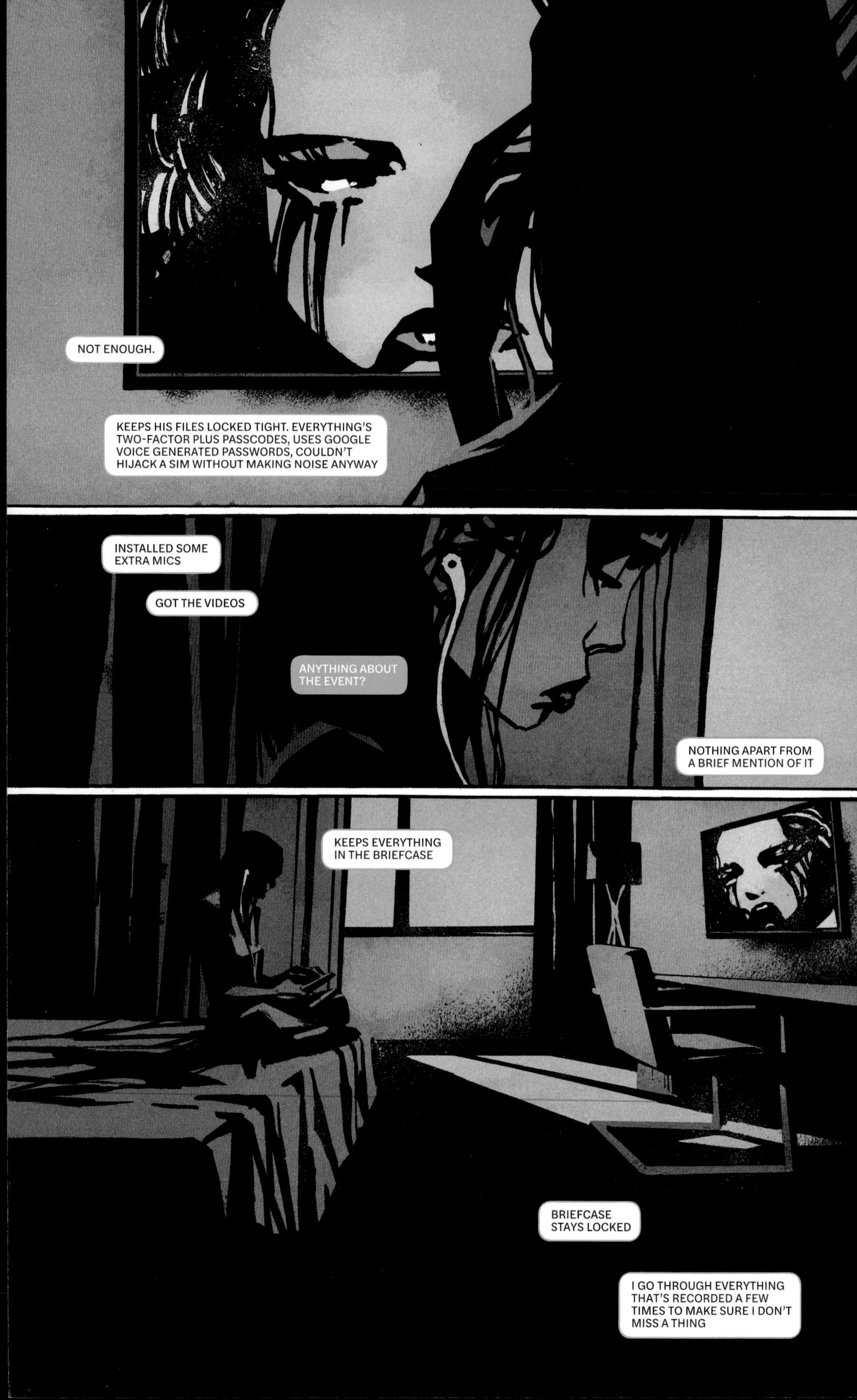
NOT ENOUGH.
KEEPS HIS FILES LOCKED TIGHT. EVERYTHING'S TWO-FACTOR PLUS PASSCODES, USES GOOGLE VOICE GENERATED PASSWORDS, COULDN'T HIJACK A SIM WITHOUT MAKING NOISE ANYWAY
INSTALLED SOME EXTRA MICS
GOT THE VIDEOS
ANYTHING ABOUT THE EVENT?
NOTHING APART FROM A BRIEF MENTION OF IT
KEEPS EVERYTHING IN THE BRIEFCASE
BRIEFCASE STAYS LOCKED
I GO THROUGH EVERYTHING THAT'S RECORDED A FEW TIMES TO MAKE SURE I DON'T MISS A THING

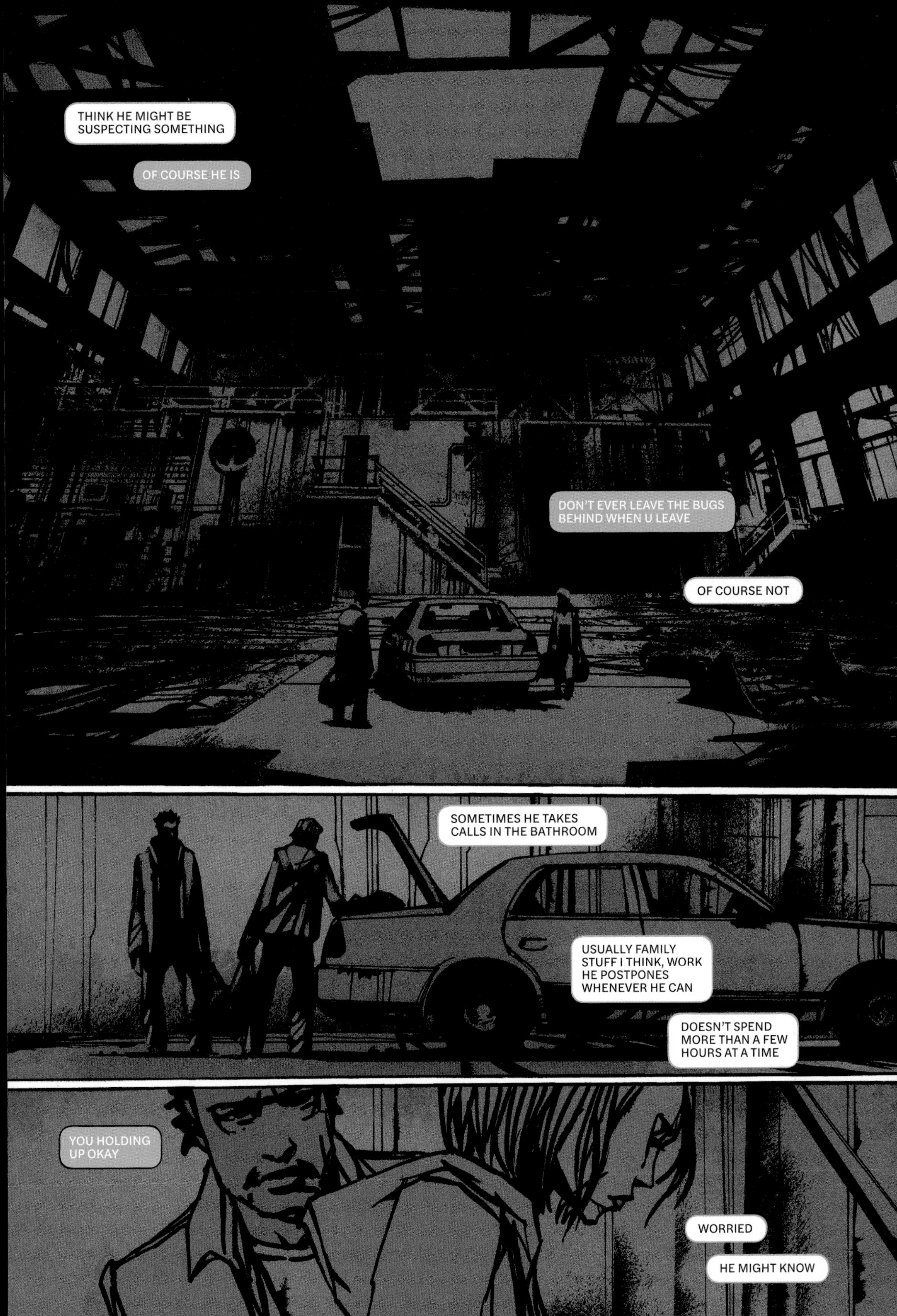
THINK HE MIGHT BE SUSPECTING SOMETHING
OF COURSE HE IS
DON'T EVER LEAVE THE BUGS BEHIND WHEN U LEAVE
OF COURSE NOT
SOMETIMES HE TAKES CALLS IN THE BATHROOM
USUALLY FAMILY STUFF I THINK, WORK HE POSTPONES WHENEVER HE CAN
DOESN'T SPEND MORE THAN A FEW HOURS AT A TIME
YOU HOLDING UP OKAY
WORRIED
HE MIGHT KNOW

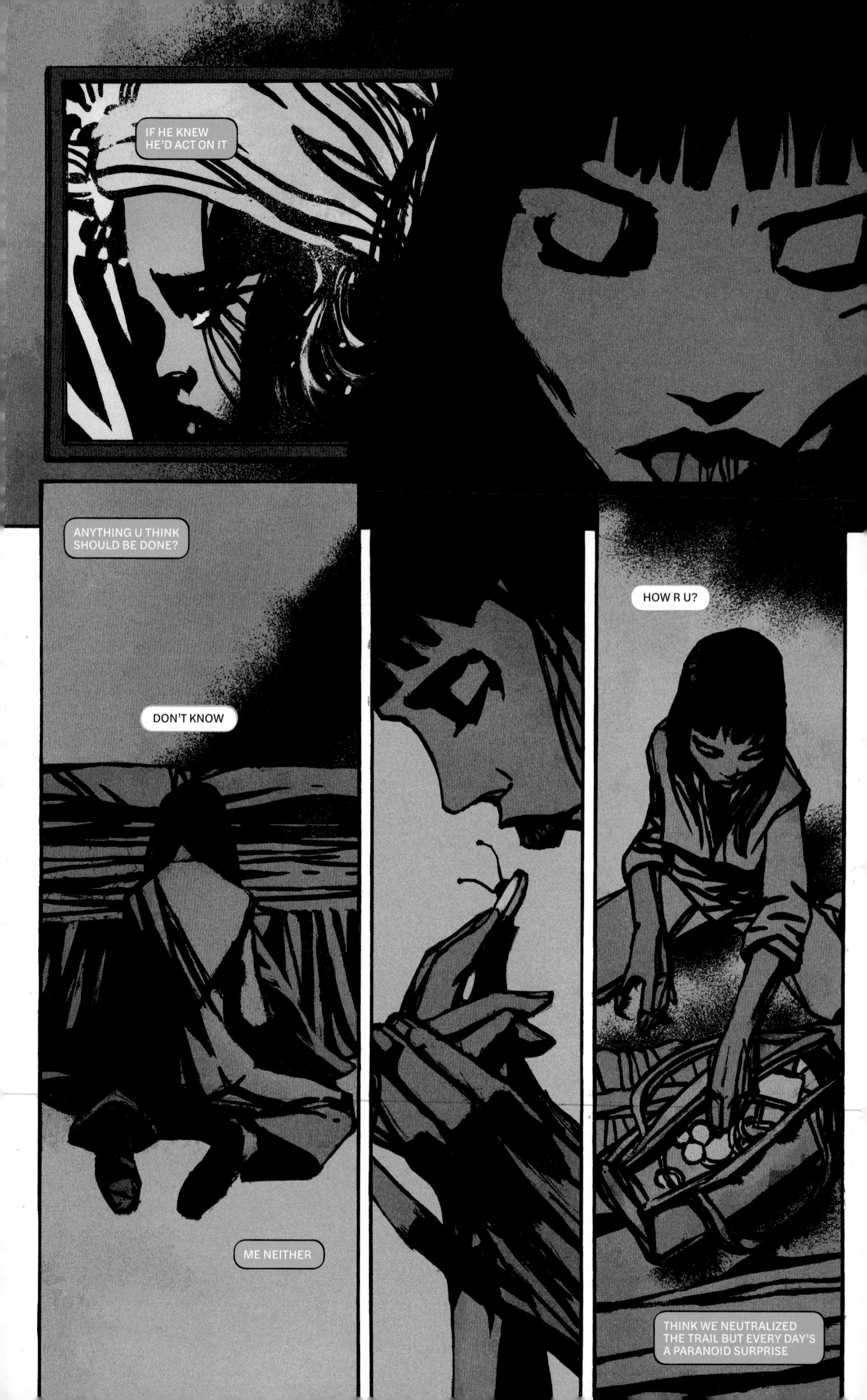
IF HE KNEW HE'D ACT ON IT
ANYTHING U THINK SHOULD BE DONE?
DON'T KNOW
ME NEITHER
HOW R U?
THINK WE NEUTRALIZED THE TRAIL BUT EVERY DAY'S A PARANOID SURPRISE

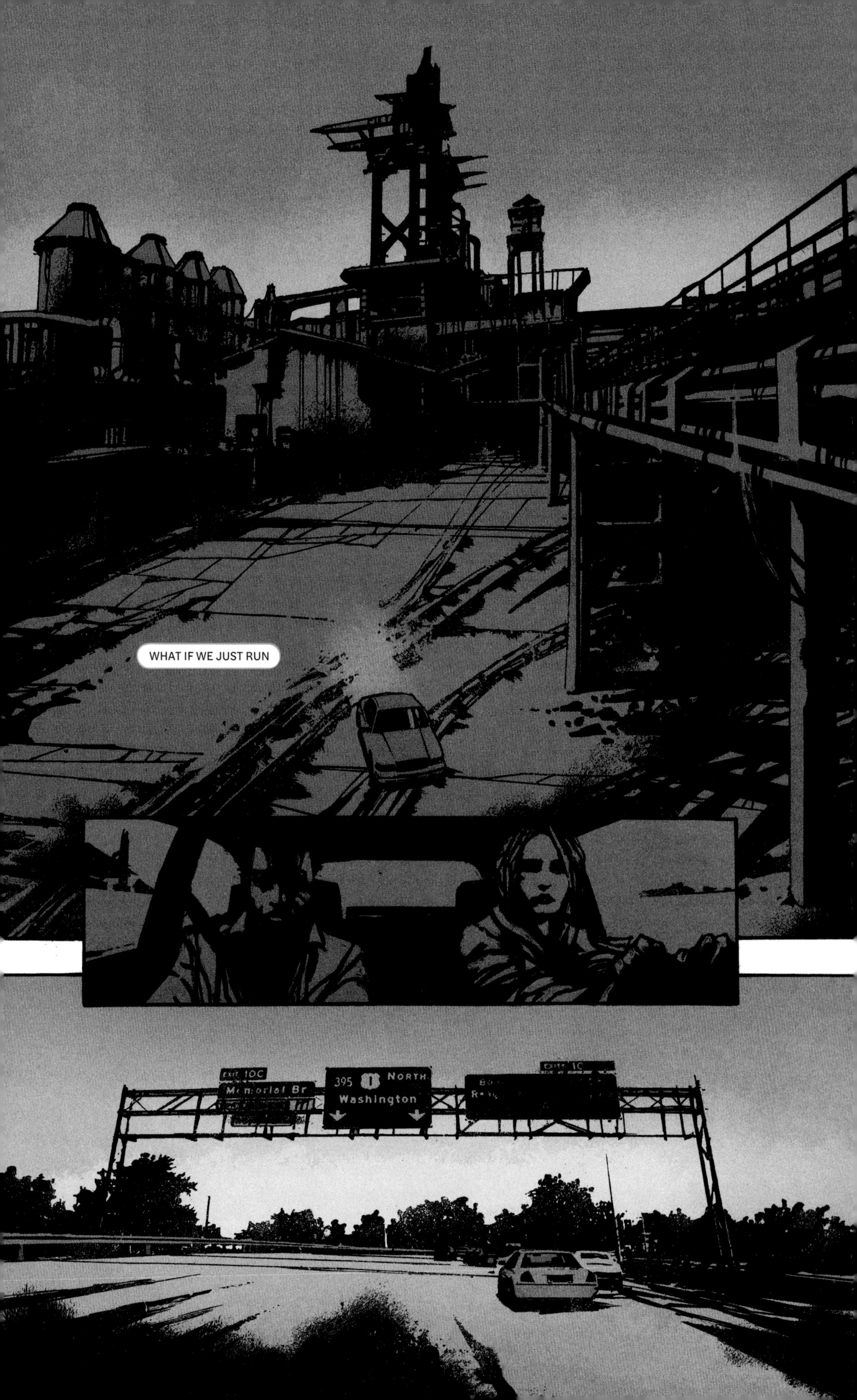
WHAT IF WE JUST RUN
EXIT 10C
Memorial Br
395 1 NORTH
Washington

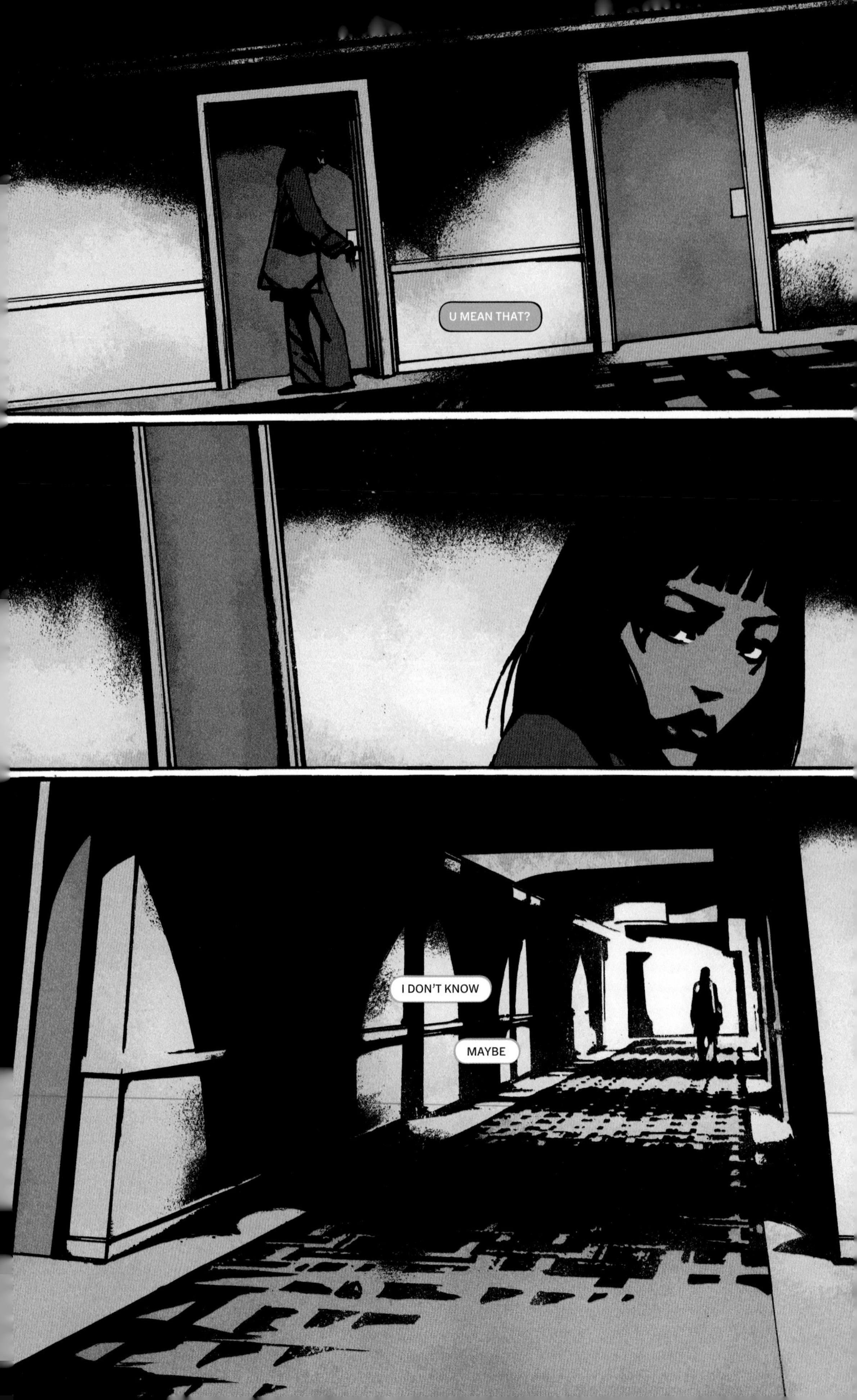
U MEAN THAT?
I DON'T KNOW
MAYBE

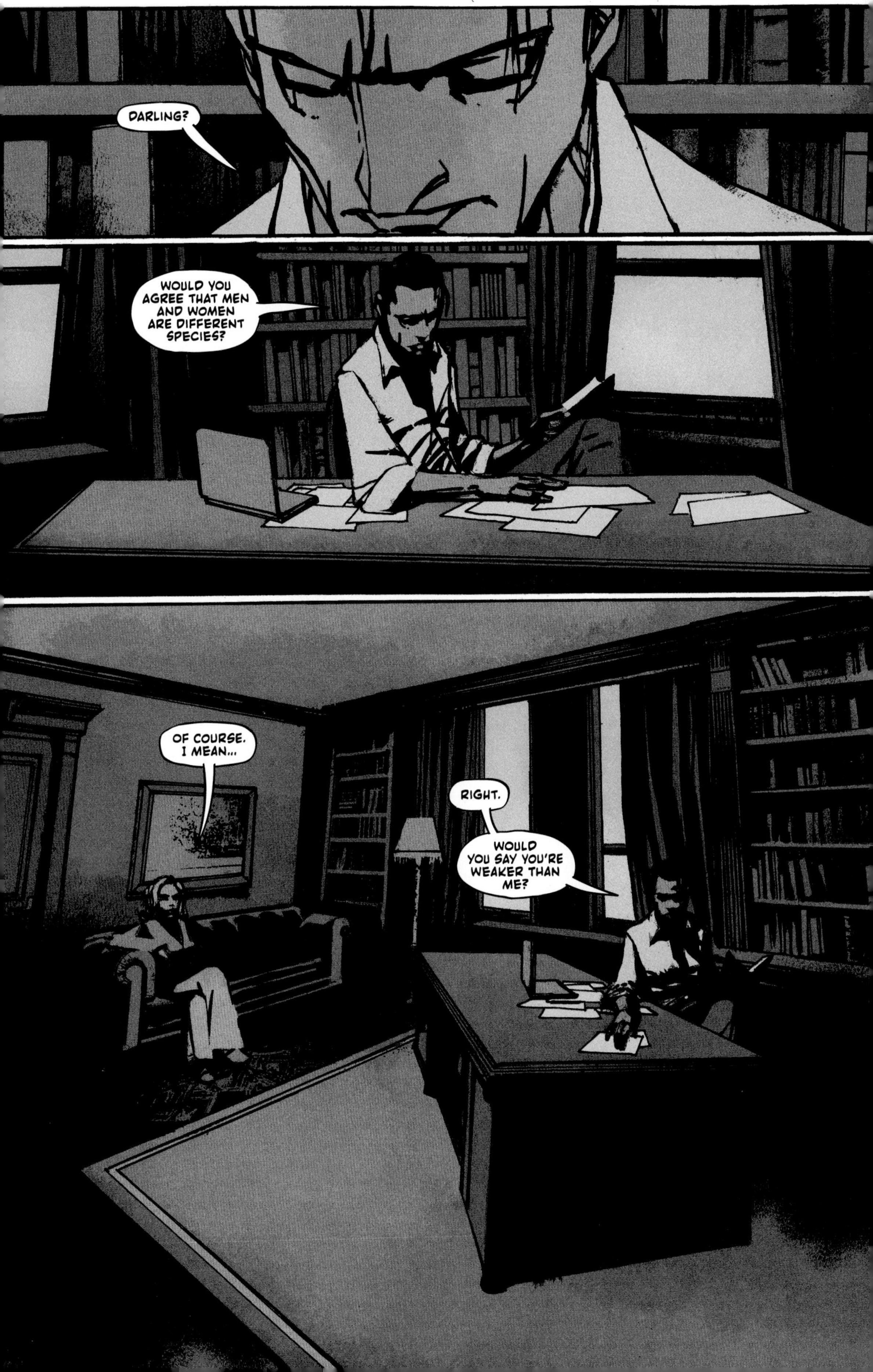
DARLING?
WOULD YOU AGREE THAT MEN AND WOMEN ARE DIFFERENT SPECIES?
OF COURSE. I MEAN...
RIGHT.
WOULD YOU SAY YOU'RE WEAKER THAN ME?

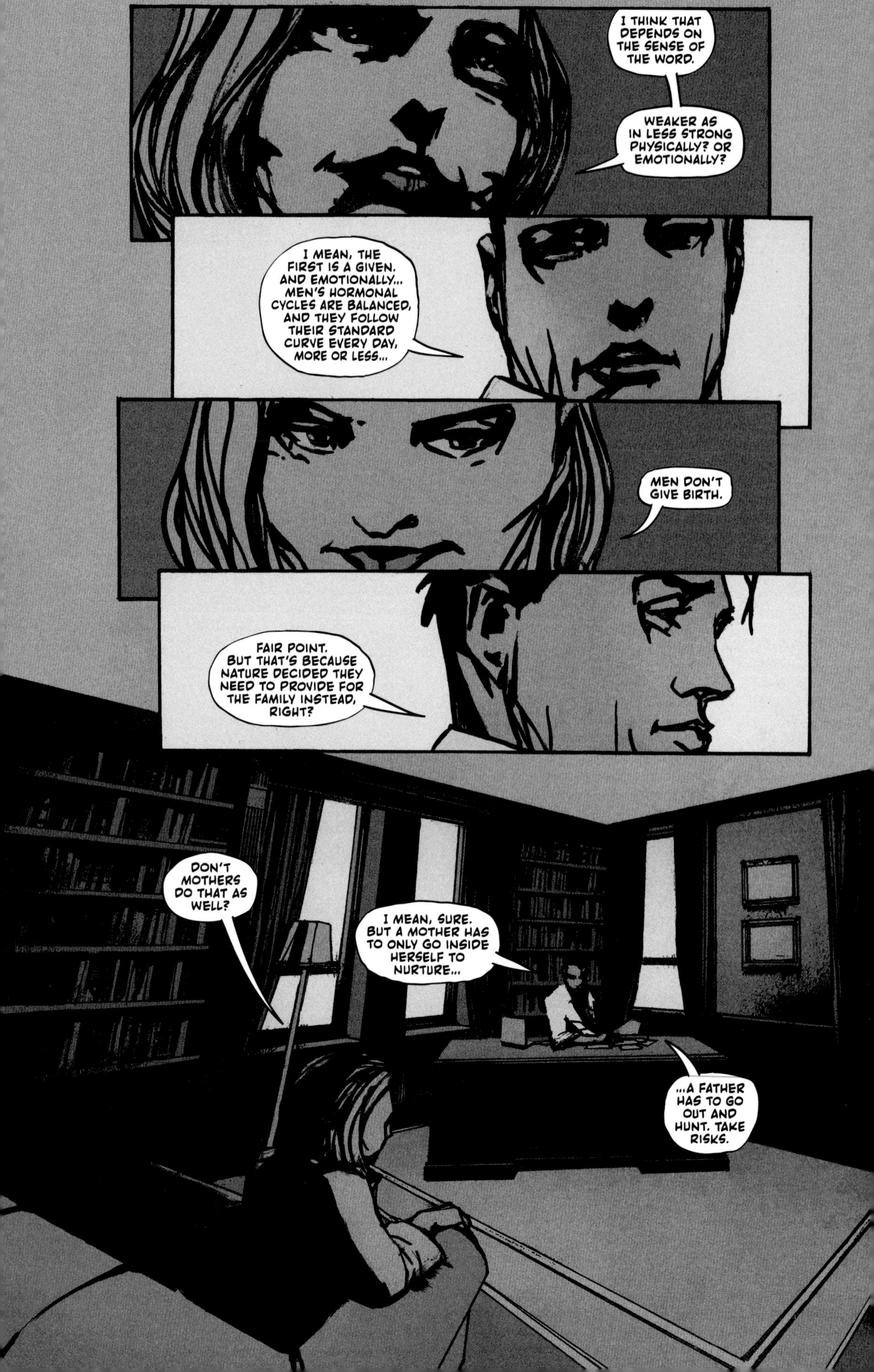
I THINK THAT DEPENDS ON THE SENSE OF THE WORD.
WEAKER AS IN LESS STRONG PHYSICALLY? OR EMOTIONALLY?
I MEAN, THE FIRST IS A GIVEN. AND EMOTIONALLY... MEN'S HORMONAL CYCLES ARE BALANCED, AND THEY FOLLOW THEIR STANDARD CURVE EVERY DAY, MORE OR LESS...
MEN DON'T GIVE BIRTH.
FAIR POINT. BUT THAT'S BECAUSE NATURE DECIDED THEY NEED TO PROVIDE FOR THE FAMILY INSTEAD, RIGHT?
DON'T MOTHERS DO THAT AS WELL?
I MEAN, SURE. BUT A MOTHER HAS TO ONLY GO INSIDE HERSELF TO NURTURE...
...A FATHER HAS TO GO OUT AND HUNT. TAKE RISKS.

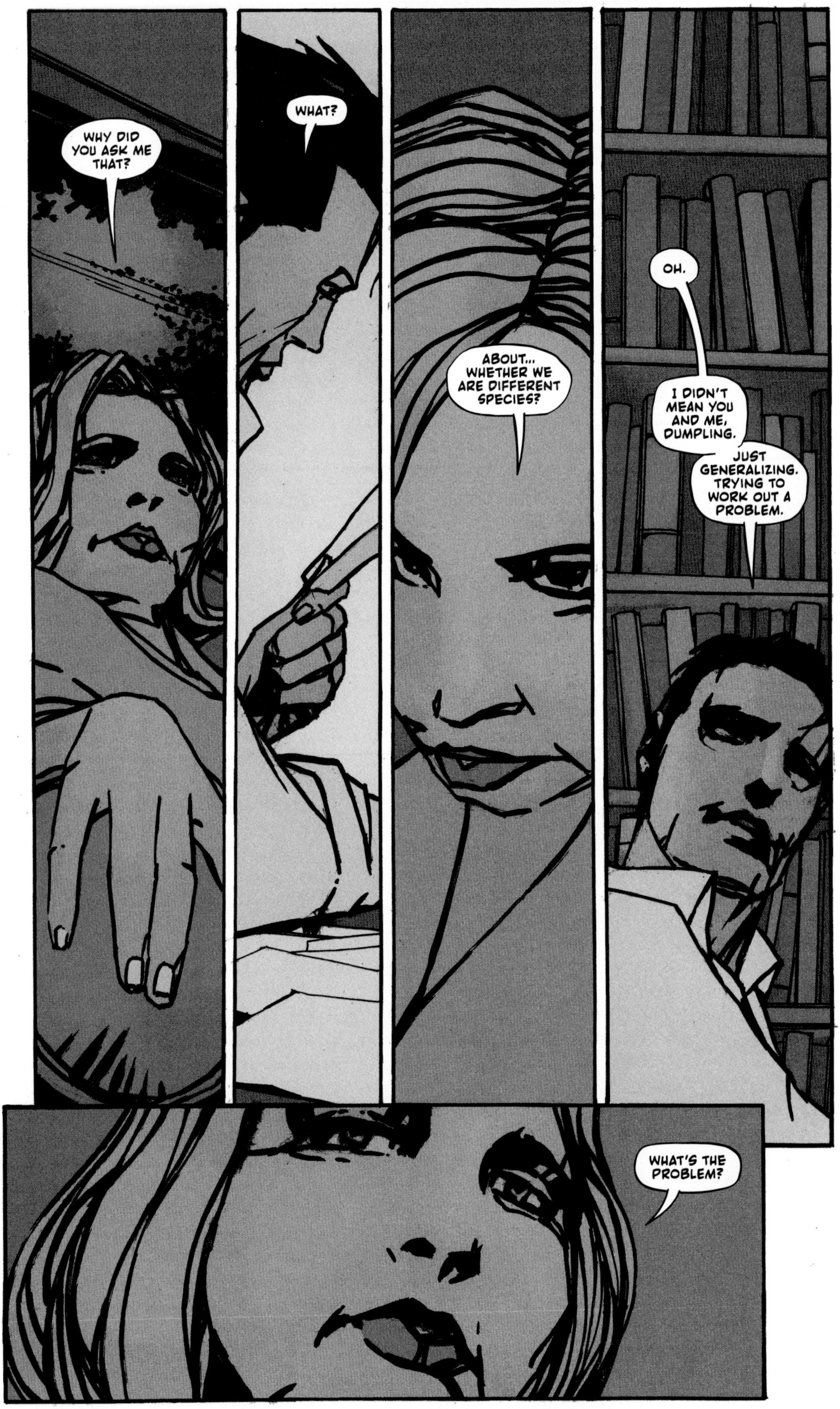
WHY DID YOU ASK ME THAT?
WHAT?
ABOUT... WHETHER WE ARE DIFFERENT SPECIES?
OH.
I DIDN'T MEAN YOU AND ME, DUMPLING.
JUST GENERALIZING. TRYING TO WORK OUT A PROBLEM.
WHAT'S THE PROBLEM?

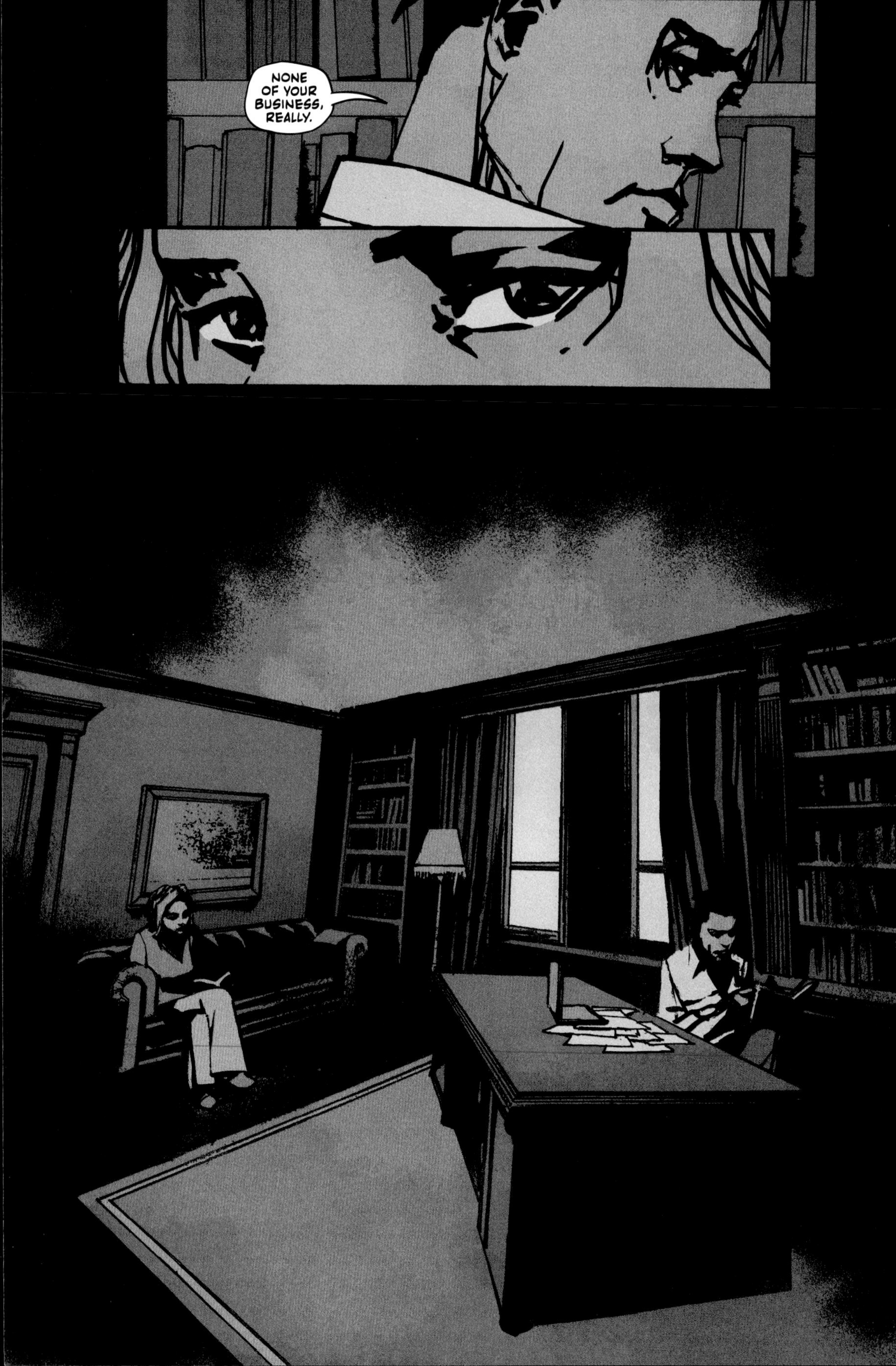
NONE OF YOUR BUSINESS, REALLY.

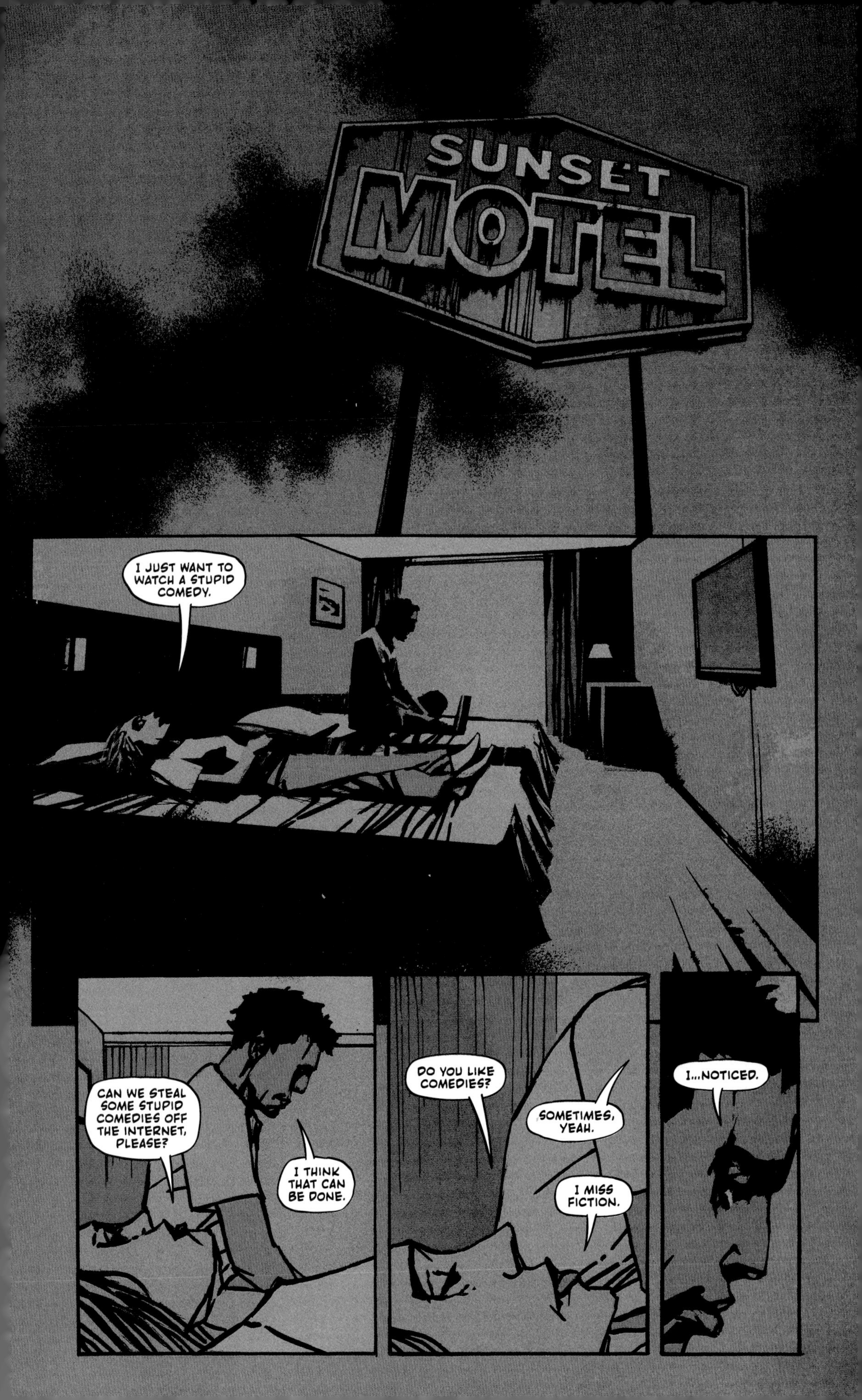
SUNSET MOTEL
I JUST WANT TO WATCH A STUPID COMEDY.
CAN WE STEAL SOME STUPID COMEDIES OFF THE INTERNET, PLEASE?
I THINK THAT CAN BE DONE.
DO YOU LIKE COMEDIES?
SOMETIMES, YEAH.
I MISS FICTION.
I...NOTICED.

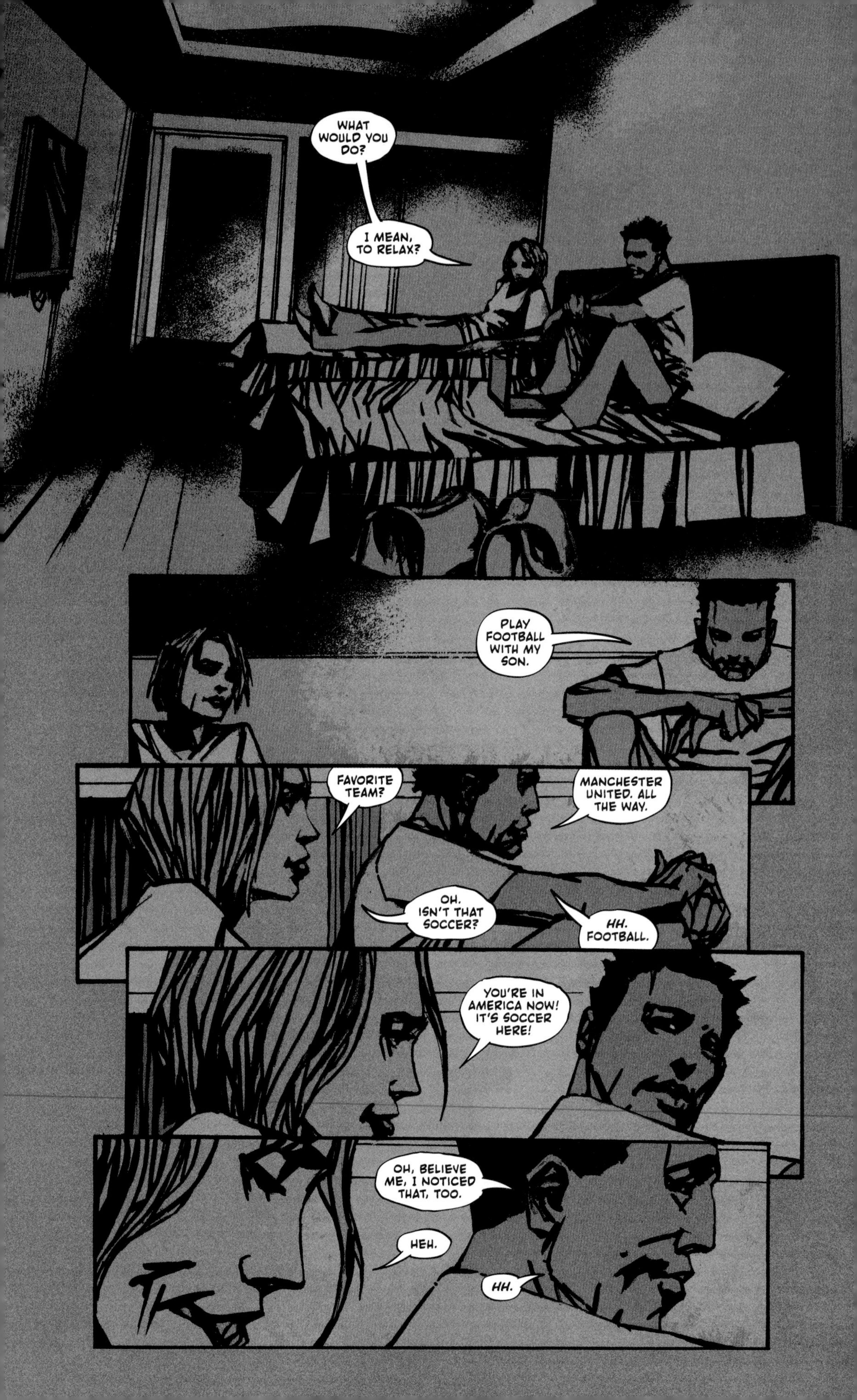
WHAT WOULD YOU DO?
I MEAN, TO RELAX?
PLAY FOOTBALL WITH MY SON.
FAVORITE TEAM?
MANCHESTER UNITED. ALL THE WAY.
OH. ISN'T THAT SOCCER?
HH. FOOTBALL.
YOU'RE IN AMERICA NOW! IT'S SOCCER HERE!
OH, BELIEVE ME, I NOTICED THAT, TOO.
HEH.
HH.

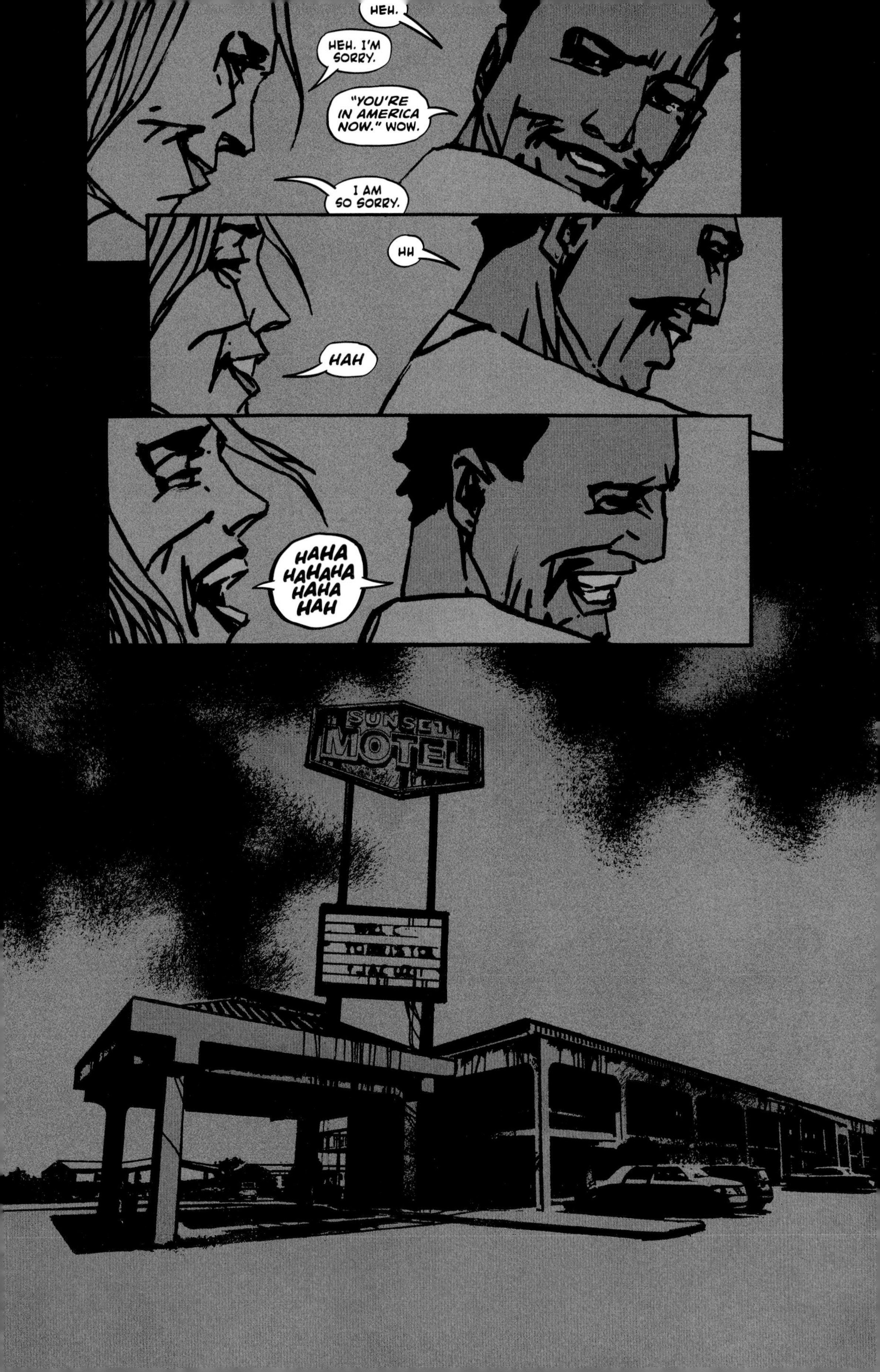
HEH.
HEH. I'M SORRY.
"YOU'RE IN AMERICA NOW." WOW.
I AM SO SORRY.
HH
HAH
HAHA HAHAHA HAHA HAH
SUNSET MOTEL

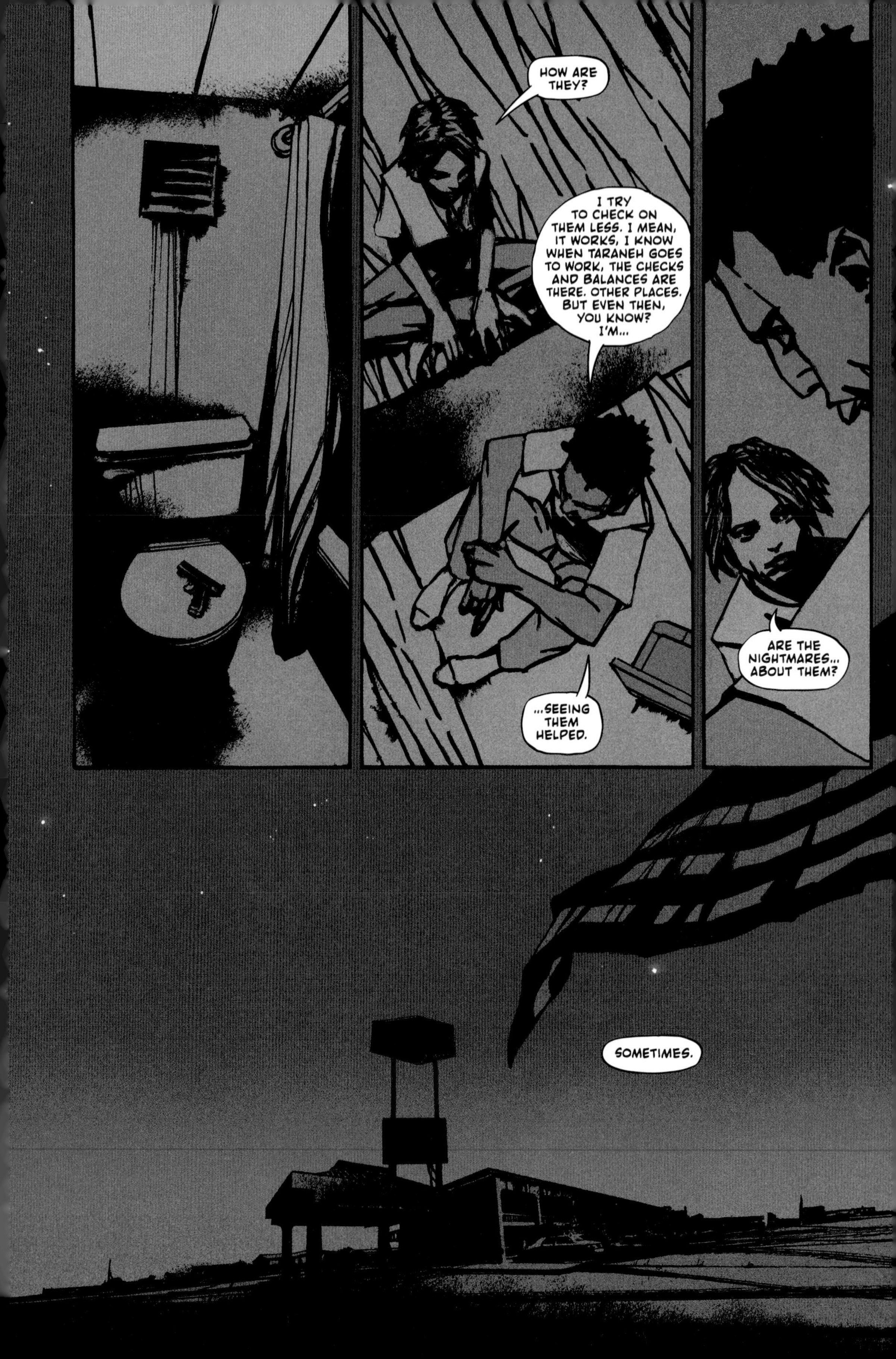
HOW ARE THEY?
I TRY TO CHECK ON THEM LESS. I MEAN, IT WORKS, I KNOW WHEN TARANEH GOES TO WORK, THE CHECKS AND BALANCES ARE THERE. OTHER PLACES. BUT EVEN THEN, YOU KNOW? I'M...
...SEEING THEM HELPED.
ARE THE NIGHTMARES... ABOUT THEM?
SOMETIMES.

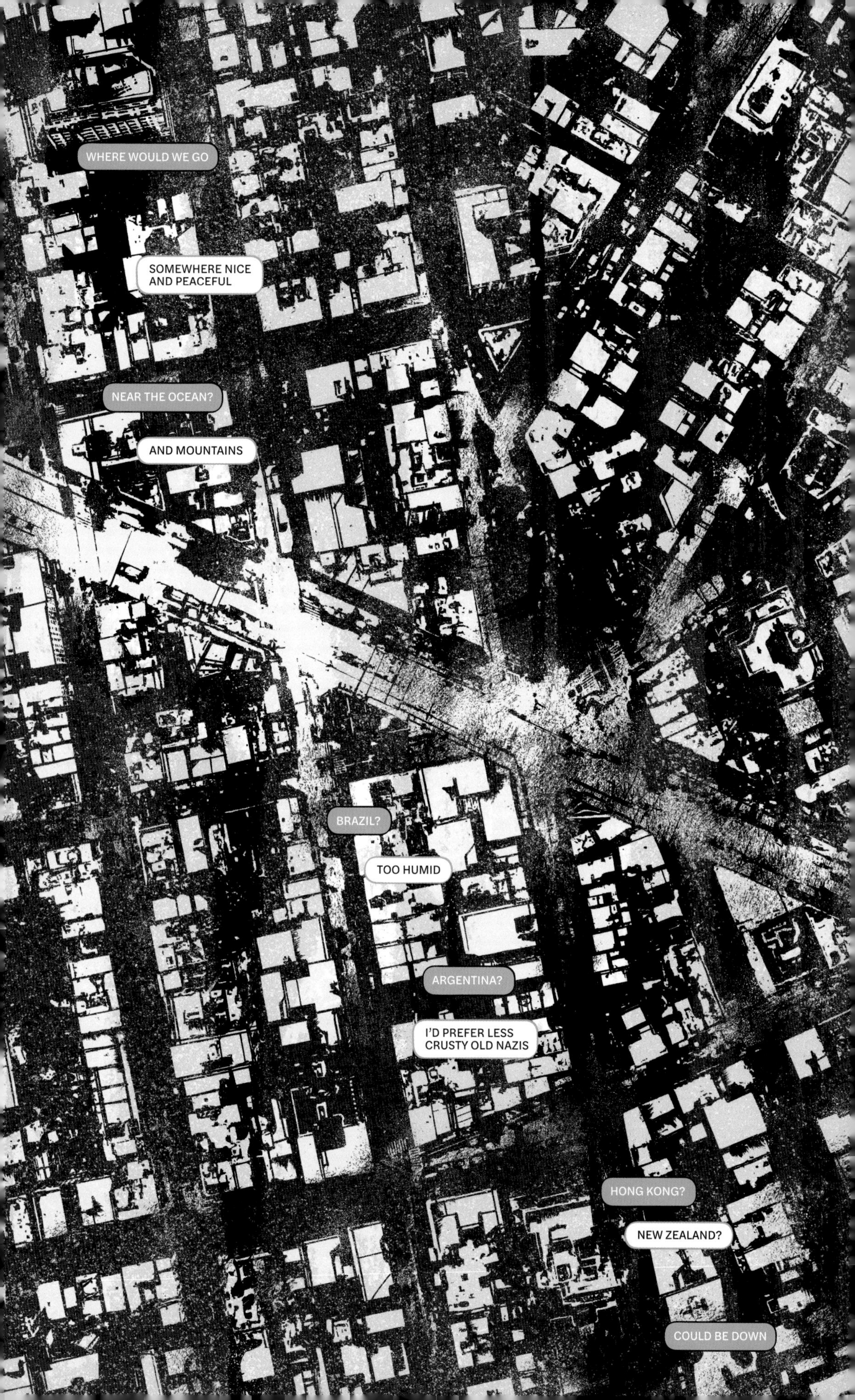
WHERE WOULD WE GO
SOMEWHERE NICE AND PEACEFUL
NEAR THE OCEAN?
AND MOUNTAINS
BRAZIL?
TOO HUMID
ARGENTINA?
I'D PREFER LESS CRUSTY OLD NAZIS
HONG KONG?
NEW ZEALAND?
COULD BE DOWN

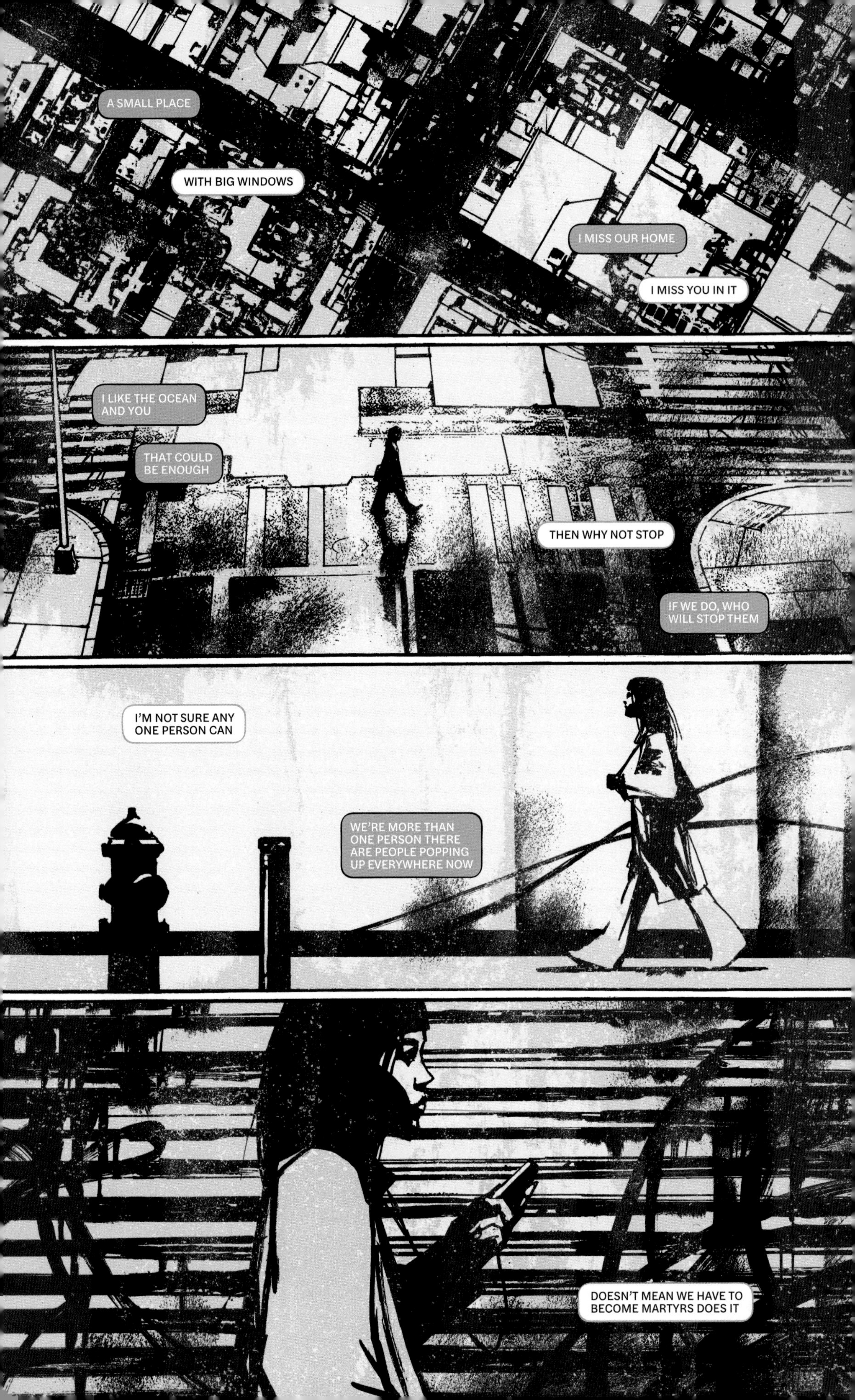
A SMALL PLACE
WITH BIG WINDOWS
I MISS OUR HOME
I MISS YOU IN IT
I LIKE THE OCEAN AND YOU
THAT COULD BE ENOUGH
THEN WHY NOT STOP
IF WE DO, WHO WILL STOP THEM
I'M NOT SURE ANY ONE PERSON CAN
WE'RE MORE THAN ONE PERSON THERE ARE PEOPLE POPPING UP EVERYWHERE NOW
DOESN'T MEAN WE HAVE TO BECOME MARTYRS DOES IT

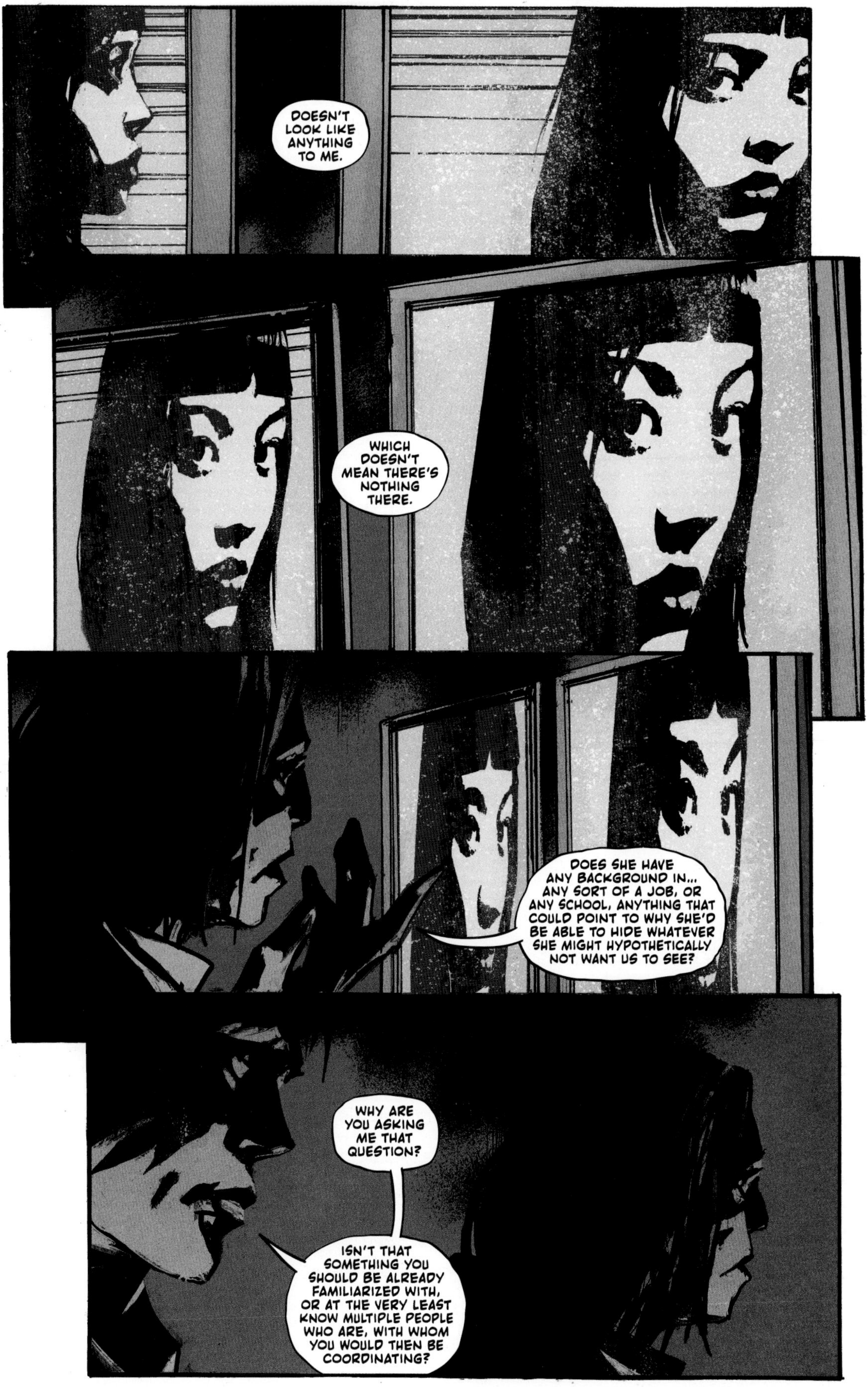
DOESN'T LOOK LIKE ANYTHING TO ME.
WHICH DOESN'T MEAN THERE'S NOTHING THERE.
DOES SHE HAVE ANY BACKGROUND IN... ANY SORT OF A JOB, OR ANY SCHOOL, ANYTHING THAT COULD POINT TO WHY SHE'D BE ABLE TO HIDE WHATEVER SHE MIGHT HYPOTHETICALLY NOT WANT US TO SEE?
WHY ARE YOU ASKING ME THAT QUESTION?
ISN'T THAT SOMETHING YOU SHOULD BE ALREADY FAMILIARIZED WITH, OR AT THE VERY LEAST KNOW MULTIPLE PEOPLE WHO ARE, WITH WHOM YOU WOULD THEN BE COORDINATING?

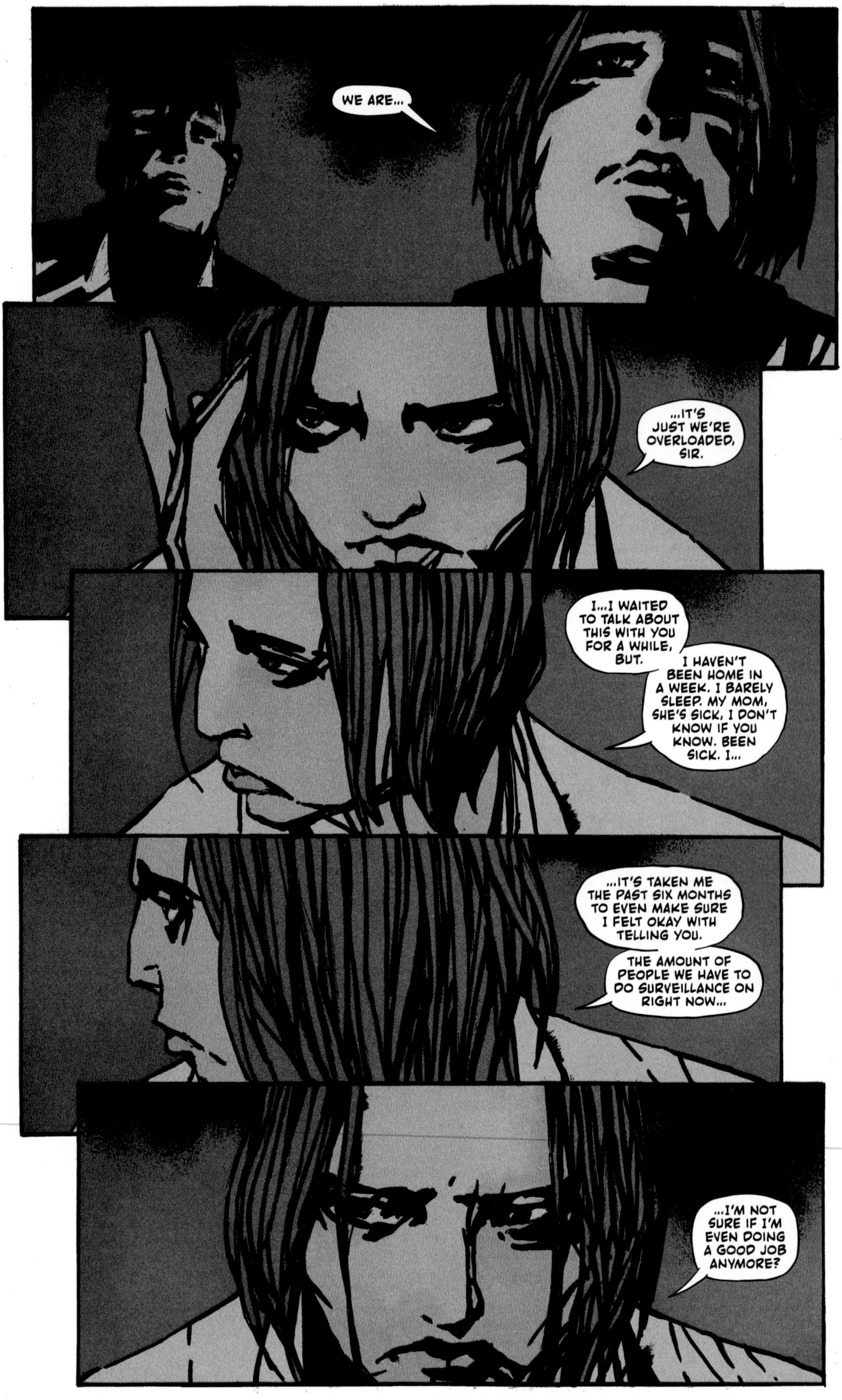
WE ARE...
...IT'S JUST WE'RE OVERLOADED, SIR.
I...I WAITED TO TALK ABOUT THIS WITH YOU FOR A WHILE, BUT.
I HAVEN'T BEEN HOME IN A WEEK. I BARELY SLEEP. MY MOM, SHE'S SICK, I DON'T KNOW IF YOU KNOW. BEEN SICK. I...
...IT'S TAKEN ME THE PAST SIX MONTHS TO EVEN MAKE SURE I FELT OKAY WITH TELLING YOU.
THE AMOUNT OF PEOPLE WE HAVE TO DO SURVEILLANCE ON RIGHT NOW...
...I'M NOT SURE IF I'M EVEN DOING A GOOD JOB ANYMORE?

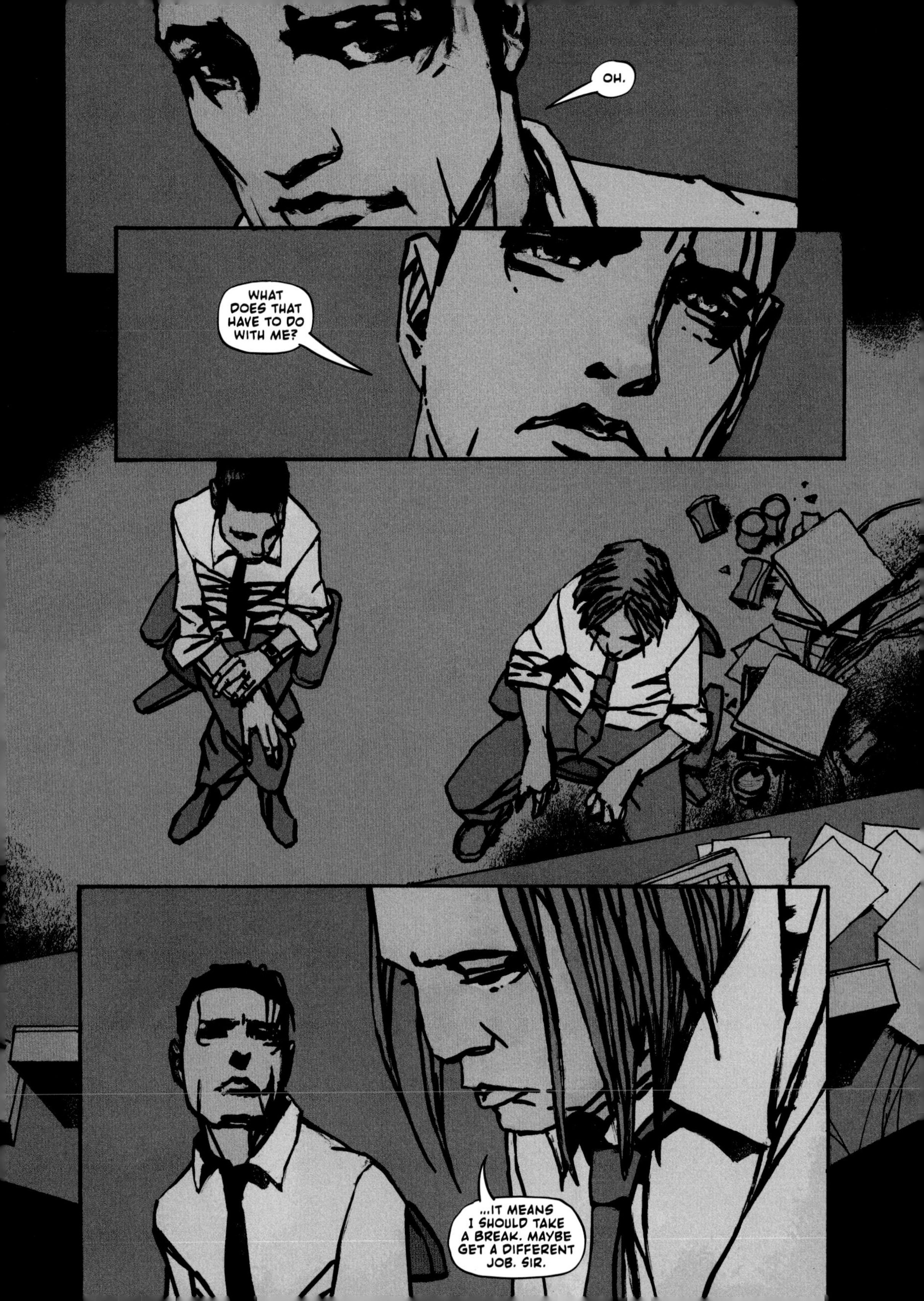
OH.
WHAT DOES THAT HAVE TO DO WITH ME?
...IT MEANS I SHOULD TAKE A BREAK. MAYBE GET A DIFFERENT JOB. SIR.

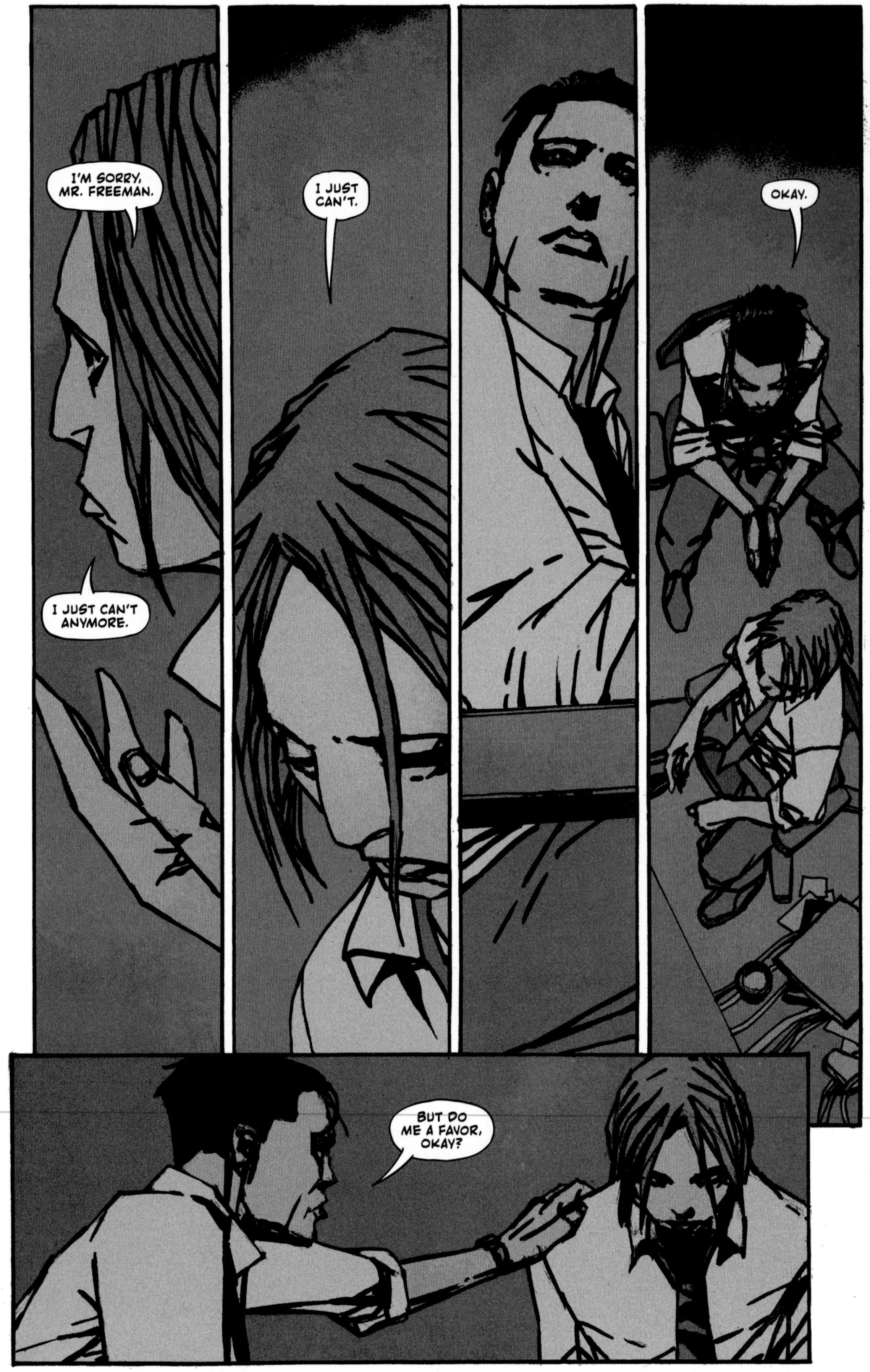
I'M SORRY, MR. FREEMAN.
I JUST CAN'T ANYMORE.
I JUST CAN'T.
OKAY.
BUT DO ME A FAVOR, OKAY?

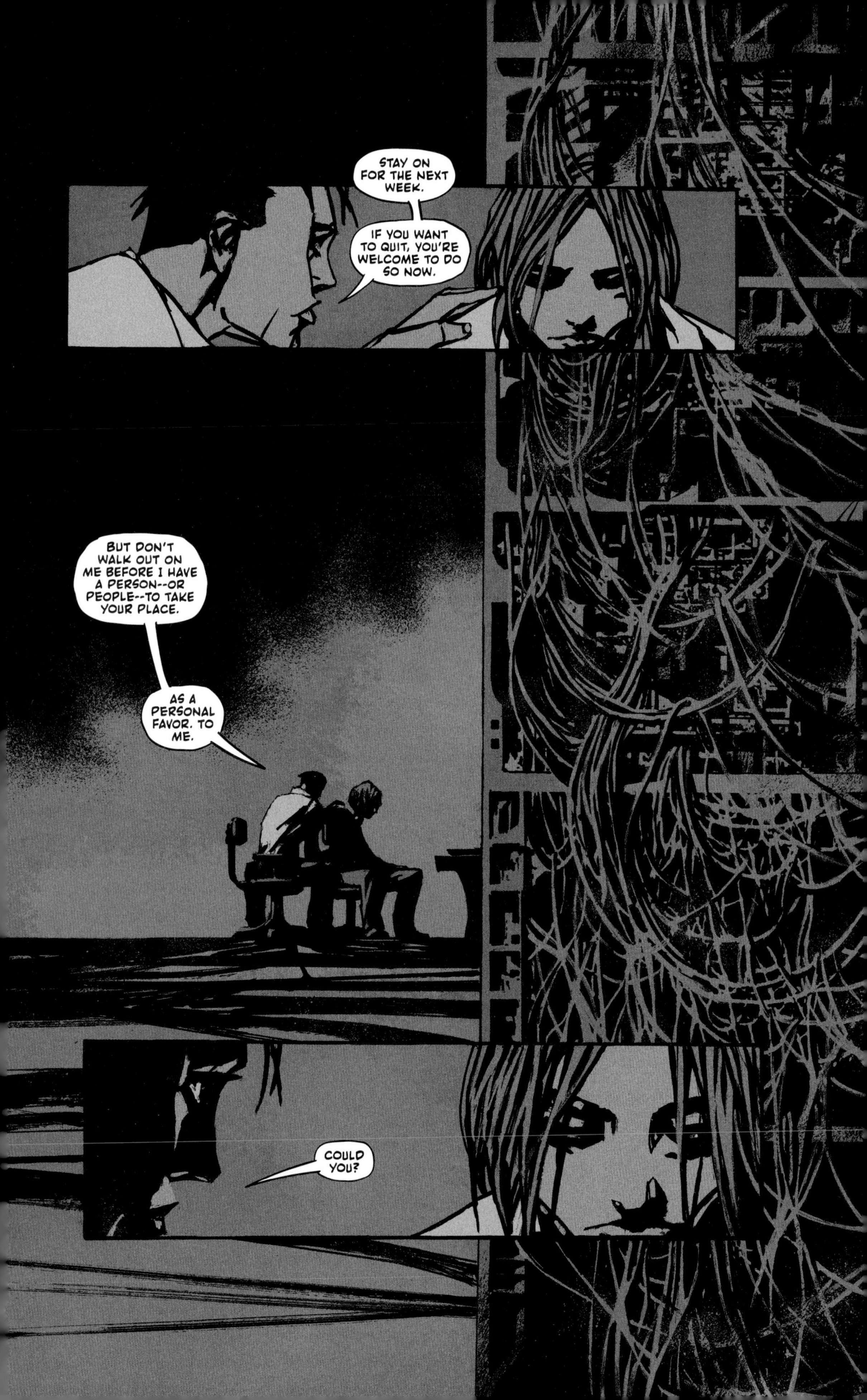
STAY ON FOR THE NEXT WEEK.
IF YOU WANT TO QUIT, YOU'RE WELCOME TO DO SO NOW.
BUT DON'T WALK OUT ON ME BEFORE I HAVE A PERSON--OR PEOPLE--TO TAKE YOUR PLACE.
AS A PERSONAL FAVOR. TO ME.
COULD YOU?

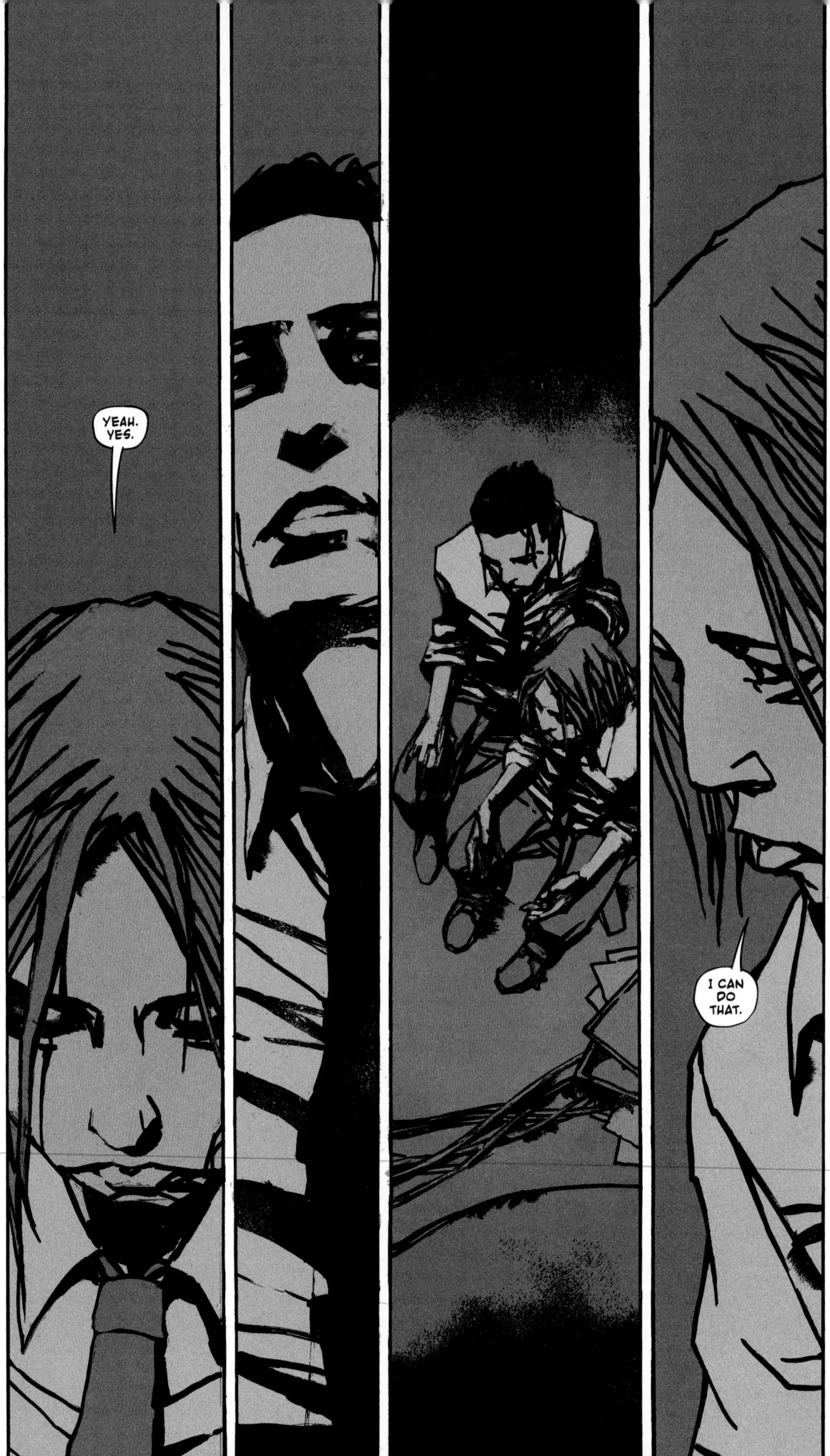
YEAH. YES.
I CAN DO THAT.

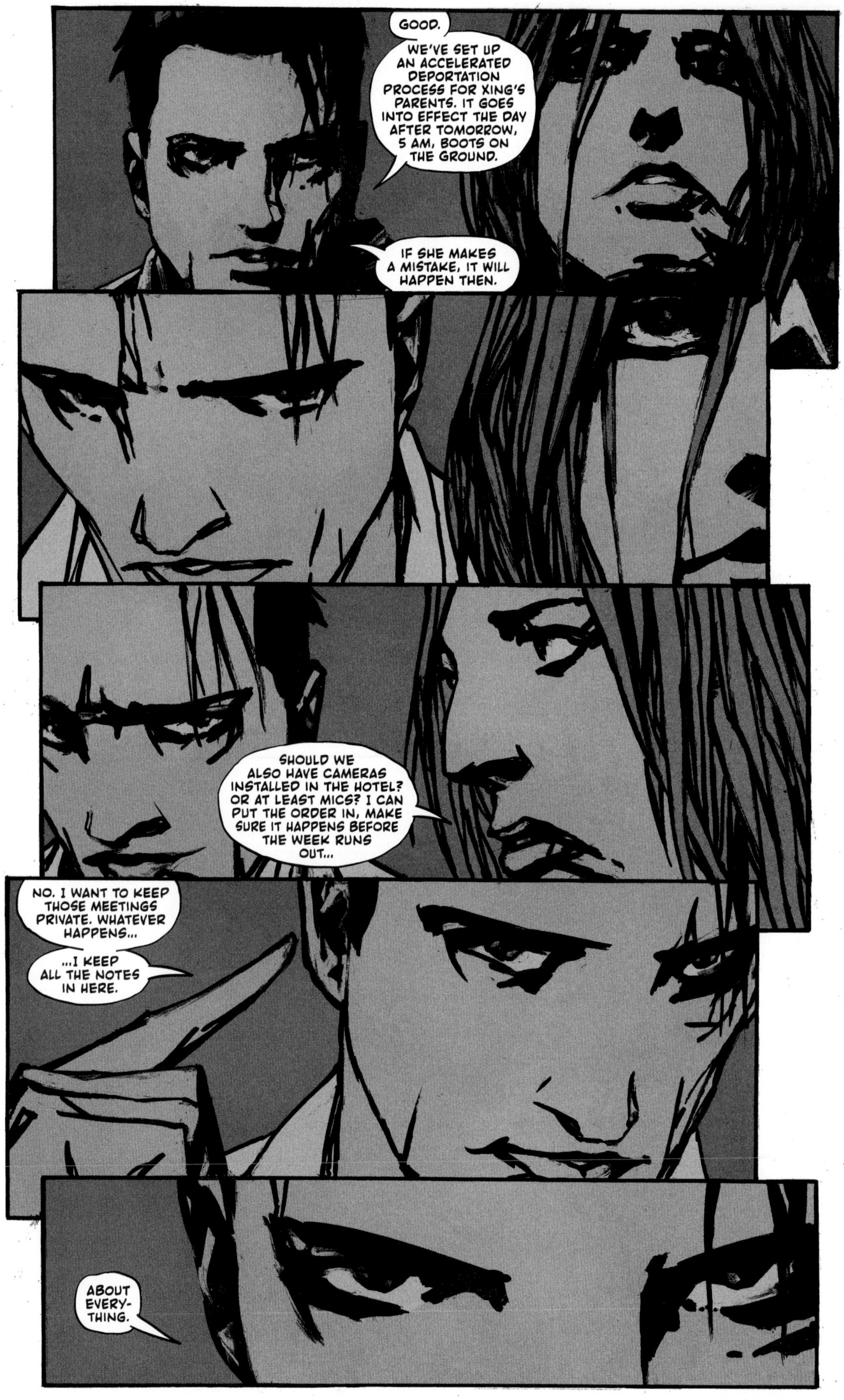
GOOD.
WE'VE SET UP AN ACCELERATED DEPORTATION PROCESS FOR XING'S PARENTS. IT GOES INTO EFFECT THE DAY AFTER TOMORROW, 5 AM, BOOTS ON THE GROUND.
IF SHE MAKES A MISTAKE, IT WILL HAPPEN THEN.
SHOULD WE ALSO HAVE CAMERAS INSTALLED IN THE HOTEL? OR AT LEAST MICS? I CAN PUT THE ORDER IN, MAKE SURE IT HAPPENS BEFORE THE WEEK RUNS OUT...
NO. I WANT TO KEEP THOSE MEETINGS PRIVATE. WHATEVER HAPPENS...
...I KEEP ALL THE NOTES IN HERE.
ABOUT EVERY-THING.

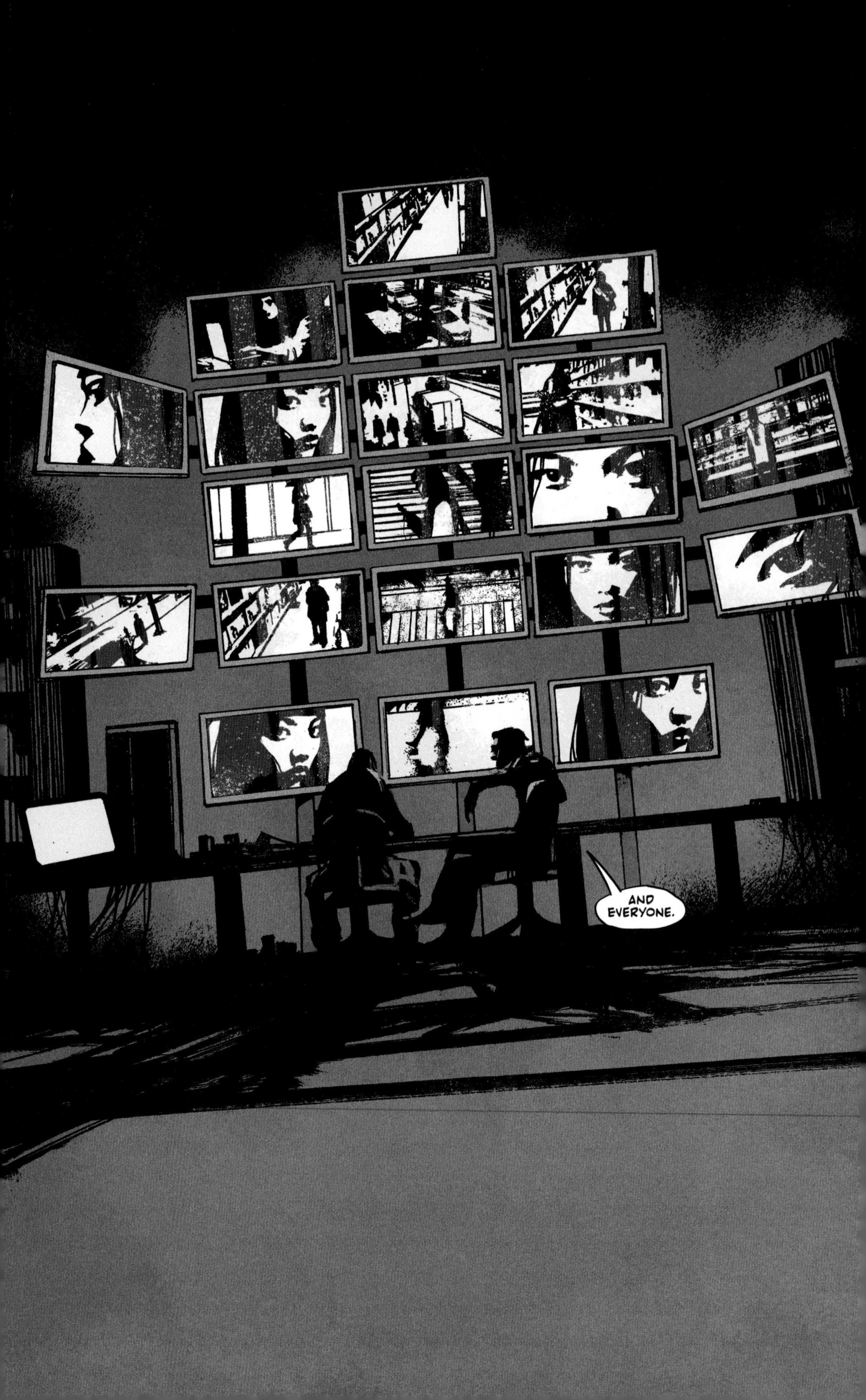
AND EVERYONE.

CHAPTER NINE:
TIRED,
TIRED,
TIRED.

*"My bones hold a stillness, the far
  Fields melt my heart."*

—Sylvia Plath, "Sheep in Fog"

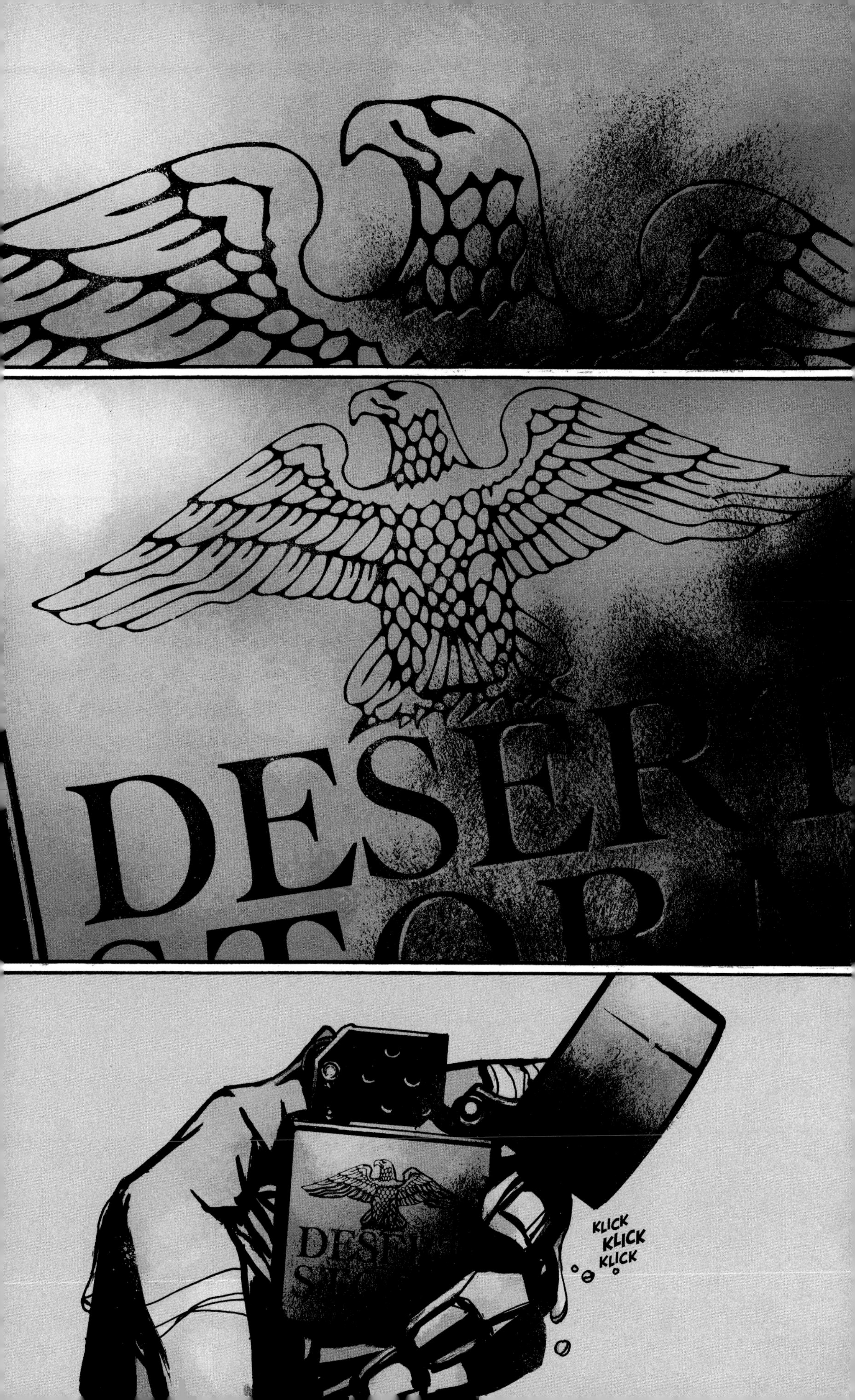
KLICK
KLICK
KLICK

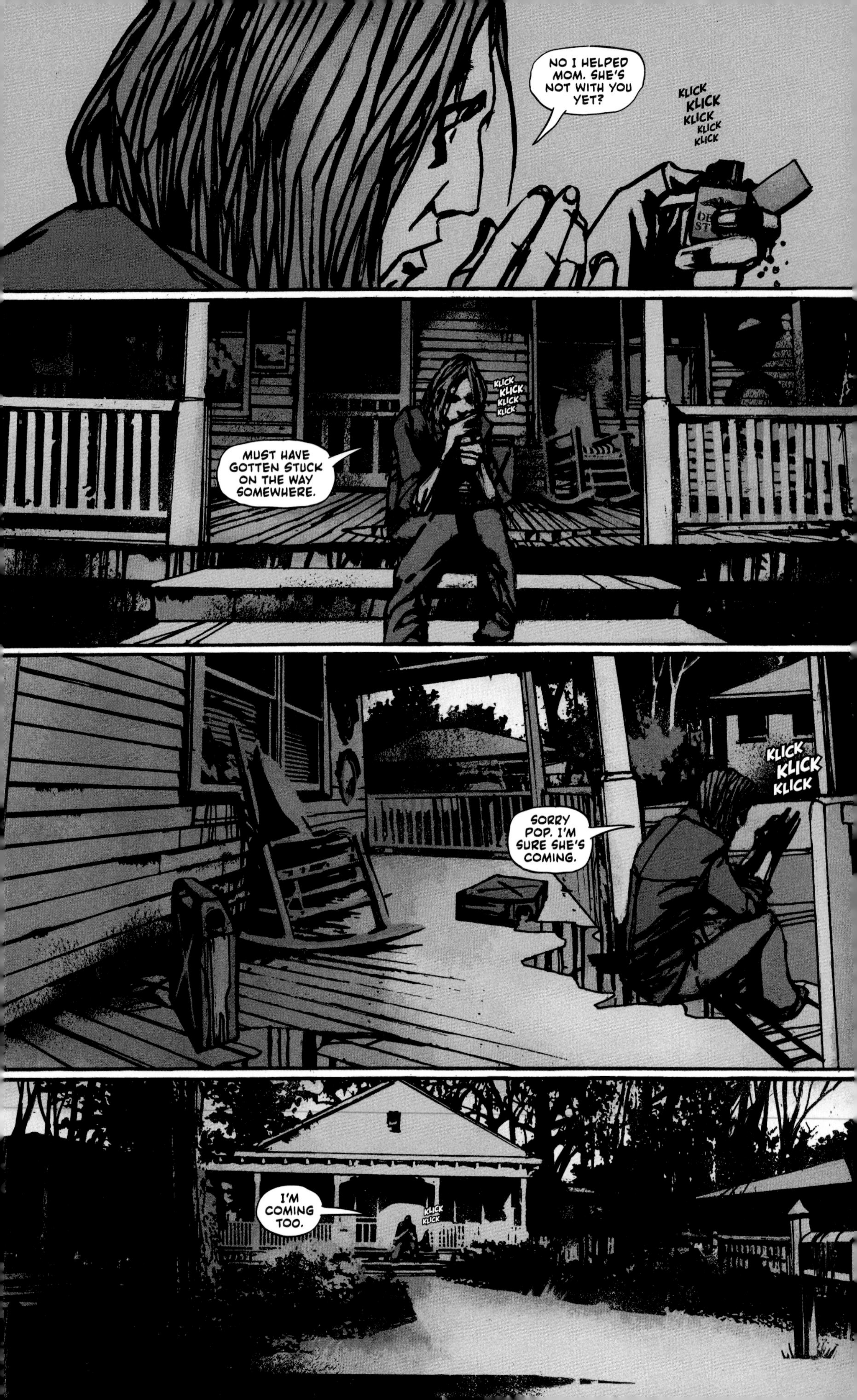
NO I HELPED MOM. SHE'S NOT WITH YOU YET?
KLICK KLICK KLICK KLICK KLICK
KLICK KLICK KLICK KLICK
MUST HAVE GOTTEN STUCK ON THE WAY SOMEWHERE.
KLICK KLICK KLICK
SORRY POP. I'M SURE SHE'S COMING.
I'M COMING TOO.
KLICK KLICK

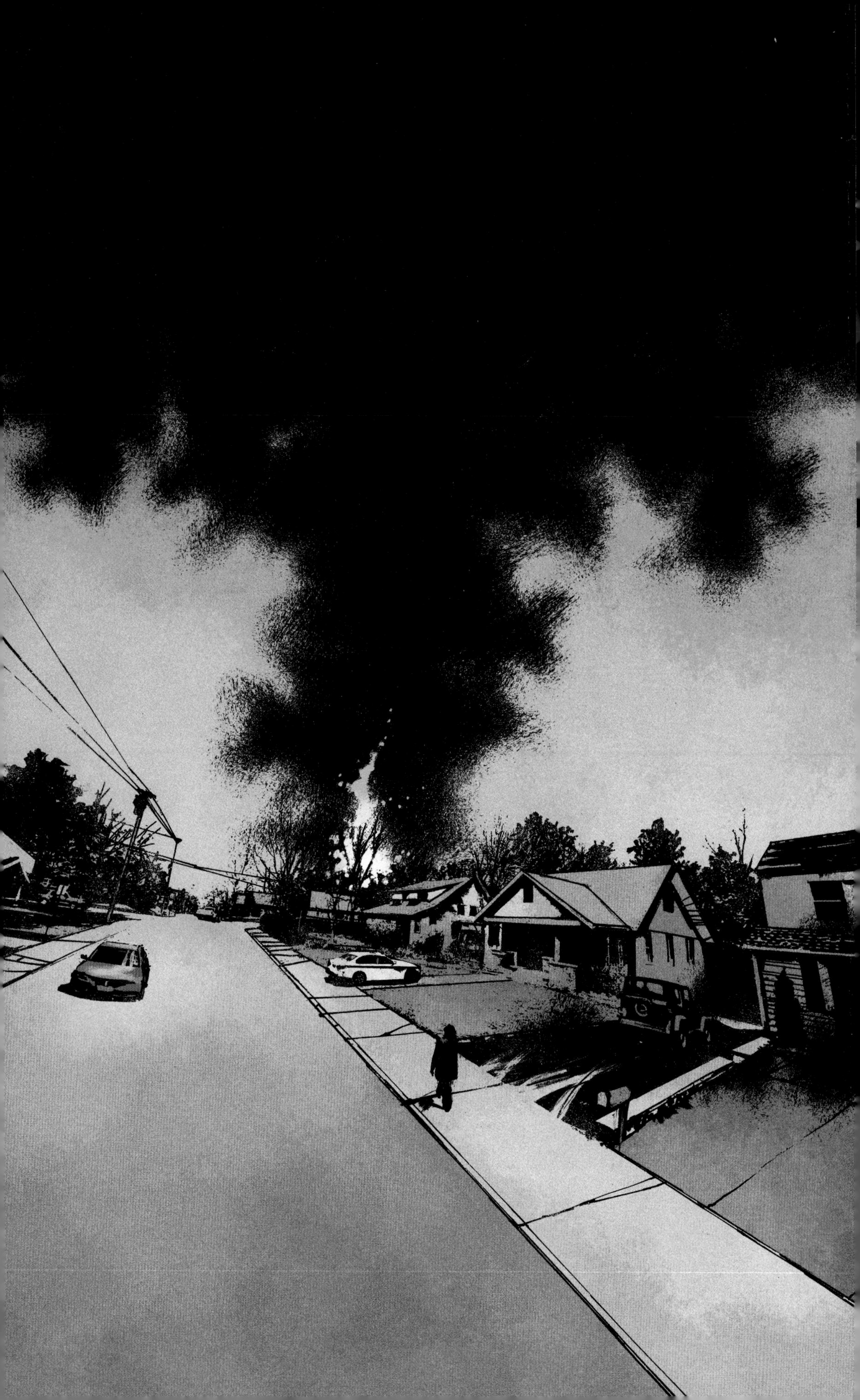

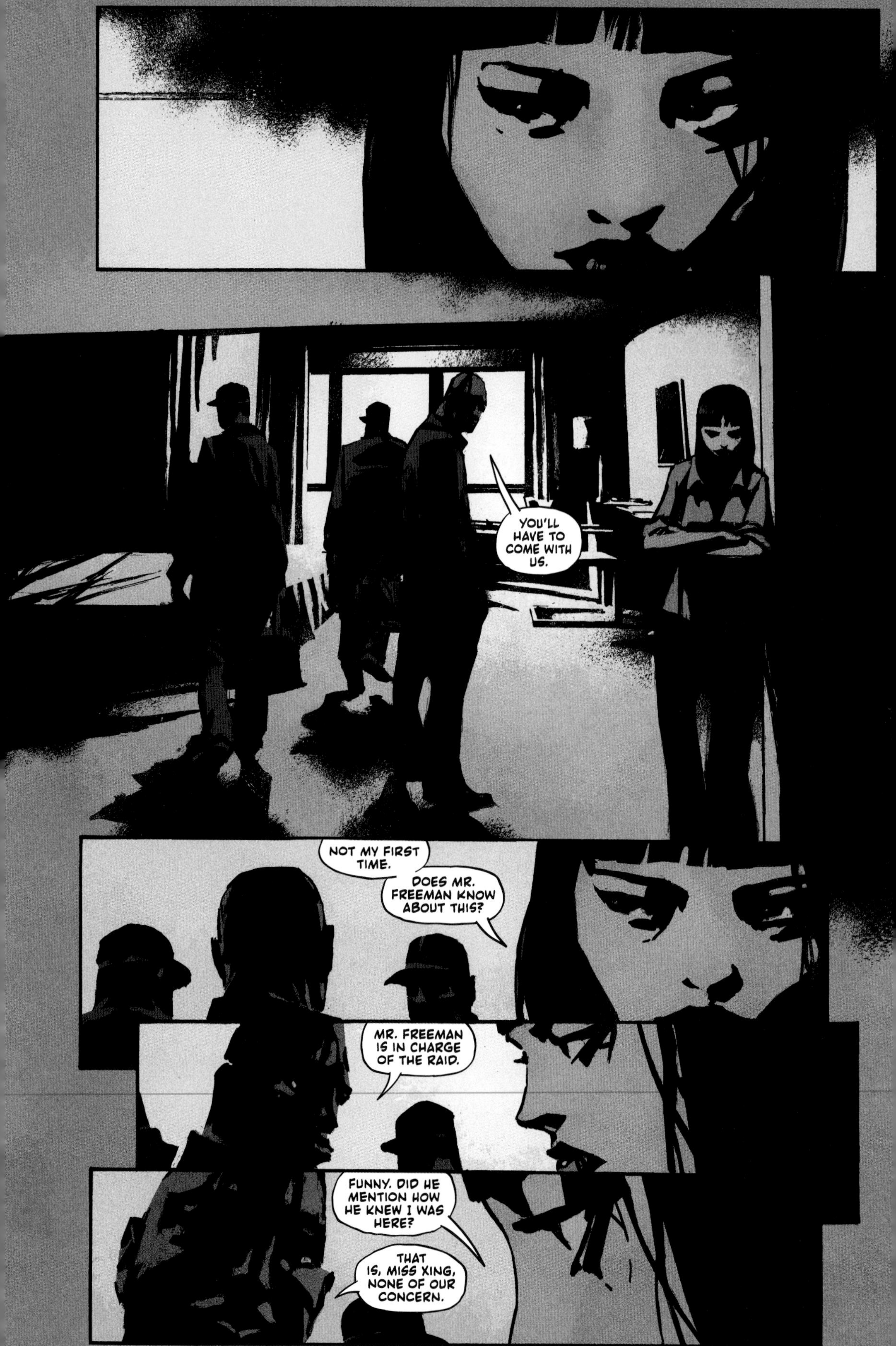
YOU'LL HAVE TO COME WITH US.
NOT MY FIRST TIME.
DOES MR. FREEMAN KNOW ABOUT THIS?
MR. FREEMAN IS IN CHARGE OF THE RAID.
FUNNY. DID HE MENTION HOW HE KNEW I WAS HERE?
THAT IS, MISS XING, NONE OF OUR CONCERN.

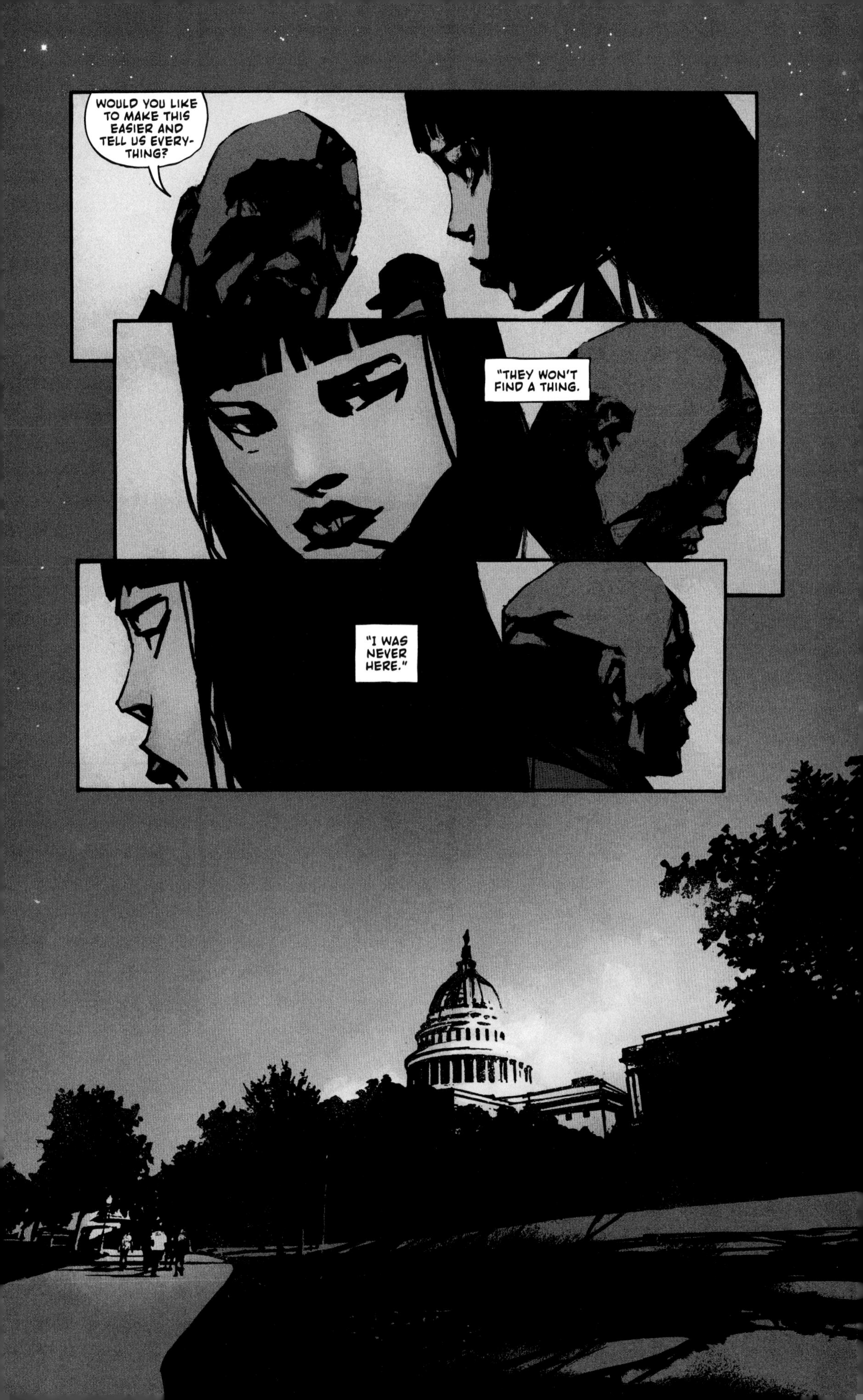
WOULD YOU LIKE TO MAKE THIS EASIER AND TELL US EVERY- THING?
"THEY WON'T FIND A THING.
"I WAS NEVER HERE."

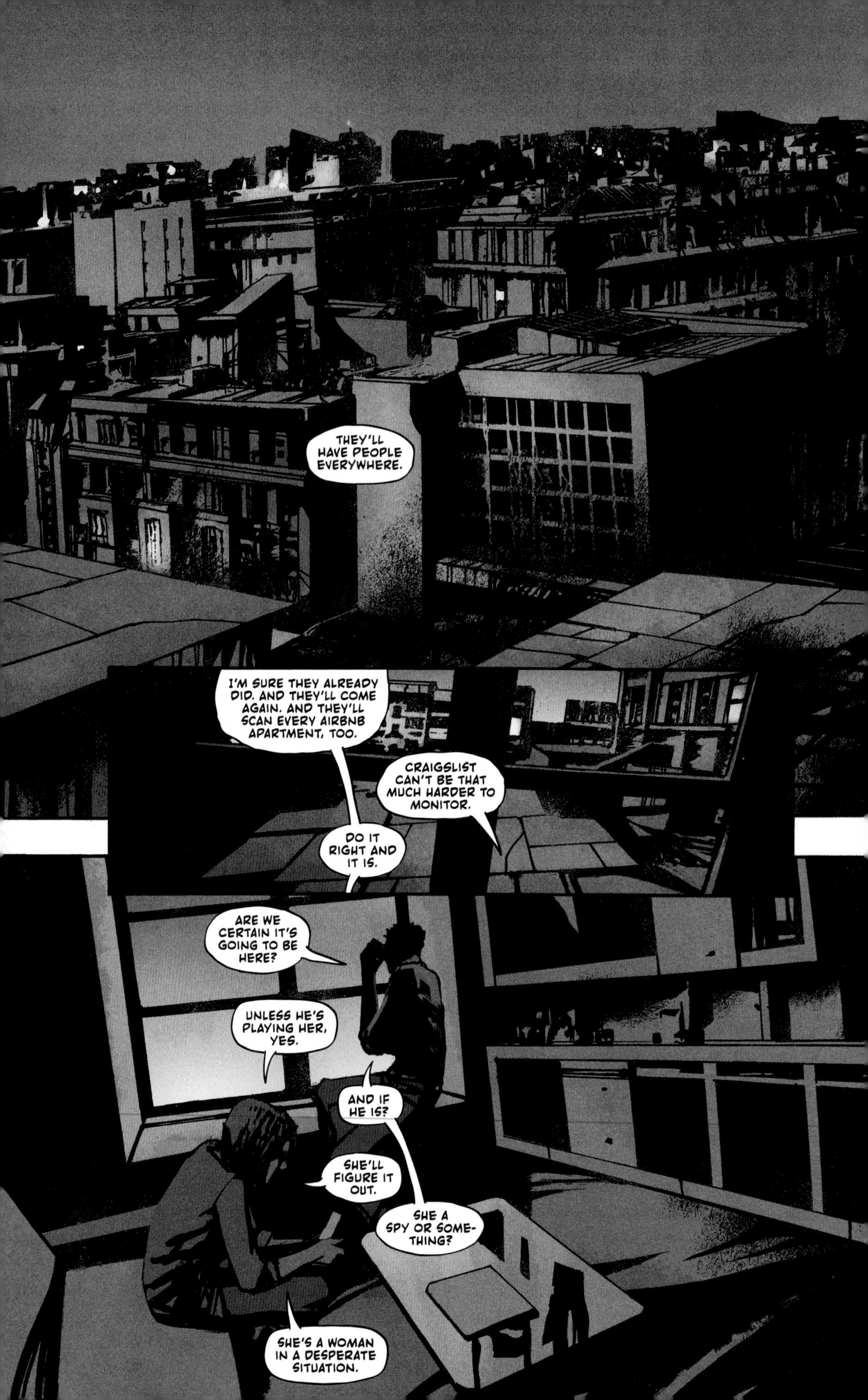
THEY'LL HAVE PEOPLE EVERYWHERE.
I'M SURE THEY ALREADY DID. AND THEY'LL COME AGAIN. AND THEY'LL SCAN EVERY AIRBNB APARTMENT, TOO.
CRAIGSLIST CAN'T BE THAT MUCH HARDER TO MONITOR.
DO IT RIGHT AND IT IS.
ARE WE CERTAIN IT'S GOING TO BE HERE?
UNLESS HE'S PLAYING HER, YES.
AND IF HE IS?
SHE'LL FIGURE IT OUT.
SHE A SPY OR SOME-THING?
SHE'S A WOMAN IN A DESPERATE SITUATION.

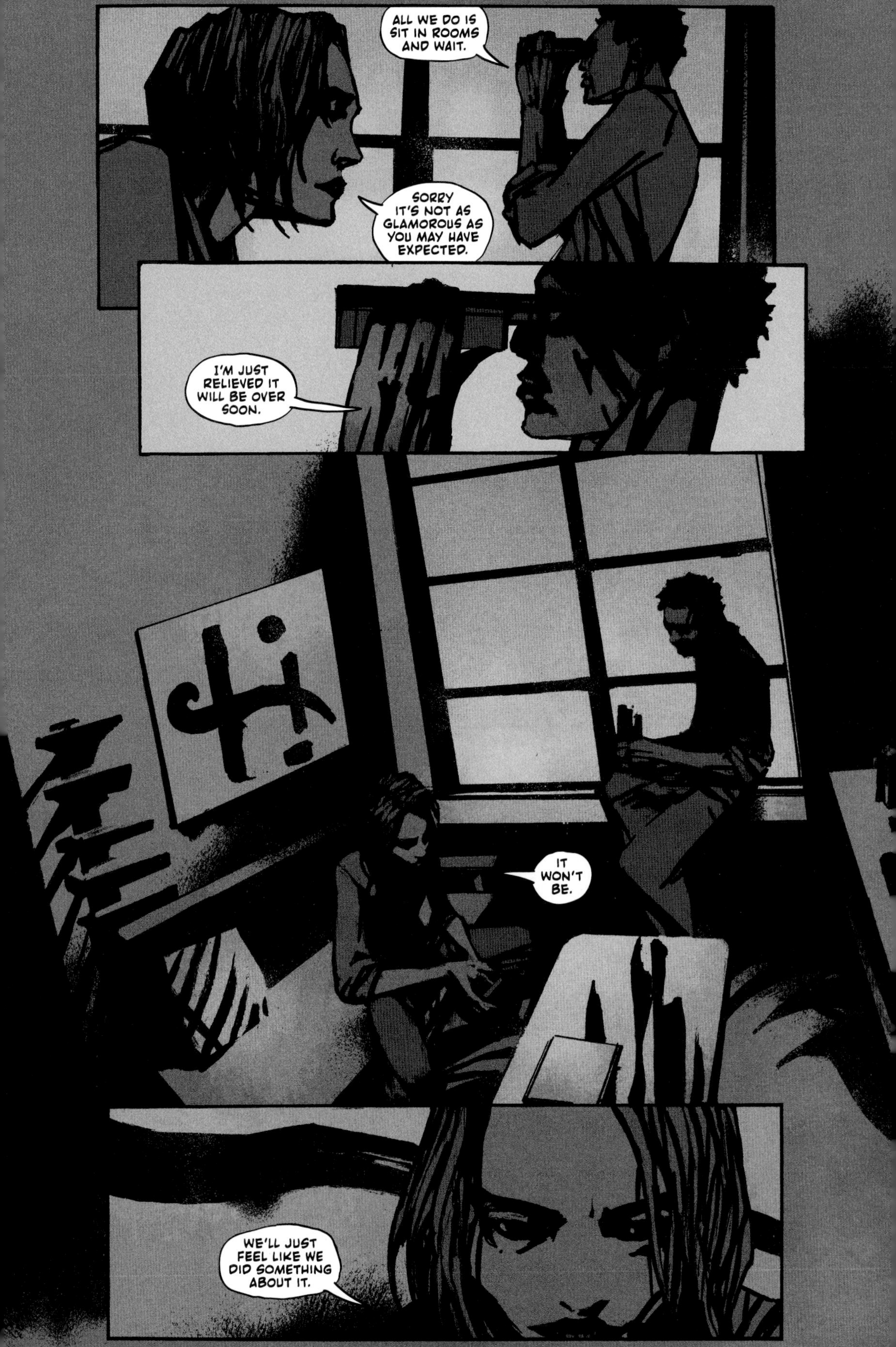
ALL WE DO IS SIT IN ROOMS AND WAIT.
SORRY IT'S NOT AS GLAMOROUS AS YOU MAY HAVE EXPECTED.
I'M JUST RELIEVED IT WILL BE OVER SOON.
IT WON'T BE.
WE'LL JUST FEEL LIKE WE DID SOMETHING ABOUT IT.

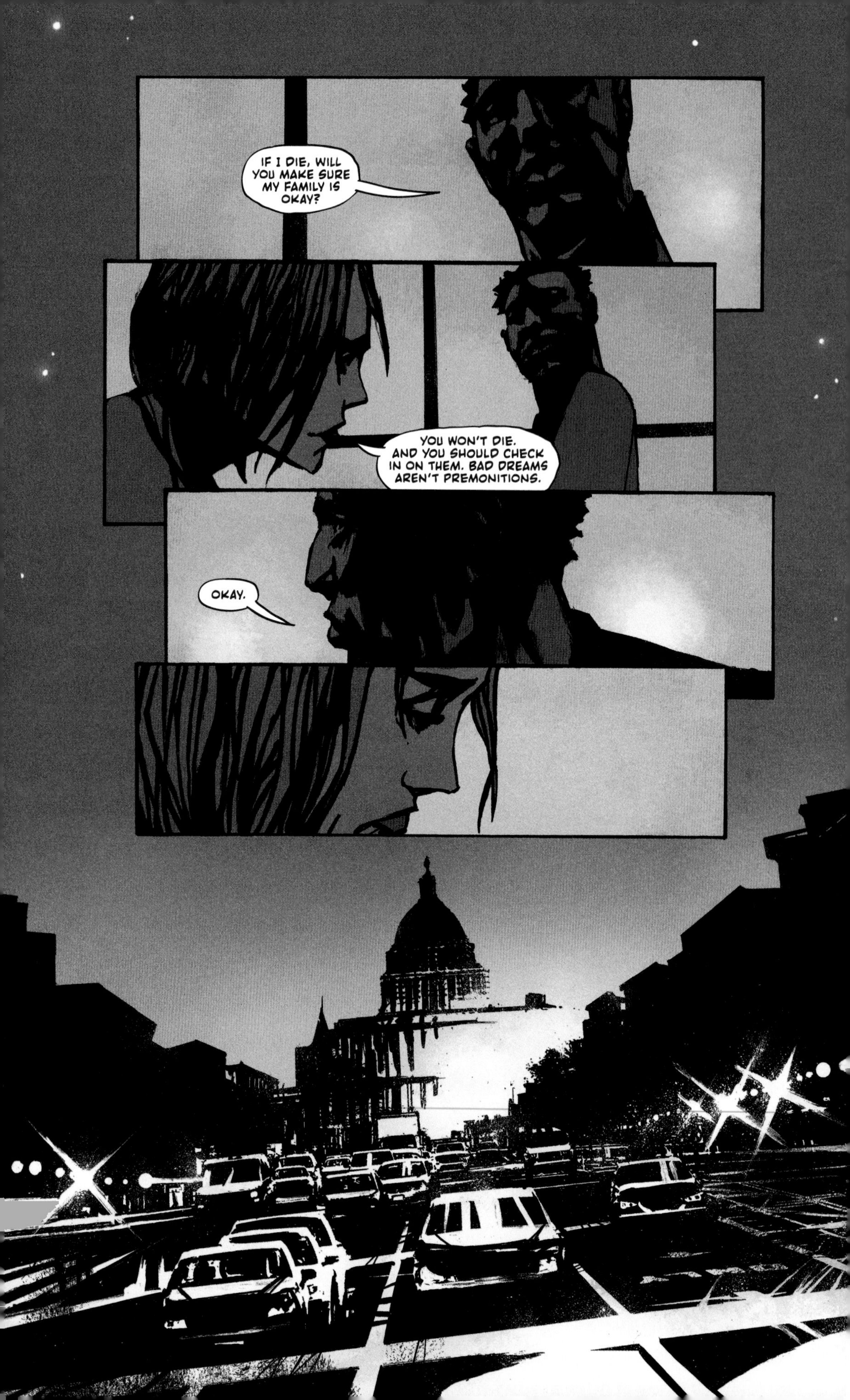
IF I DIE, WILL YOU MAKE SURE MY FAMILY IS OKAY?
YOU WON'T DIE. AND YOU SHOULD CHECK IN ON THEM. BAD DREAMS AREN'T PREMONITIONS.
OKAY.

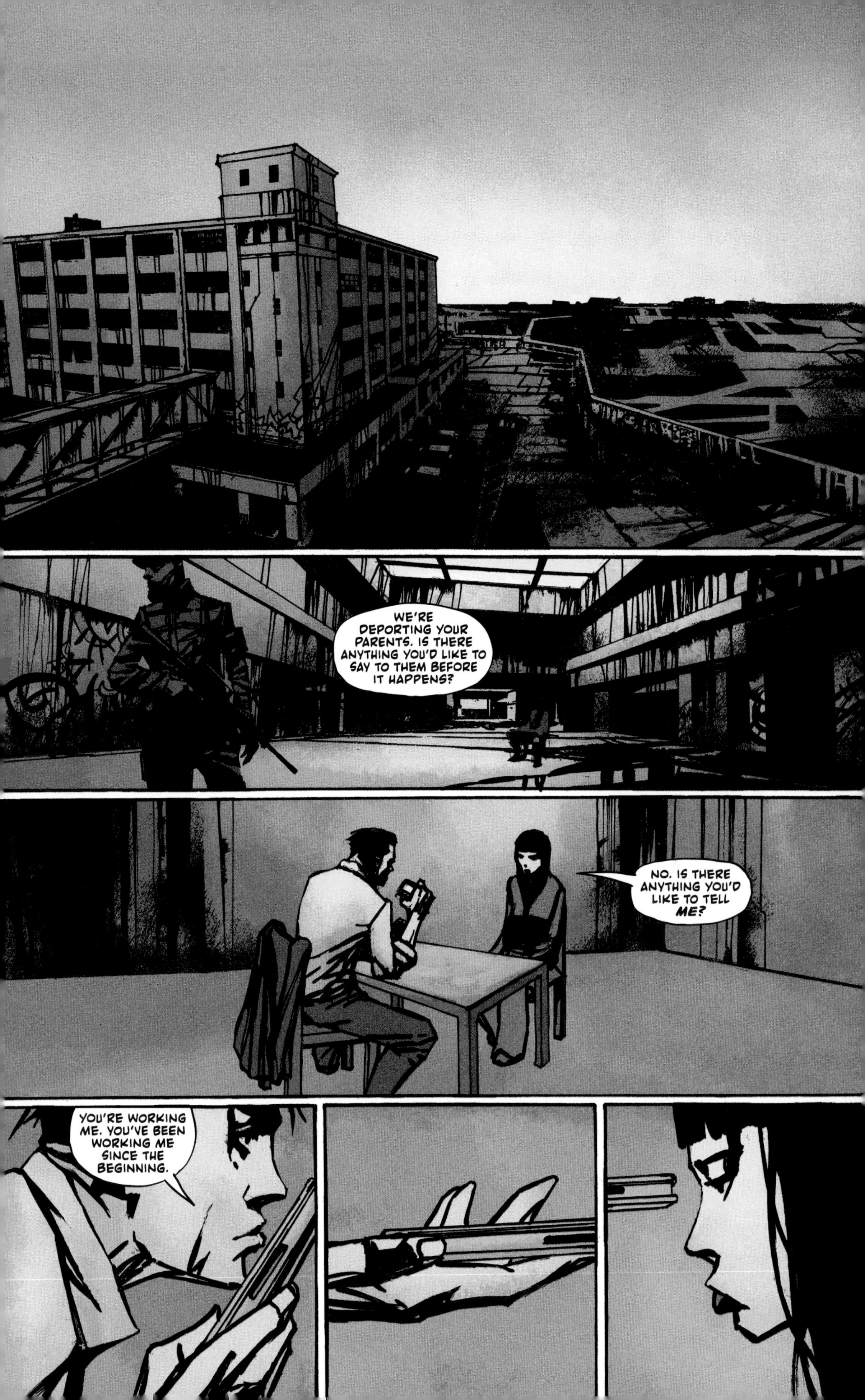
WE'RE DEPORTING YOUR PARENTS. IS THERE ANYTHING YOU'D LIKE TO SAY TO THEM BEFORE IT HAPPENS?
NO. IS THERE ANYTHING YOU'D LIKE TO TELL ME?
YOU'RE WORKING ME. YOU'VE BEEN WORKING ME SINCE THE BEGINNING.

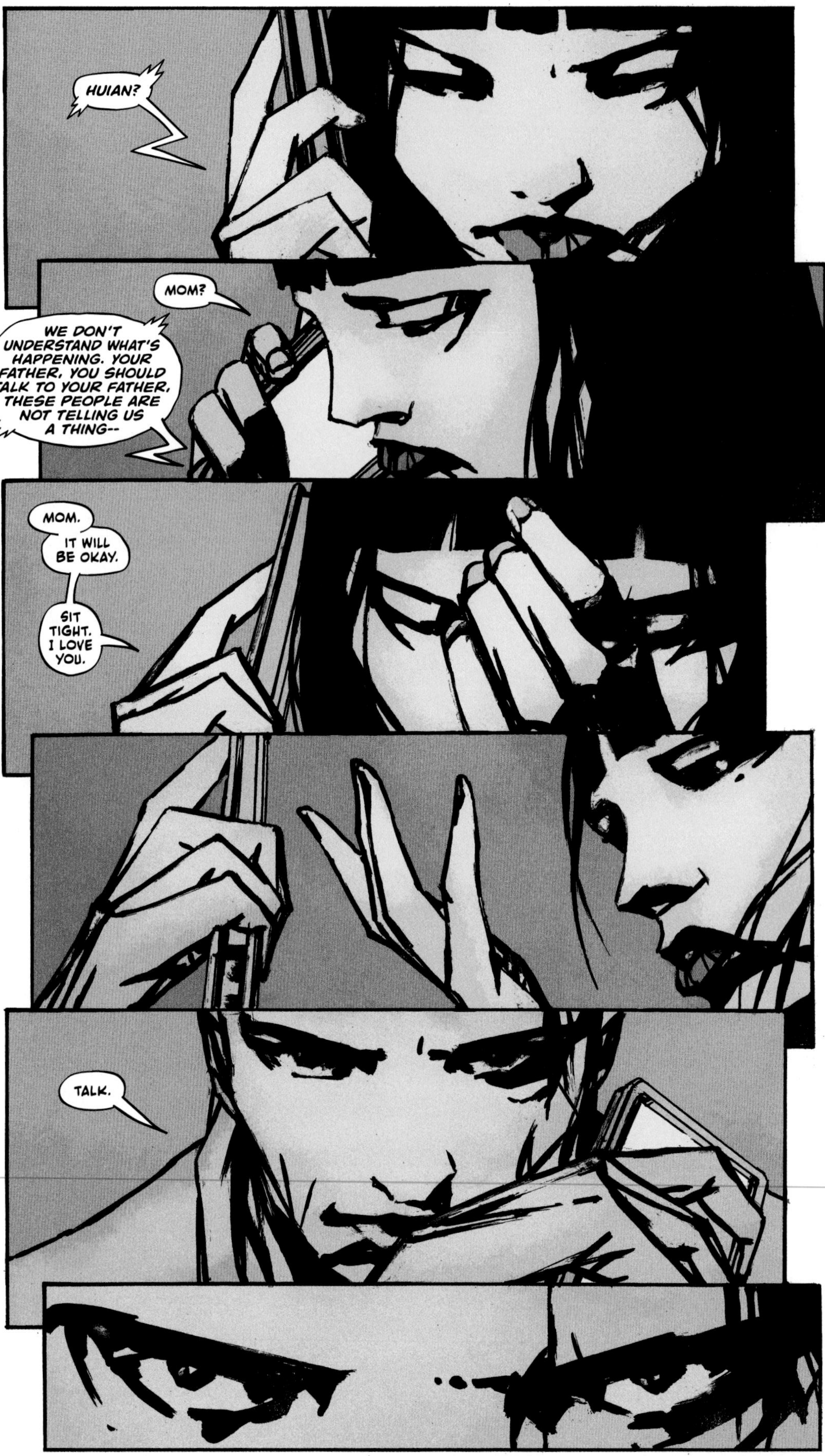
HUIAN?
MOM?
WE DON'T UNDERSTAND WHAT'S HAPPENING. YOUR FATHER, YOU SHOULD TALK TO YOUR FATHER, THESE PEOPLE ARE NOT TELLING US A THING--
MOM.
IT WILL BE OKAY.
SIT TIGHT. I LOVE YOU.
TALK.

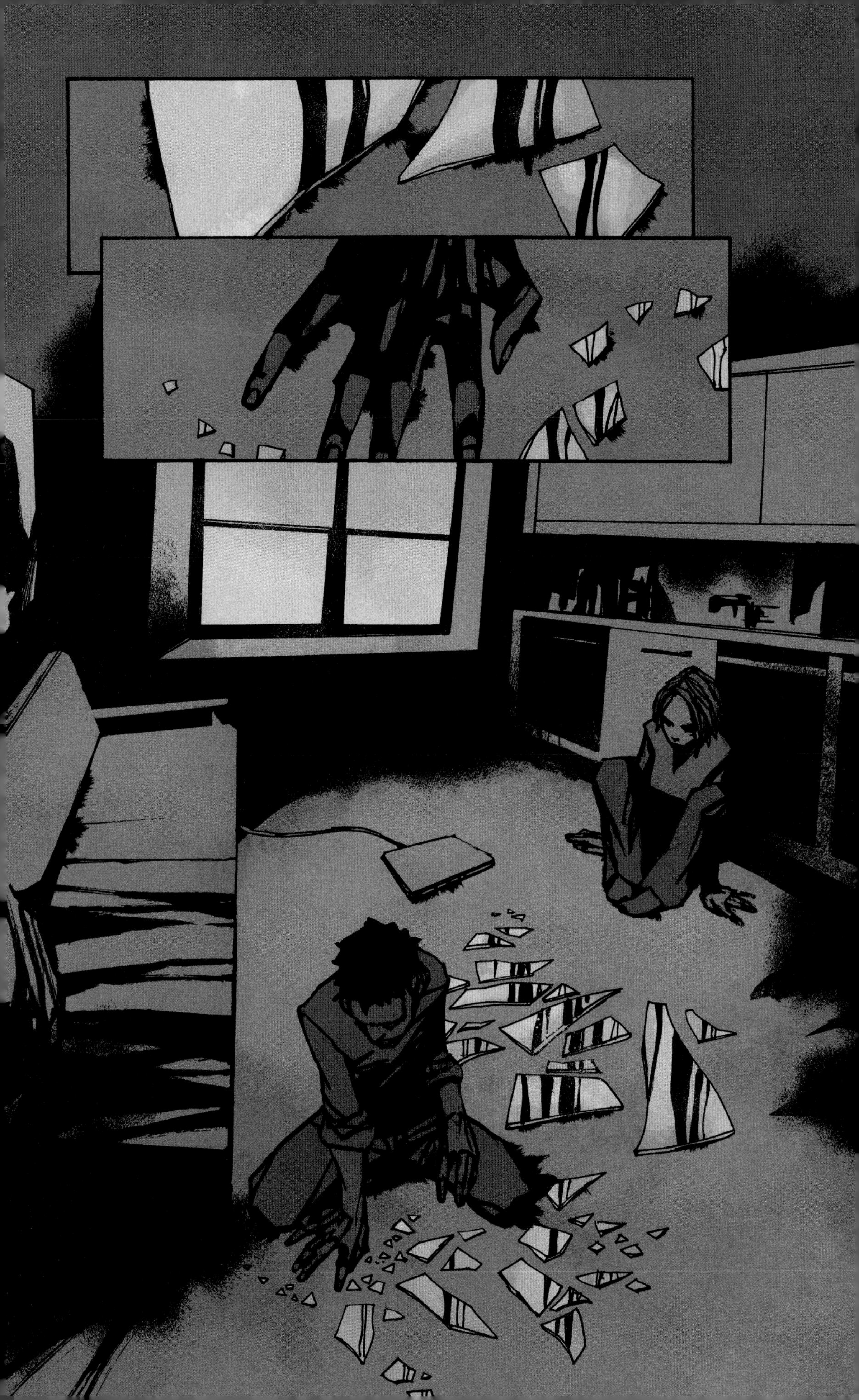

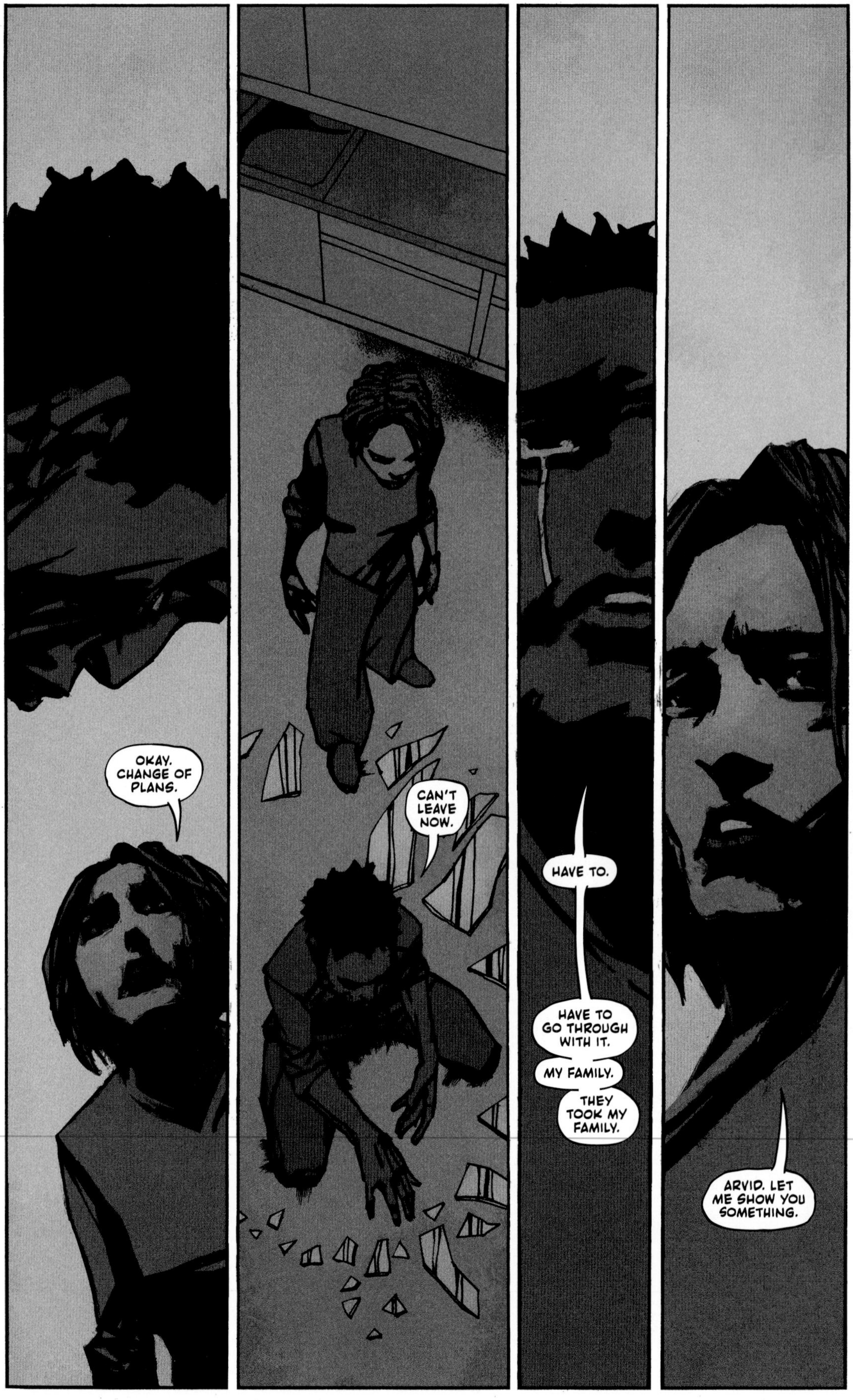
OKAY. CHANGE OF PLANS.
CAN'T LEAVE NOW.
HAVE TO.
HAVE TO GO THROUGH WITH IT.
MY FAMILY.
THEY TOOK MY FAMILY.
ARVID. LET ME SHOW YOU SOMETHING.

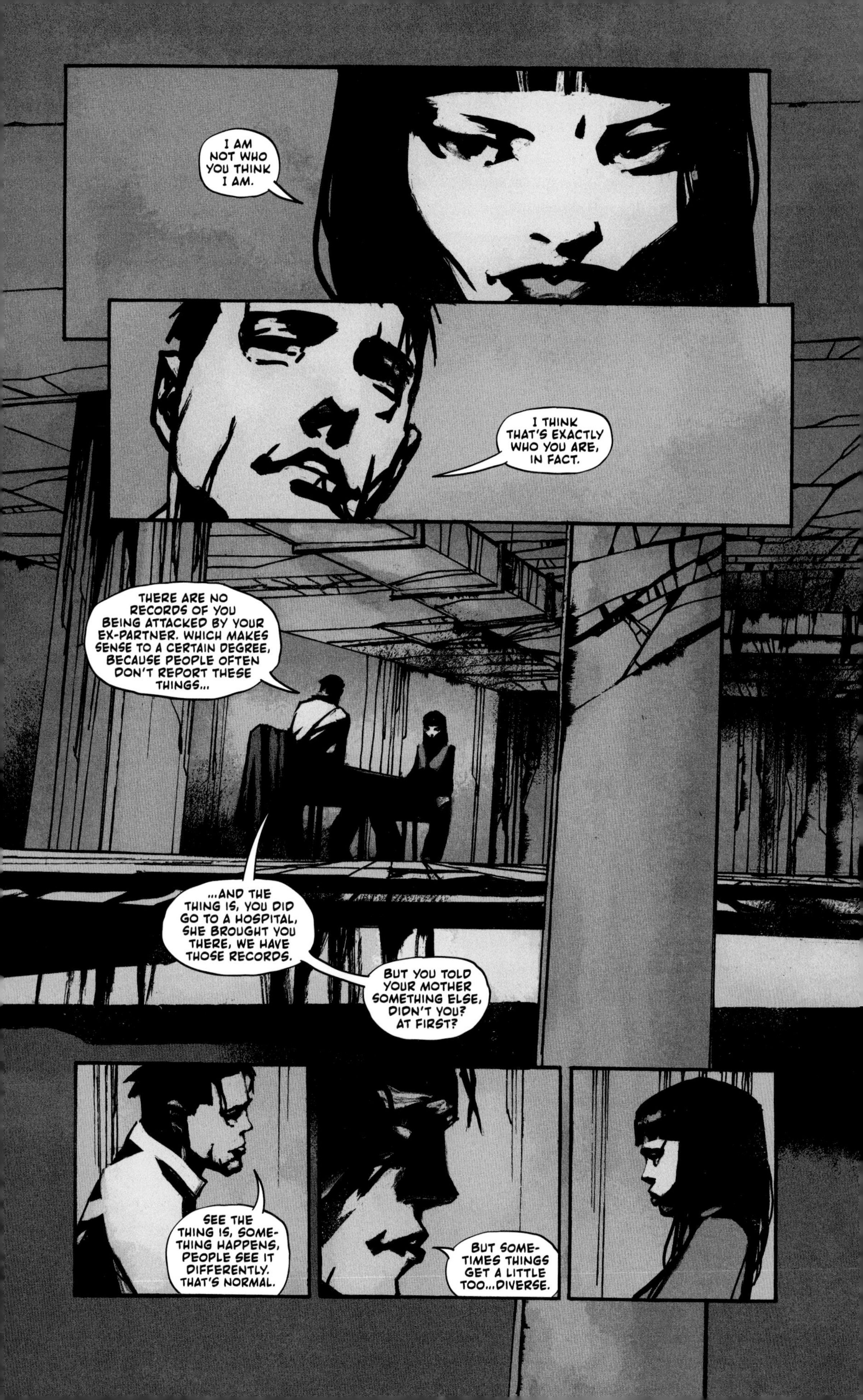
I AM NOT WHO YOU THINK I AM.
I THINK THAT'S EXACTLY WHO YOU ARE, IN FACT.
THERE ARE NO RECORDS OF YOU BEING ATTACKED BY YOUR EX-PARTNER. WHICH MAKES SENSE TO A CERTAIN DEGREE, BECAUSE PEOPLE OFTEN DON'T REPORT THESE THINGS...
...AND THE THING IS, YOU DID GO TO A HOSPITAL, SHE BROUGHT YOU THERE, WE HAVE THOSE RECORDS.
BUT YOU TOLD YOUR MOTHER SOMETHING ELSE, DIDN'T YOU? AT FIRST?
SEE THE THING IS, SOME-THING HAPPENS, PEOPLE SEE IT DIFFERENTLY. THAT'S NORMAL.
BUT SOME-TIMES THINGS GET A LITTLE TOO...DIVERSE.

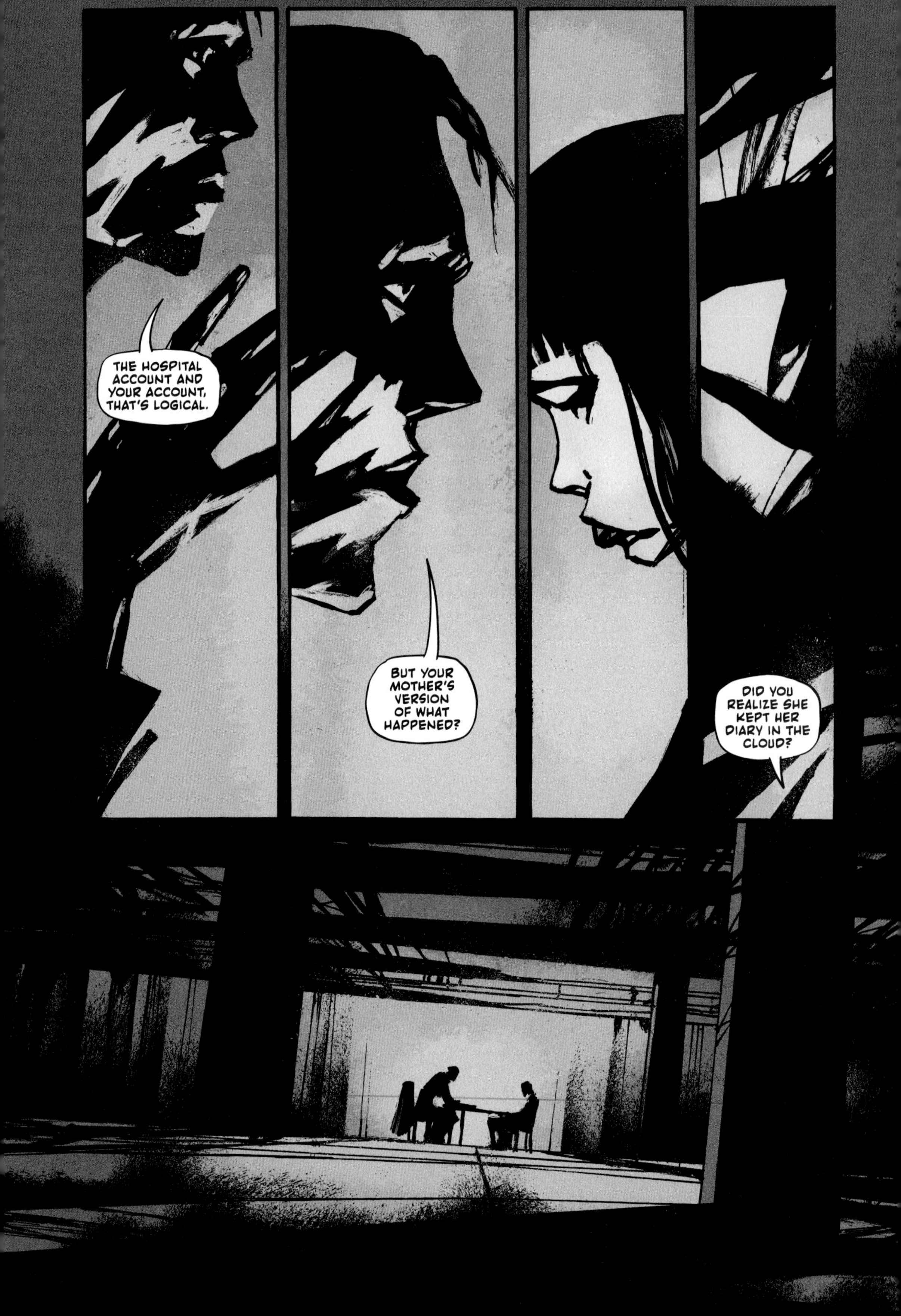
THE HOSPITAL ACCOUNT AND YOUR ACCOUNT, THAT'S LOGICAL.
BUT YOUR MOTHER'S VERSION OF WHAT HAPPENED?
DID YOU REALIZE SHE KEPT HER DIARY IN THE CLOUD?

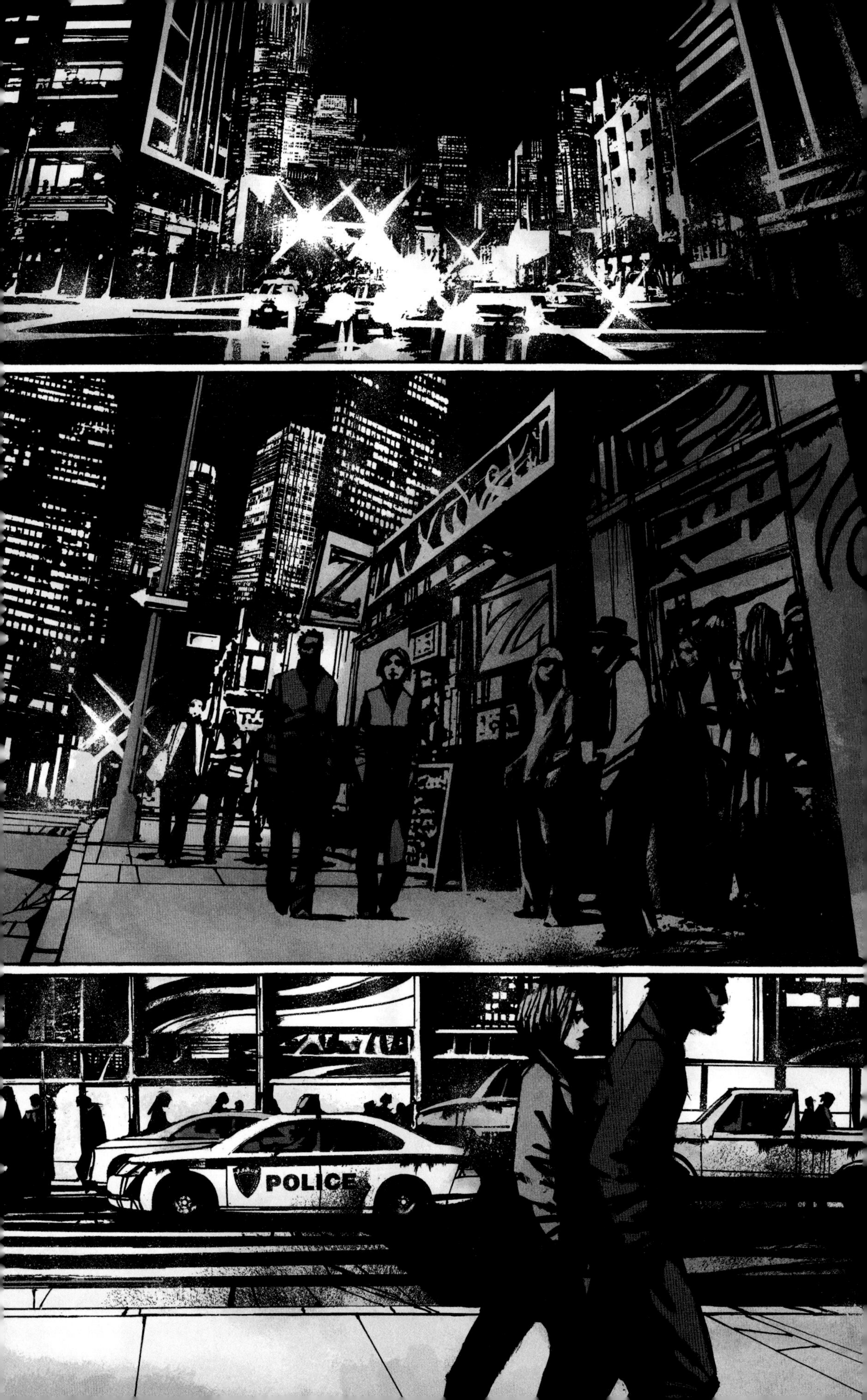
POLICE

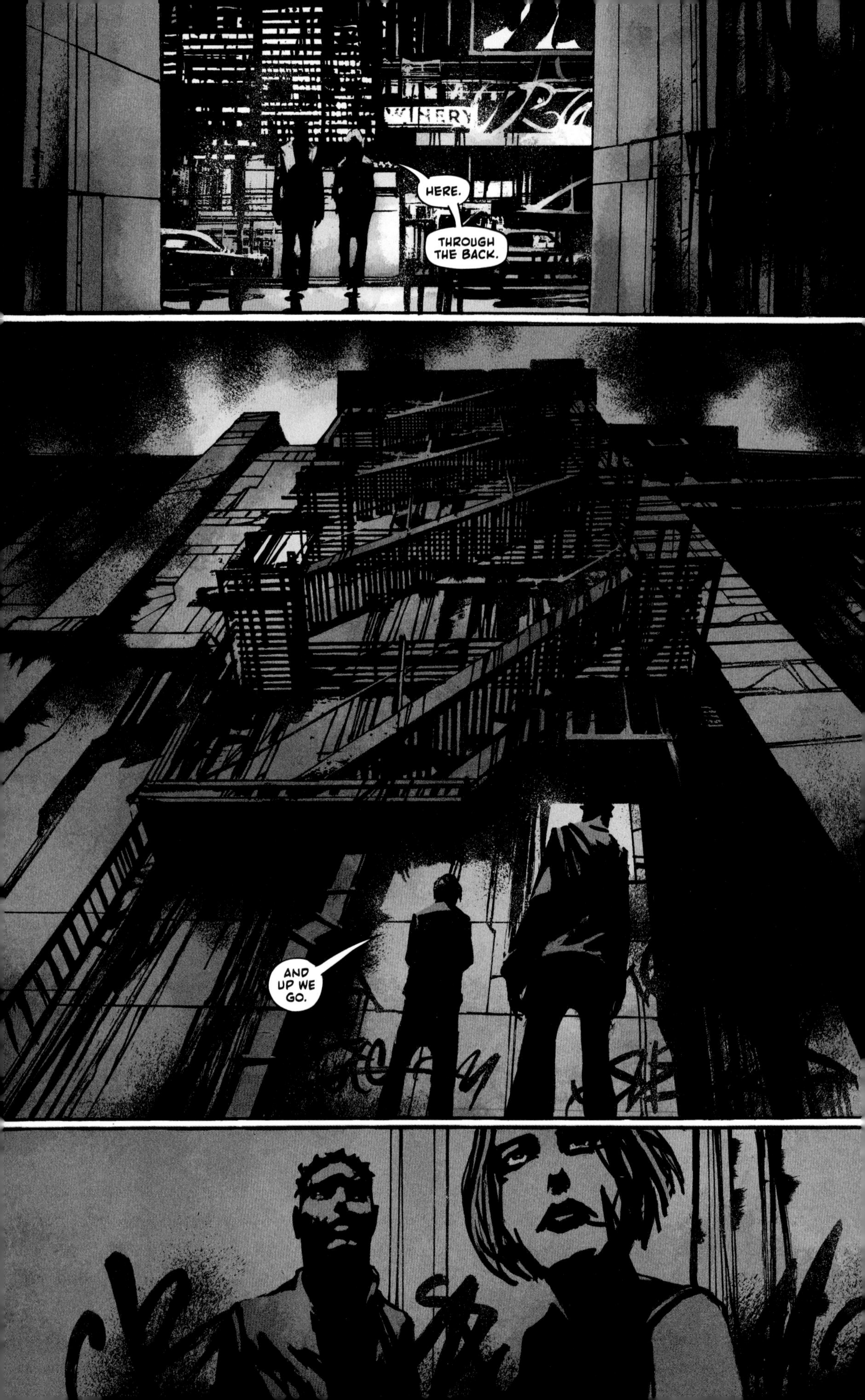

WINERY
HERE.
THROUGH THE BACK.
AND UP WE GO.

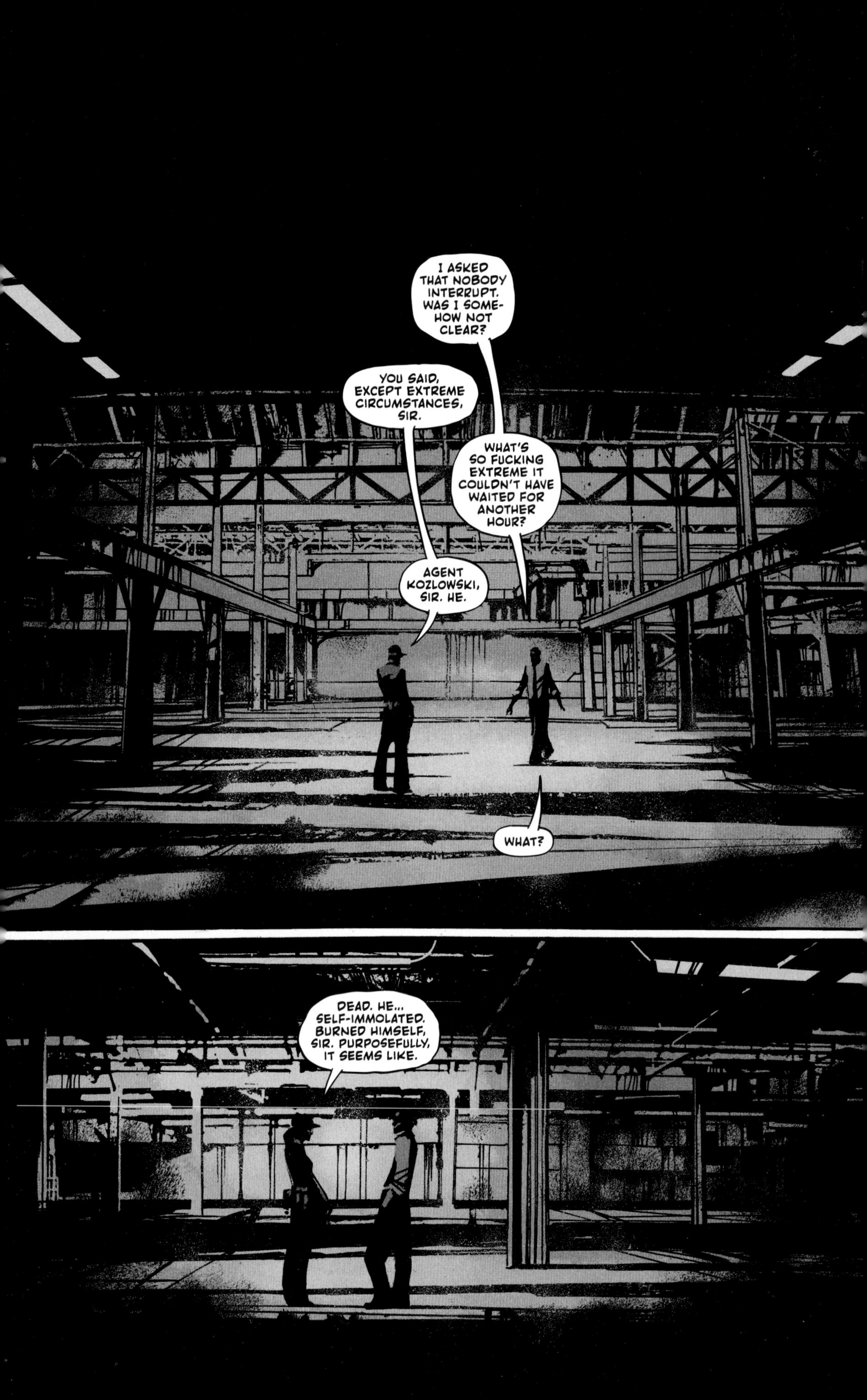
I ASKED THAT NOBODY INTERRUPT. WAS I SOME-HOW NOT CLEAR?
YOU SAID, EXCEPT EXTREME CIRCUMSTANCES, SIR.
WHAT'S SO FUCKING EXTREME IT COULDN'T HAVE WAITED FOR ANOTHER HOUR?
AGENT KOZLOWSKI, SIR. HE.
WHAT?
DEAD. HE... SELF-IMMOLATED. BURNED HIMSELF, SIR. PURPOSEFULLY, IT SEEMS LIKE.

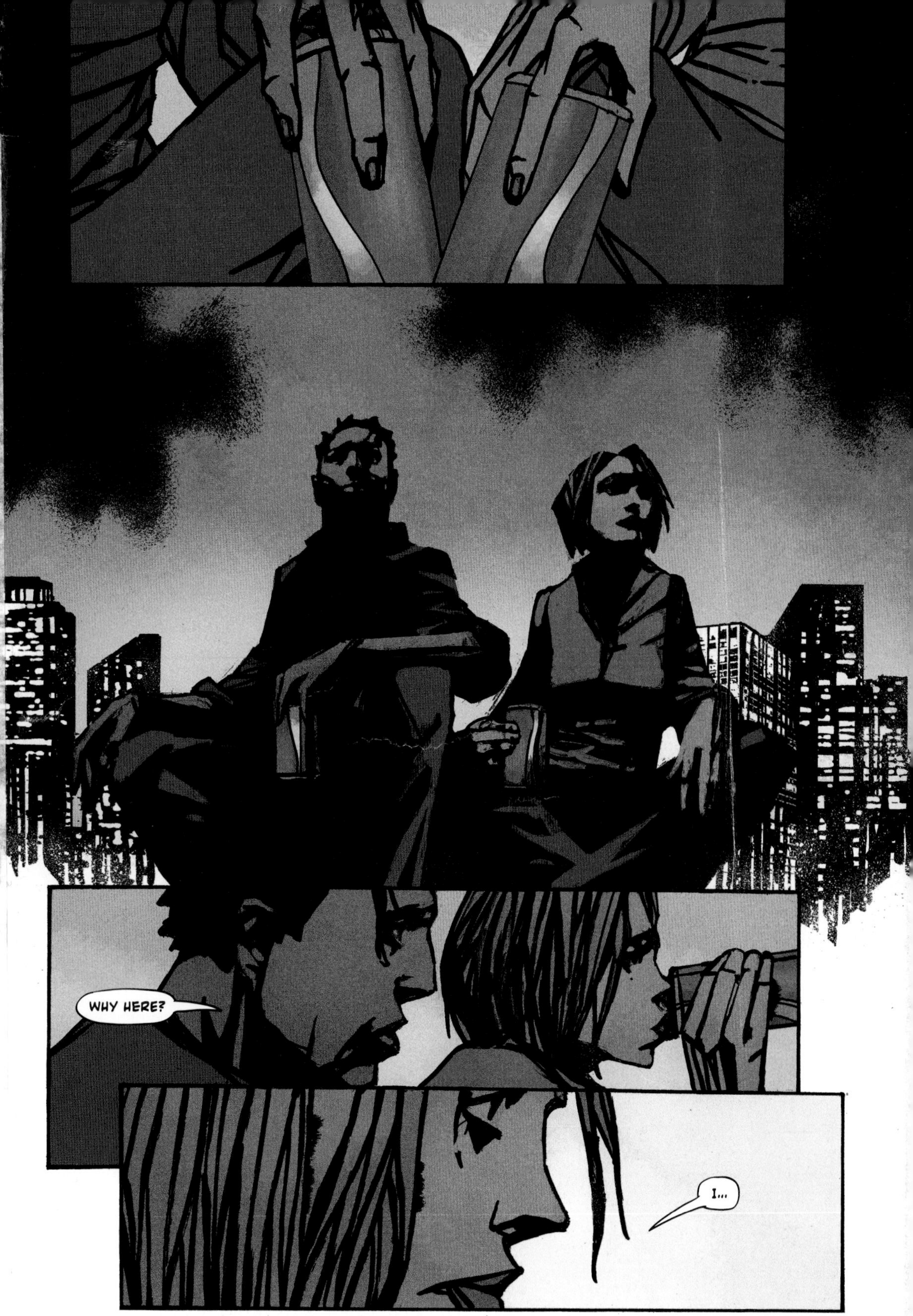
WHY HERE?
I...

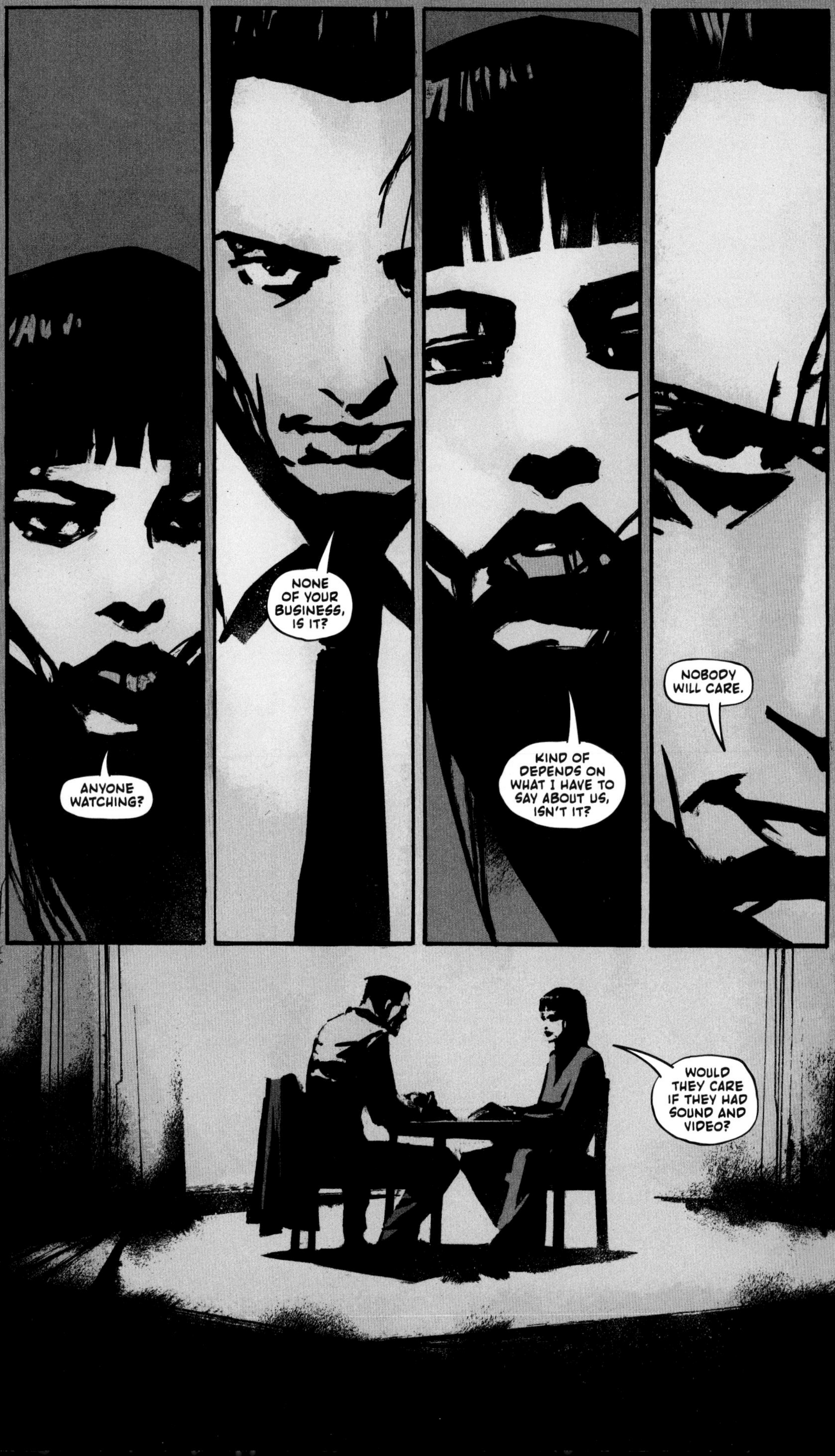
ANYONE WATCHING?
NONE OF YOUR BUSINESS, IS IT?
KIND OF DEPENDS ON WHAT I HAVE TO SAY ABOUT US, ISN'T IT?
NOBODY WILL CARE.
WOULD THEY CARE IF THEY HAD SOUND AND VIDEO?

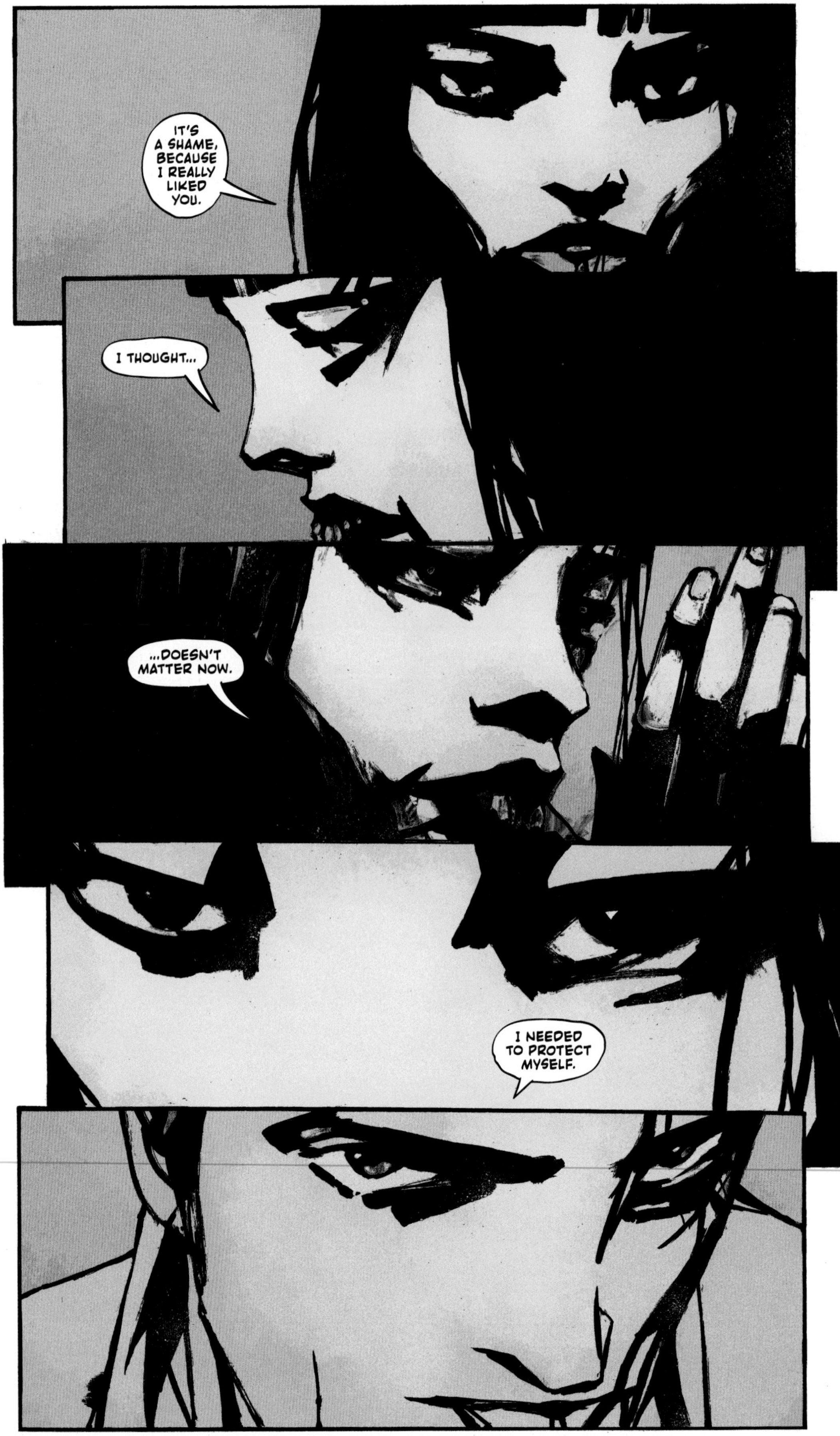
IT'S A SHAME, BECAUSE I REALLY LIKED YOU.
I THOUGHT...
...DOESN'T MATTER NOW.
I NEEDED TO PROTECT MYSELF.

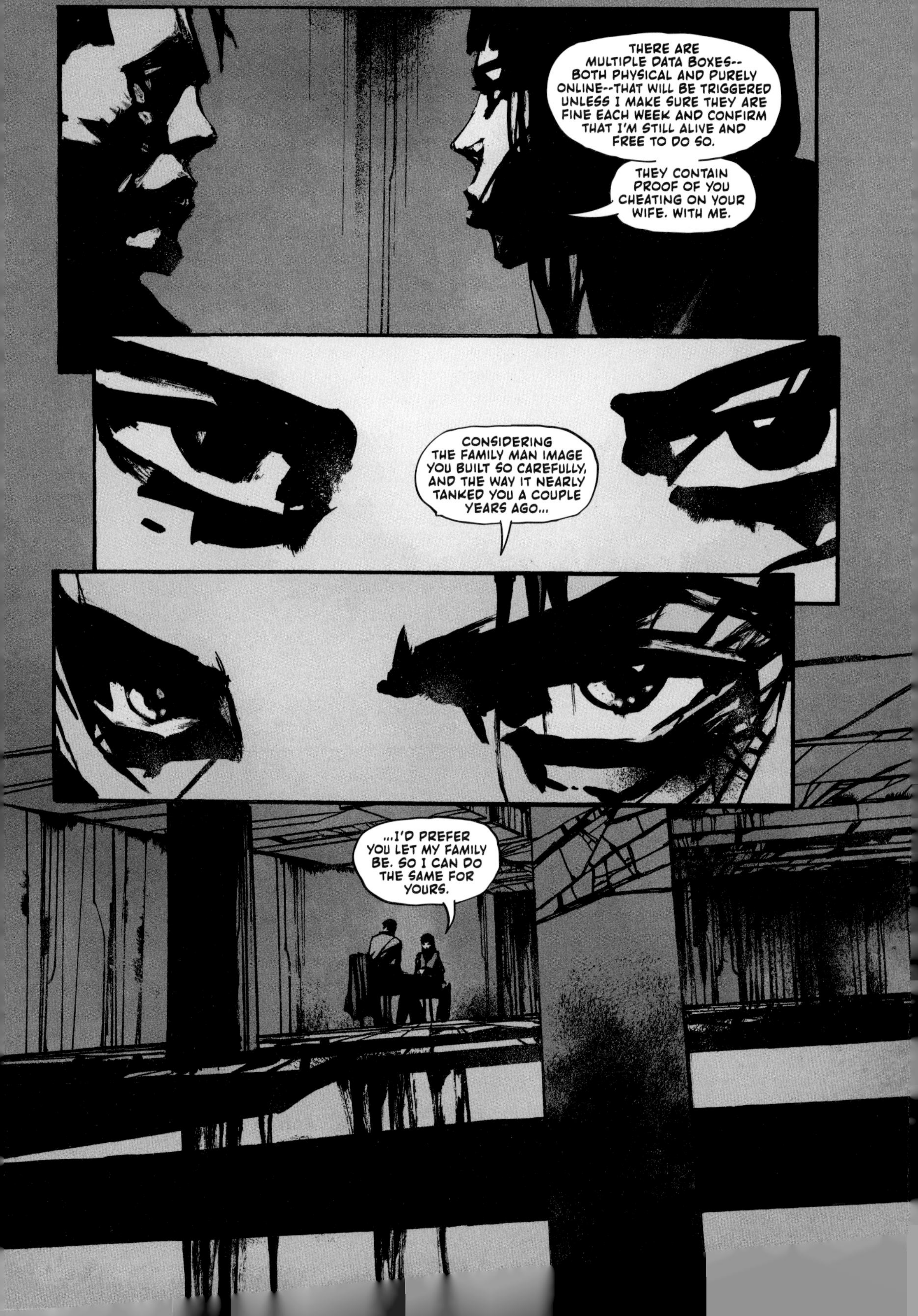
THERE ARE MULTIPLE DATA BOXES--BOTH PHYSICAL AND PURELY ONLINE--THAT WILL BE TRIGGERED UNLESS I MAKE SURE THEY ARE FINE EACH WEEK AND CONFIRM THAT I'M STILL ALIVE AND FREE TO DO SO.
THEY CONTAIN PROOF OF YOU CHEATING ON YOUR WIFE. WITH ME.
CONSIDERING THE FAMILY MAN IMAGE YOU BUILT SO CAREFULLY, AND THE WAY IT NEARLY TANKED YOU A COUPLE YEARS AGO...
...I'D PREFER YOU LET MY FAMILY BE. SO I CAN DO THE SAME FOR YOURS.

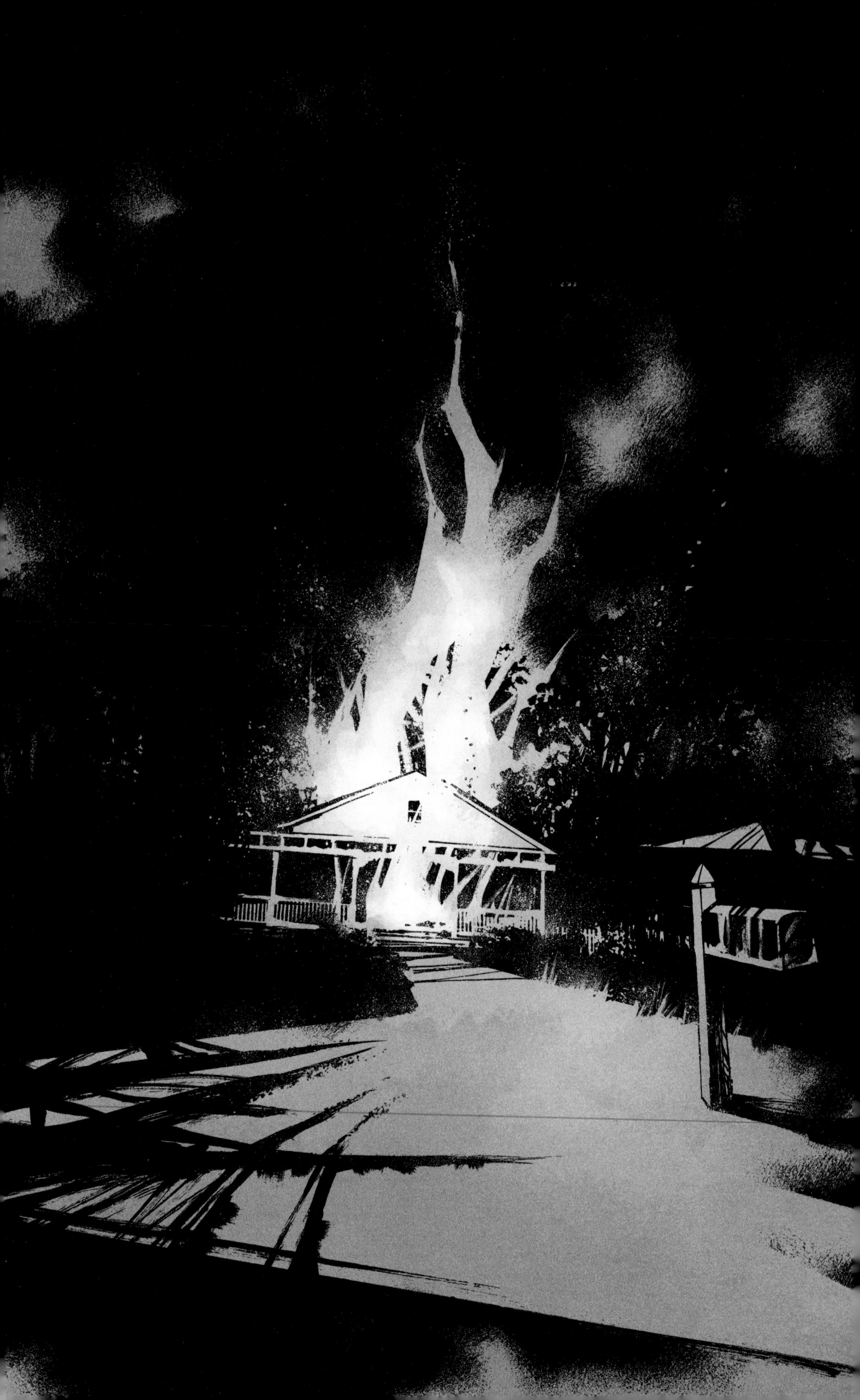

CHAPTER TEN:
ARMY OF SHADOWS

"Every pig has its butcher."

—Czech proverb

ONE DAY BEFORE
THE EVENT.

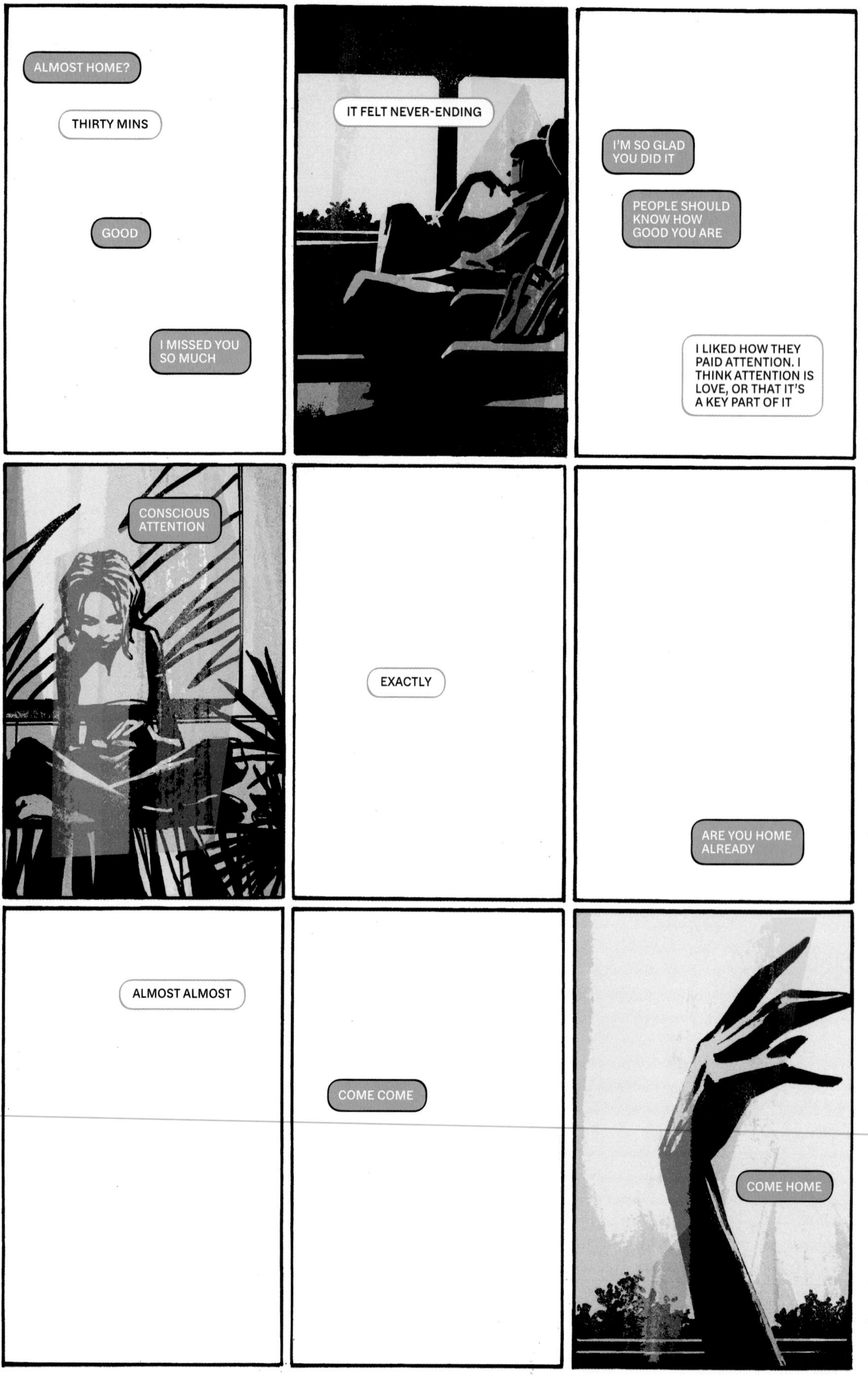
ALMOST HOME?
THIRTY MINS
GOOD
I MISSED YOU SO MUCH
IT FELT NEVER-ENDING
I'M SO GLAD YOU DID IT
PEOPLE SHOULD KNOW HOW GOOD YOU ARE
I LIKED HOW THEY PAID ATTENTION. I THINK ATTENTION IS LOVE, OR THAT IT'S A KEY PART OF IT
CONSCIOUS ATTENTION
EXACTLY
ARE YOU HOME ALREADY
ALMOST ALMOST
COME COME
COME HOME

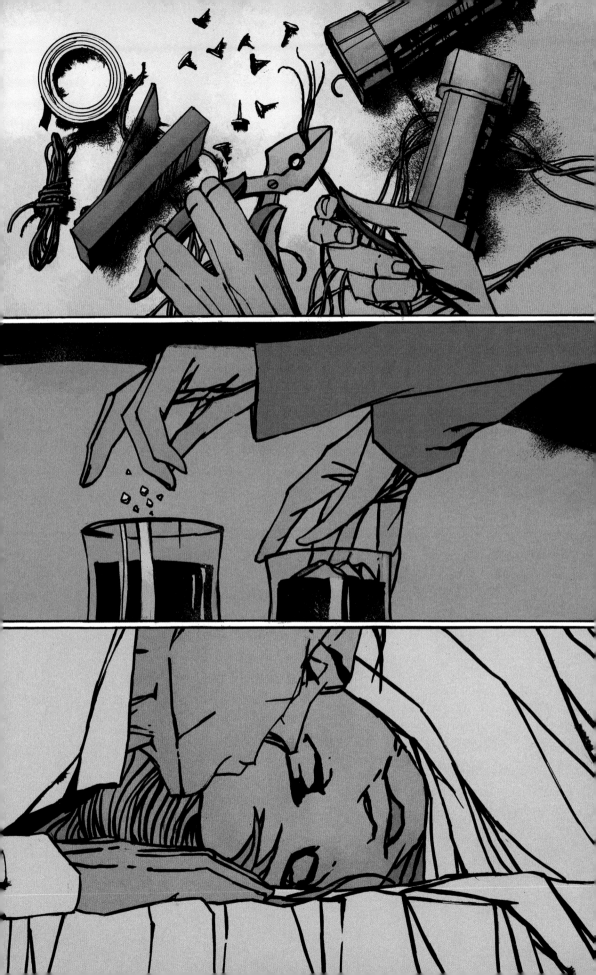

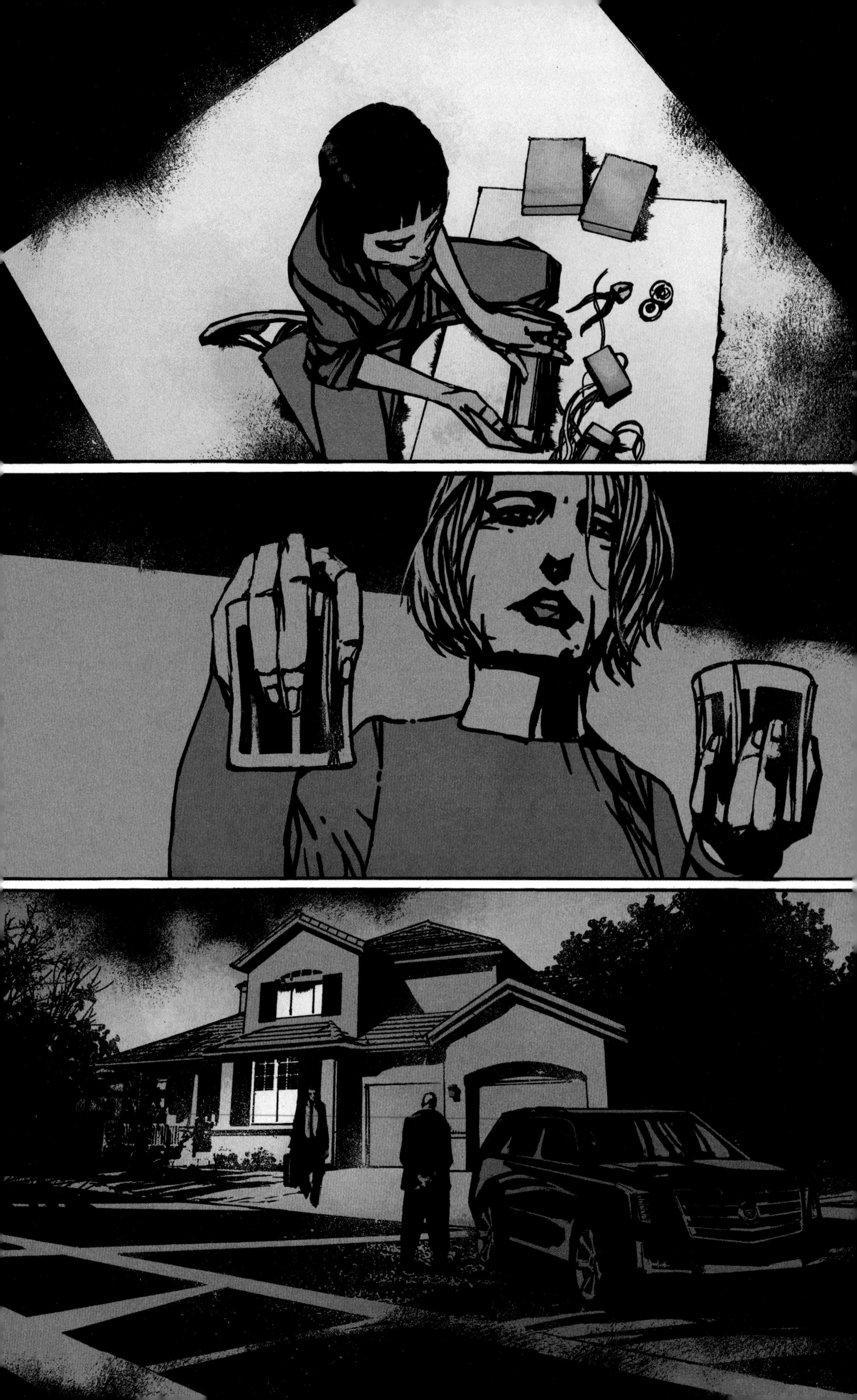

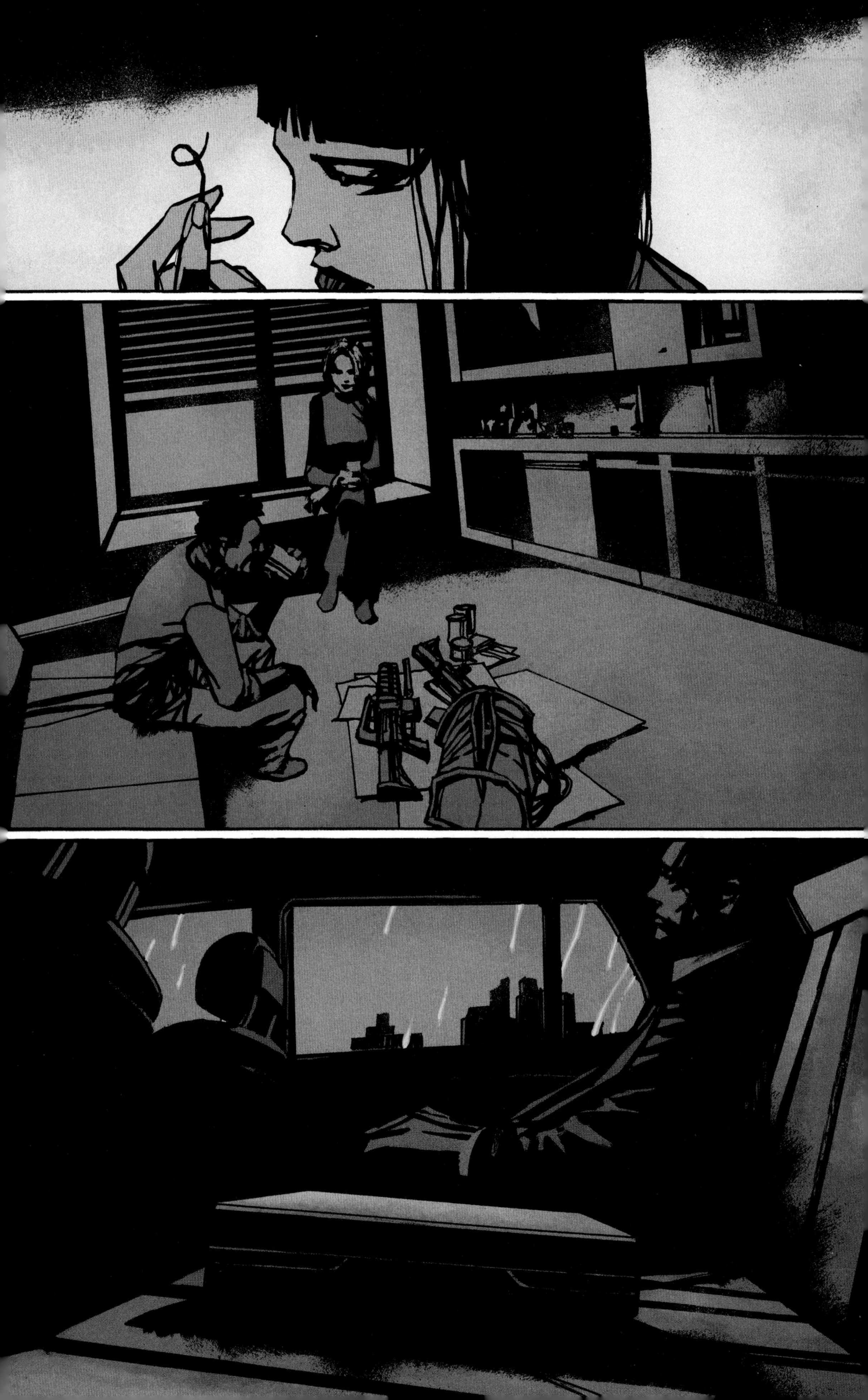

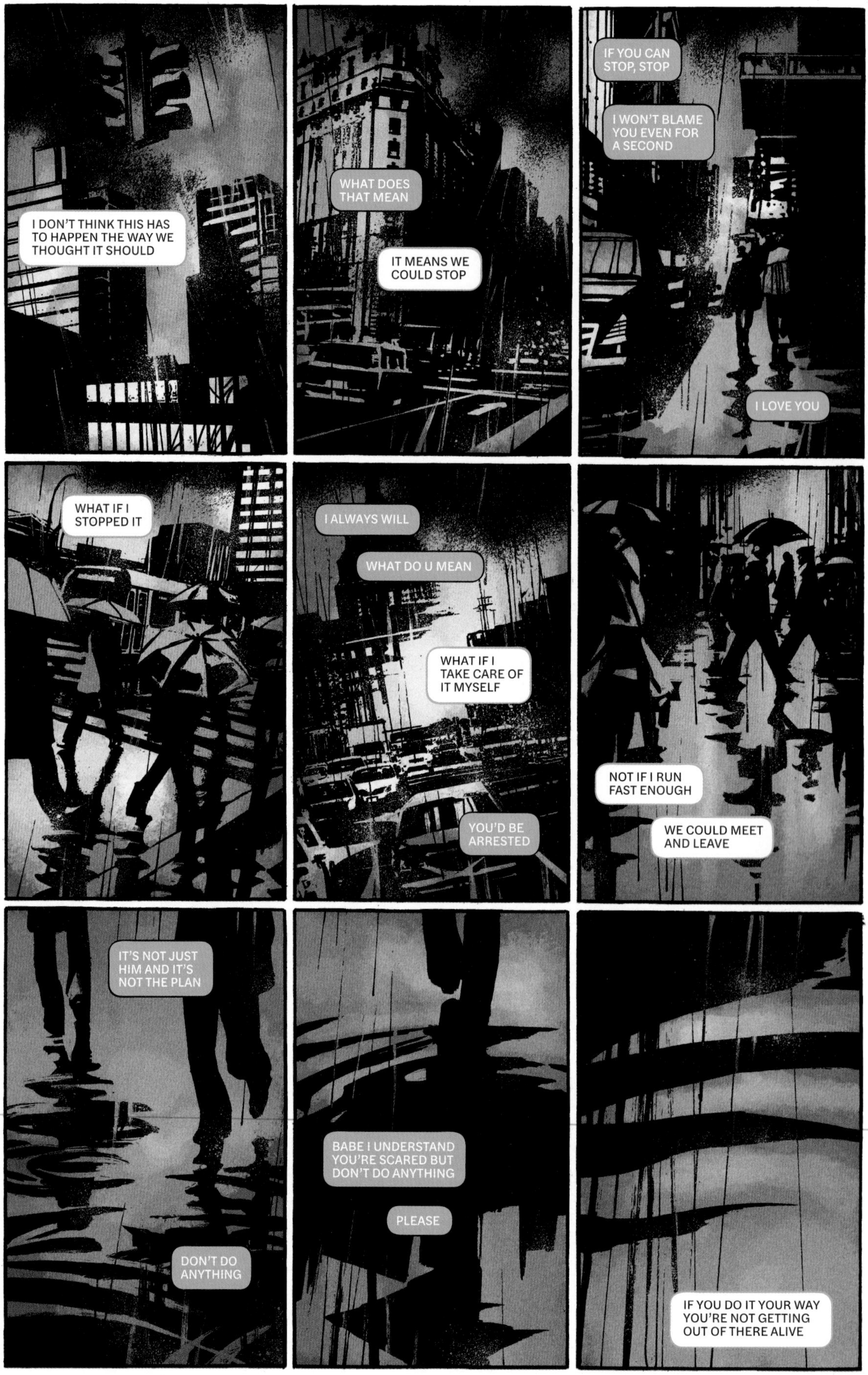
I DON'T THINK THIS HAS TO HAPPEN THE WAY WE THOUGHT IT SHOULD
WHAT DOES THAT MEAN
IT MEANS WE COULD STOP
IF YOU CAN STOP, STOP
I WON'T BLAME YOU EVEN FOR A SECOND
I LOVE YOU
WHAT IF I STOPPED IT
I ALWAYS WILL
WHAT DO U MEAN
WHAT IF I TAKE CARE OF IT MYSELF
YOU'D BE ARRESTED
NOT IF I RUN FAST ENOUGH
WE COULD MEET AND LEAVE
IT'S NOT JUST HIM AND IT'S NOT THE PLAN
DON'T DO ANYTHING
BABE I UNDERSTAND YOU'RE SCARED BUT DON'T DO ANYTHING
PLEASE
IF YOU DO IT YOUR WAY YOU'RE NOT GETTING OUT OF THERE ALIVE

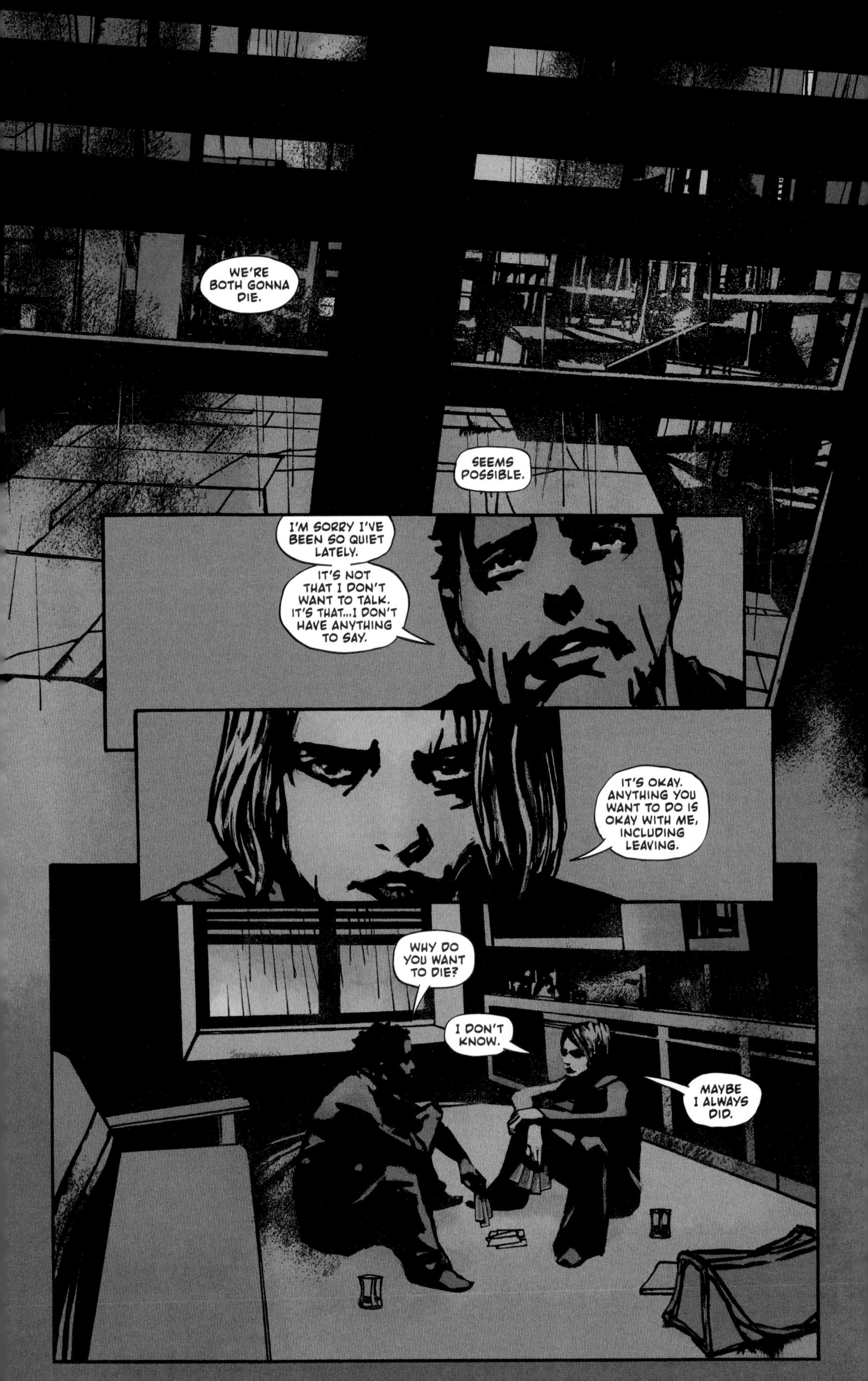
WE'RE BOTH GONNA DIE.
SEEMS POSSIBLE.
I'M SORRY I'VE BEEN SO QUIET LATELY.
IT'S NOT THAT I DON'T WANT TO TALK. IT'S THAT...I DON'T HAVE ANYTHING TO SAY.
IT'S OKAY. ANYTHING YOU WANT TO DO IS OKAY WITH ME, INCLUDING LEAVING.
WHY DO YOU WANT TO DIE?
I DON'T KNOW.
MAYBE I ALWAYS DID.

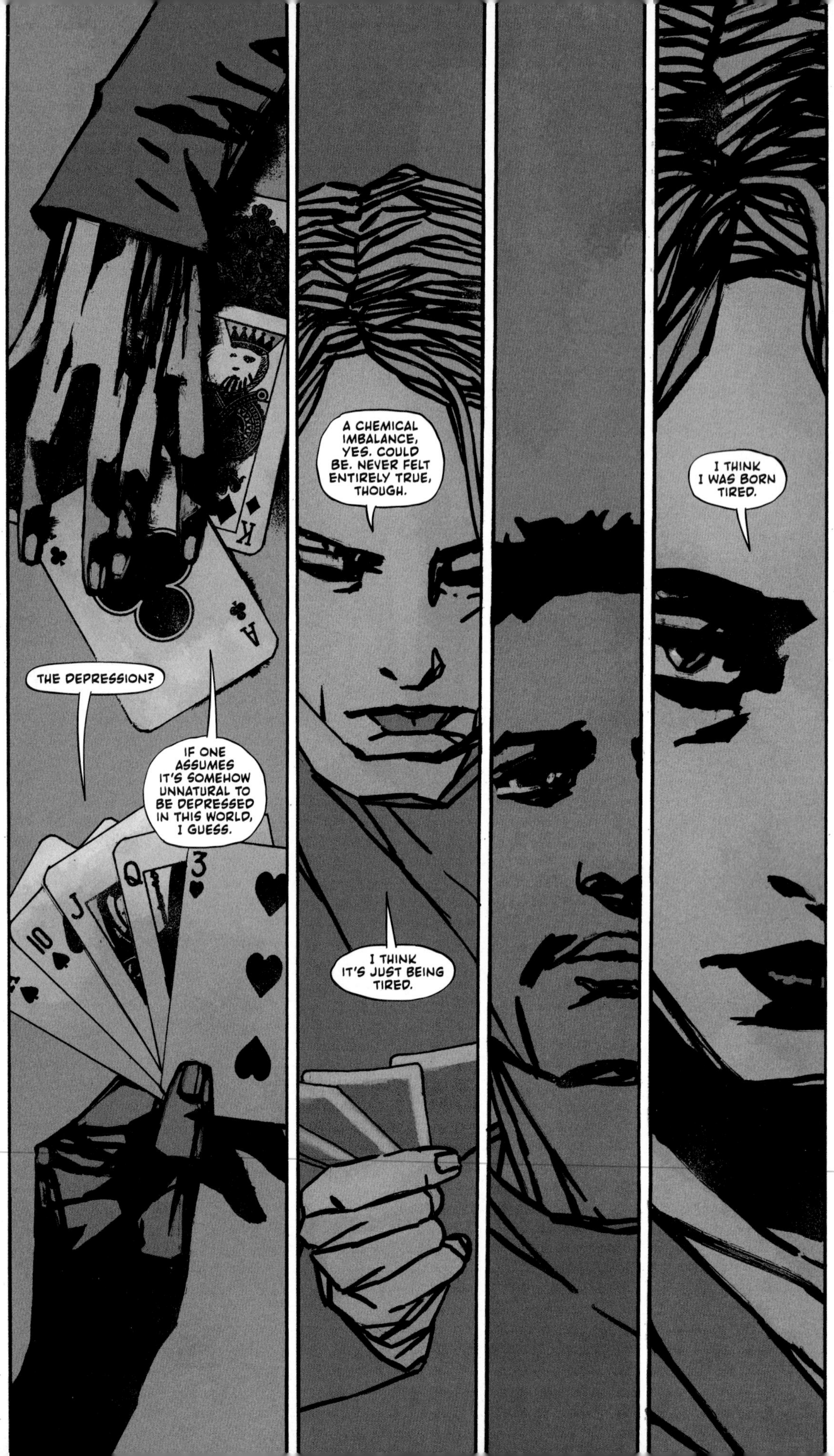
THE DEPRESSION?
IF ONE ASSUMES IT'S SOMEHOW UNNATURAL TO BE DEPRESSED IN THIS WORLD, I GUESS.
A CHEMICAL IMBALANCE, YES. COULD BE. NEVER FELT ENTIRELY TRUE, THOUGH.
I THINK IT'S JUST BEING TIRED.
I THINK I WAS BORN TIRED.

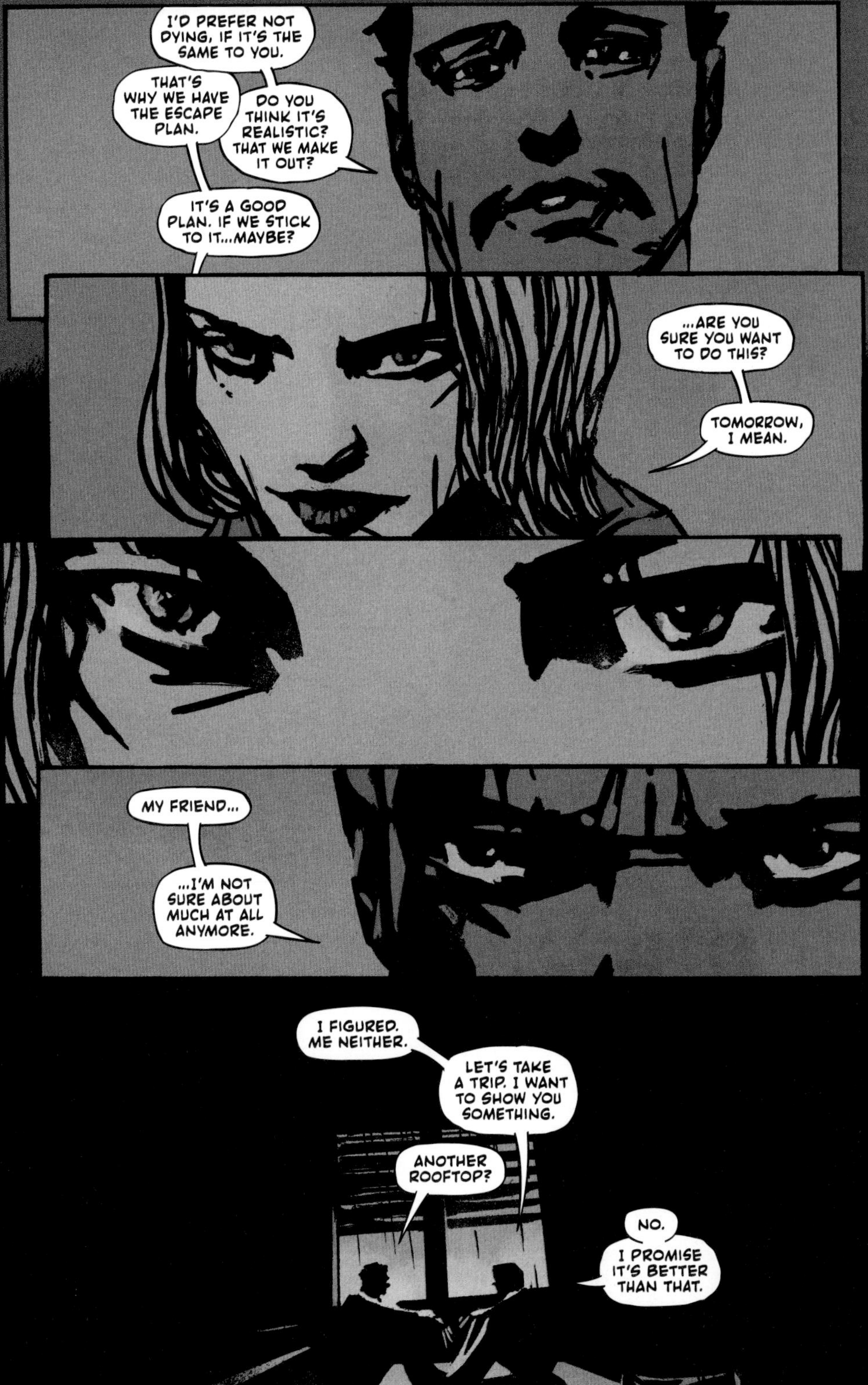
I'D PREFER NOT DYING, IF IT'S THE SAME TO YOU.
THAT'S WHY WE HAVE THE ESCAPE PLAN.
DO YOU THINK IT'S REALISTIC? THAT WE MAKE IT OUT?
IT'S A GOOD PLAN. IF WE STICK TO IT...MAYBE?
...ARE YOU SURE YOU WANT TO DO THIS?
TOMORROW, I MEAN.
MY FRIEND...
...I'M NOT SURE ABOUT MUCH AT ALL ANYMORE.
I FIGURED. ME NEITHER.
LET'S TAKE A TRIP. I WANT TO SHOW YOU SOMETHING.
ANOTHER ROOFTOP?
NO.
I PROMISE IT'S BETTER THAN THAT.

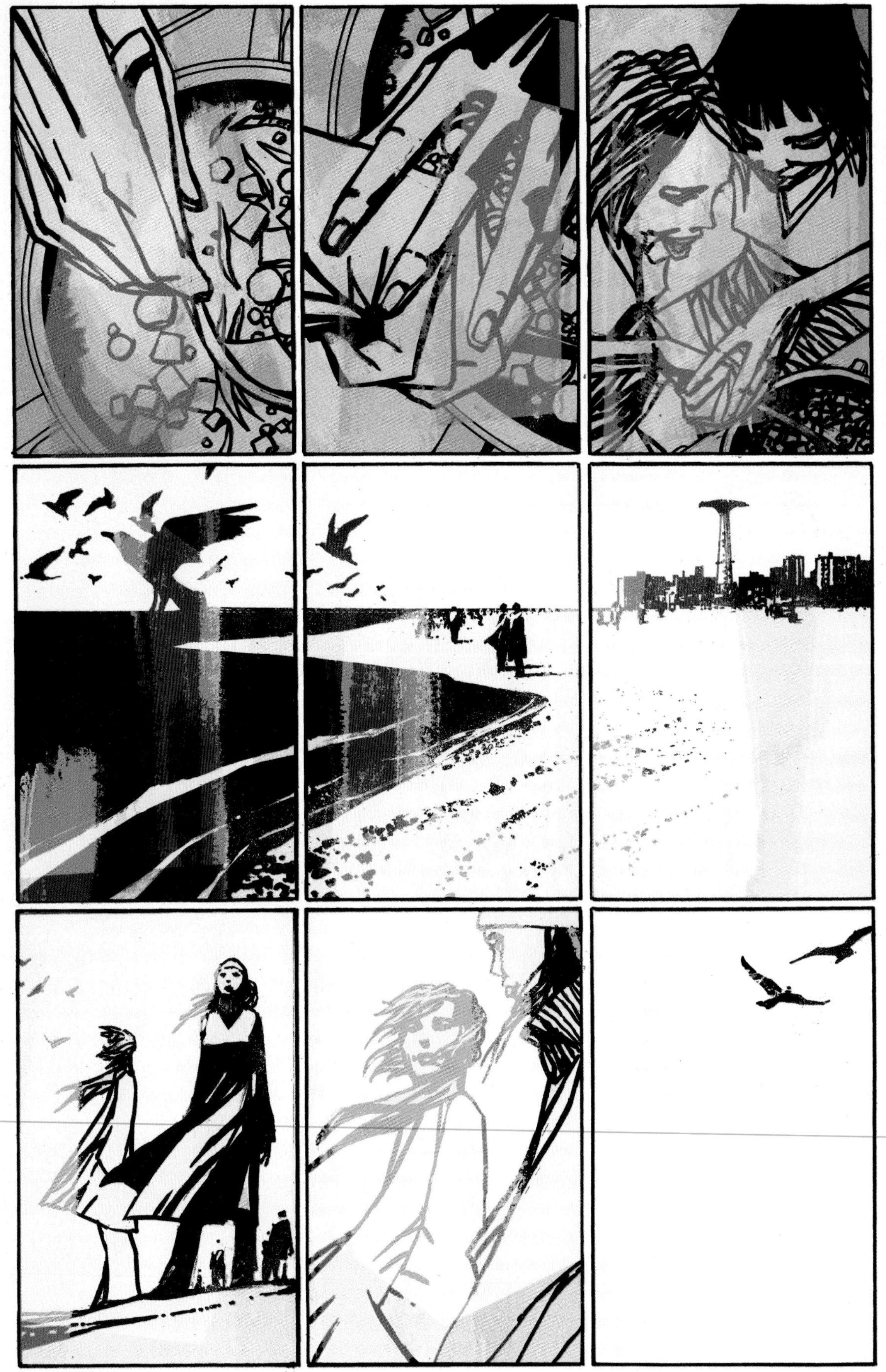

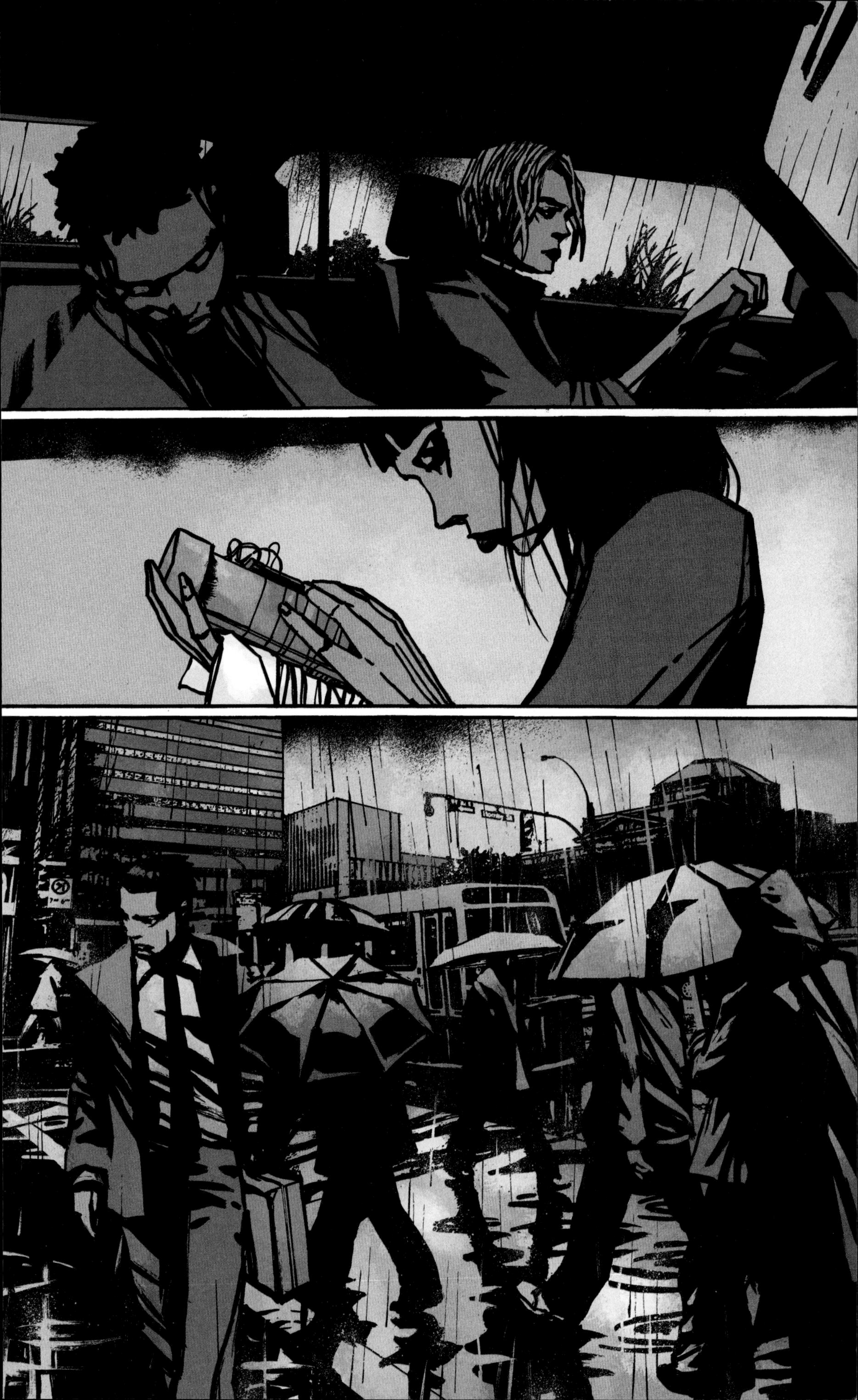

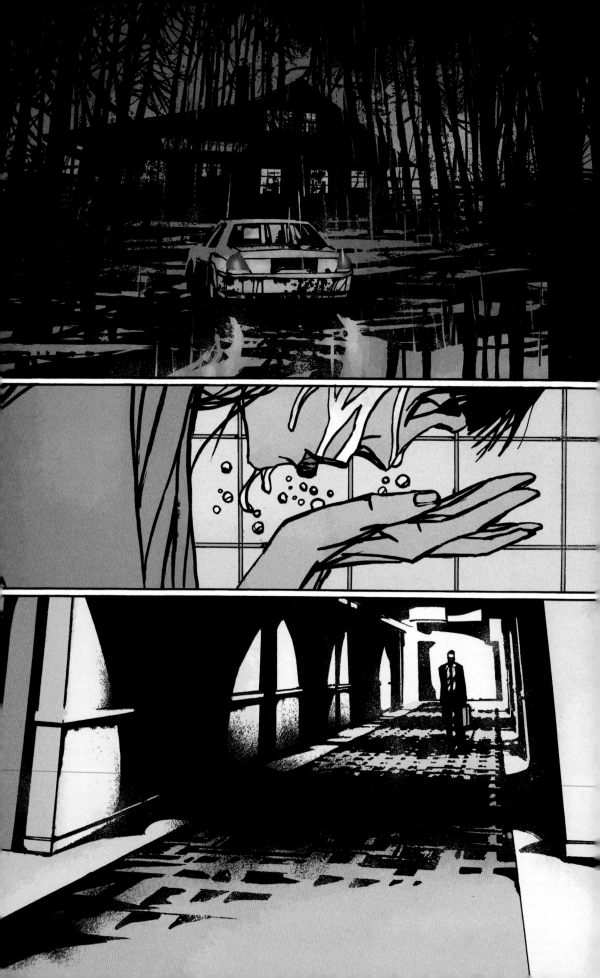

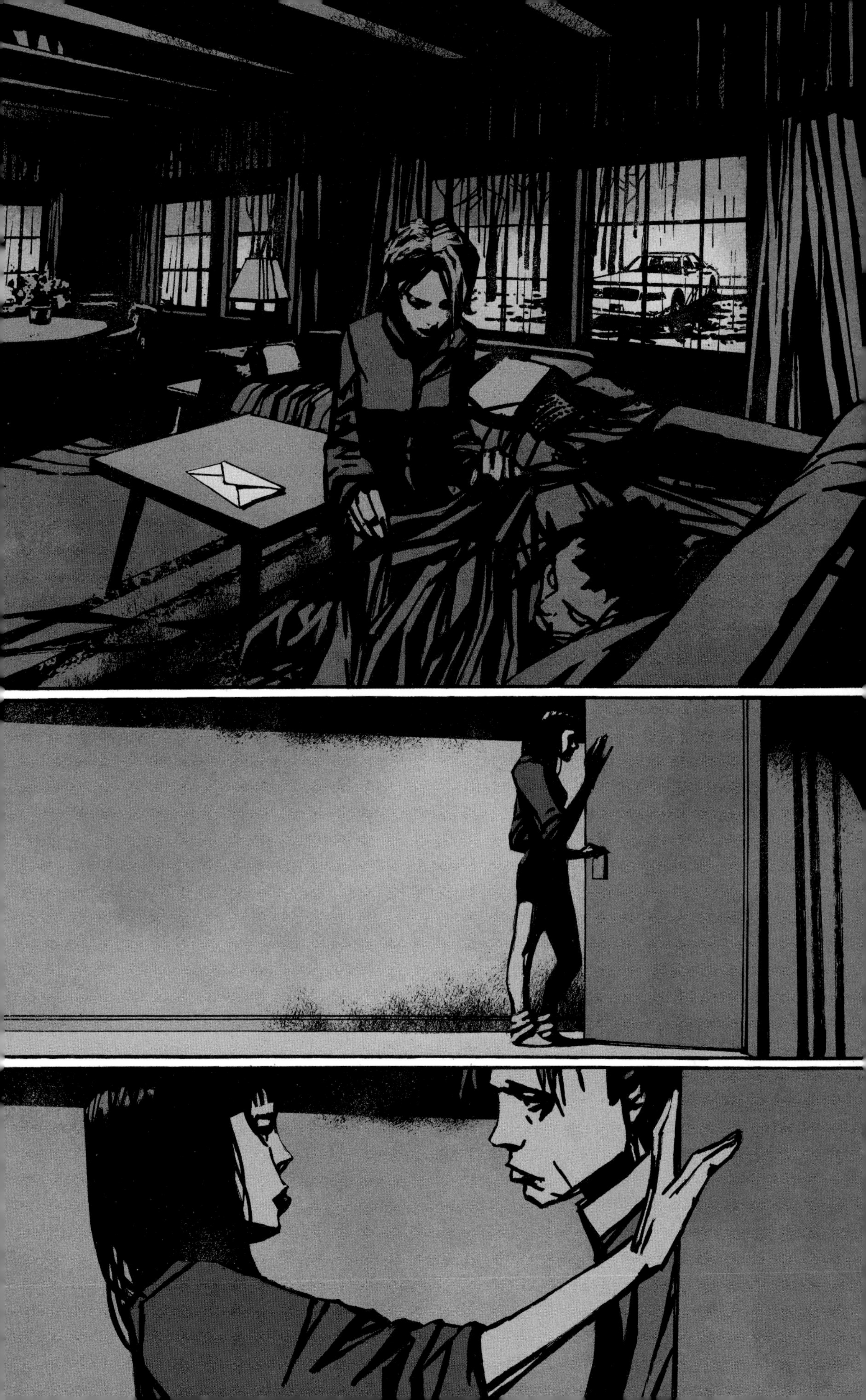

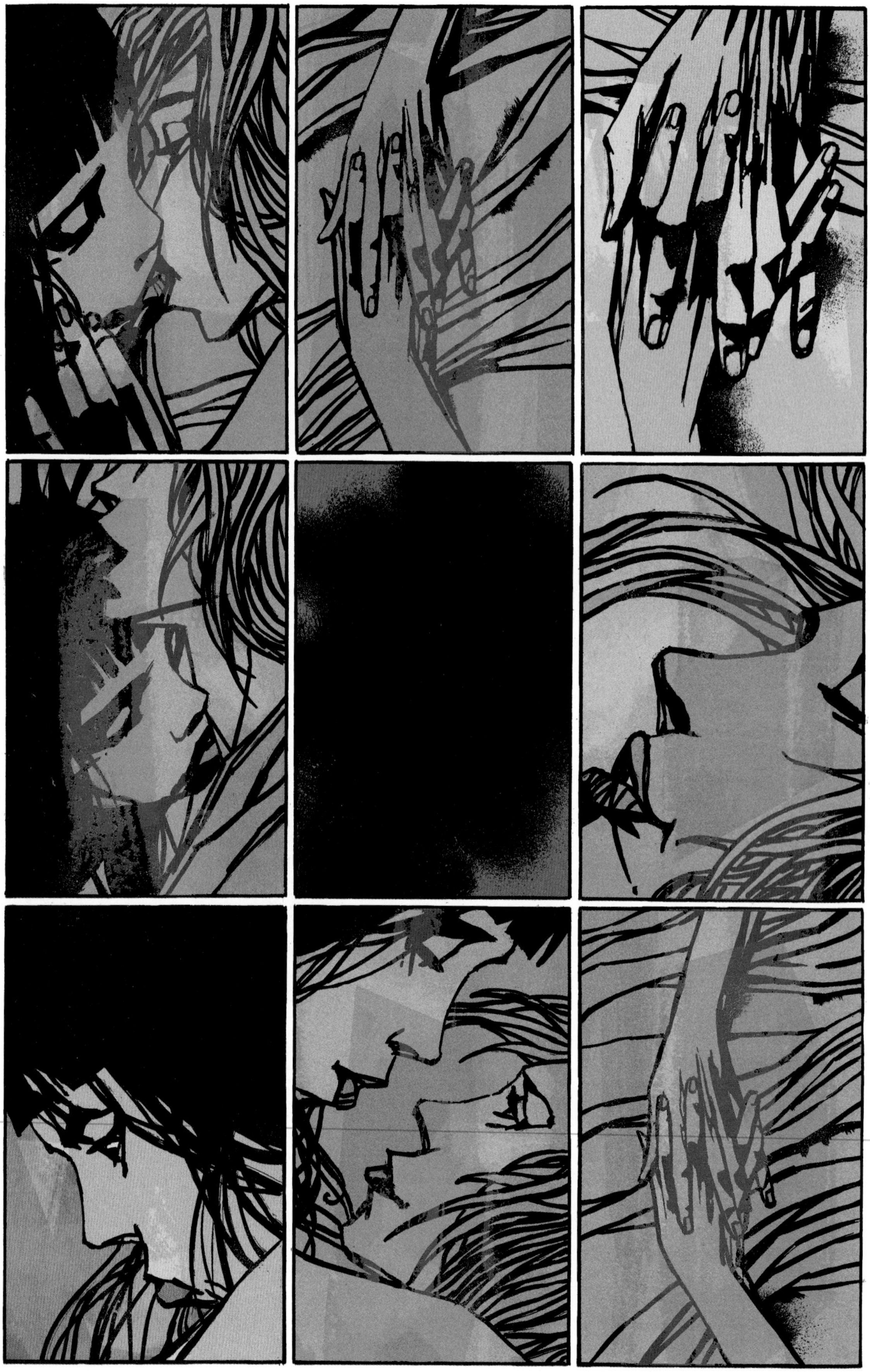

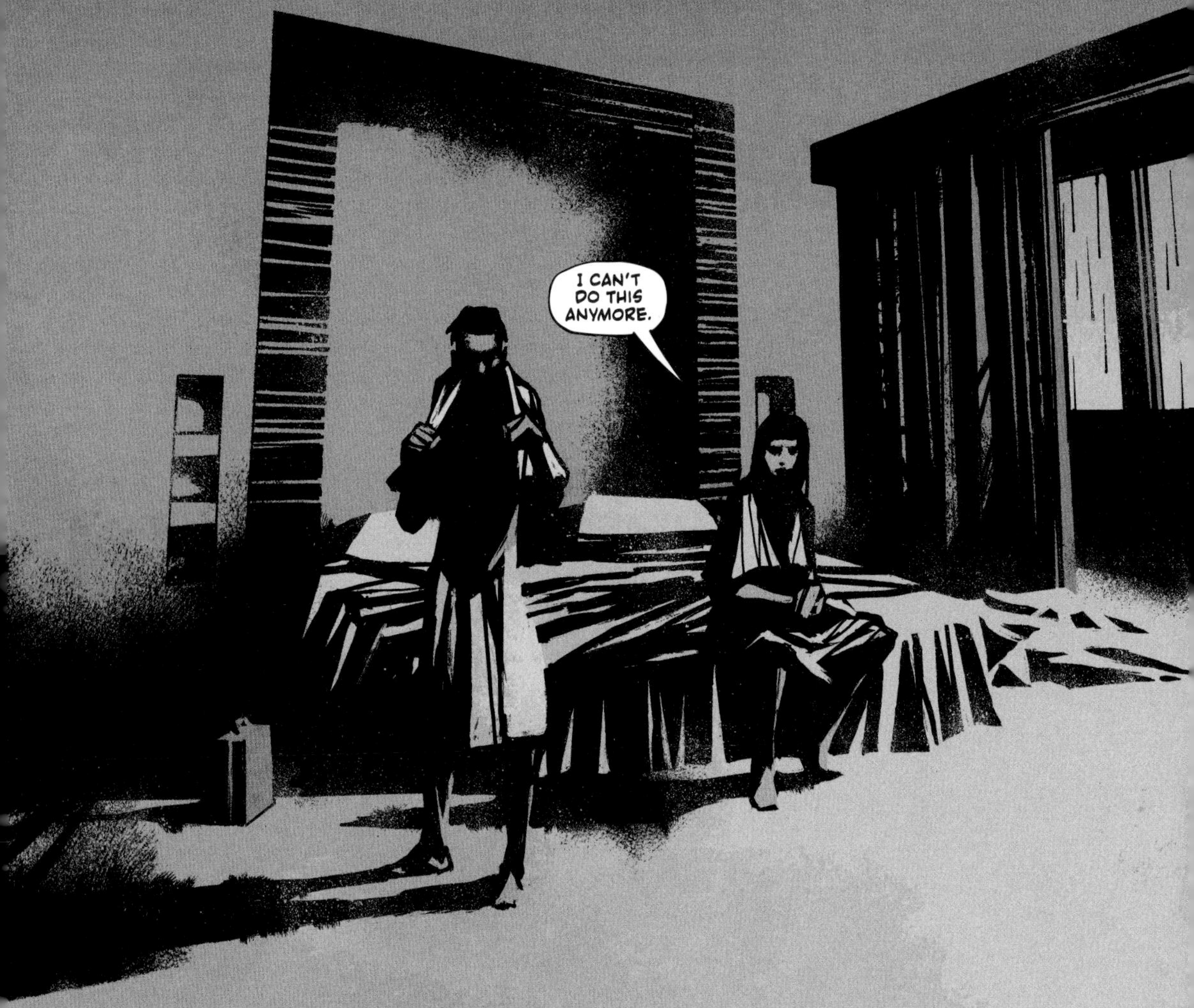
I CAN'T DO THIS ANYMORE.
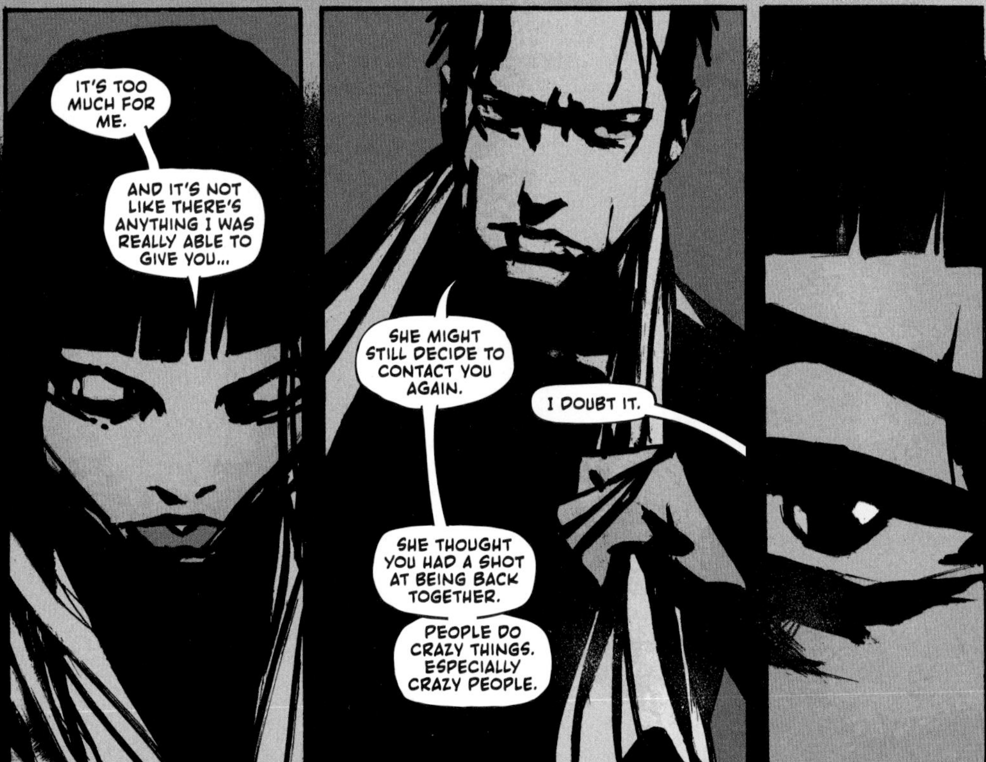
IT'S TOO MUCH FOR ME.
AND IT'S NOT LIKE THERE'S ANYTHING I WAS REALLY ABLE TO GIVE YOU...
SHE MIGHT STILL DECIDE TO CONTACT YOU AGAIN.
I DOUBT IT.
SHE THOUGHT YOU HAD A SHOT AT BEING BACK TOGETHER.
PEOPLE DO CRAZY THINGS. ESPECIALLY CRAZY PEOPLE.

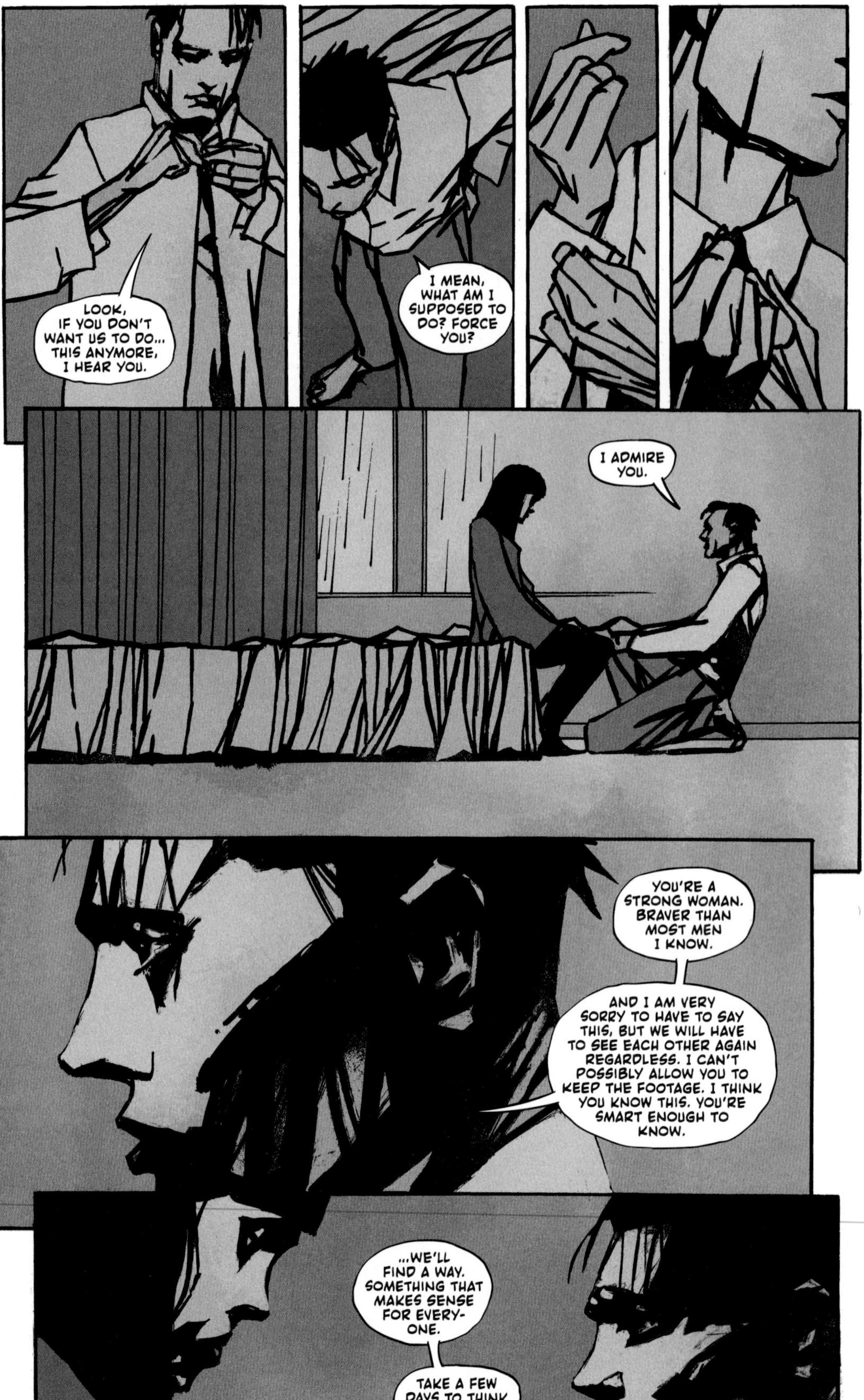
LOOK, IF YOU DON'T WANT US TO DO... THIS ANYMORE, I HEAR YOU.
I MEAN, WHAT AM I SUPPOSED TO DO? FORCE YOU?
I ADMIRE YOU.
YOU'RE A STRONG WOMAN. BRAVER THAN MOST MEN I KNOW.
AND I AM VERY SORRY TO HAVE TO SAY THIS, BUT WE WILL HAVE TO SEE EACH OTHER AGAIN REGARDLESS. I CAN'T POSSIBLY ALLOW YOU TO KEEP THE FOOTAGE. I THINK YOU KNOW THIS. YOU'RE SMART ENOUGH TO KNOW.
...WE'LL FIND A WAY. SOMETHING THAT MAKES SENSE FOR EVERY-ONE.
TAKE A FEW DAYS TO THINK ABOUT IT?

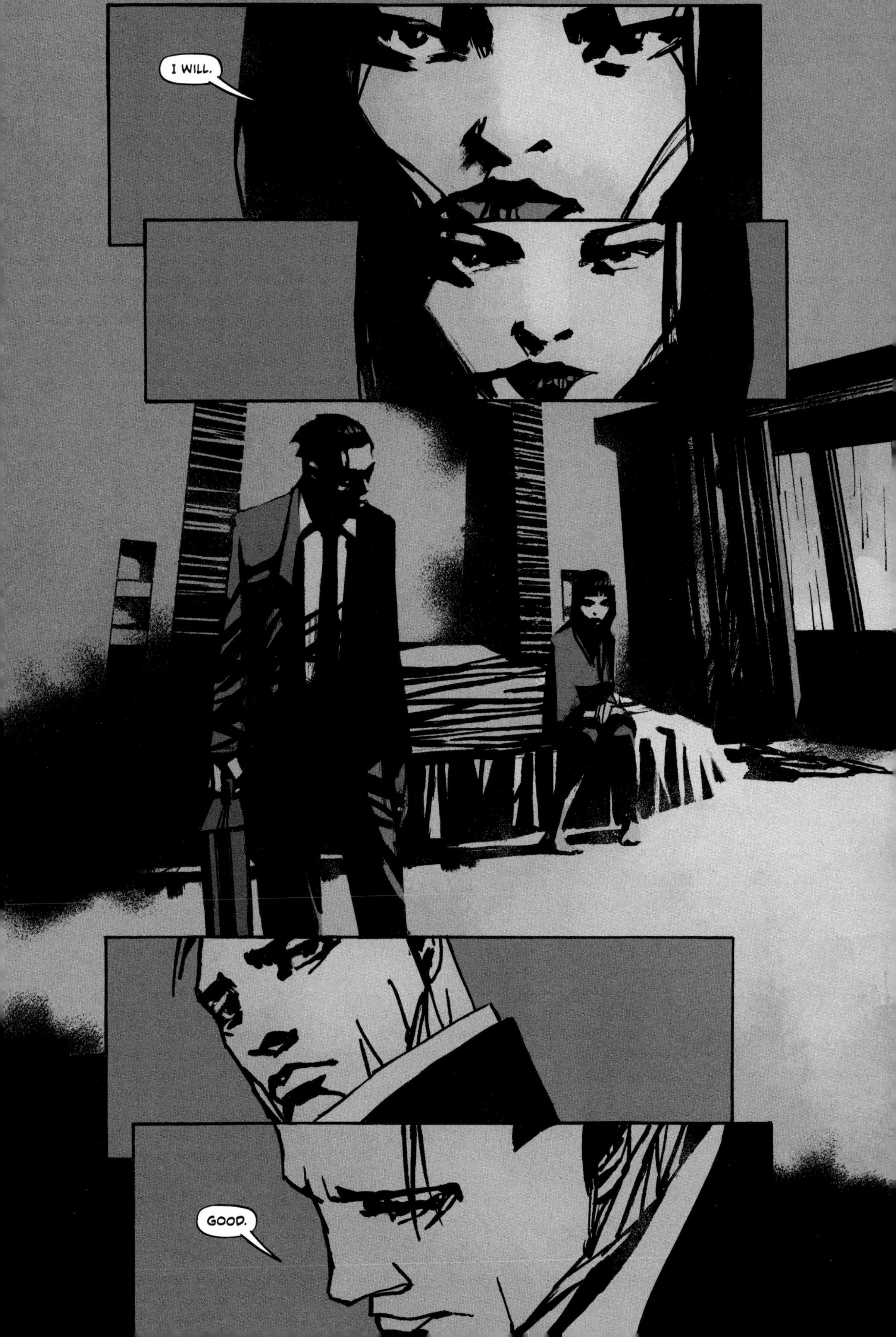
I WILL.
GOOD.

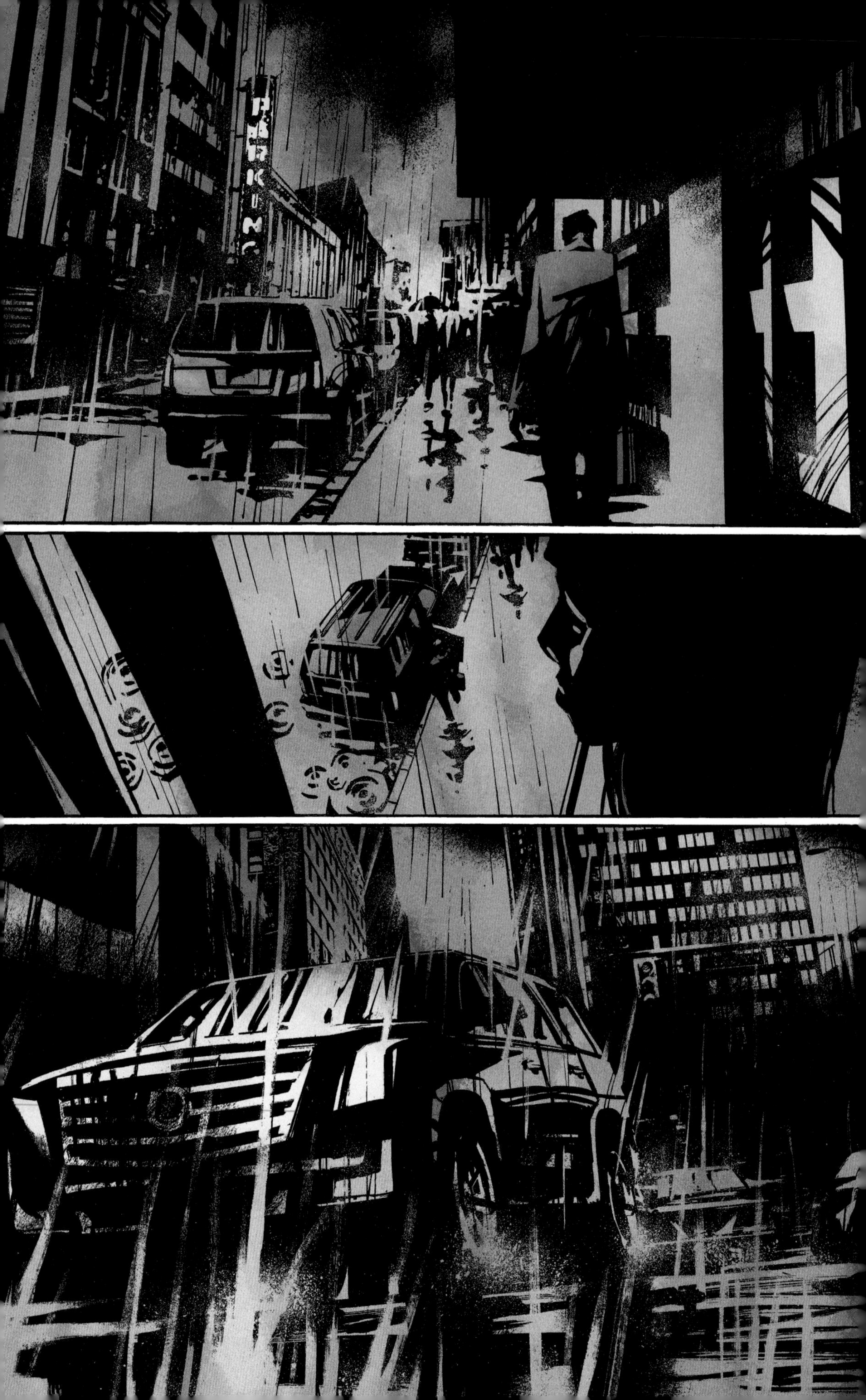

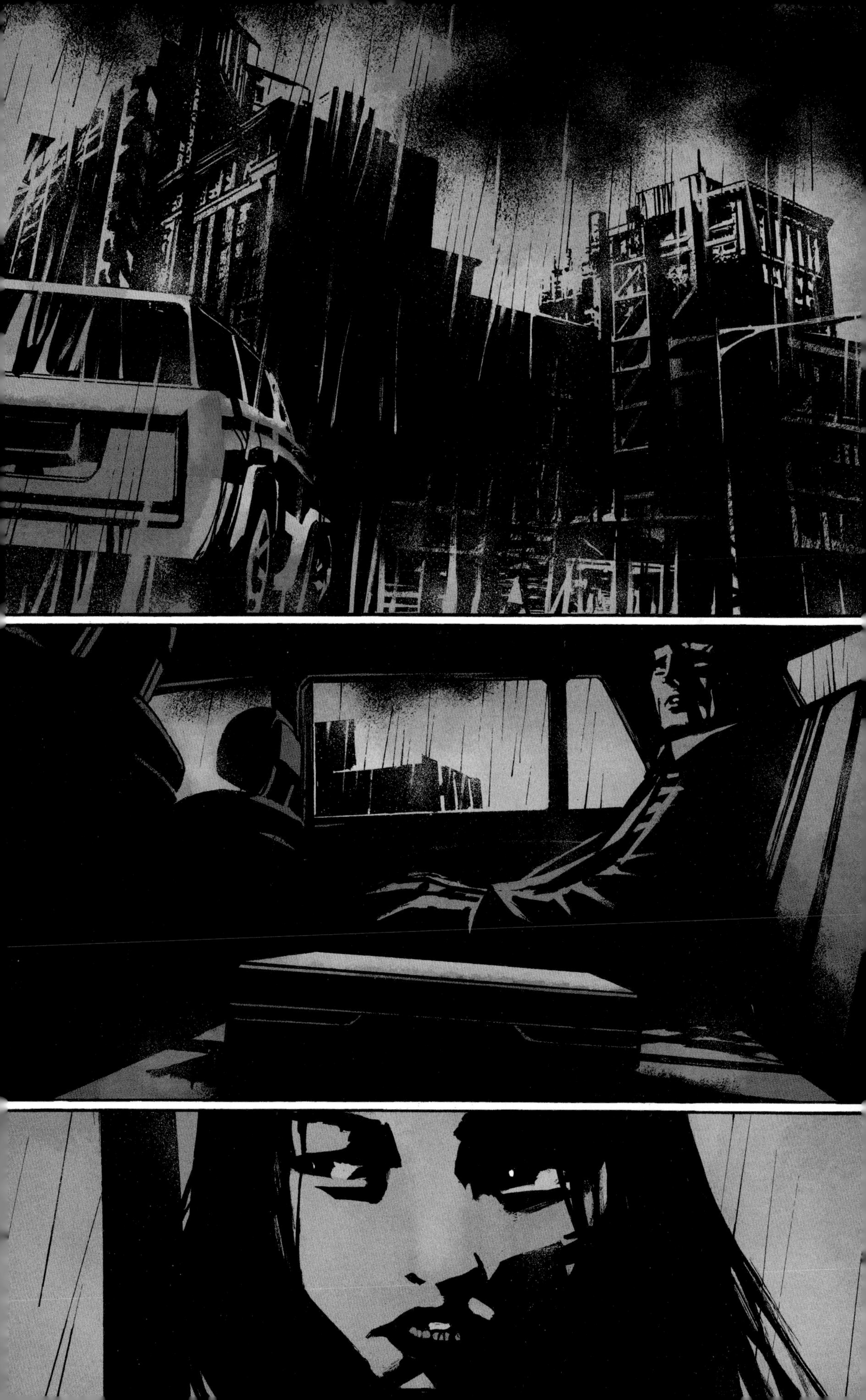

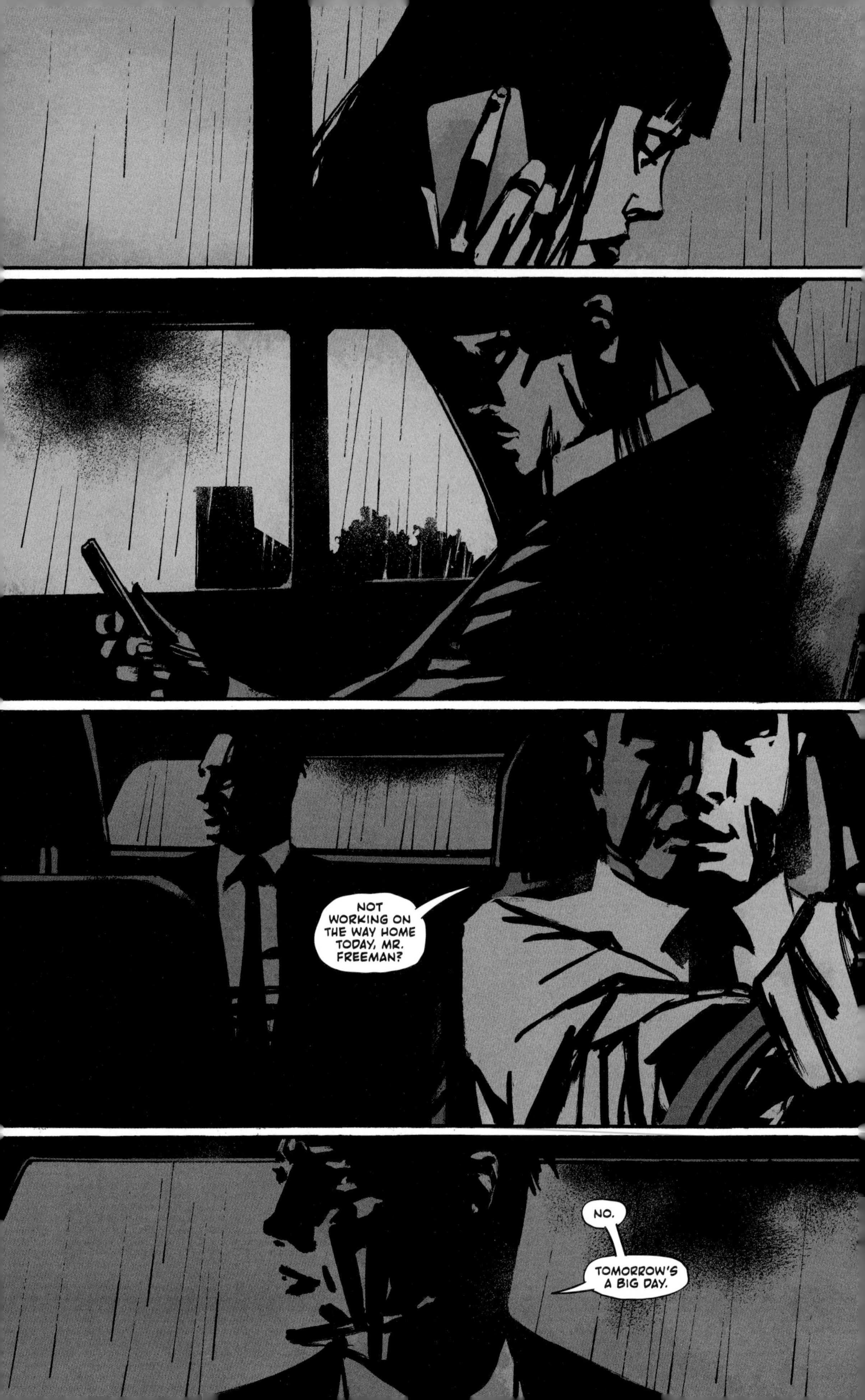
NOT WORKING ON THE WAY HOME TODAY, MR. FREEMAN?
NO.
TOMORROW'S A BIG DAY.

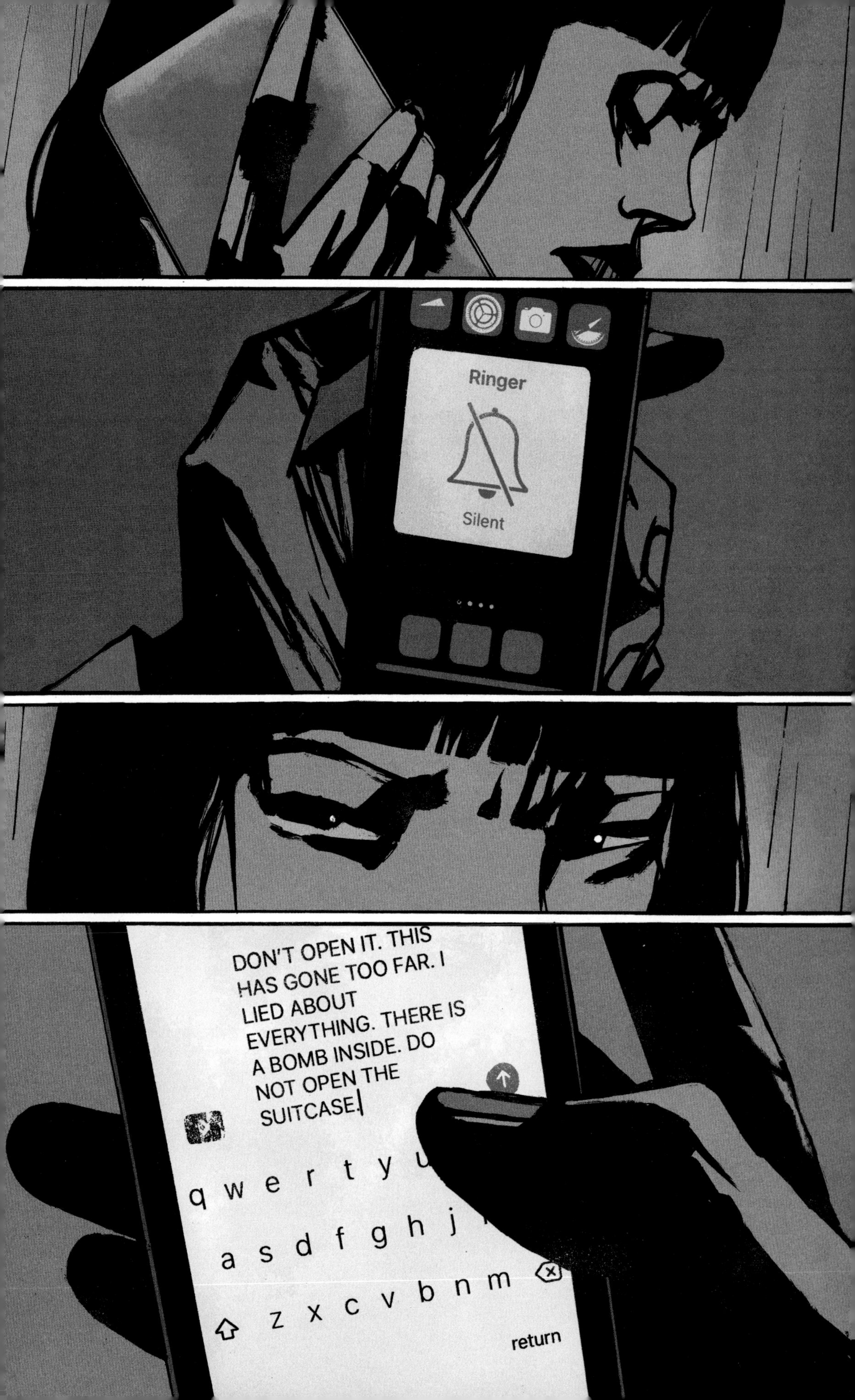
Ringer
Silent
DON'T OPEN IT. THIS HAS GONE TOO FAR. I LIED ABOUT EVERYTHING. THERE IS A BOMB INSIDE. DO NOT OPEN THE SUITCASE.
q w e r t y u
a s d f g h j
z x c v b n m
return

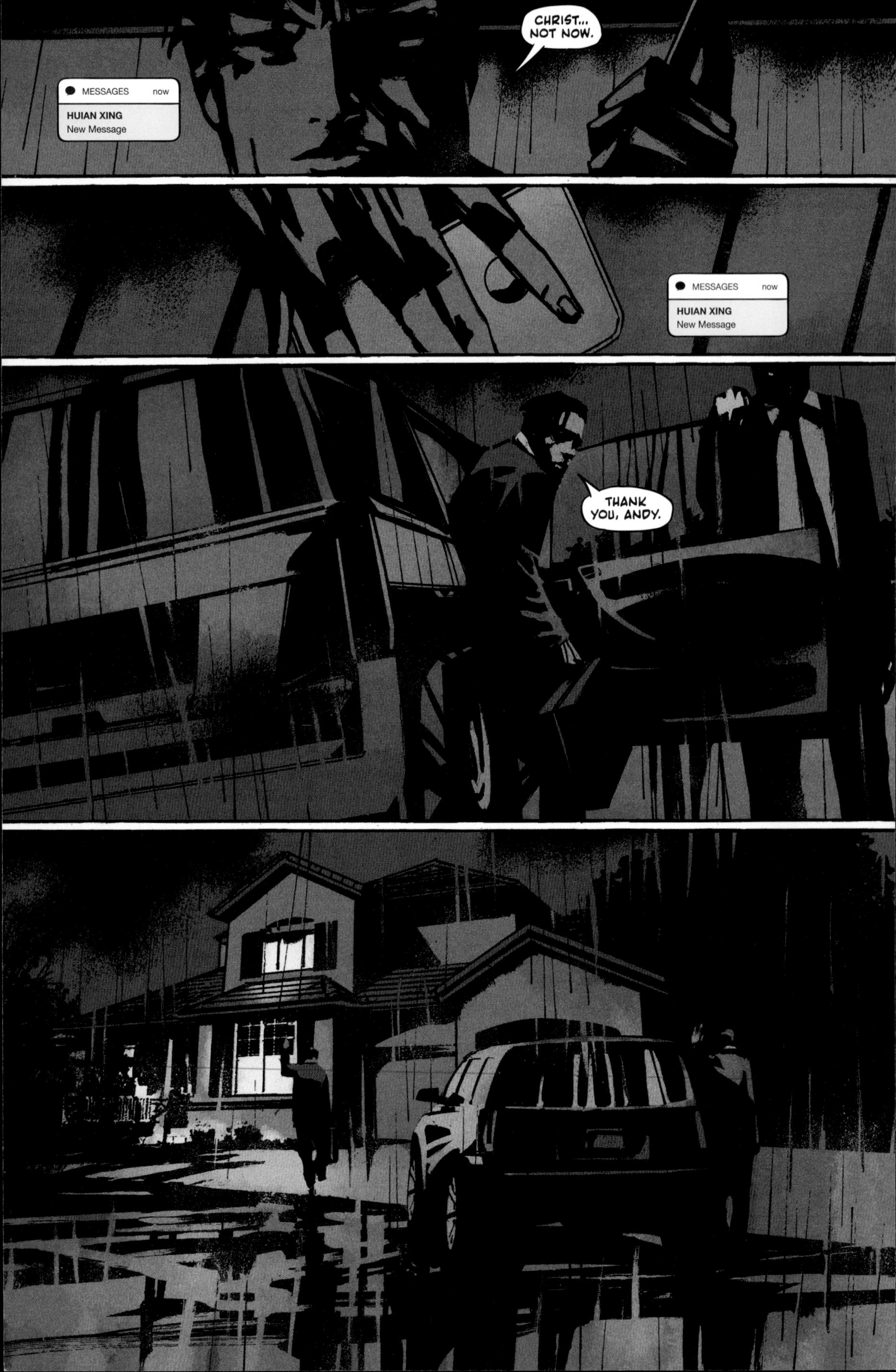
MESSAGES now
HUIAN XING
New Message
CHRIST... NOT NOW.
MESSAGES now
HUIAN XING
New Message
THANK YOU, ANDY.

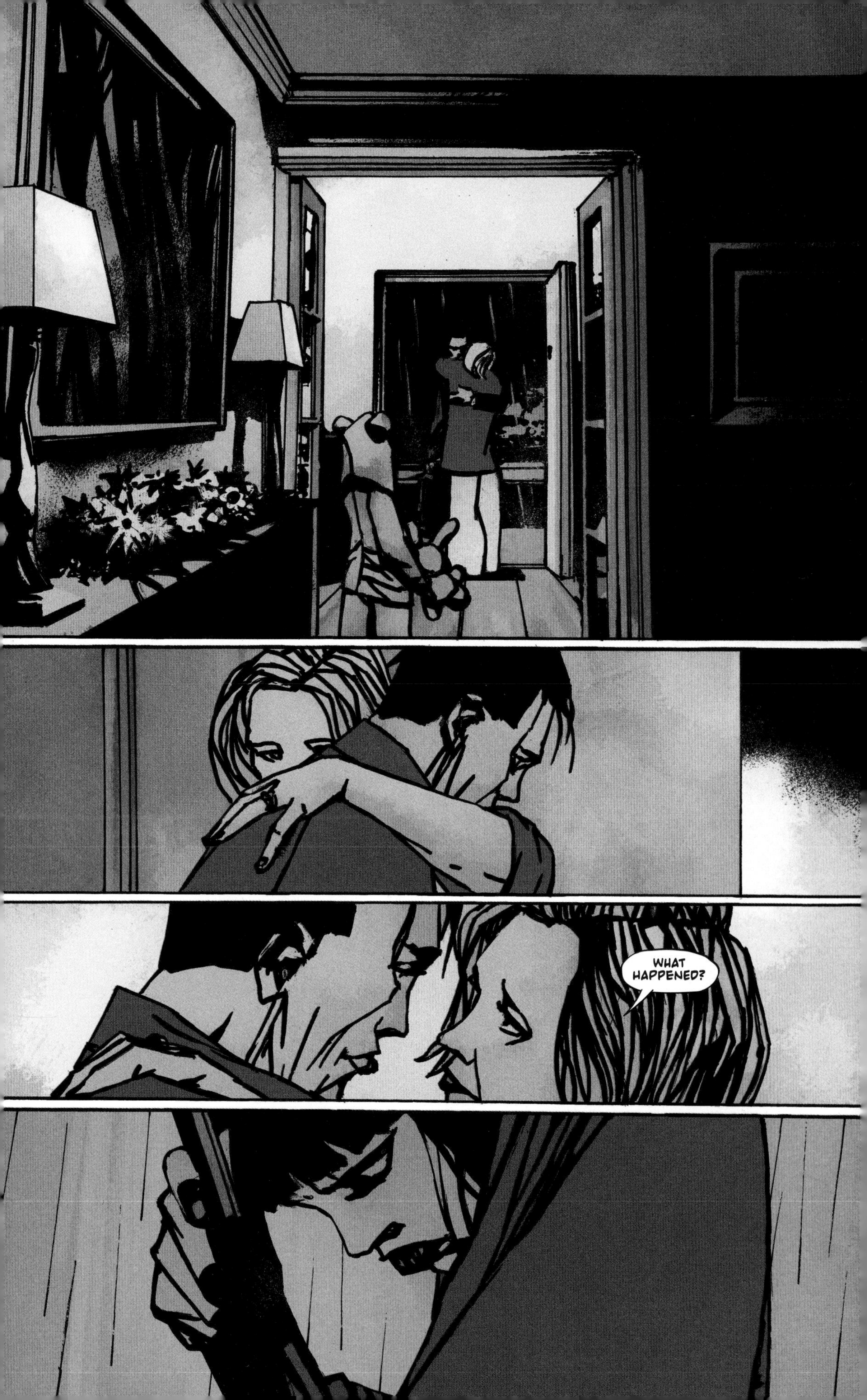
WHAT HAPPENED?

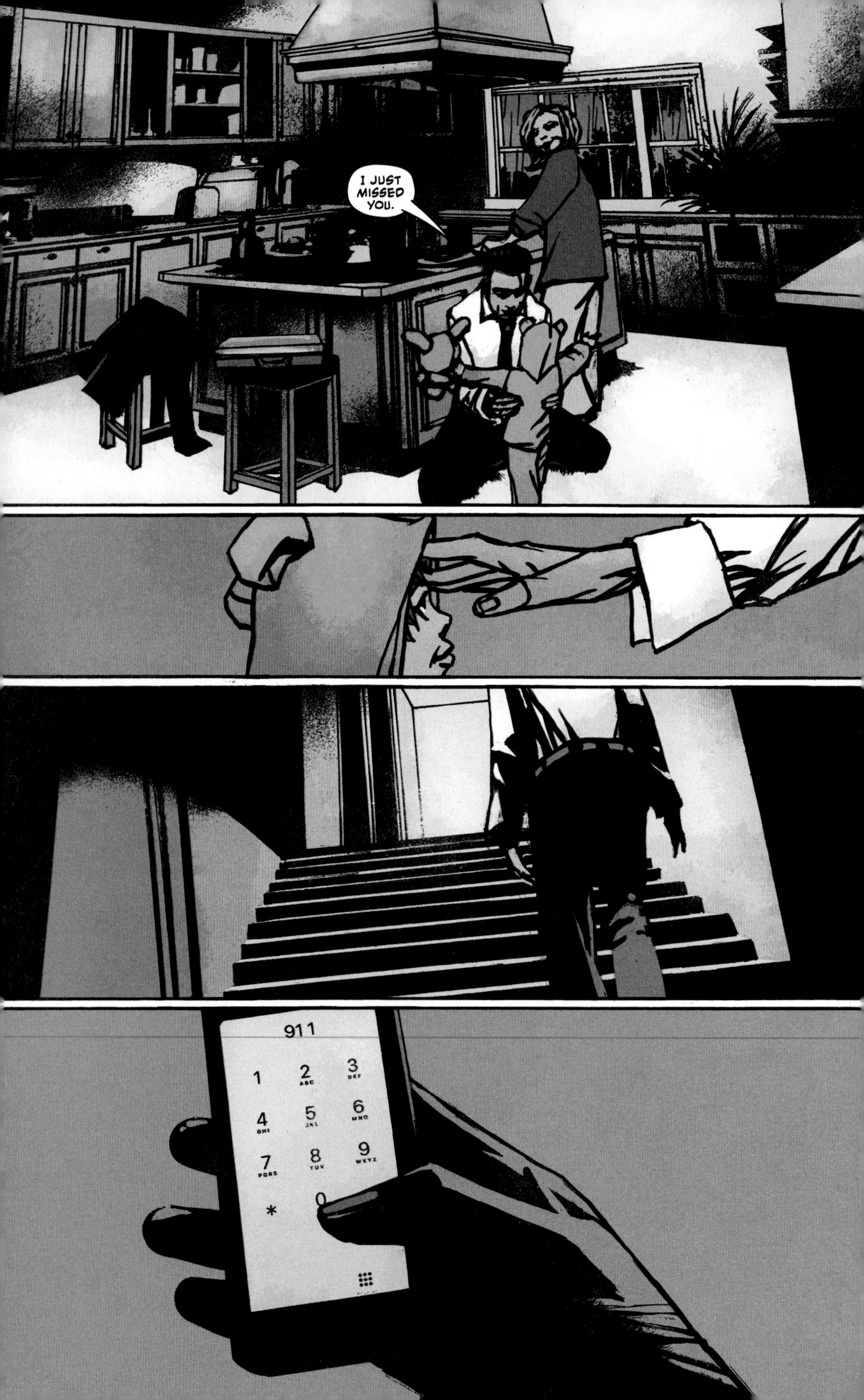
I JUST MISSED YOU.
911

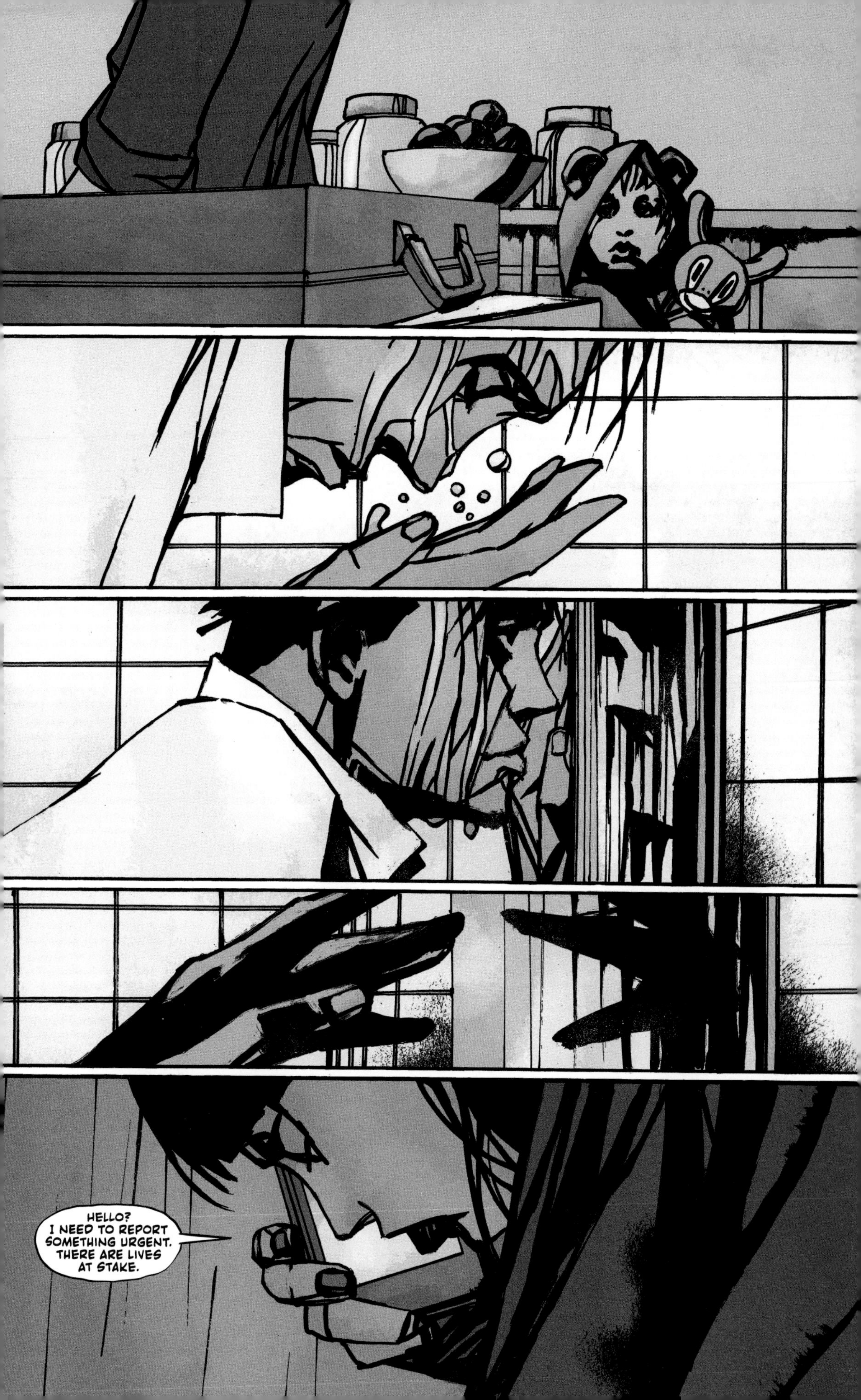
HELLO? I NEED TO REPORT SOMETHING URGENT. THERE ARE LIVES AT STAKE.

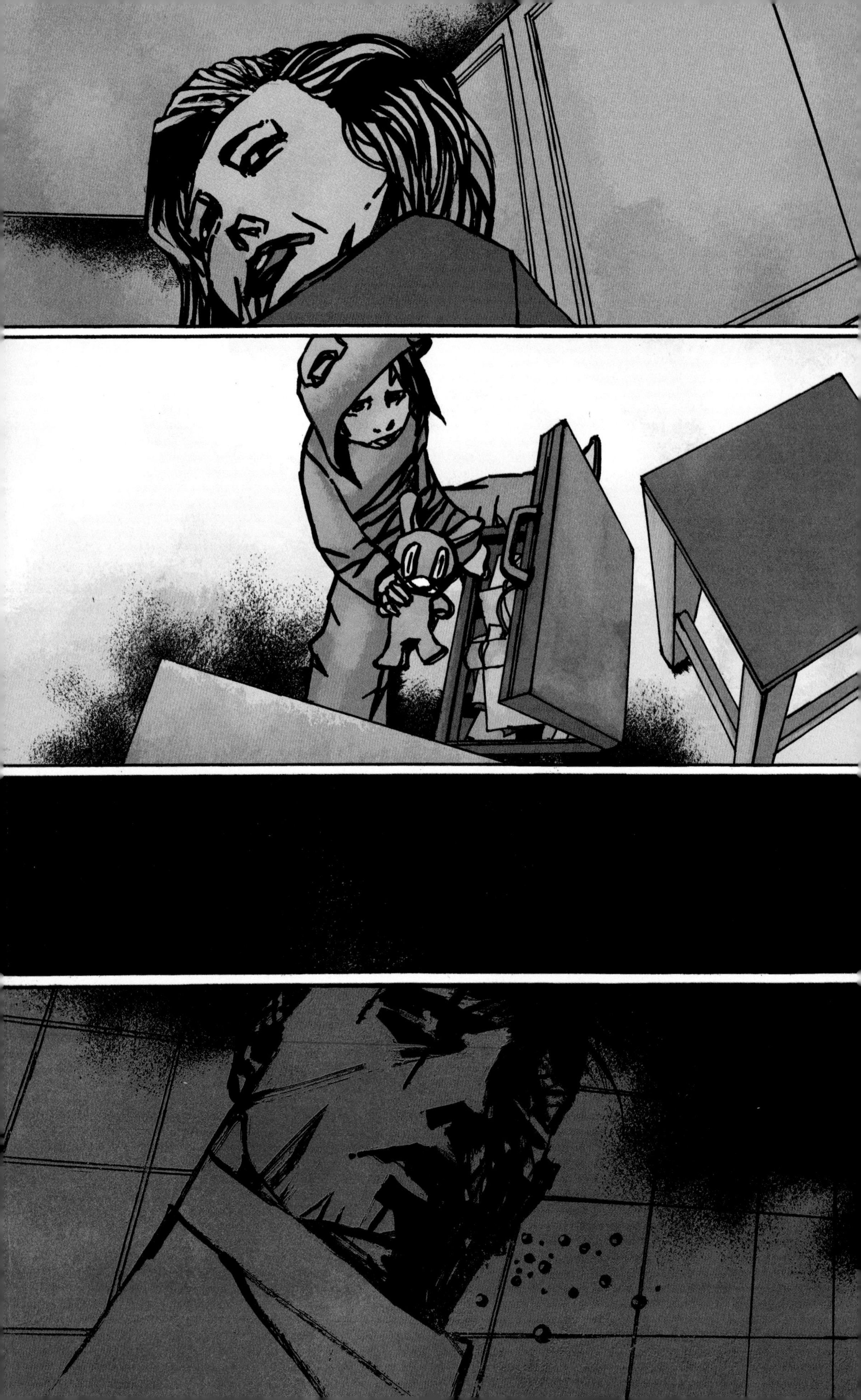

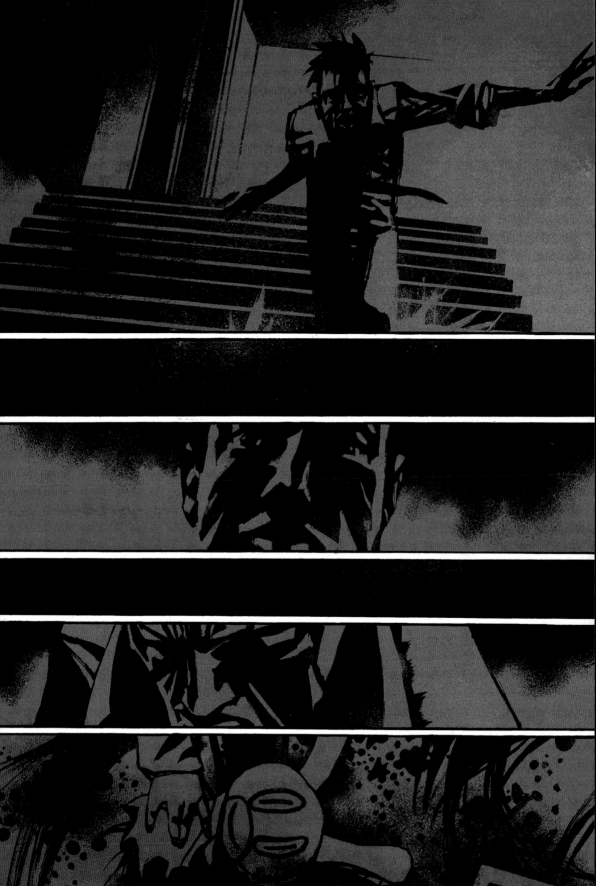

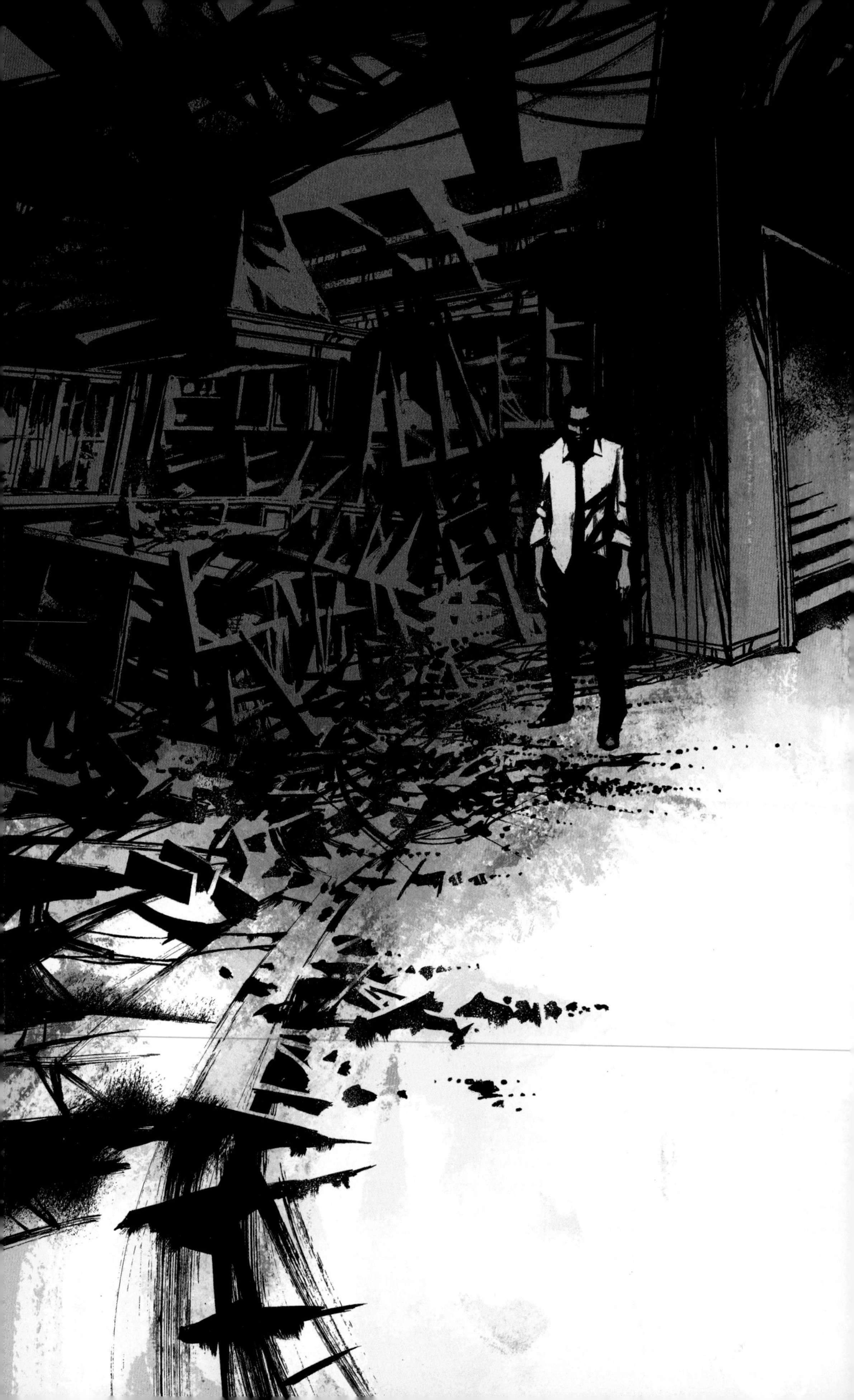

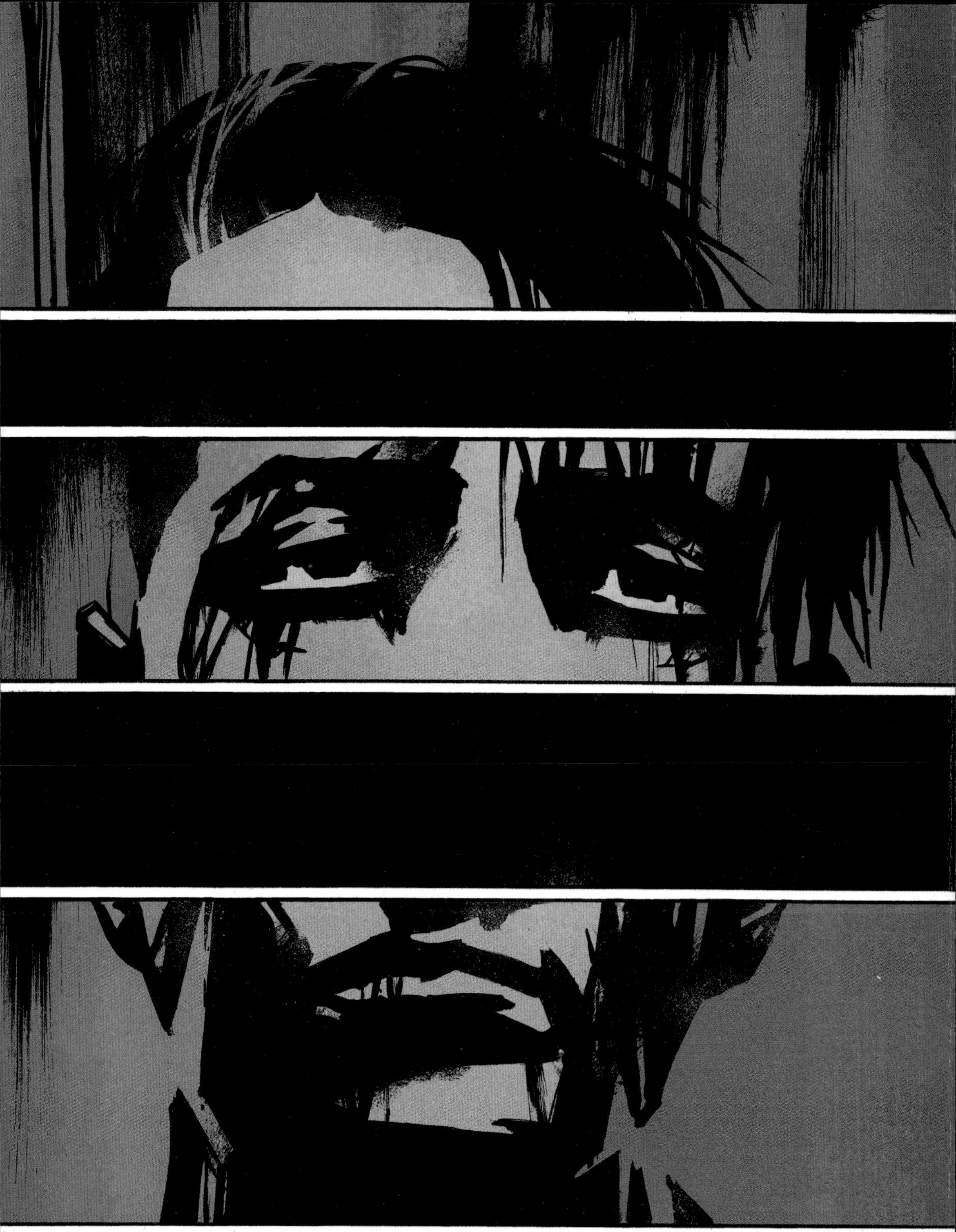

CHAPTER ELEVEN:
AMERICANA

"A year after his (Milgram's) experiment, researchers at Northwestern University found that, unlike your average human, rhesus monkeys would starve themselves rather than pull a chain that administers an electric shock to a companion."

—Kristin Dombek,
The Selfishness of Others

"It was a good hanging."

—George Orwell,
1984

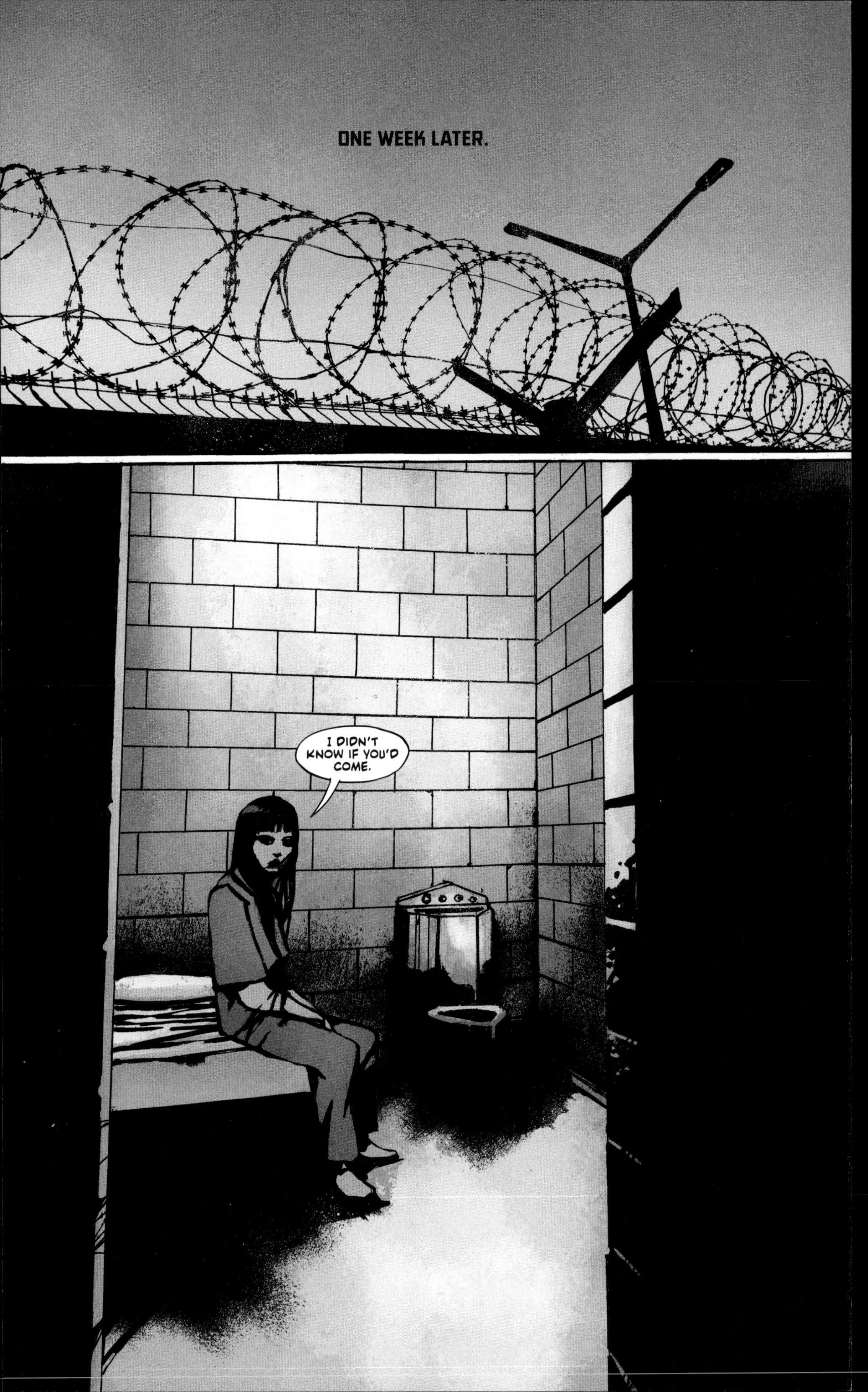
ONE WEEK LATER.
I DIDN'T KNOW IF YOU'D COME.

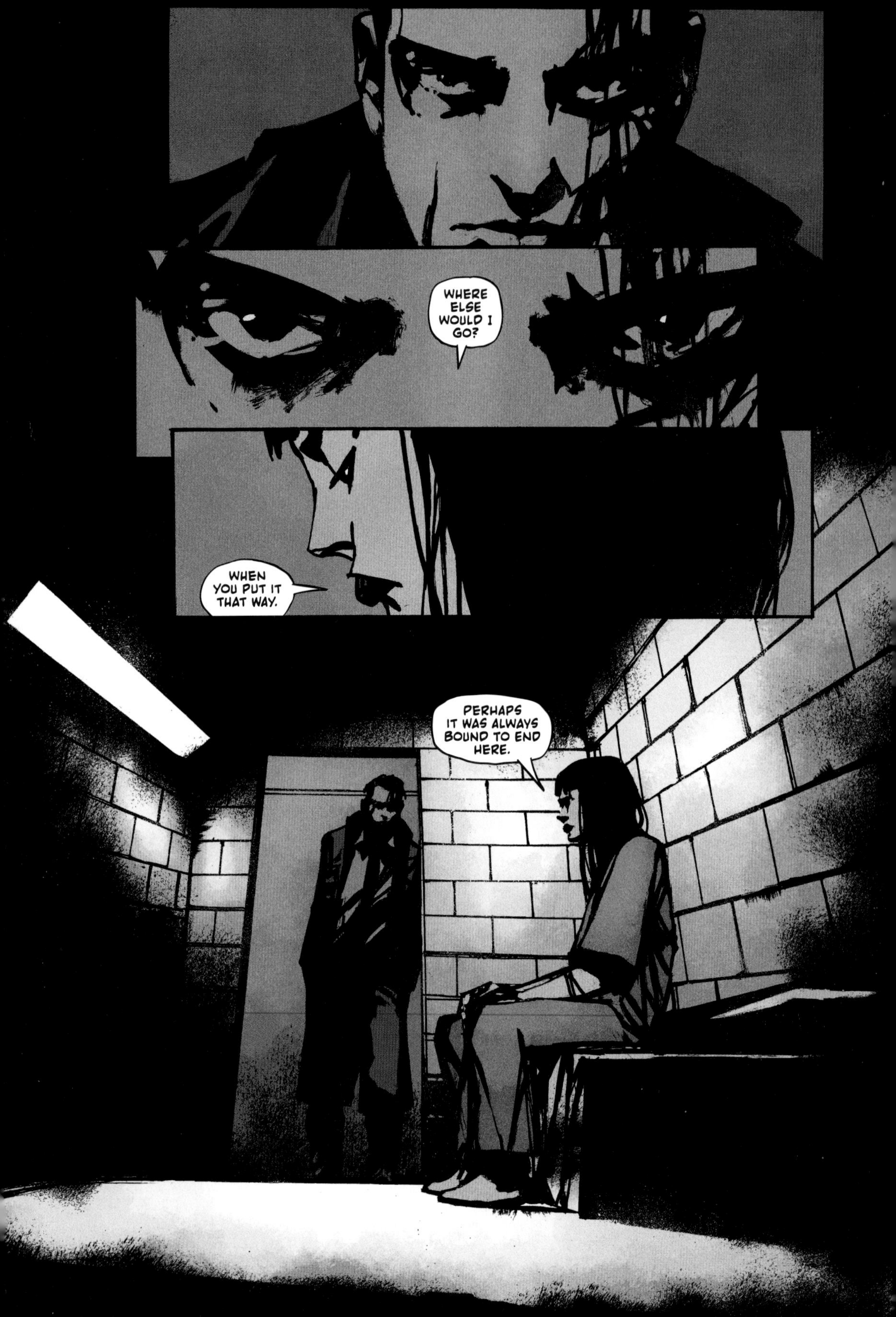
WHERE ELSE WOULD I GO?
WHEN YOU PUT IT THAT WAY.
PERHAPS IT WAS ALWAYS BOUND TO END HERE.

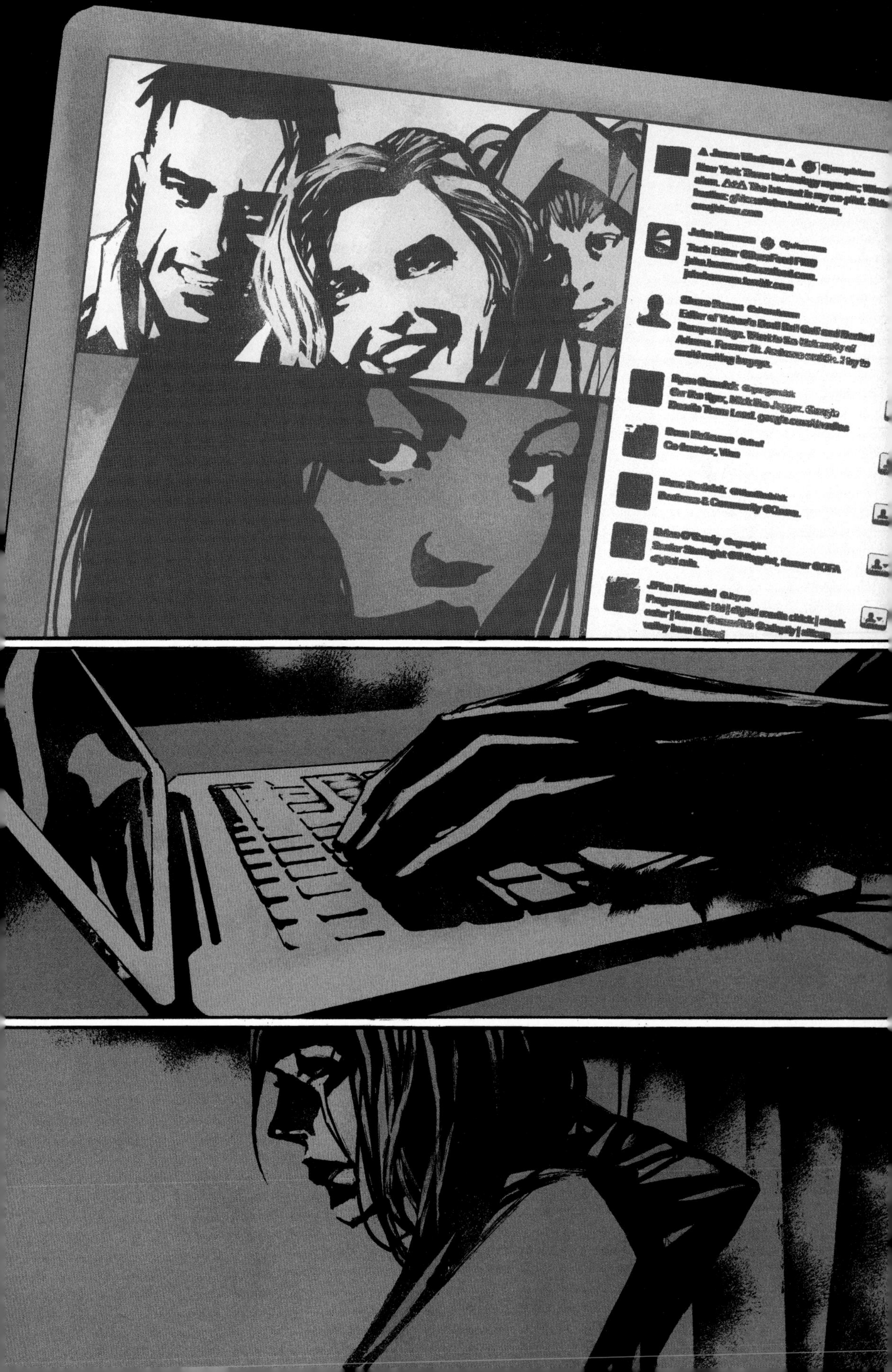

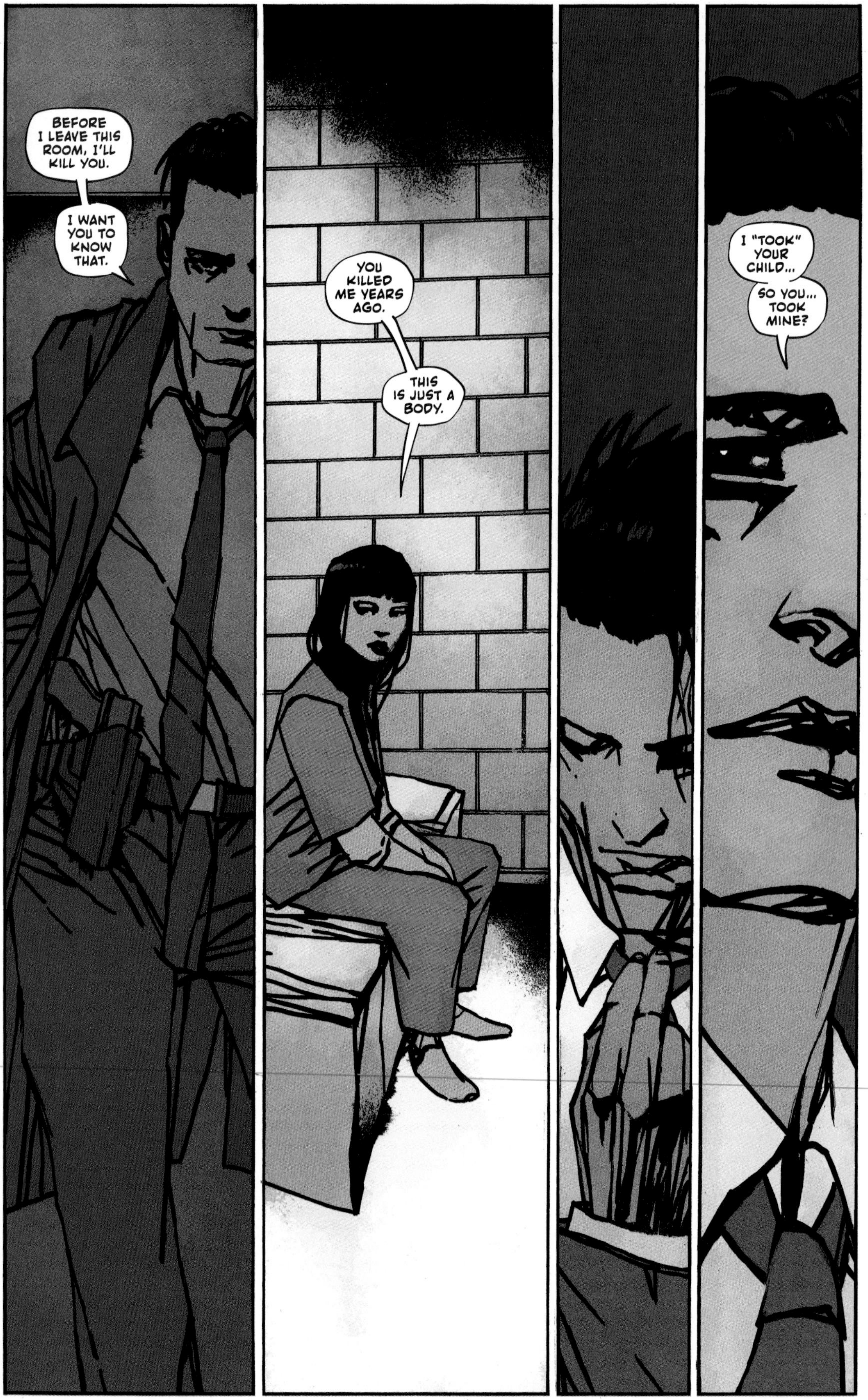
BEFORE I LEAVE THIS ROOM, I'LL KILL YOU.
I WANT YOU TO KNOW THAT.
YOU KILLED ME YEARS AGO.
THIS IS JUST A BODY.
I "TOOK" YOUR CHILD...
SO YOU... TOOK MINE?

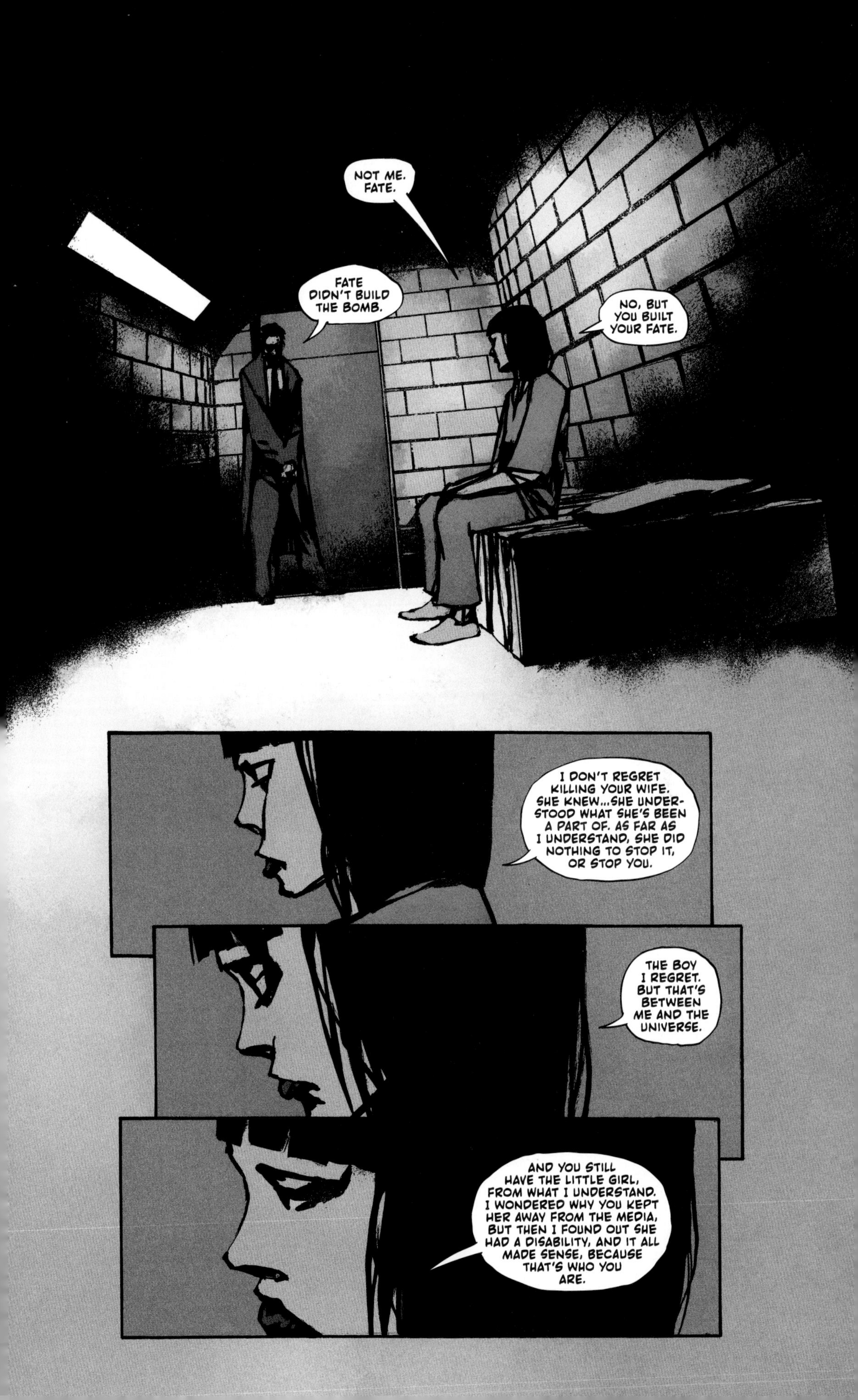
NOT ME. FATE.
FATE DIDN'T BUILD THE BOMB.
NO, BUT YOU BUILT YOUR FATE.
I DON'T REGRET KILLING YOUR WIFE. SHE KNEW...SHE UNDER-STOOD WHAT SHE'S BEEN A PART OF. AS FAR AS I UNDERSTAND, SHE DID NOTHING TO STOP IT, OR STOP YOU.
THE BOY I REGRET. BUT THAT'S BETWEEN ME AND THE UNIVERSE.
AND YOU STILL HAVE THE LITTLE GIRL, FROM WHAT I UNDERSTAND. I WONDERED WHY YOU KEPT HER AWAY FROM THE MEDIA, BUT THEN I FOUND OUT SHE HAD A DISABILITY, AND IT ALL MADE SENSE, BECAUSE THAT'S WHO YOU ARE.

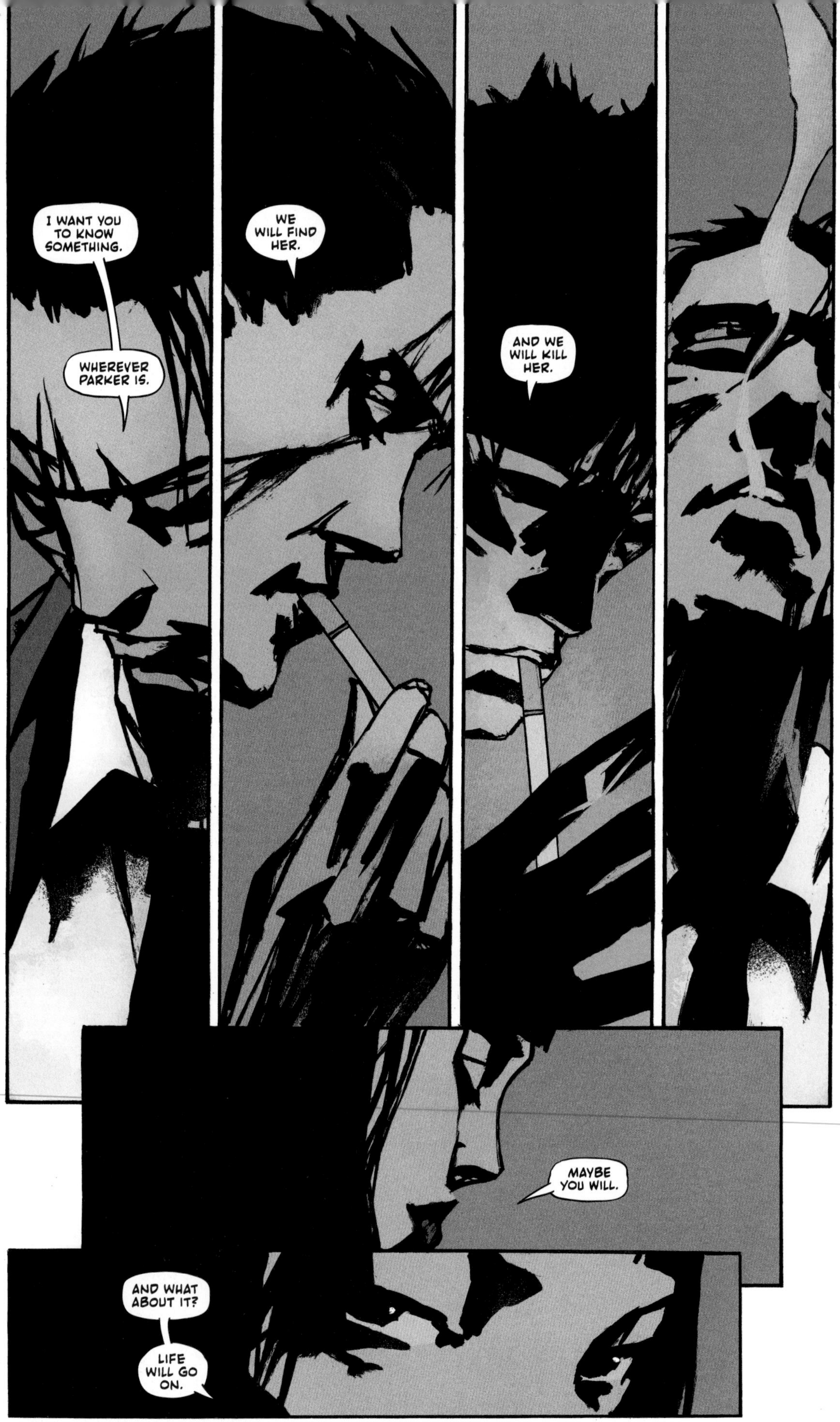
I WANT YOU TO KNOW SOMETHING.
WHEREVER PARKER IS.
WE WILL FIND HER.
AND WE WILL KILL HER.
MAYBE YOU WILL.
AND WHAT ABOUT IT?
LIFE WILL GO ON.

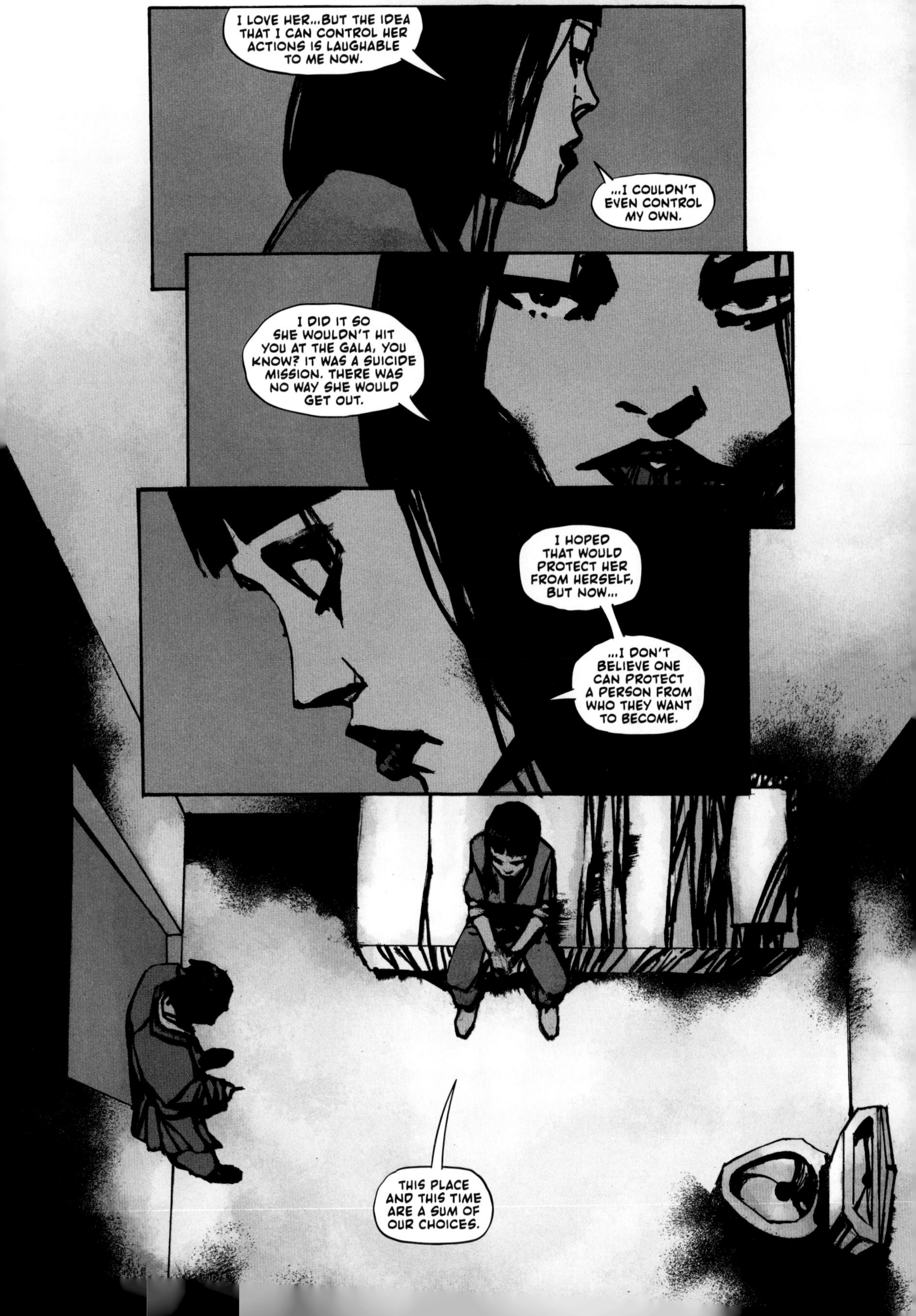
I LOVE HER...BUT THE IDEA THAT I CAN CONTROL HER ACTIONS IS LAUGHABLE TO ME NOW.
...I COULDN'T EVEN CONTROL MY OWN.
I DID IT SO SHE WOULDN'T HIT YOU AT THE GALA, YOU KNOW? IT WAS A SUICIDE MISSION. THERE WAS NO WAY SHE WOULD GET OUT.
I HOPED THAT WOULD PROTECT HER FROM HERSELF, BUT NOW...
...I DON'T BELIEVE ONE CAN PROTECT A PERSON FROM WHO THEY WANT TO BECOME.
THIS PLACE AND THIS TIME ARE A SUM OF OUR CHOICES.

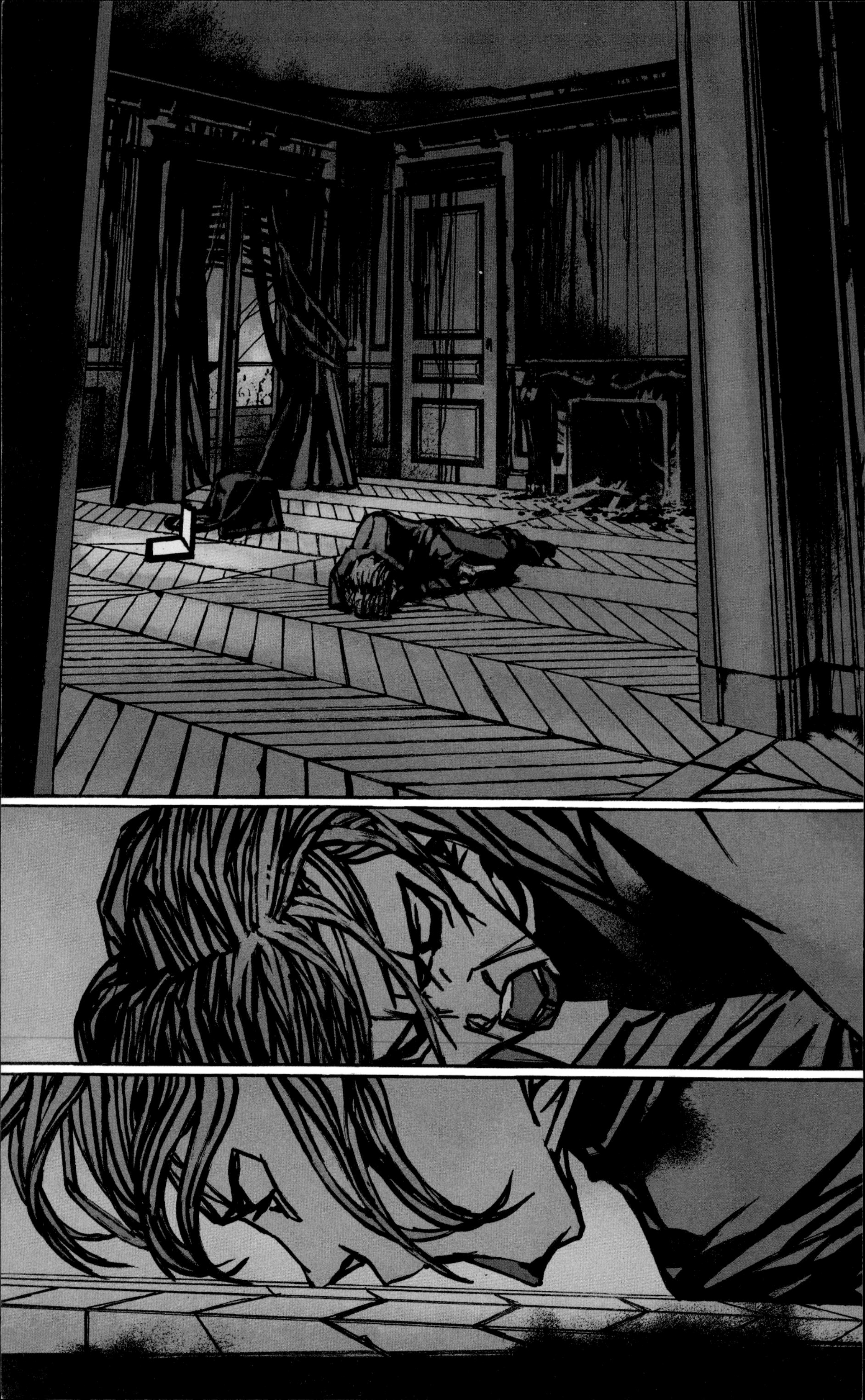

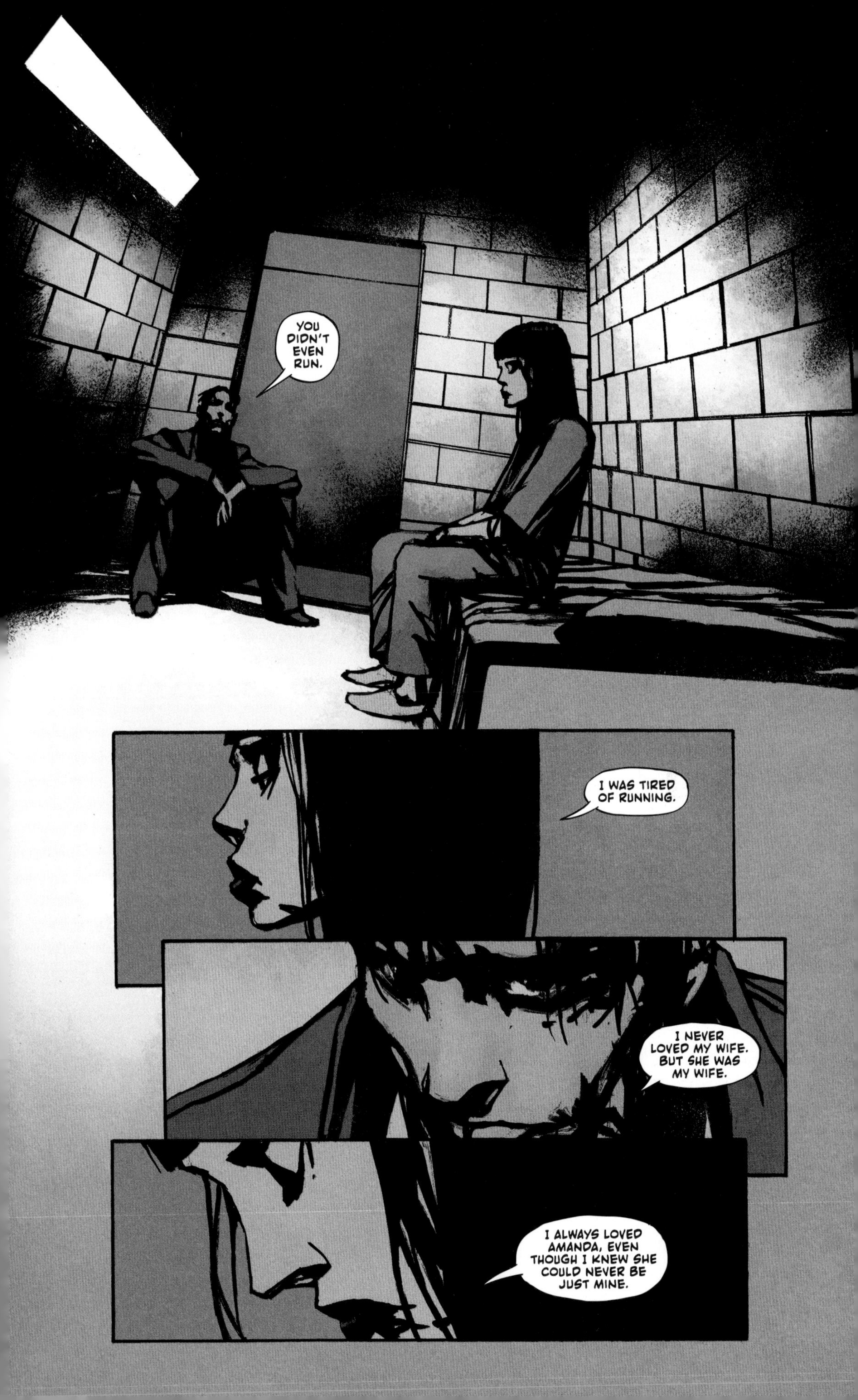
YOU DIDN'T EVEN RUN.
I WAS TIRED OF RUNNING.
I NEVER LOVED MY WIFE. BUT SHE WAS MY WIFE.
I ALWAYS LOVED AMANDA, EVEN THOUGH I KNEW SHE COULD NEVER BE JUST MINE.

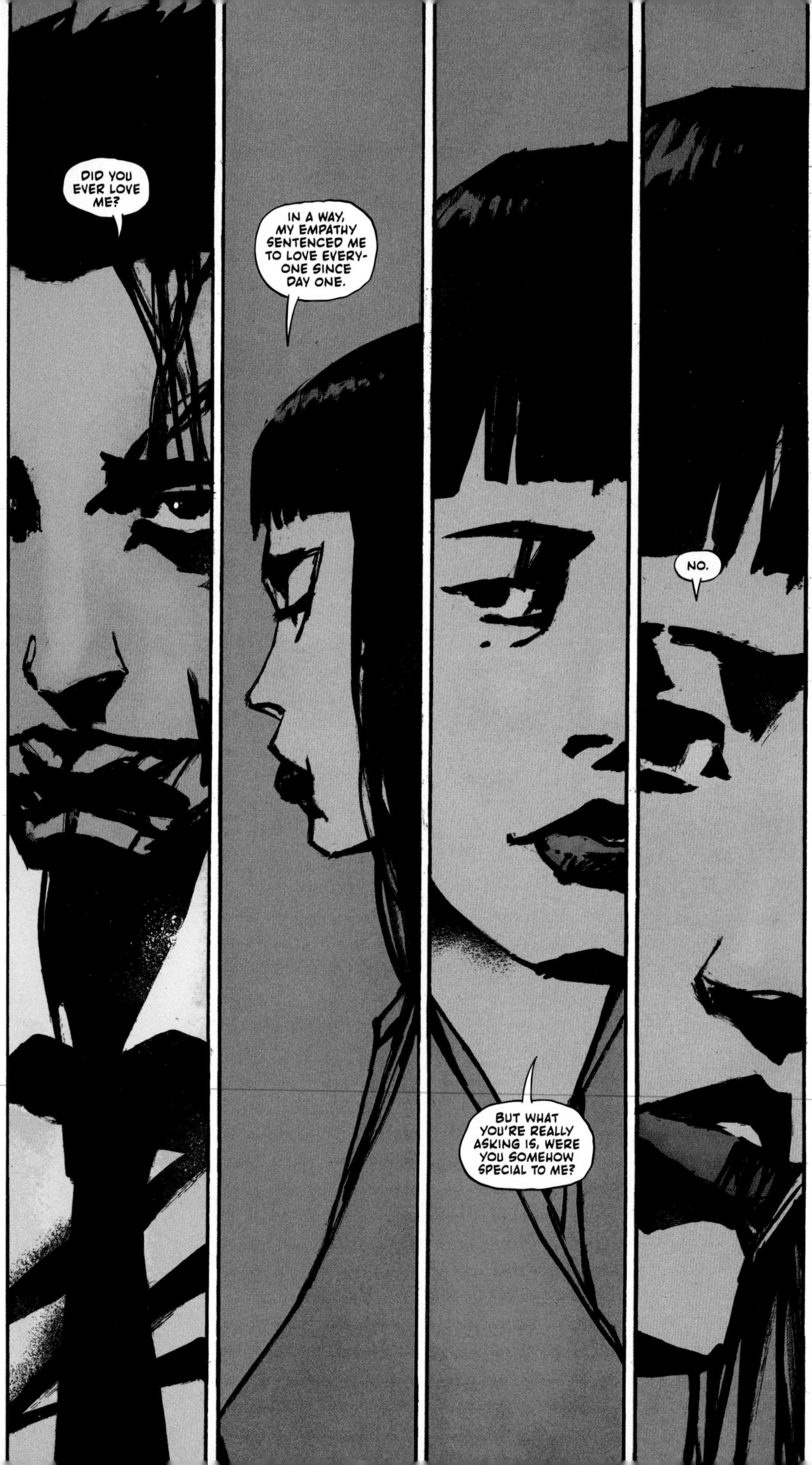
DID YOU EVER LOVE ME?
IN A WAY, MY EMPATHY SENTENCED ME TO LOVE EVERY-ONE SINCE DAY ONE.
BUT WHAT YOU'RE REALLY ASKING IS, WERE YOU SOMEHOW SPECIAL TO ME?
NO.

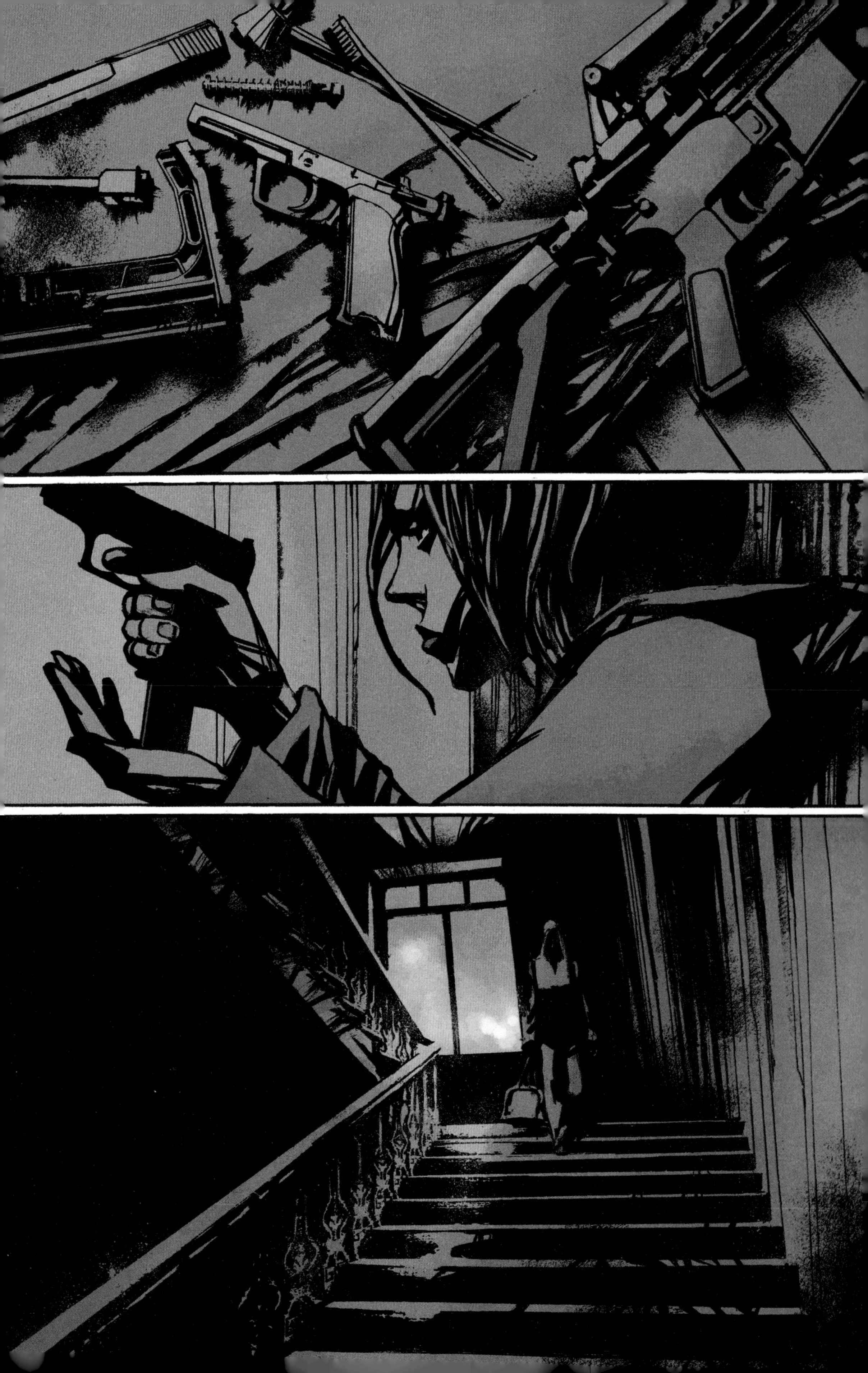

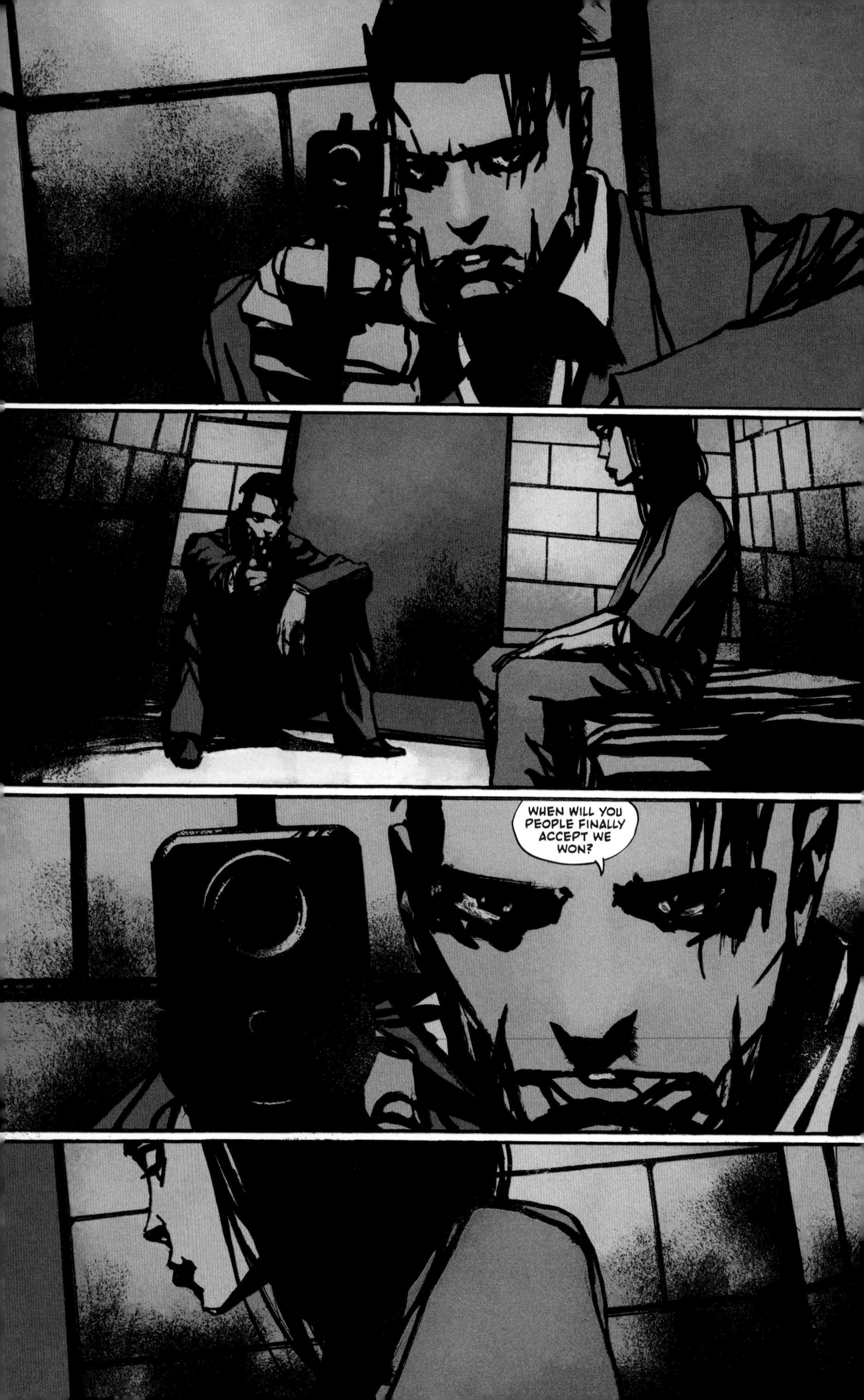
WHEN WILL YOU PEOPLE FINALLY ACCEPT WE WON?

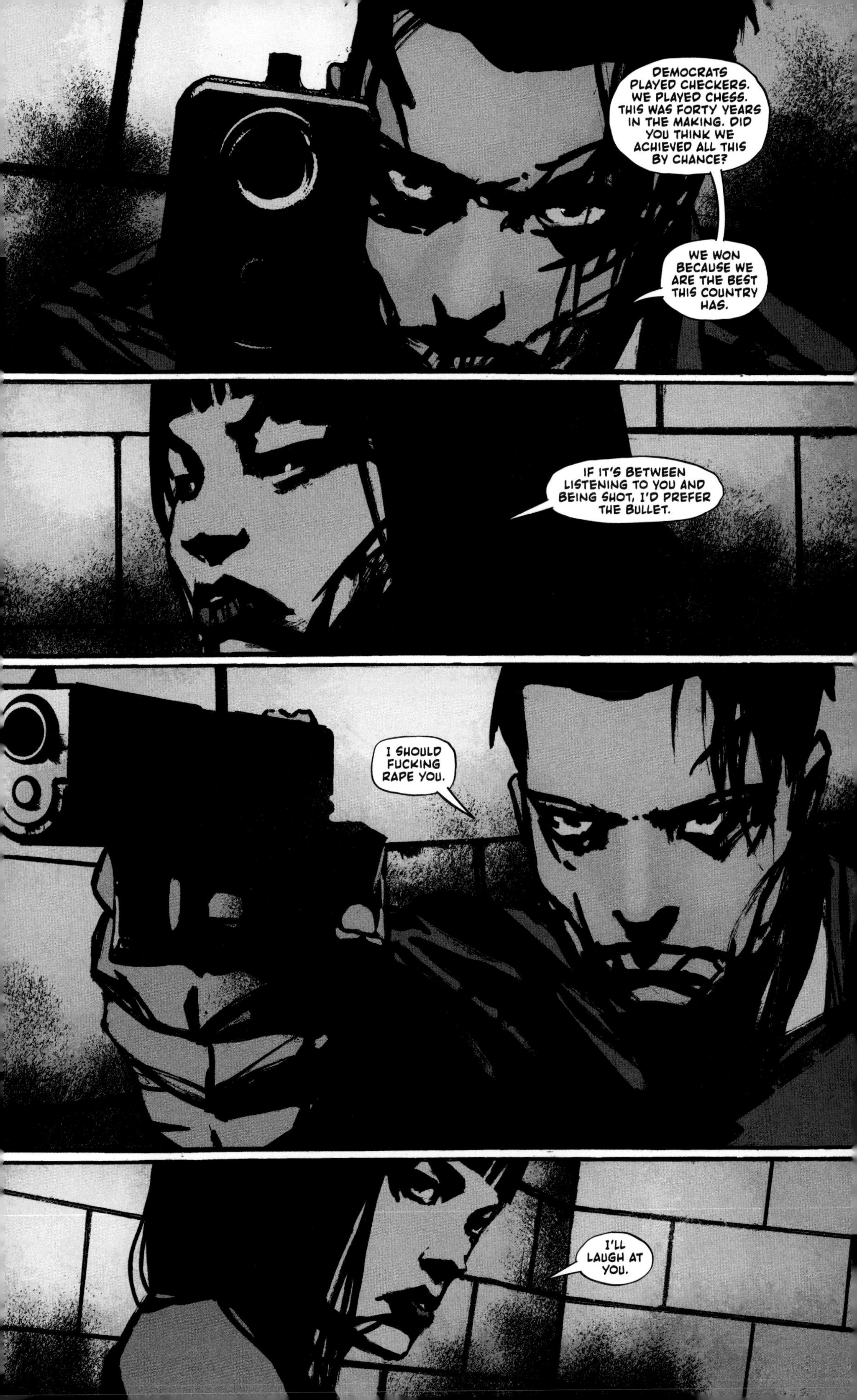
DEMOCRATS PLAYED CHECKERS. WE PLAYED CHESS. THIS WAS FORTY YEARS IN THE MAKING. DID YOU THINK WE ACHIEVED ALL THIS BY CHANCE?
WE WON BECAUSE WE ARE THE BEST THIS COUNTRY HAS.
IF IT'S BETWEEN LISTENING TO YOU AND BEING SHOT, I'D PREFER THE BULLET.
I SHOULD FUCKING RAPE YOU.
I'LL LAUGH AT YOU.

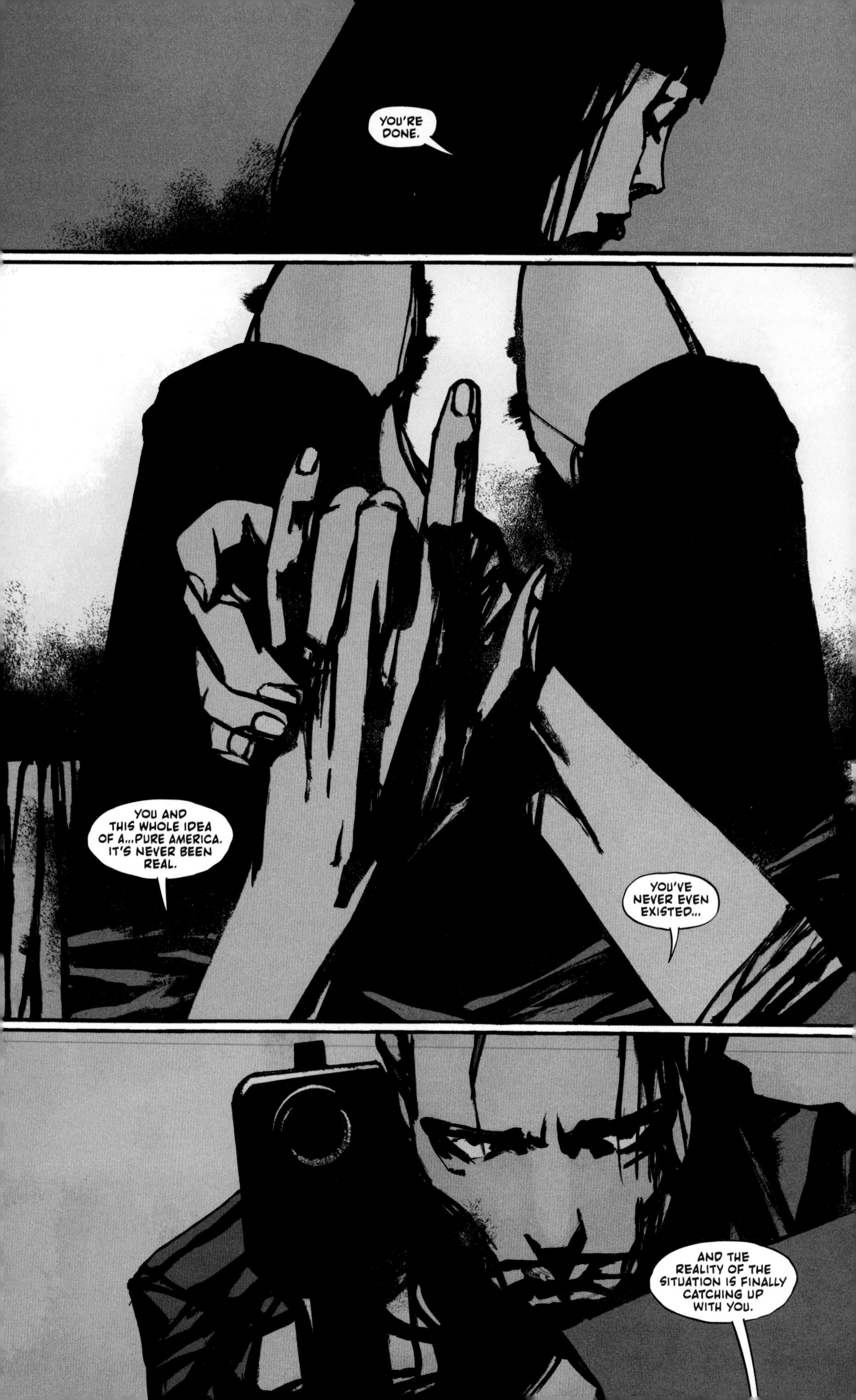
YOU'RE DONE.
YOU AND THIS WHOLE IDEA OF A...PURE AMERICA. IT'S NEVER BEEN REAL.
YOU'VE NEVER EVEN EXISTED...
AND THE REALITY OF THE SITUATION IS FINALLY CATCHING UP WITH YOU.

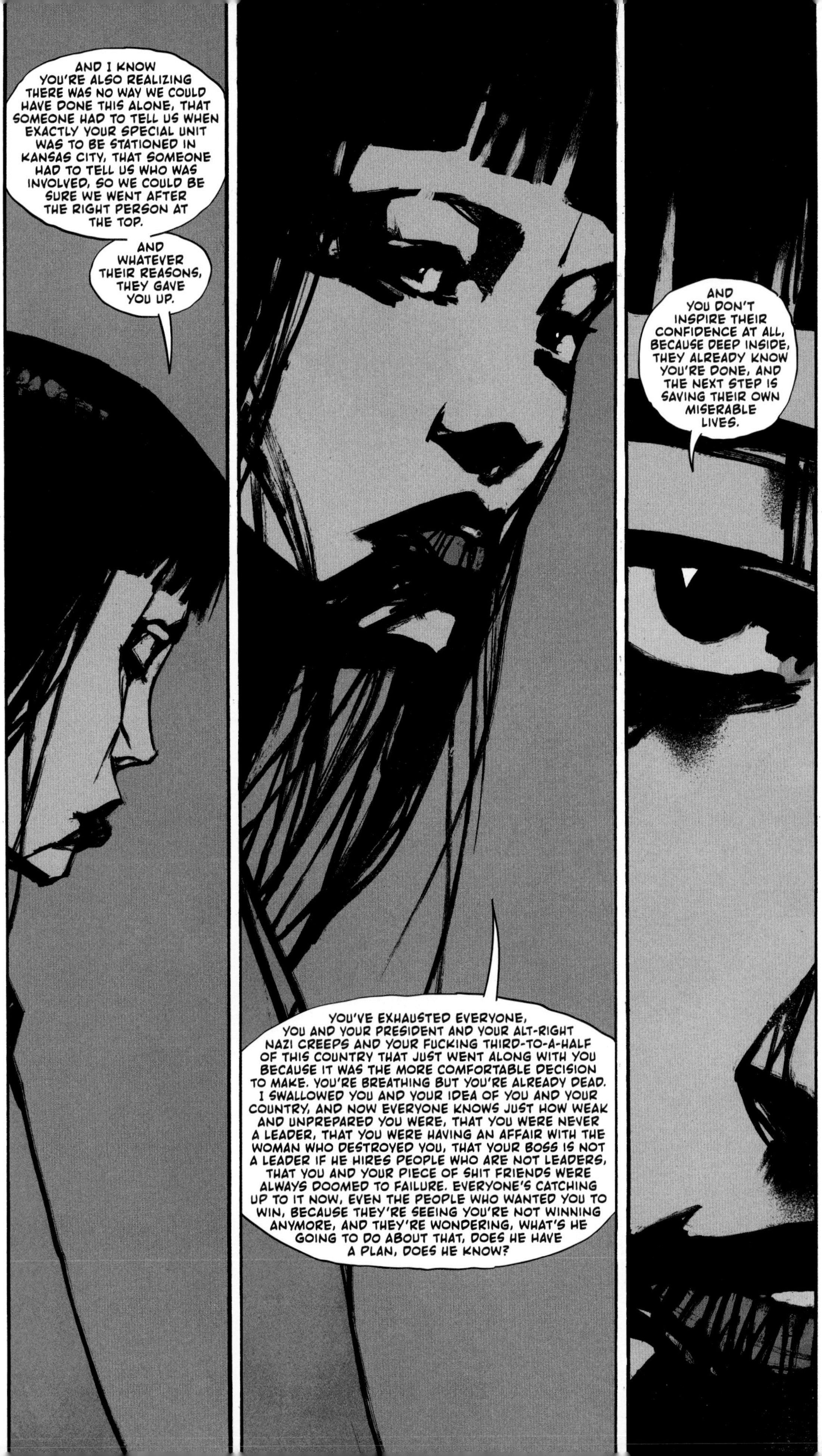
AND I KNOW YOU'RE ALSO REALIZING THERE WAS NO WAY WE COULD HAVE DONE THIS ALONE, THAT SOMEONE HAD TO TELL US WHEN EXACTLY YOUR SPECIAL UNIT WAS TO BE STATIONED IN KANSAS CITY, THAT SOMEONE HAD TO TELL US WHO WAS INVOLVED, SO WE COULD BE SURE WE WENT AFTER THE RIGHT PERSON AT THE TOP.
AND WHATEVER THEIR REASONS, THEY GAVE YOU UP.
YOU'VE EXHAUSTED EVERYONE, YOU AND YOUR PRESIDENT AND YOUR ALT-RIGHT NAZI CREEPS AND YOUR FUCKING THIRD-TO-A-HALF OF THIS COUNTRY THAT JUST WENT ALONG WITH YOU BECAUSE IT WAS THE MORE COMFORTABLE DECISION TO MAKE. YOU'RE BREATHING BUT YOU'RE ALREADY DEAD. I SWALLOWED YOU AND YOUR IDEA OF YOU AND YOUR COUNTRY, AND NOW EVERYONE KNOWS JUST HOW WEAK AND UNPREPARED YOU WERE, THAT YOU WERE NEVER A LEADER, THAT YOU WERE HAVING AN AFFAIR WITH THE WOMAN WHO DESTROYED YOU, THAT YOUR BOSS IS NOT A LEADER IF HE HIRES PEOPLE WHO ARE NOT LEADERS, THAT YOU AND YOUR PIECE OF SHIT FRIENDS WERE ALWAYS DOOMED TO FAILURE. EVERYONE'S CATCHING UP TO IT NOW, EVEN THE PEOPLE WHO WANTED YOU TO WIN, BECAUSE THEY'RE SEEING YOU'RE NOT WINNING ANYMORE, AND THEY'RE WONDERING, WHAT'S HE GOING TO DO ABOUT THAT, DOES HE HAVE A PLAN, DOES HE KNOW?
AND YOU DON'T INSPIRE THEIR CONFIDENCE AT ALL, BECAUSE DEEP INSIDE, THEY ALREADY KNOW YOU'RE DONE, AND THE NEXT STEP IS SAVING THEIR OWN MISERABLE LIVES.

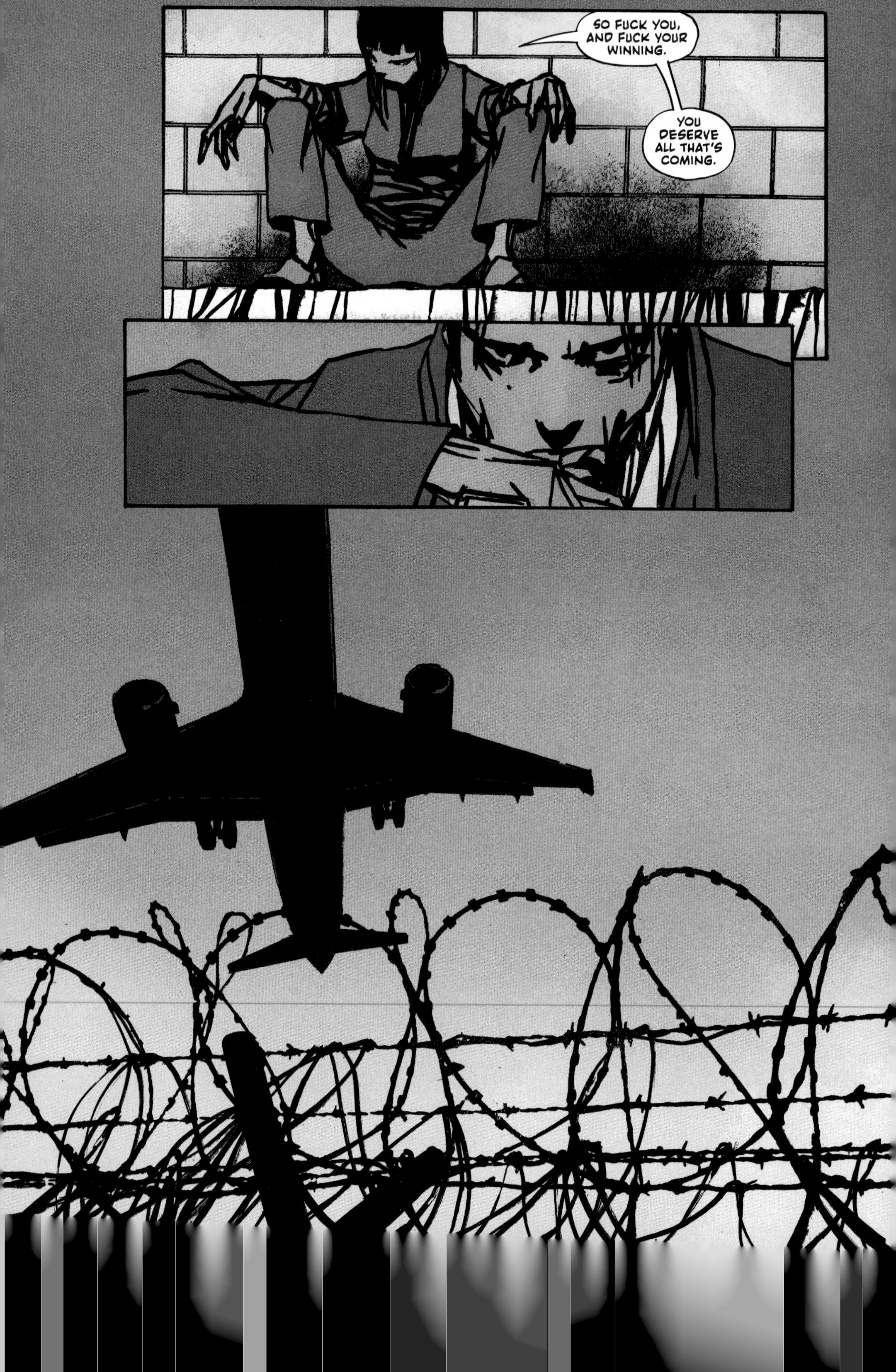
SO FUCK YOU, AND FUCK YOUR WINNING.
YOU DESERVE ALL THAT'S COMING.

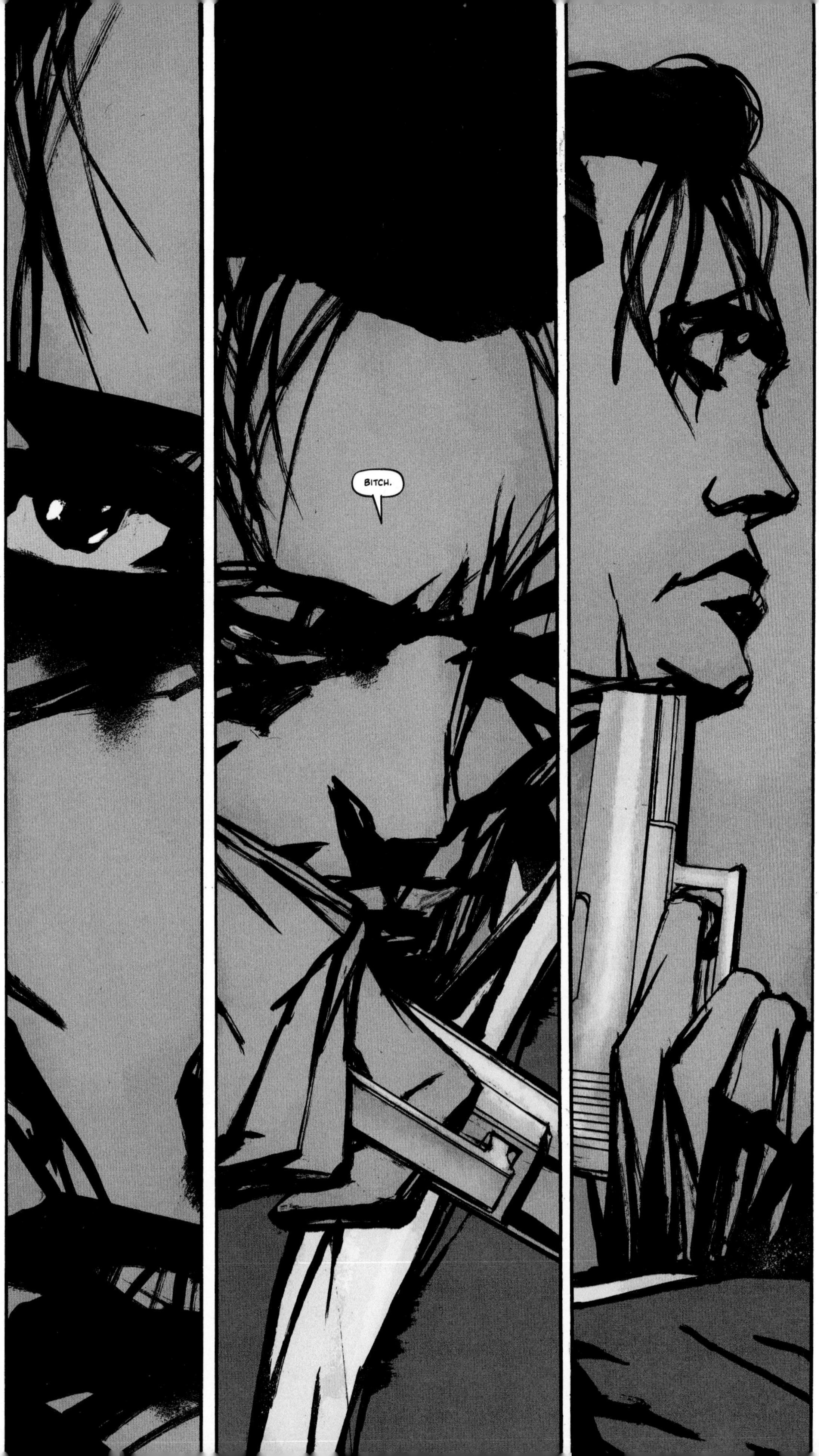
BITCH.

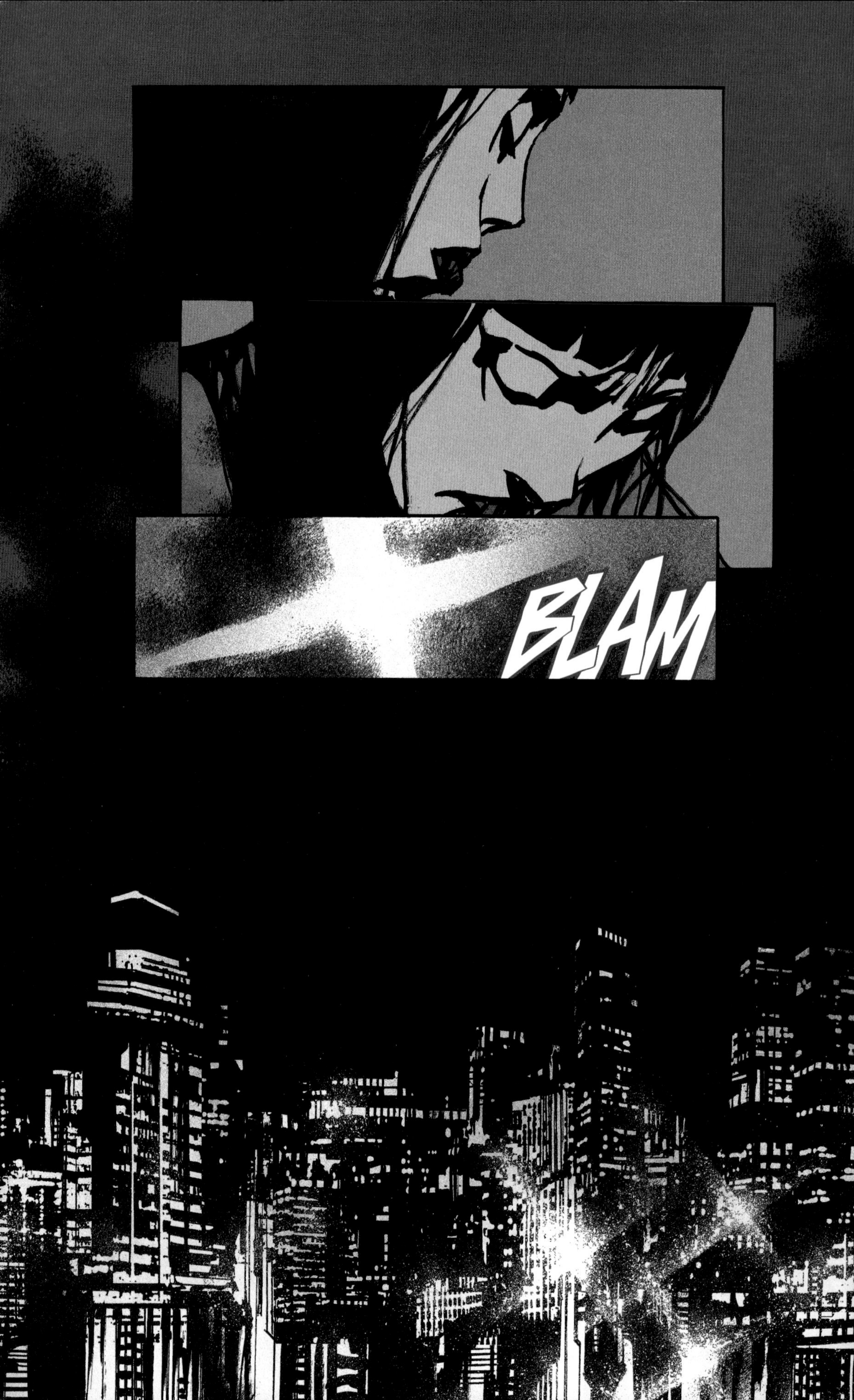
BLAM

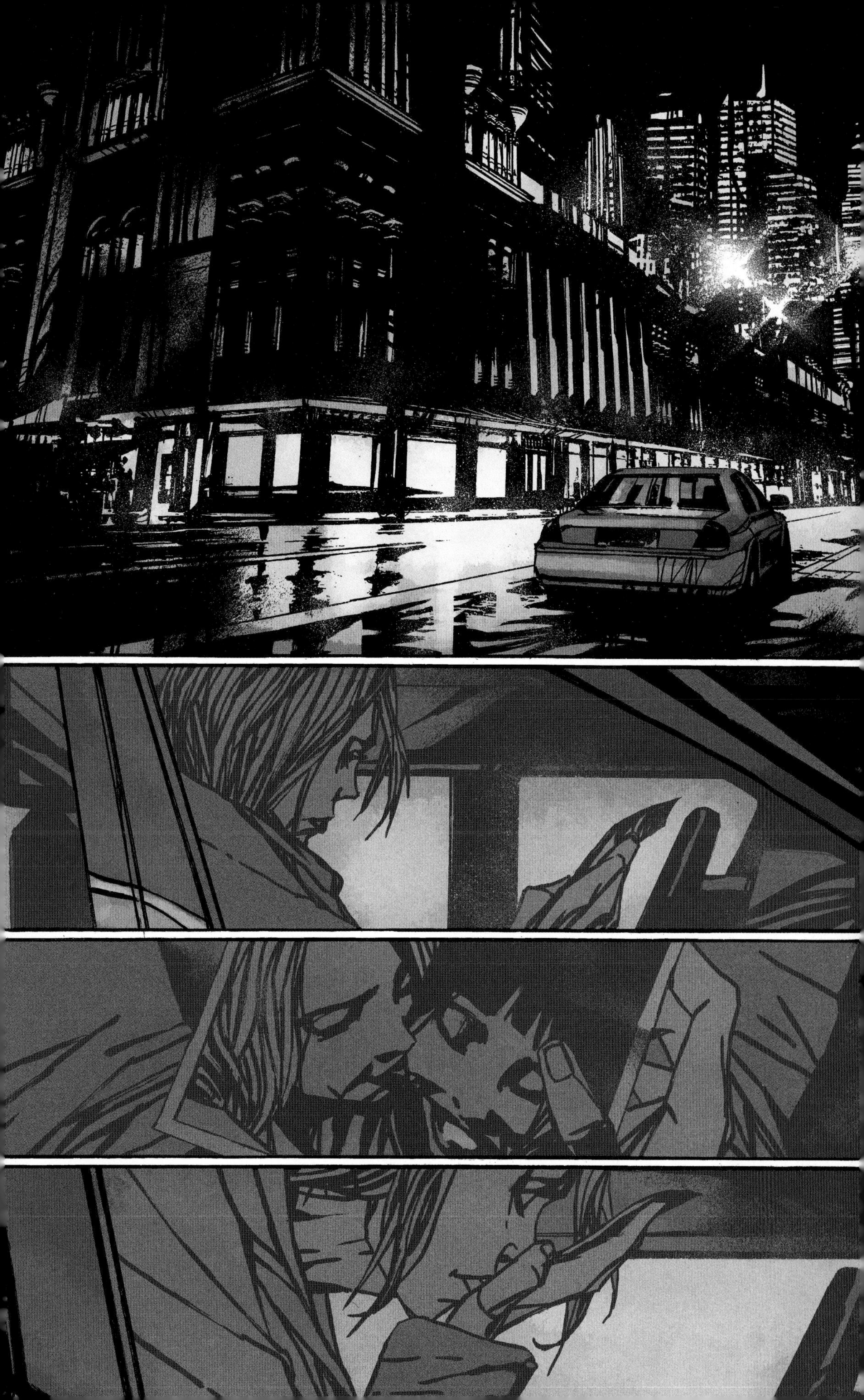

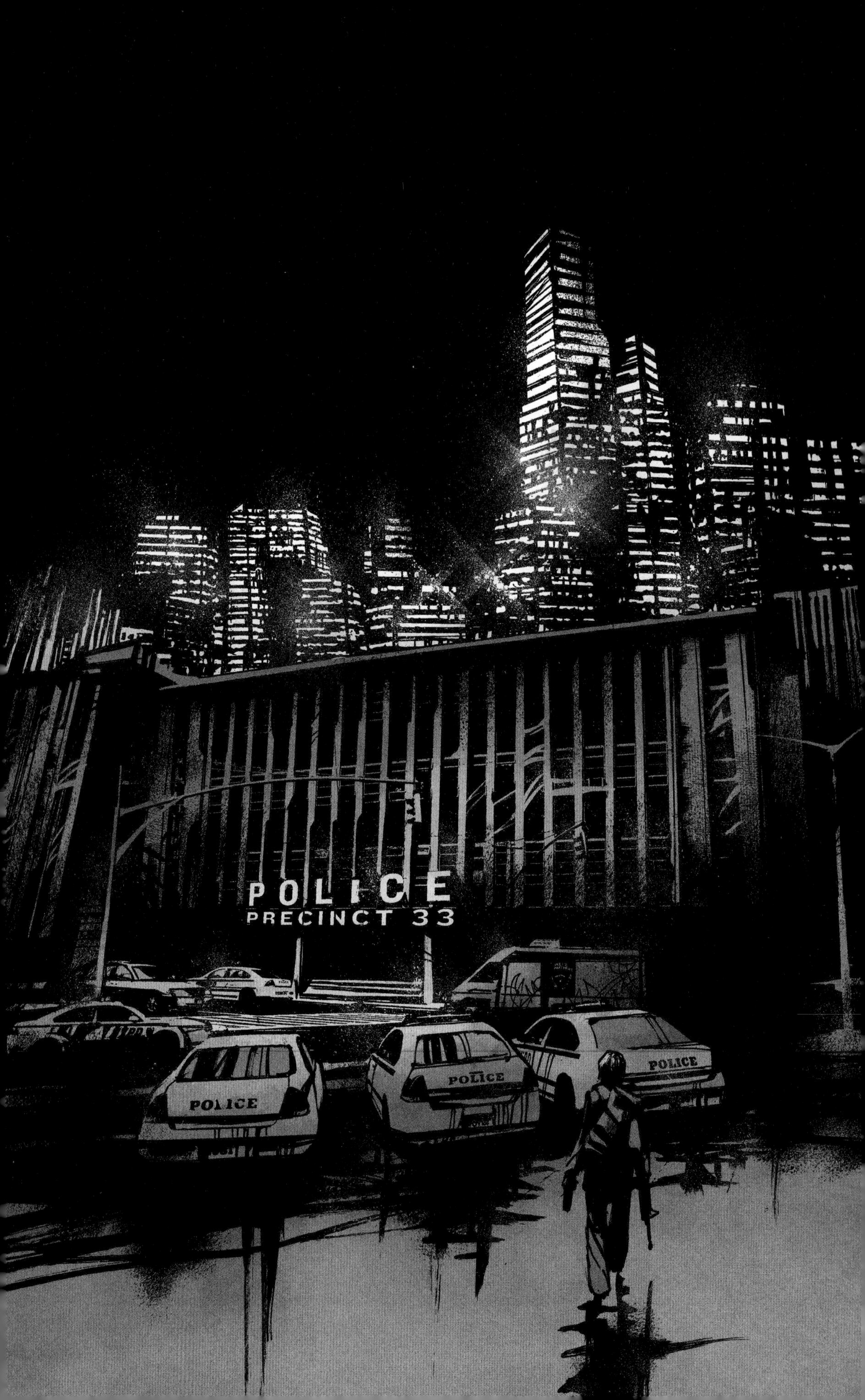
POLICE
PRECINCT 33
POLICE
POLICE
POLICE

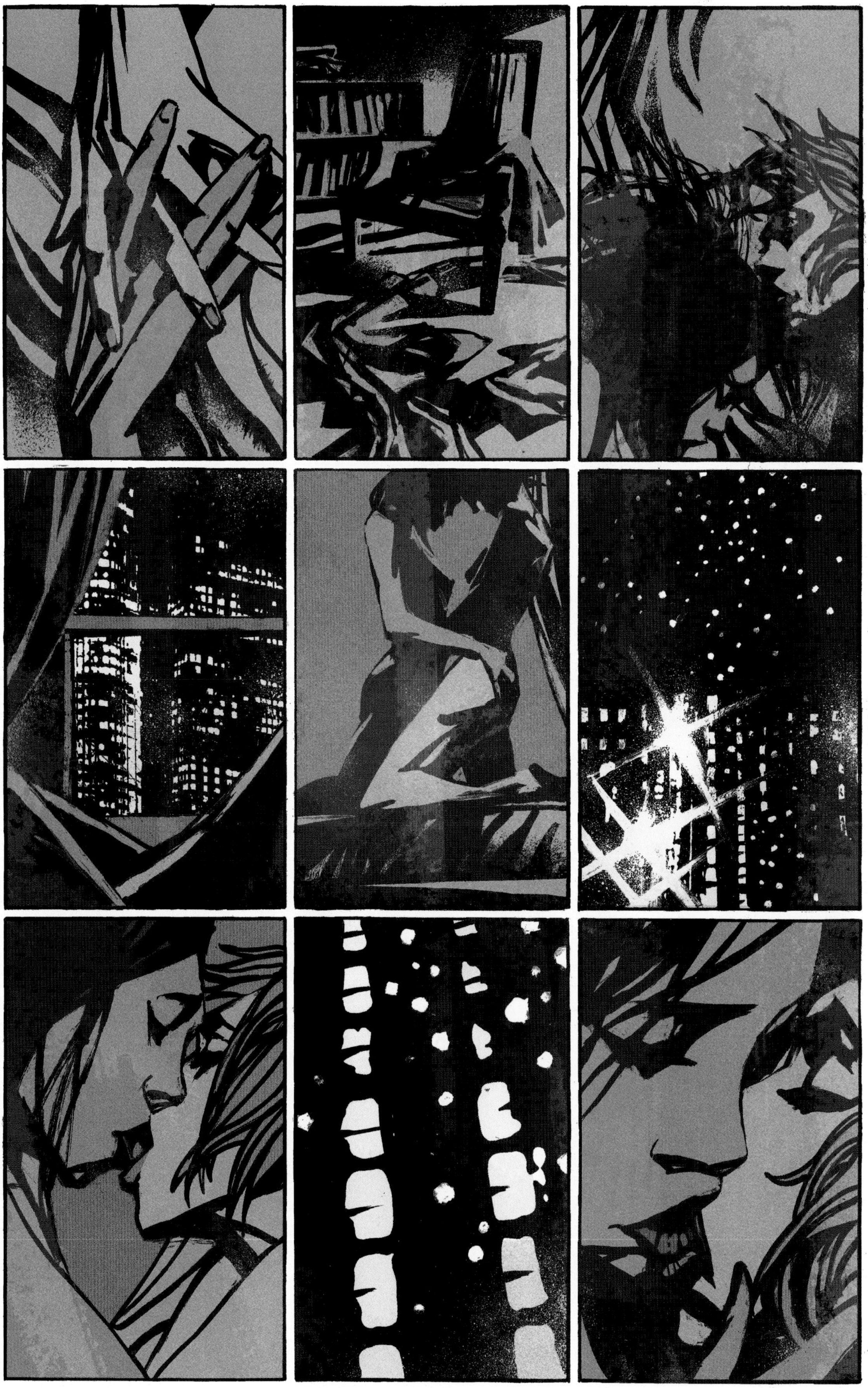

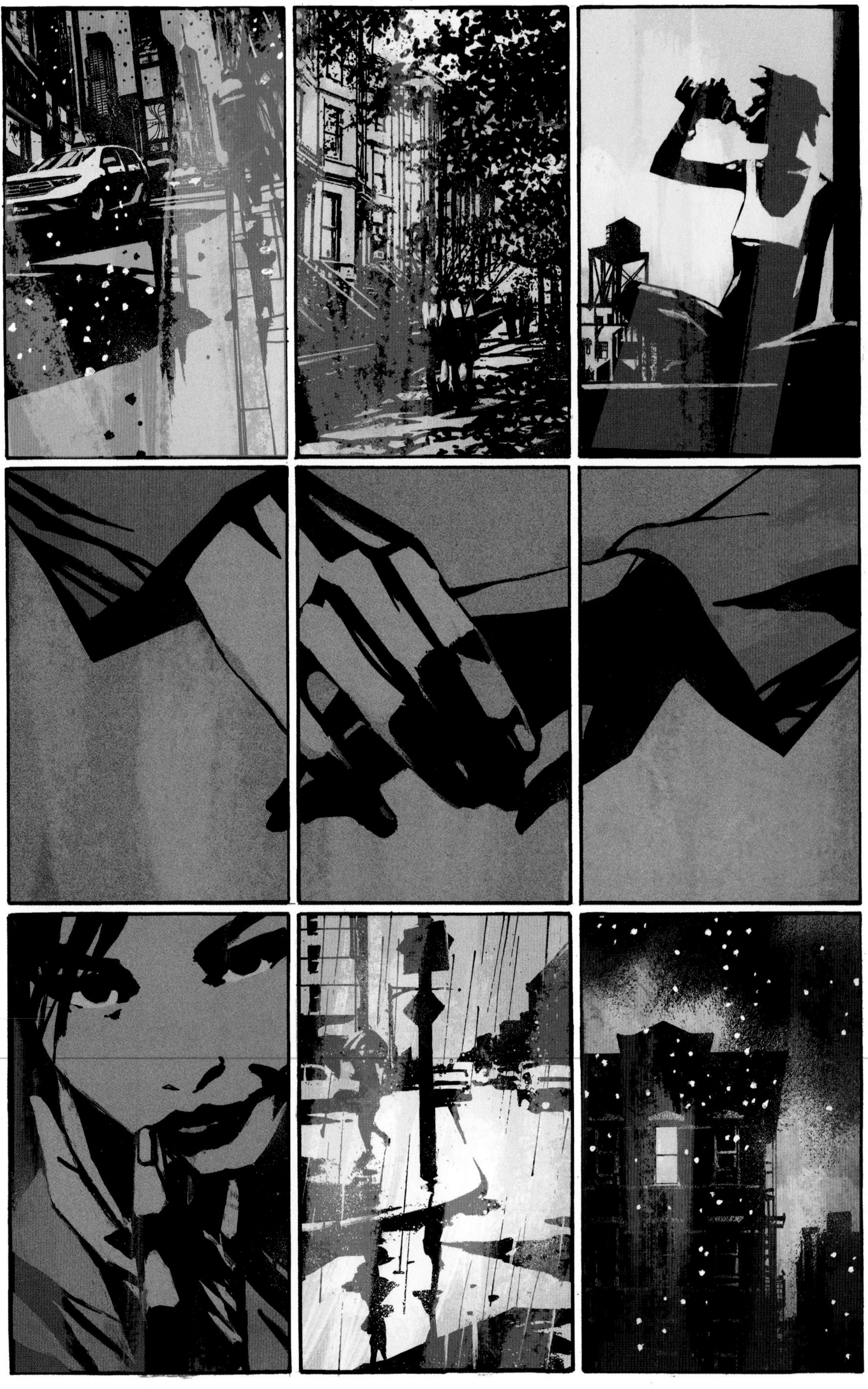

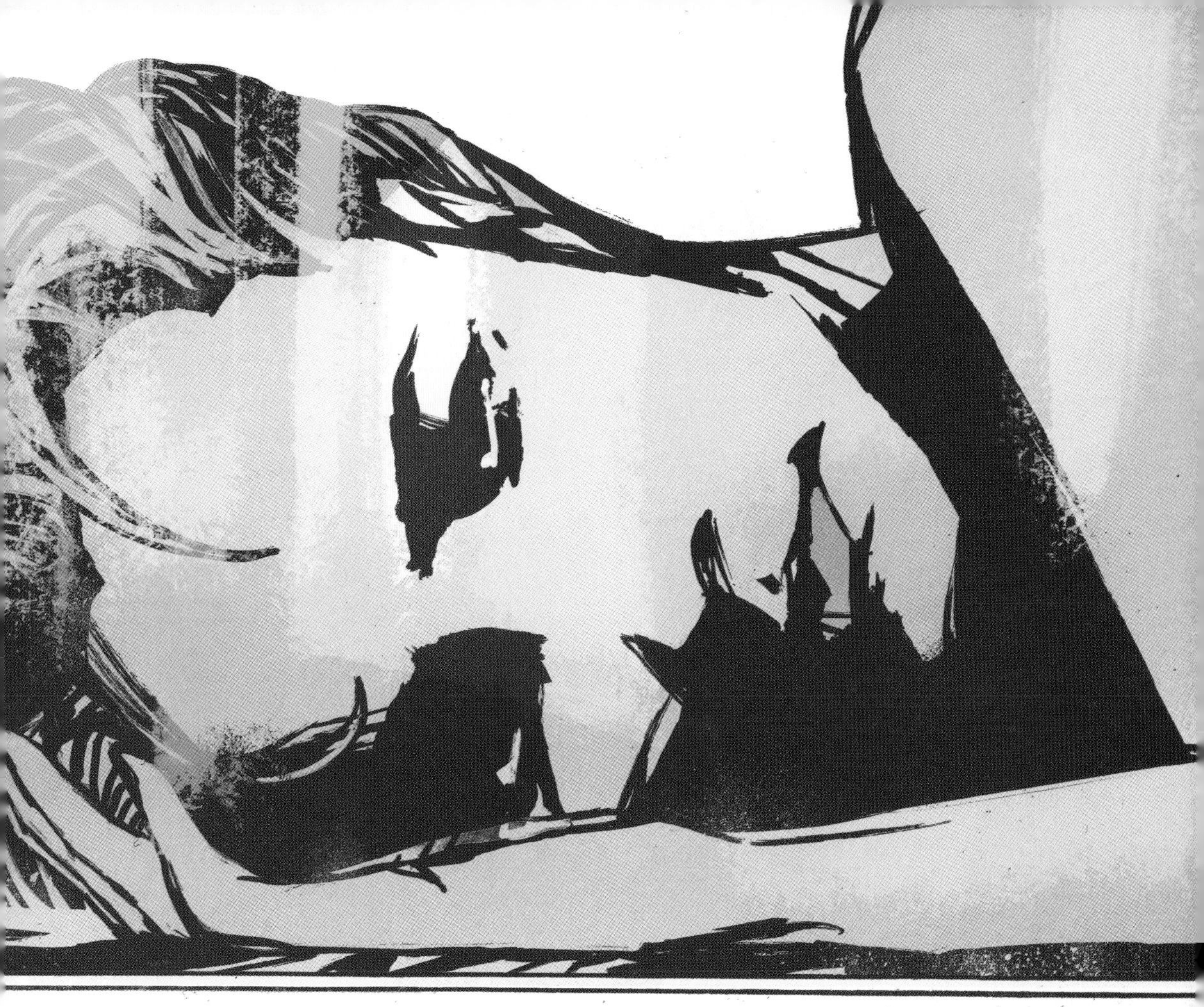

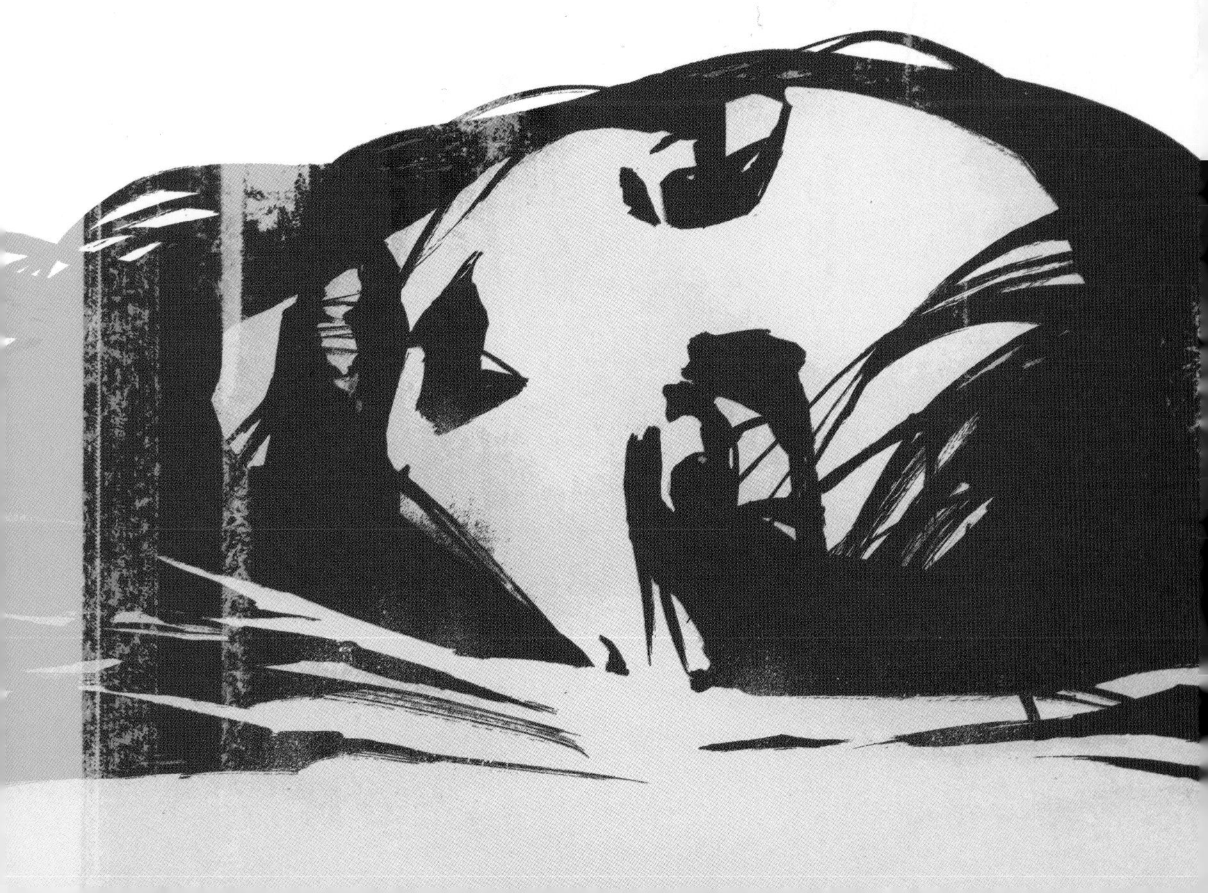

CHAPTER TWELVE:
ANTHEM FOR NO STATE

"The past is not for living in"

—John Berger,
Ways of Seeing

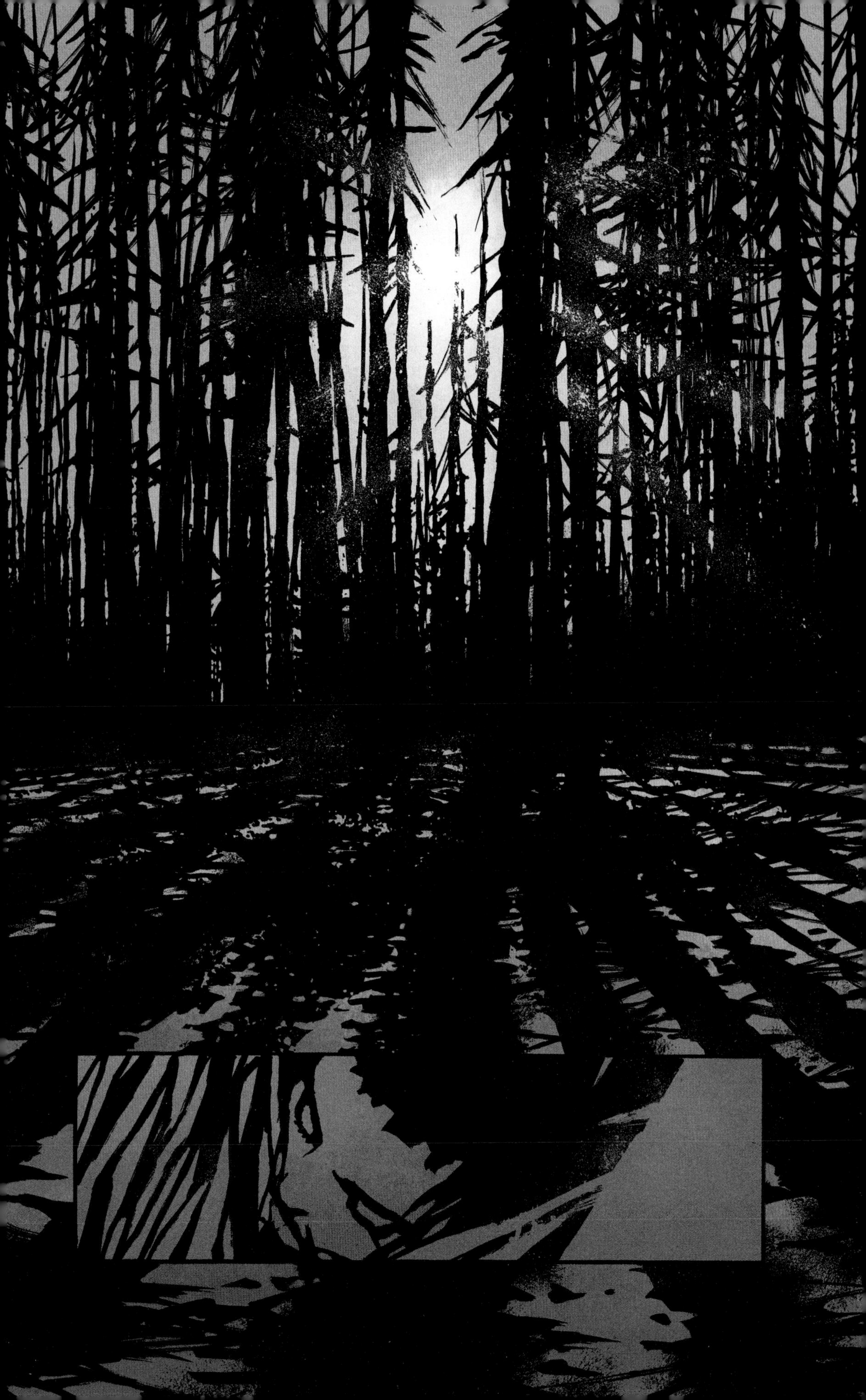

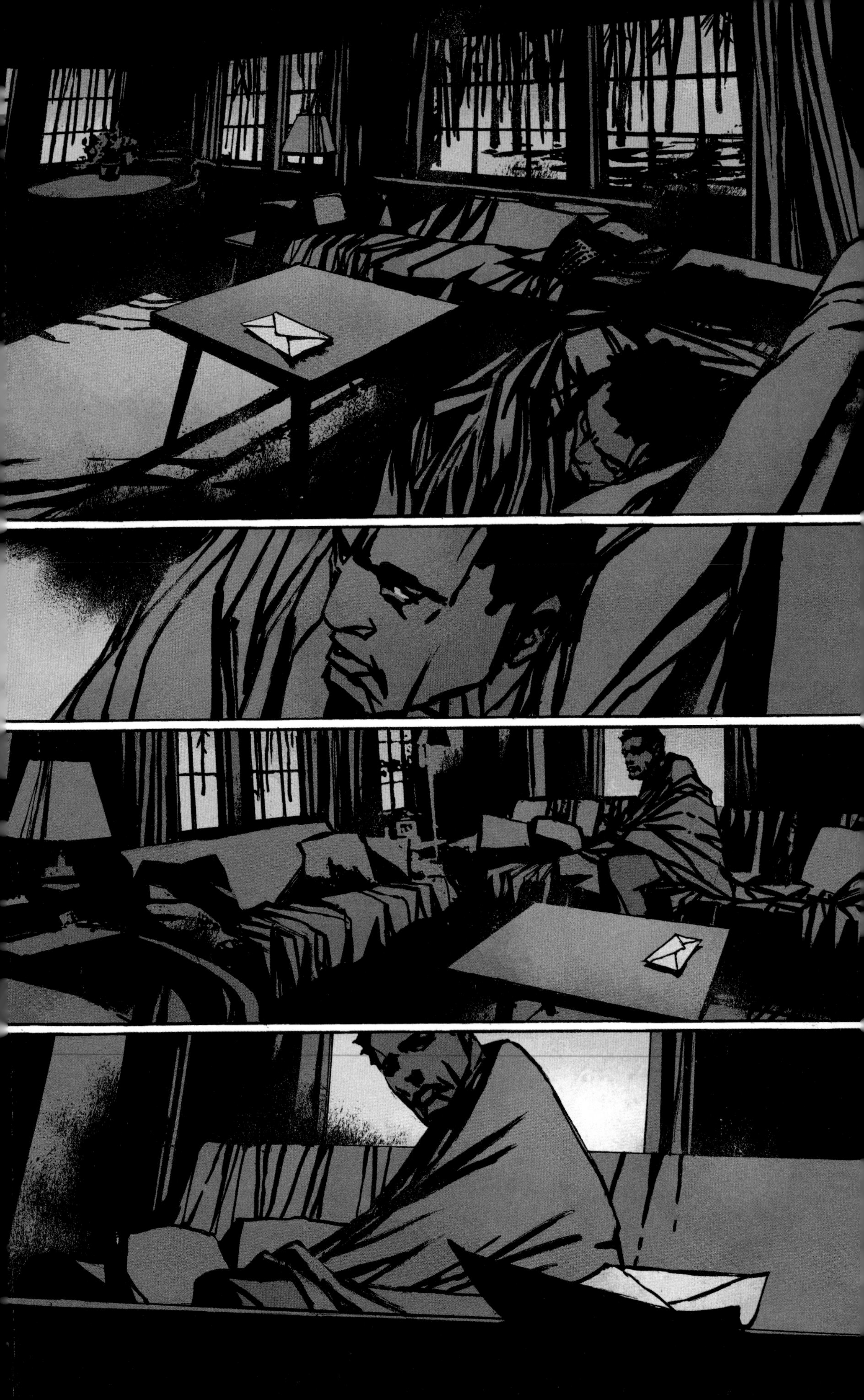

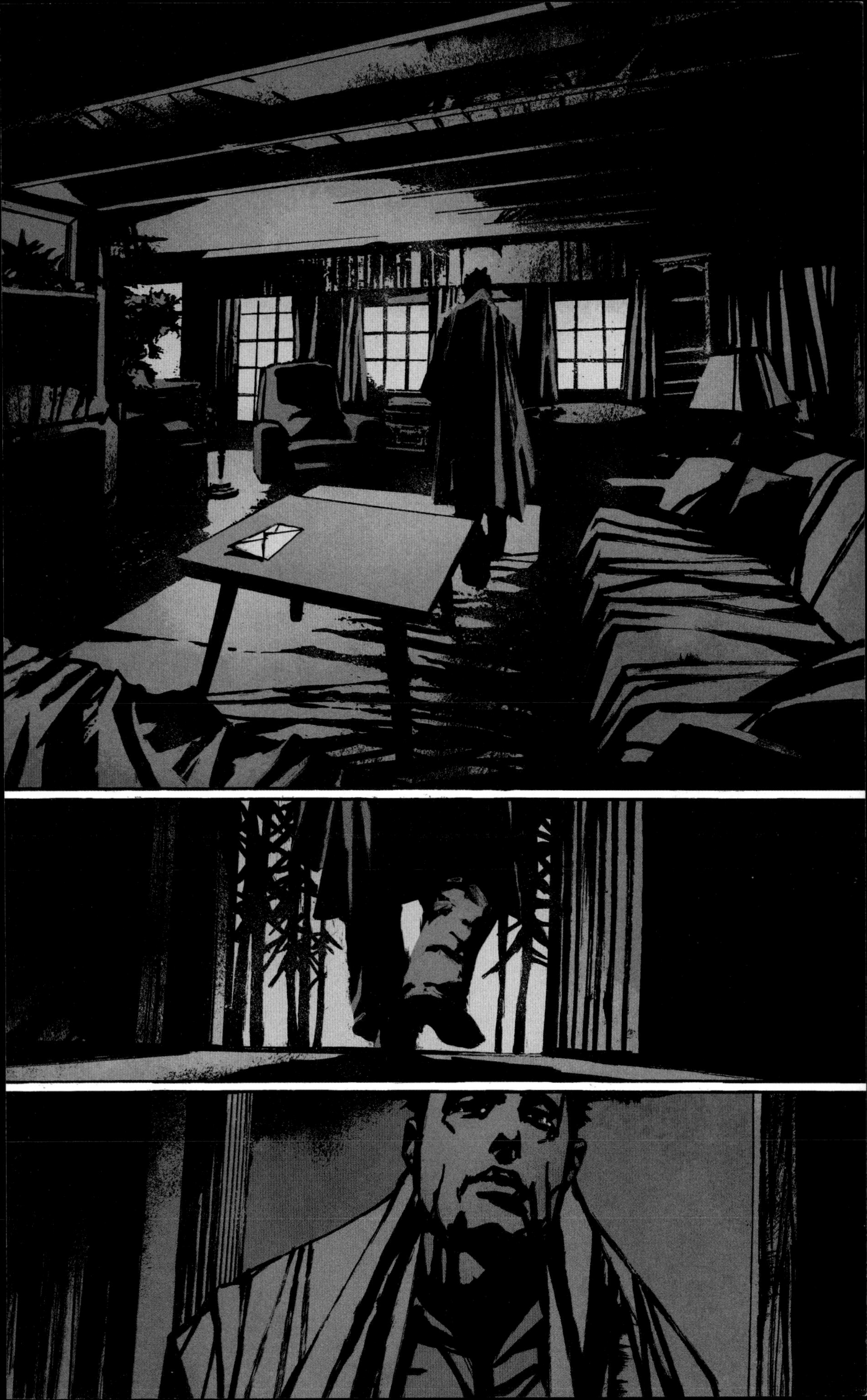

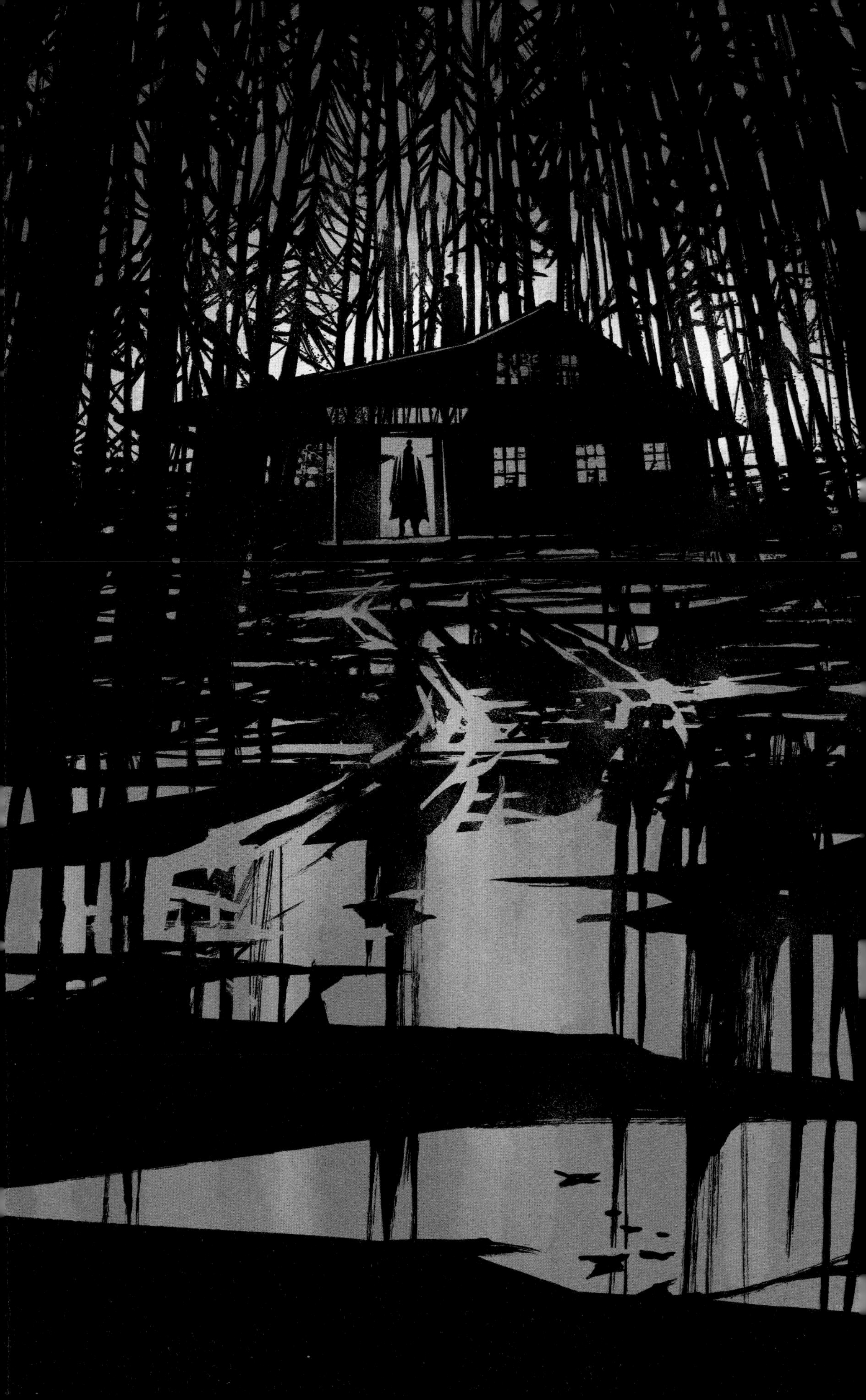

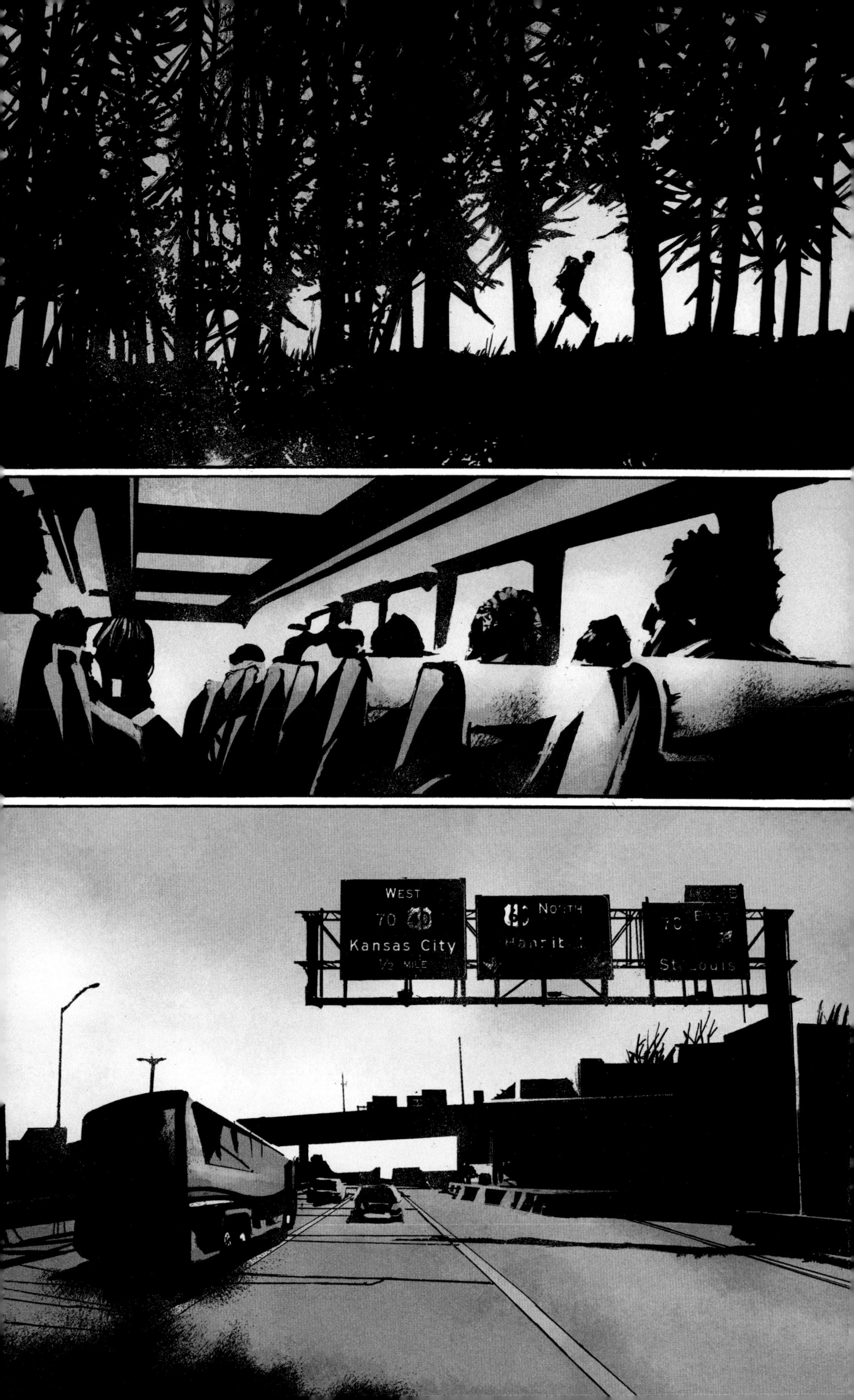
WEST
70
Kansas City
½ MILE
NORTH
70

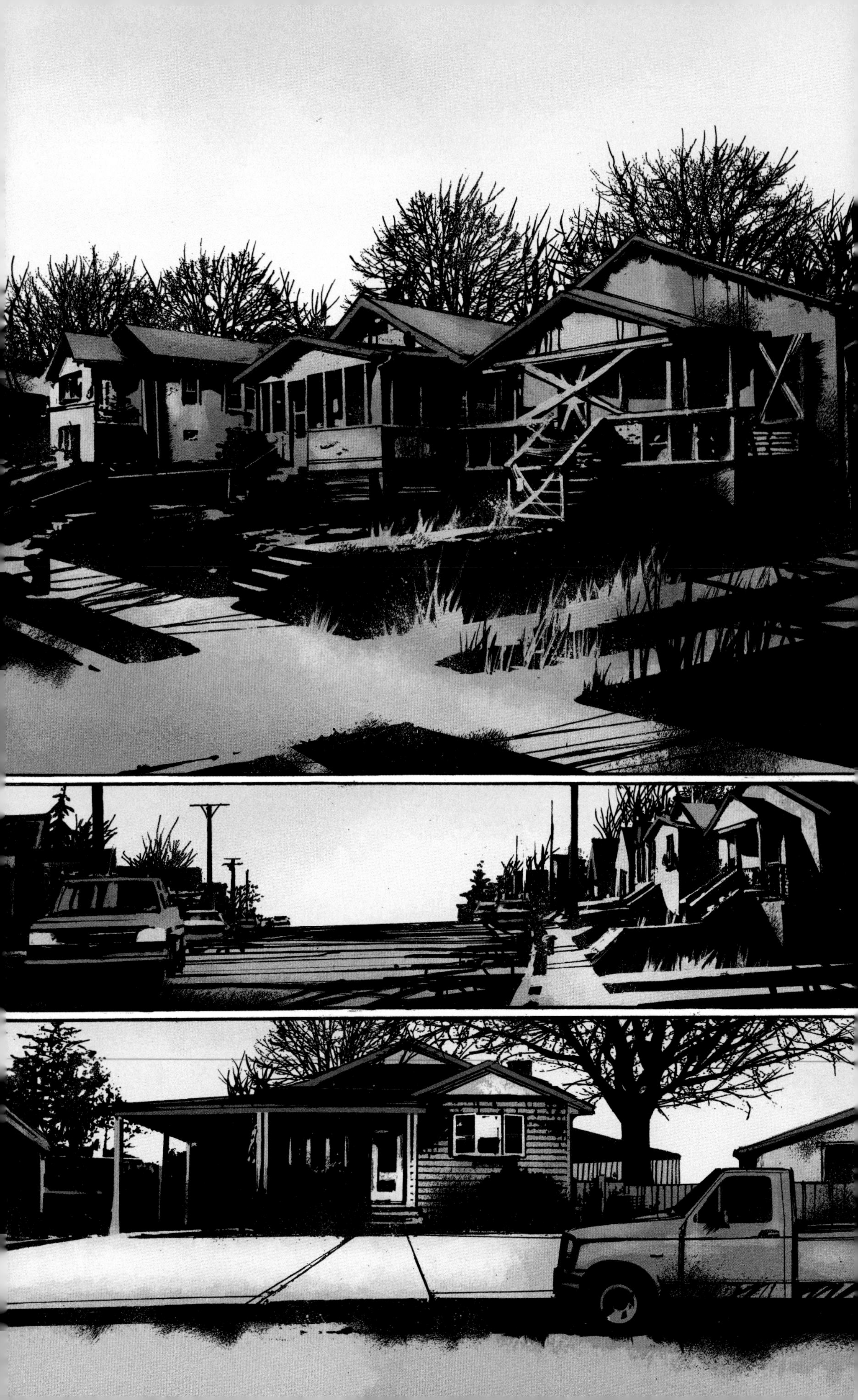

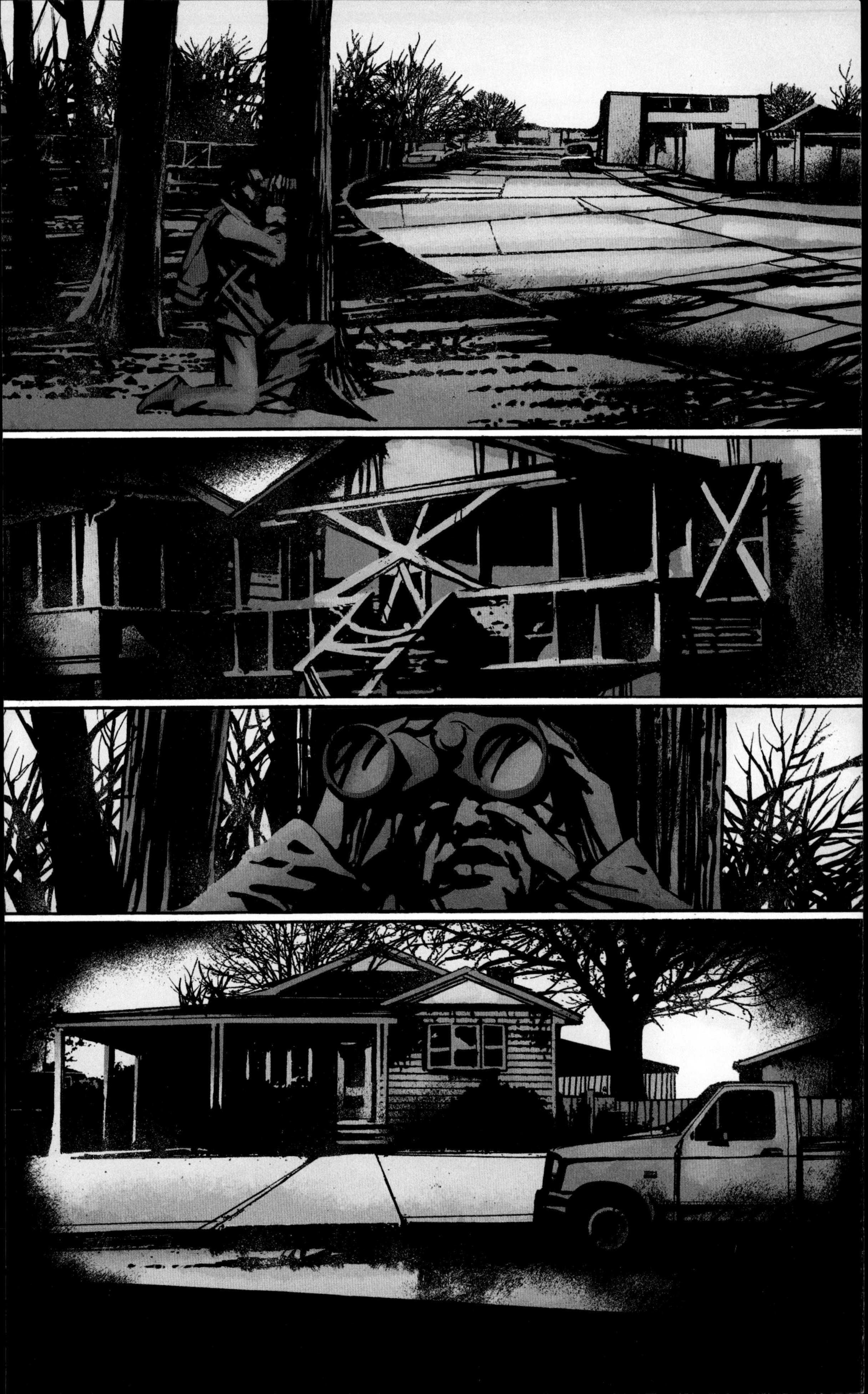

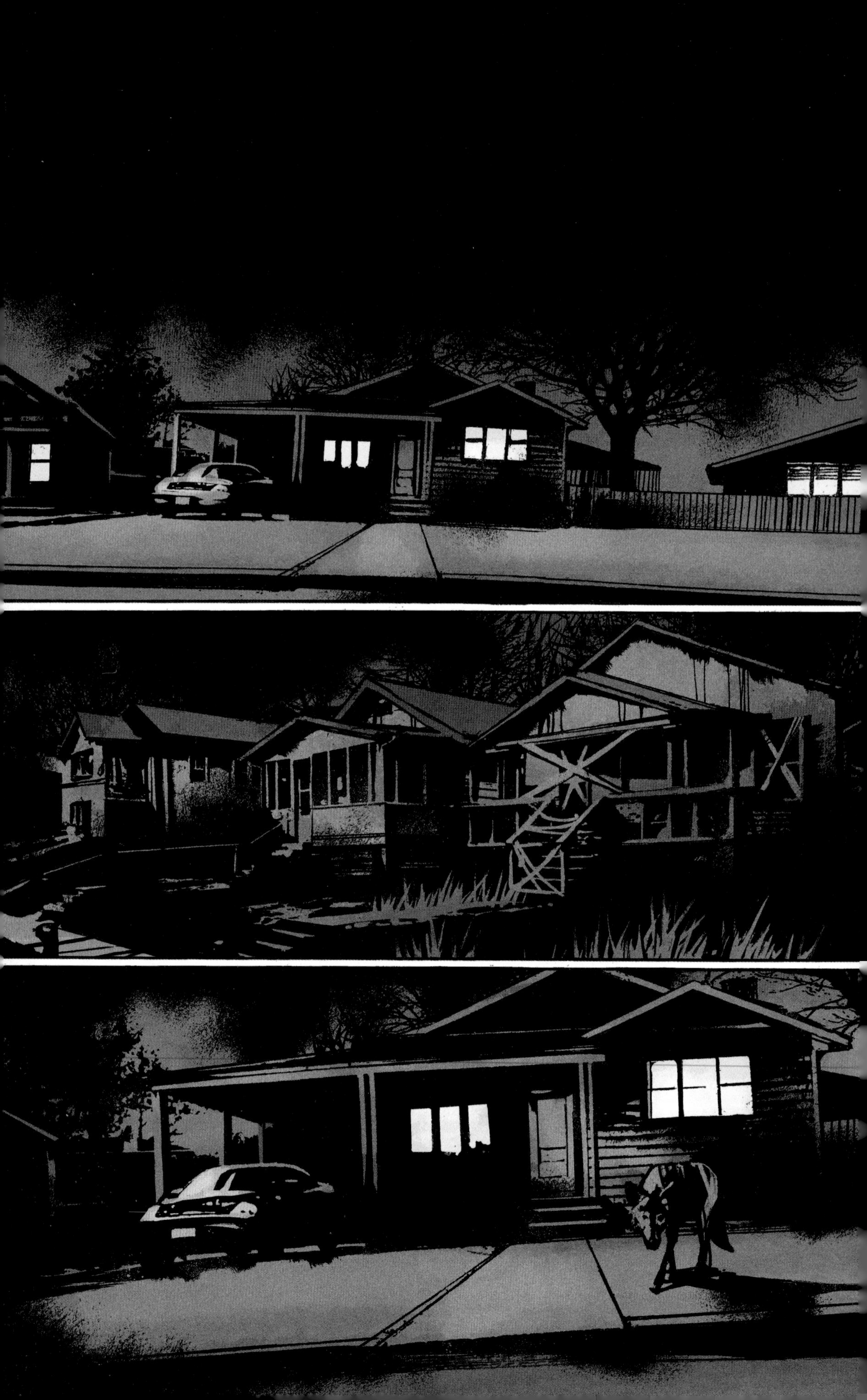

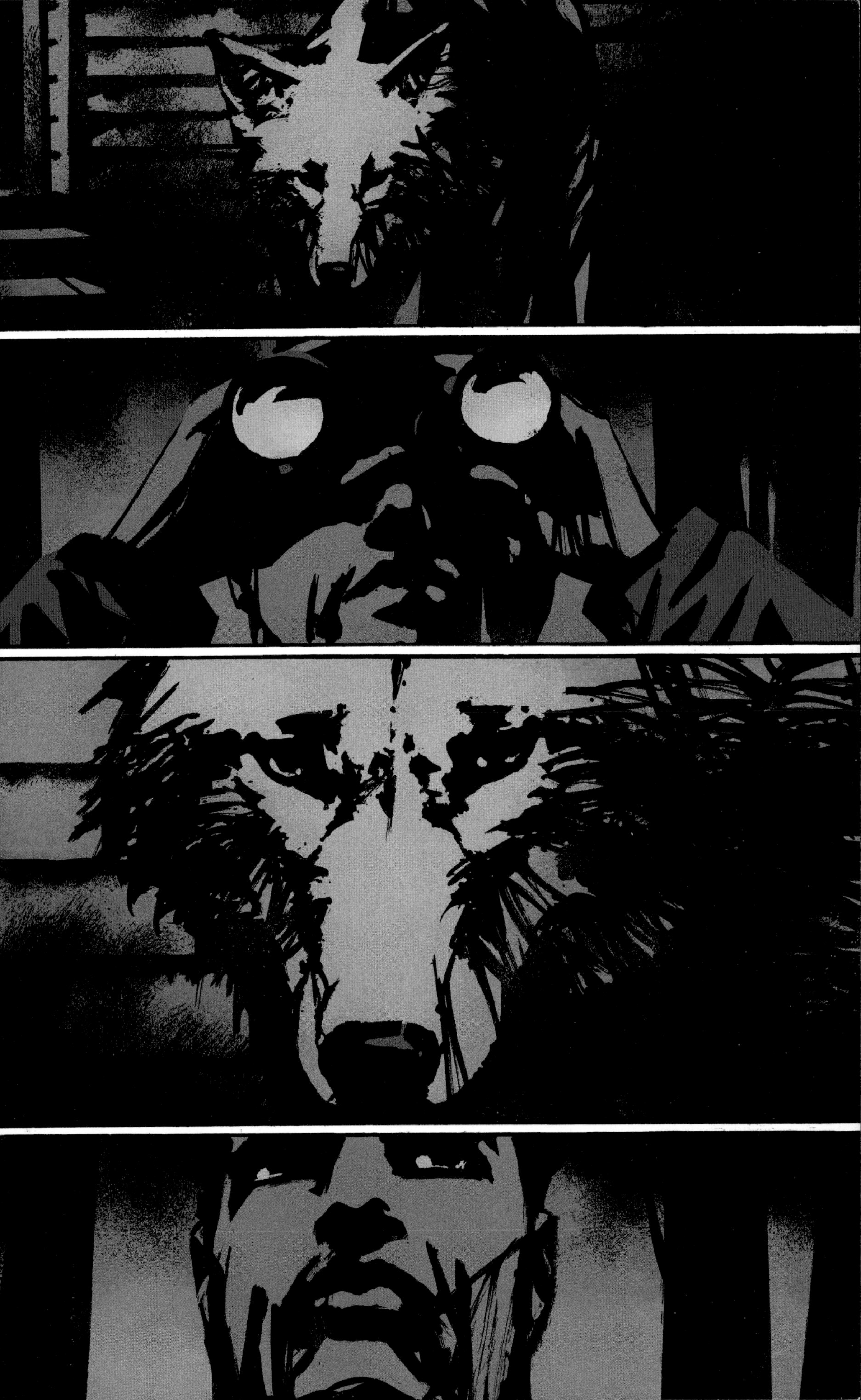

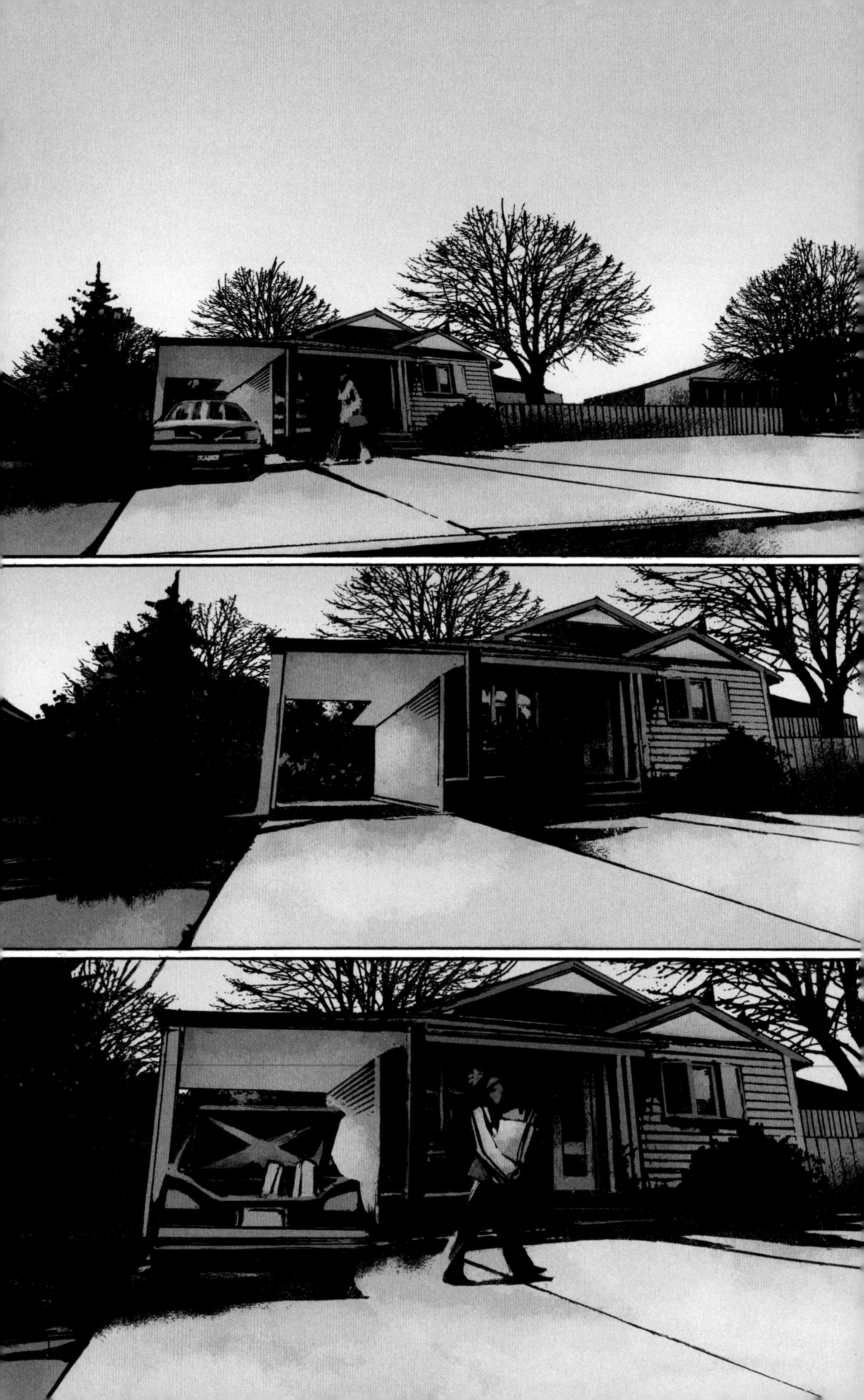

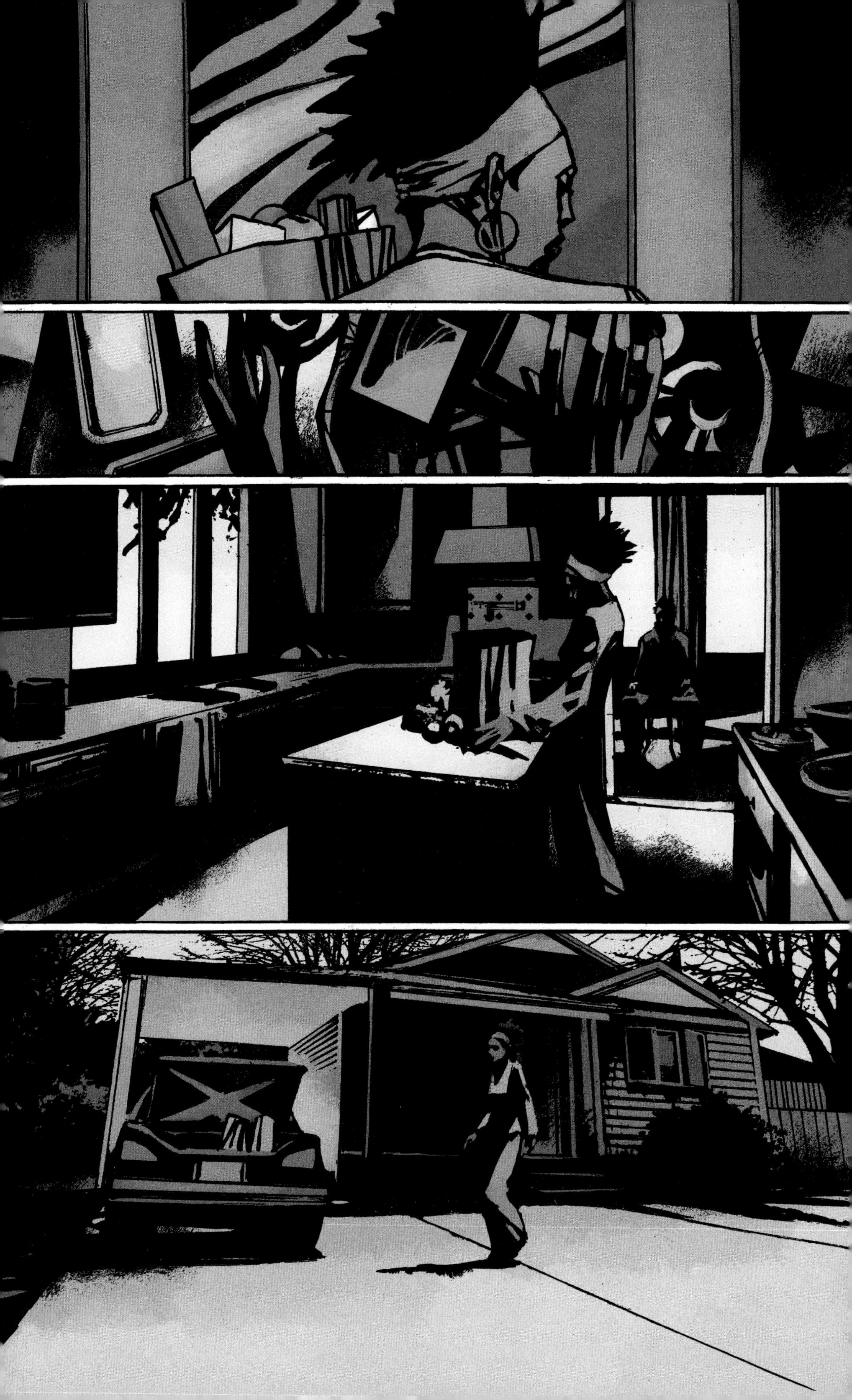

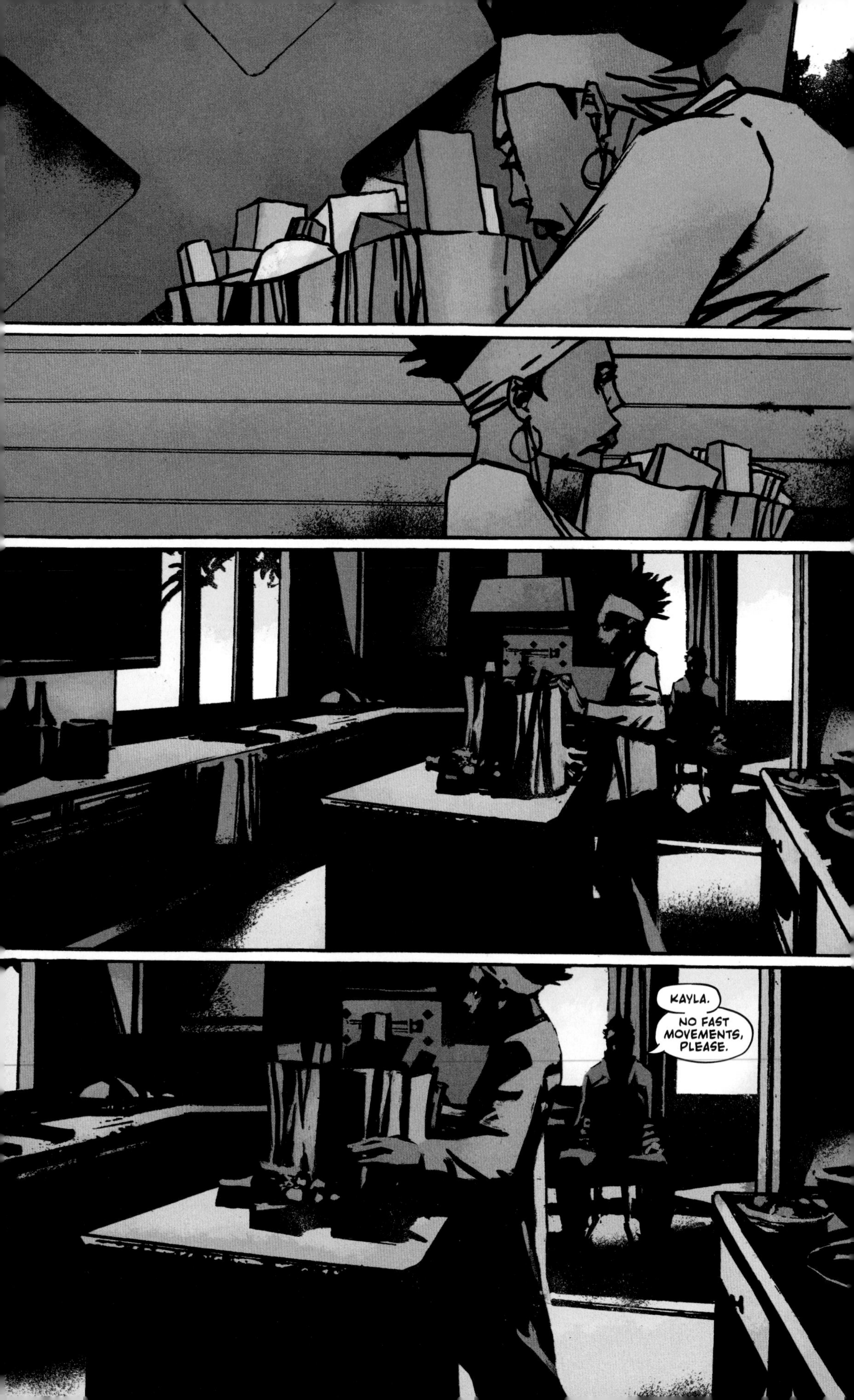
KAYLA.
NO FAST MOVEMENTS, PLEASE.

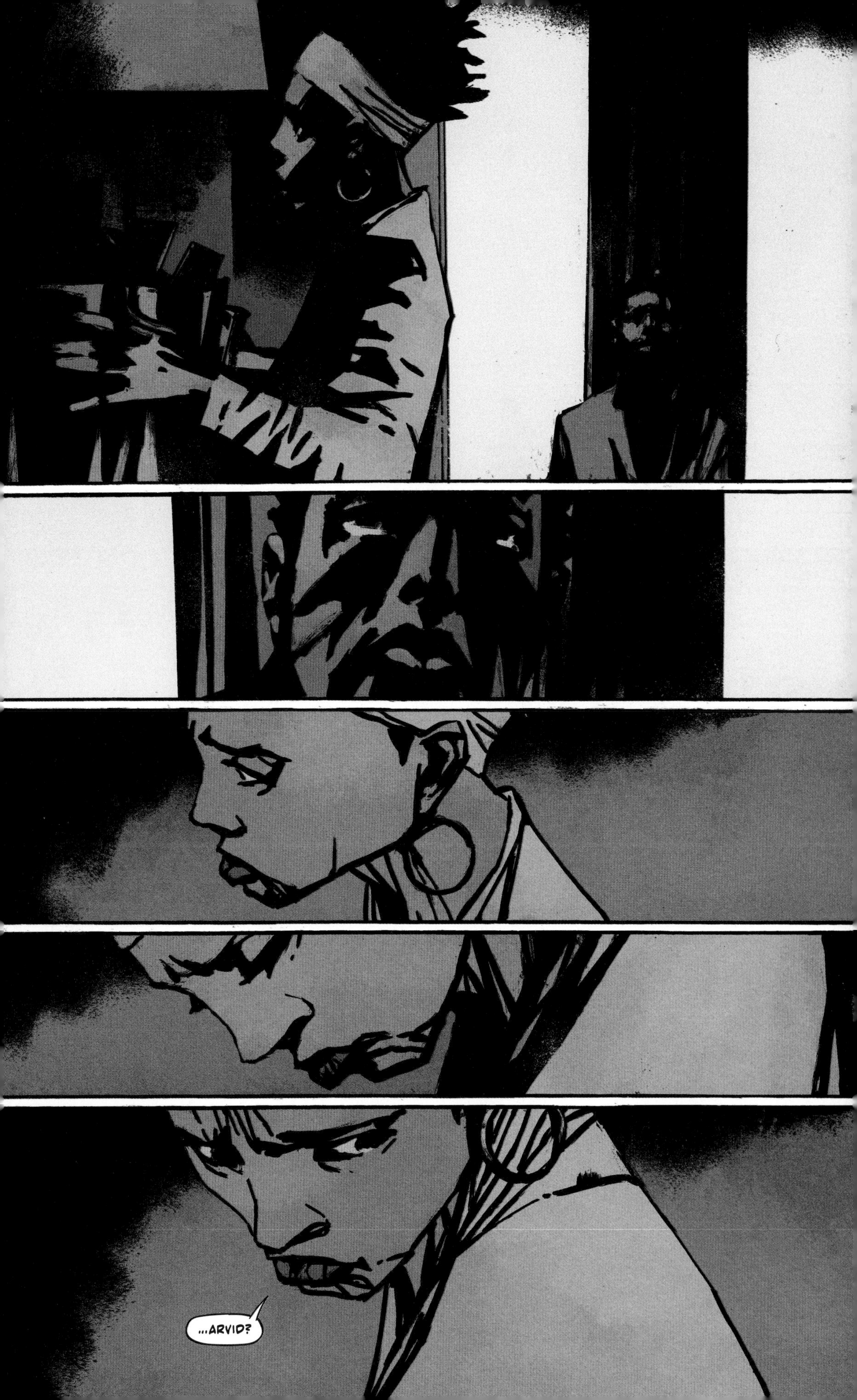
...ARVID?

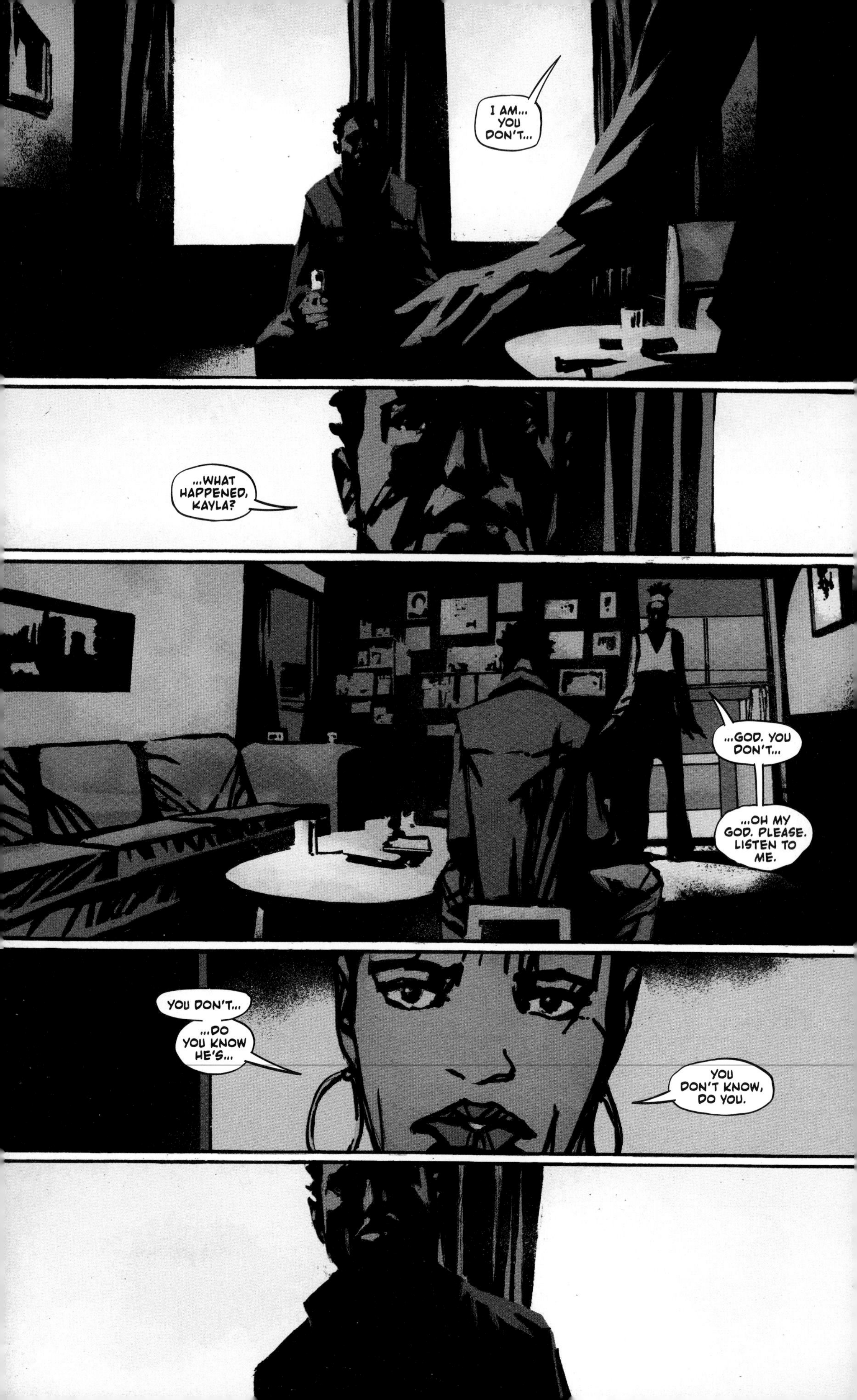
I AM... YOU DON'T...
...WHAT HAPPENED, KAYLA?
...GOD. YOU DON'T...
...OH MY GOD. PLEASE. LISTEN TO ME.
YOU DON'T...
...DO YOU KNOW HE'S...
YOU DON'T KNOW, DO YOU.

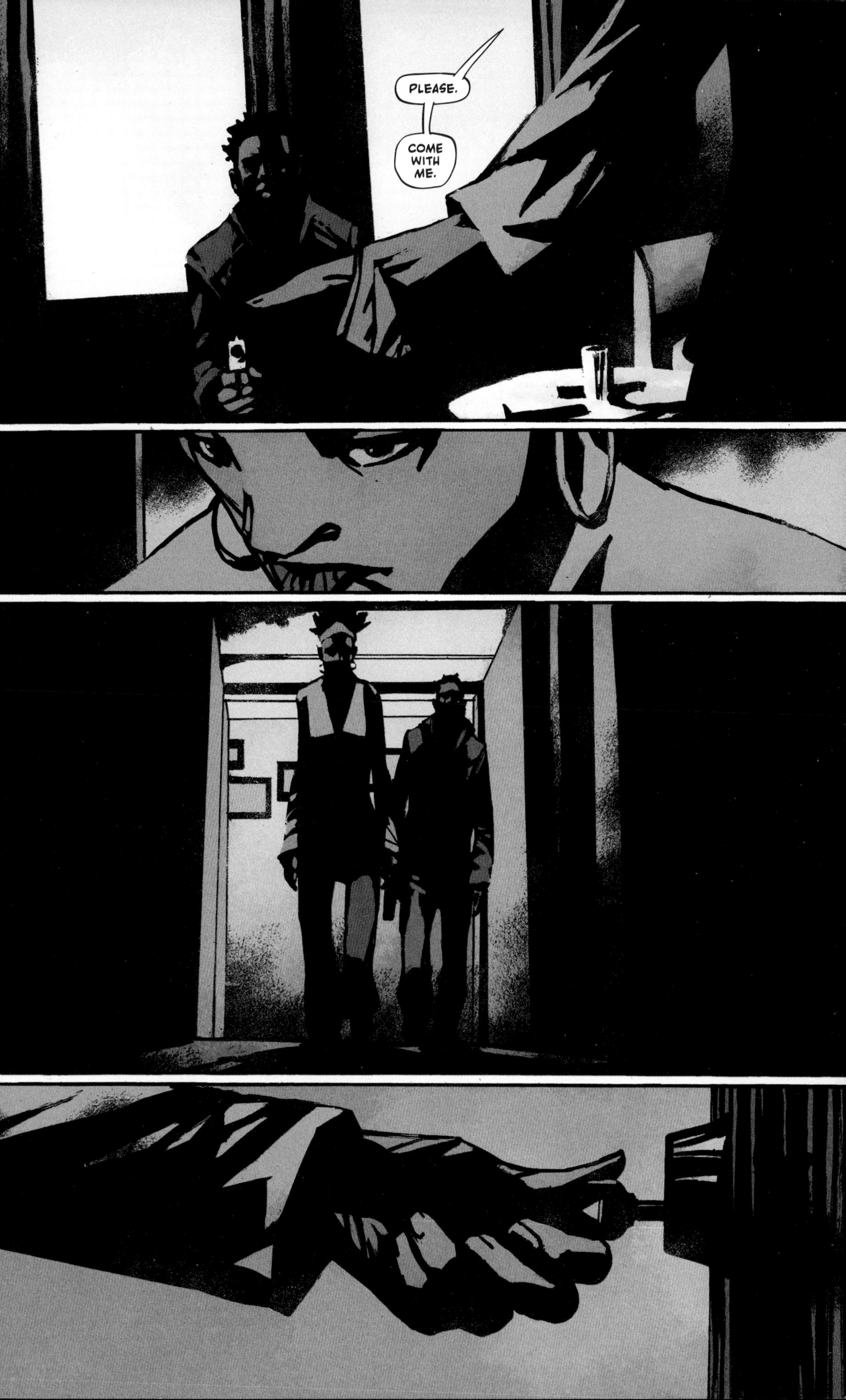
PLEASE.
COME WITH ME.

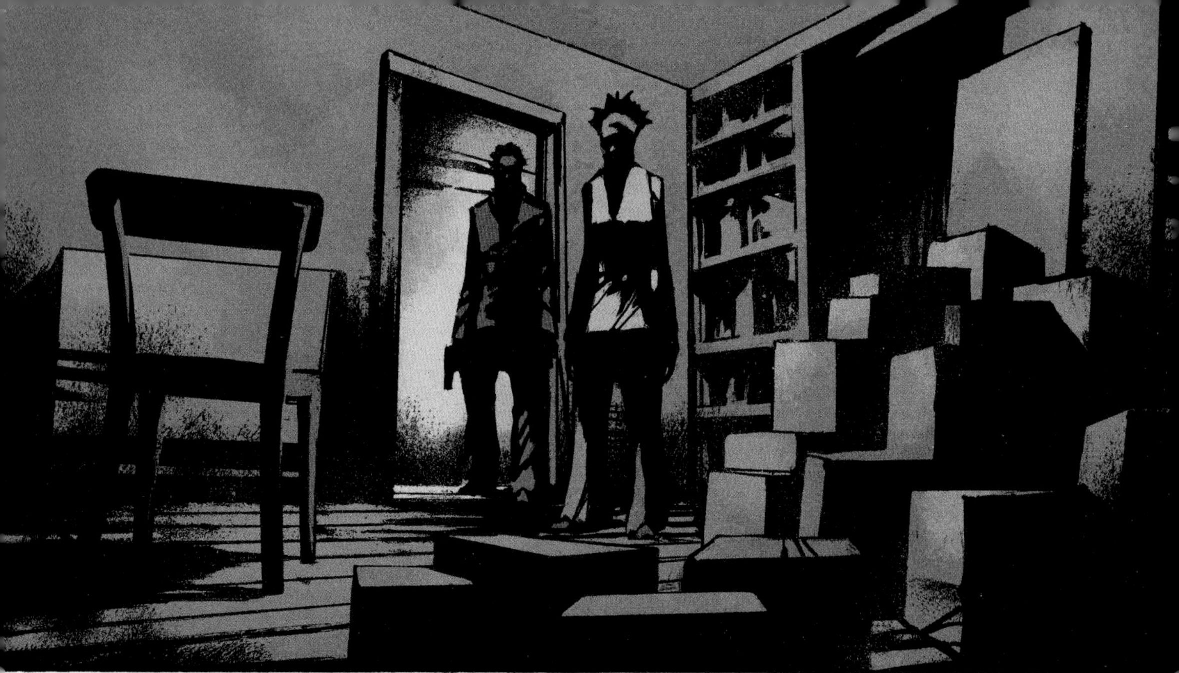

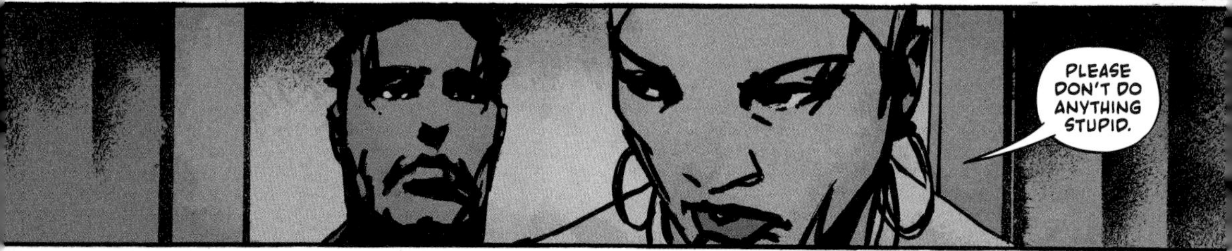
PLEASE DON'T DO ANYTHING STUPID.

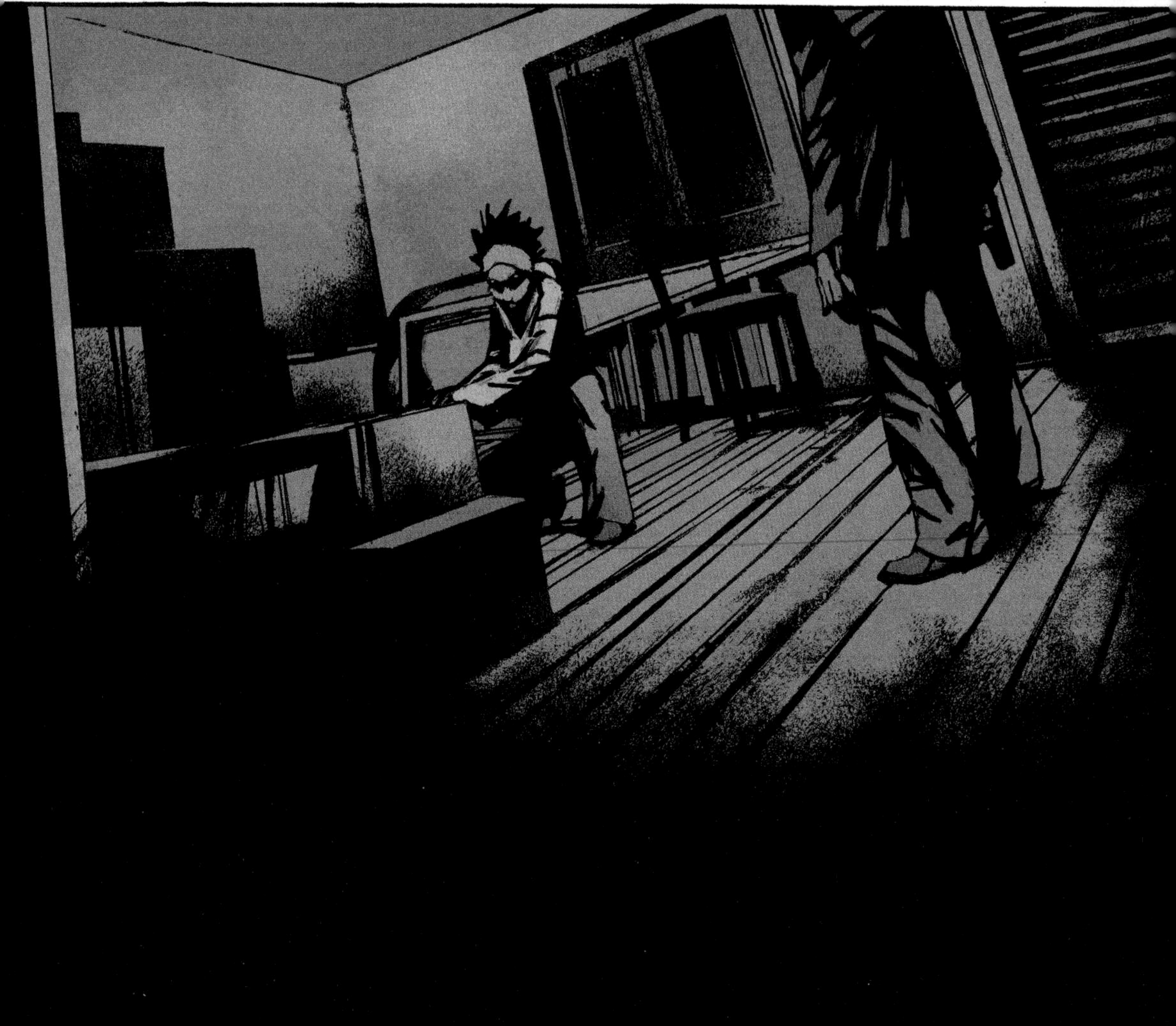

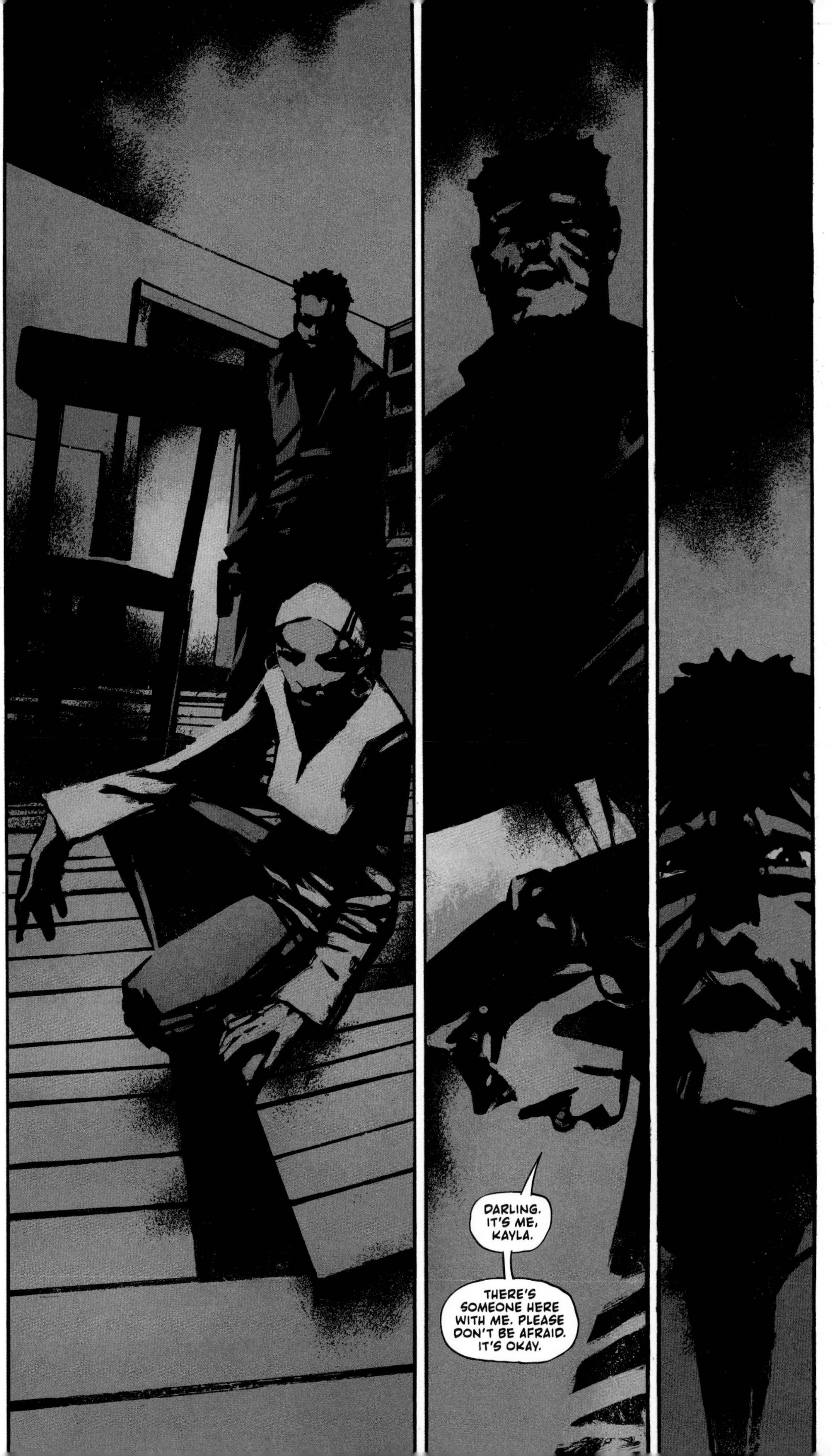
DARLING. IT'S ME, KAYLA.
THERE'S SOMEONE HERE WITH ME. PLEASE DON'T BE AFRAID. IT'S OKAY.

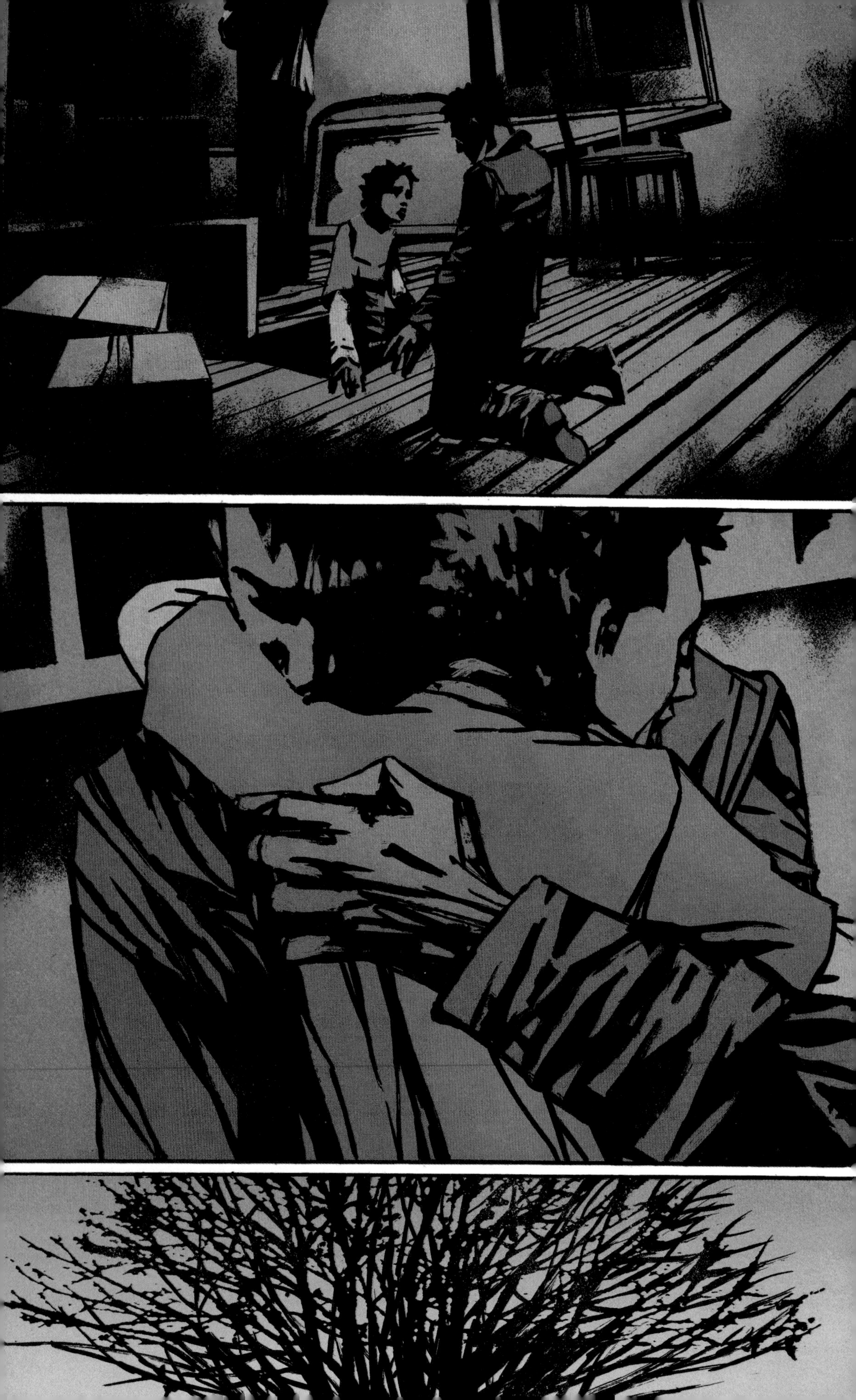

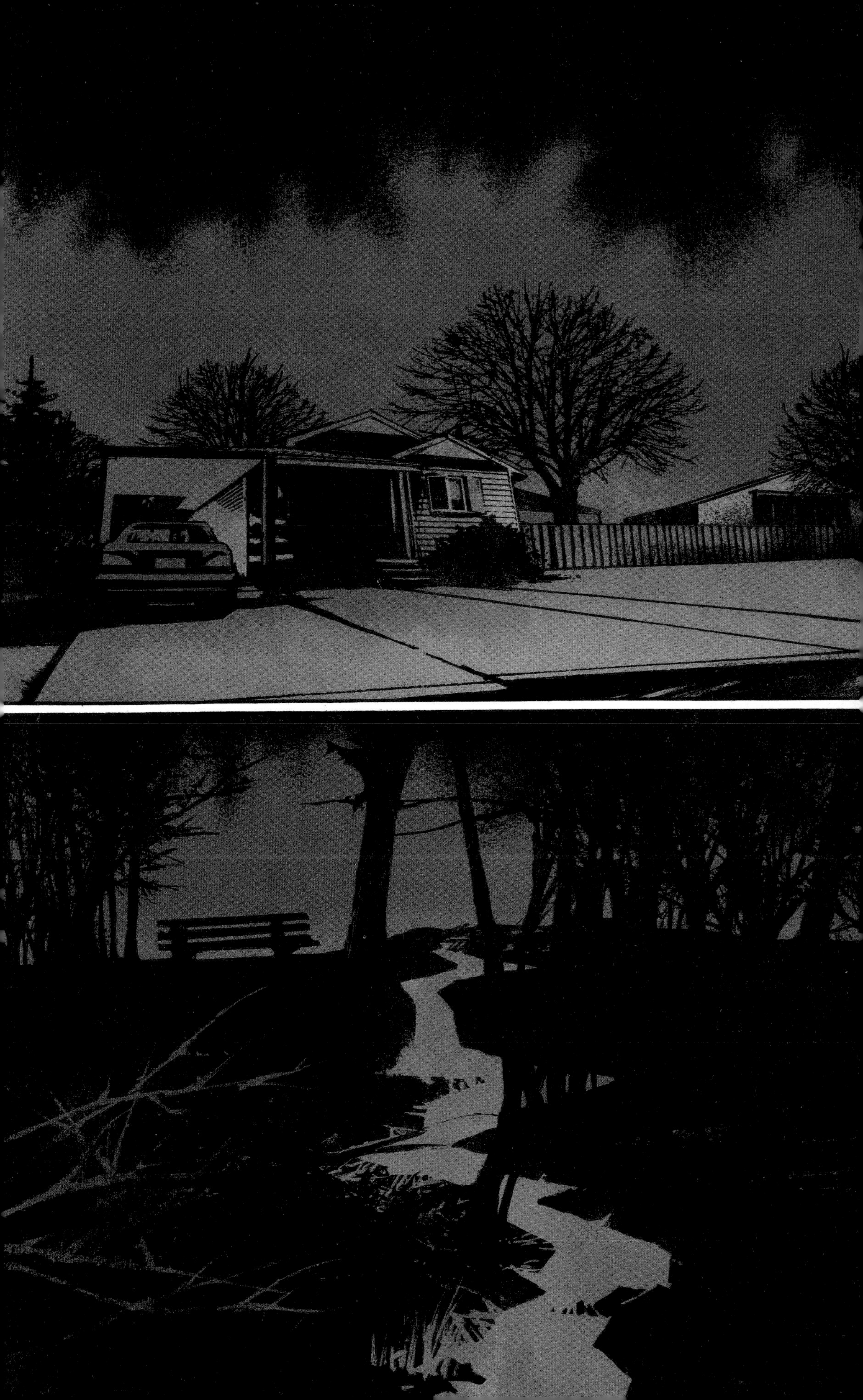

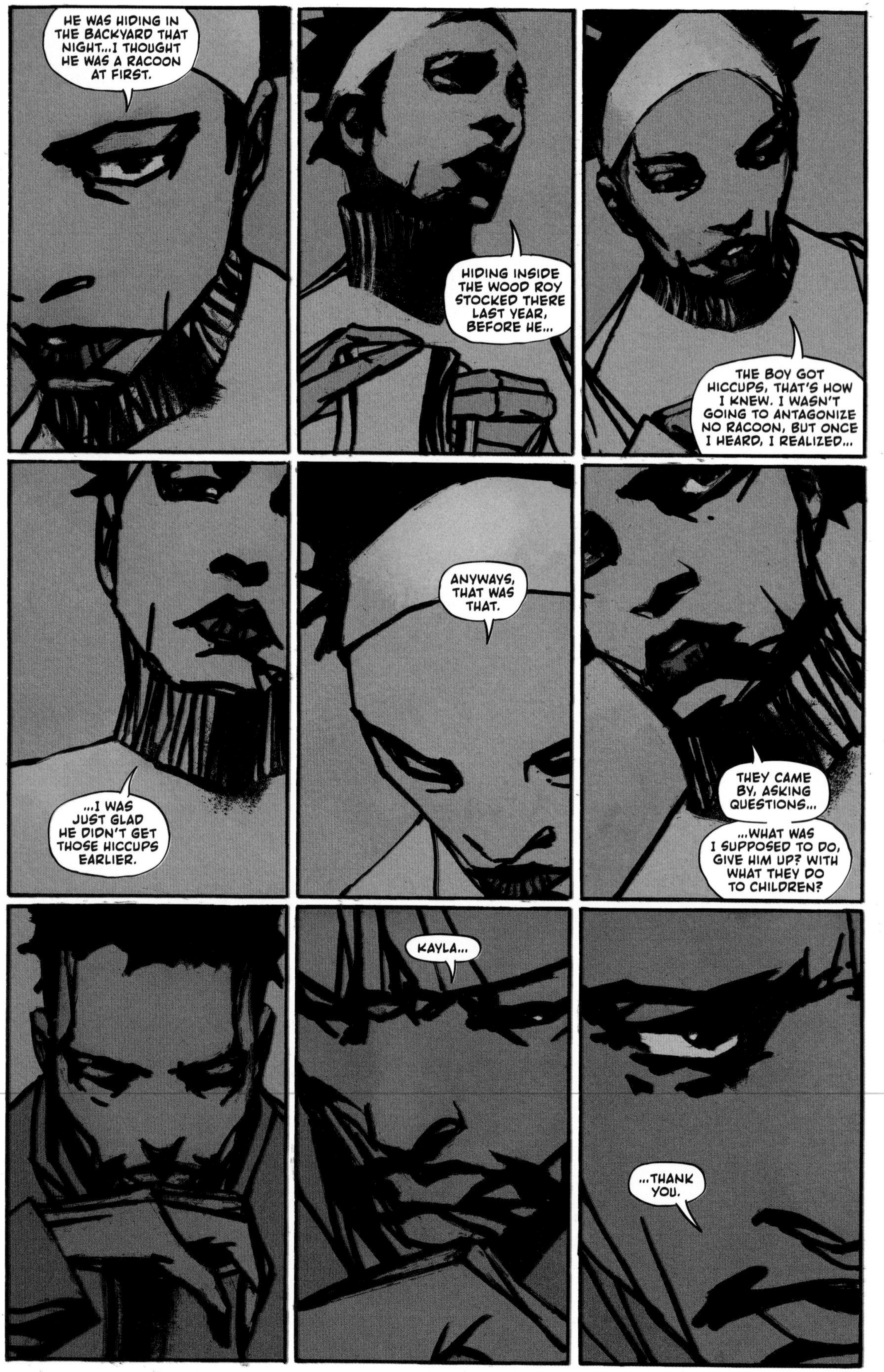
HE WAS HIDING IN THE BACKYARD THAT NIGHT...I THOUGHT HE WAS A RACOON AT FIRST.
HIDING INSIDE THE WOOD ROY STOCKED THERE LAST YEAR, BEFORE HE...
THE BOY GOT HICCUPS, THAT'S HOW I KNEW. I WASN'T GOING TO ANTAGONIZE NO RACOON, BUT ONCE I HEARD, I REALIZED...
...I WAS JUST GLAD HE DIDN'T GET THOSE HICCUPS EARLIER.
ANYWAYS, THAT WAS THAT.
THEY CAME BY, ASKING QUESTIONS...
...WHAT WAS I SUPPOSED TO DO, GIVE HIM UP? WITH WHAT THEY DO TO CHILDREN?
KAYLA...
...THANK YOU.

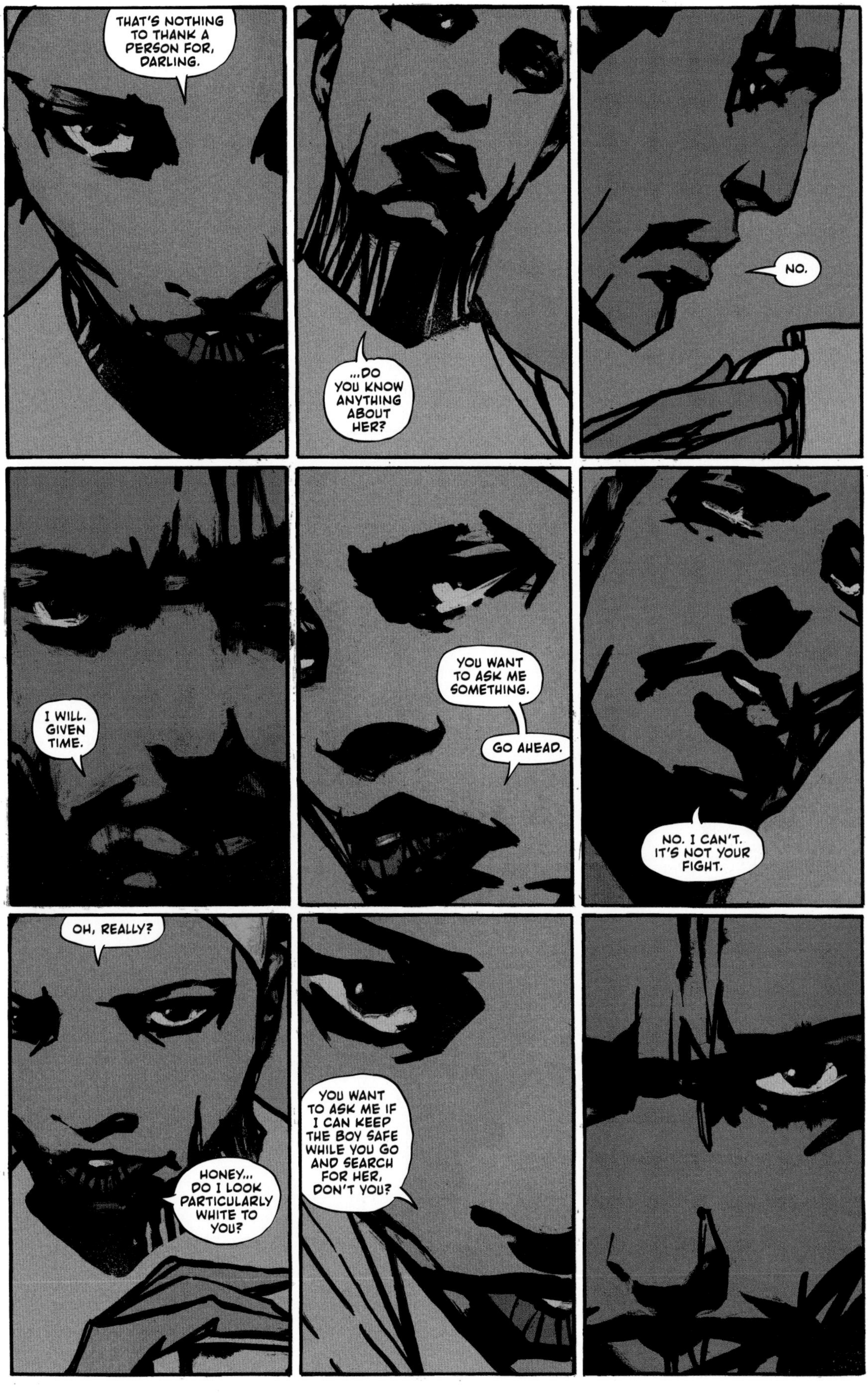
THAT'S NOTHING TO THANK A PERSON FOR, DARLING.
...DO YOU KNOW ANYTHING ABOUT HER?
NO.
I WILL. GIVEN TIME.
YOU WANT TO ASK ME SOMETHING.
GO AHEAD.
NO. I CAN'T. IT'S NOT YOUR FIGHT.
OH, REALLY?
HONEY... DO I LOOK PARTICULARLY WHITE TO YOU?
YOU WANT TO ASK ME IF I CAN KEEP THE BOY SAFE WHILE YOU GO AND SEARCH FOR HER, DON'T YOU?

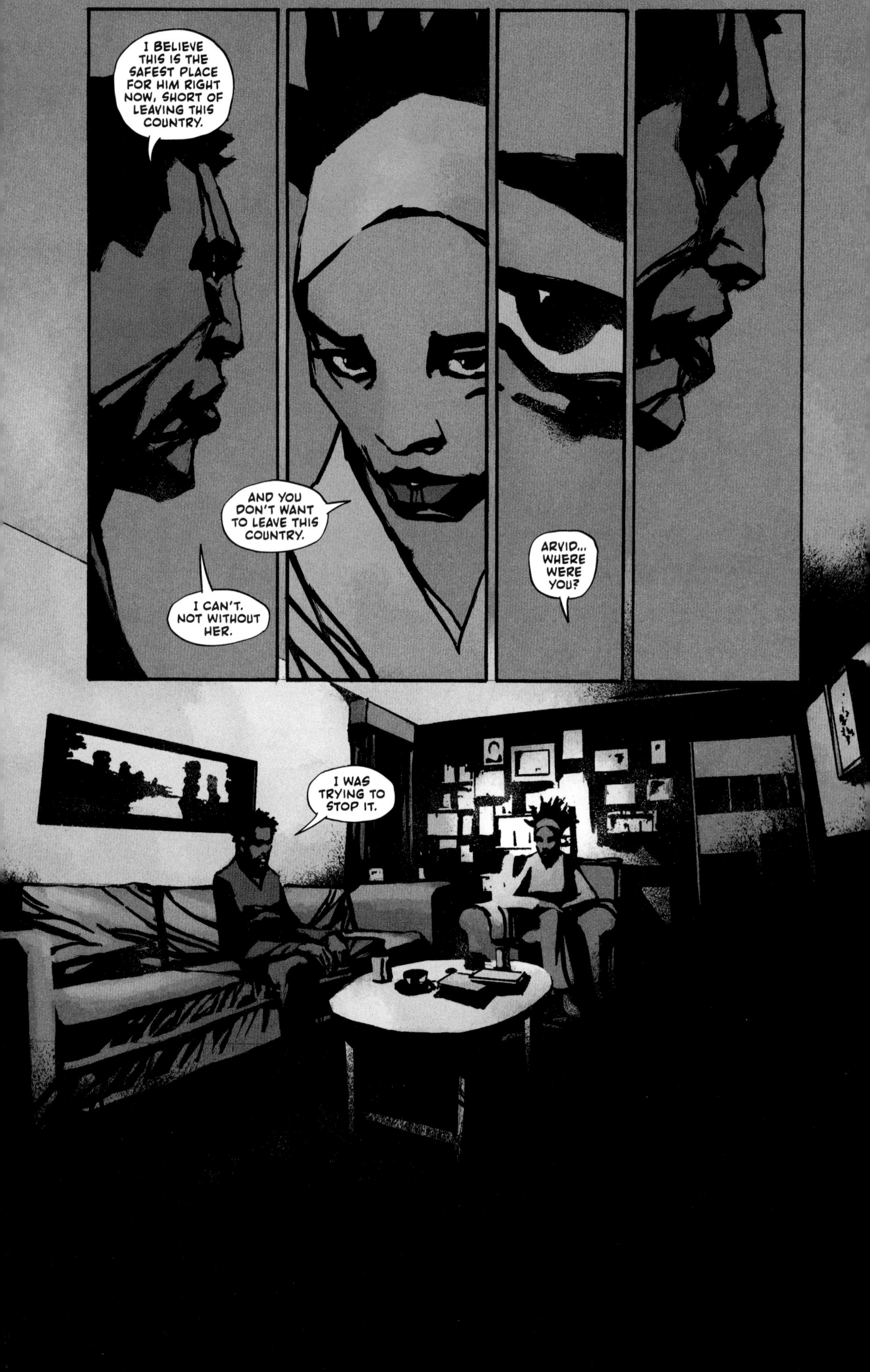
I BELIEVE THIS IS THE SAFEST PLACE FOR HIM RIGHT NOW, SHORT OF LEAVING THIS COUNTRY.
AND YOU DON'T WANT TO LEAVE THIS COUNTRY.
I CAN'T. NOT WITHOUT HER.
ARVID... WHERE WERE YOU?
I WAS TRYING TO STOP IT.

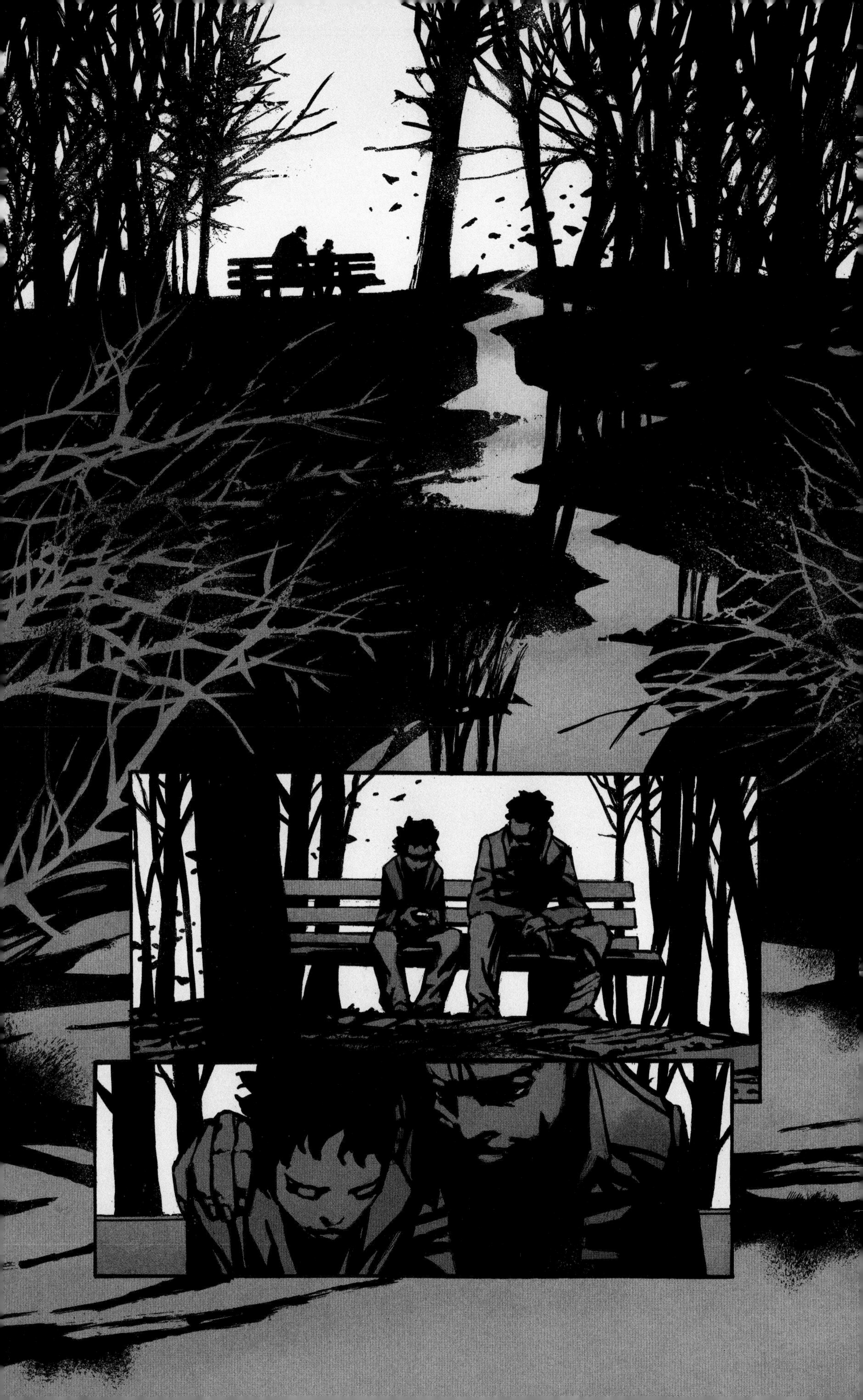

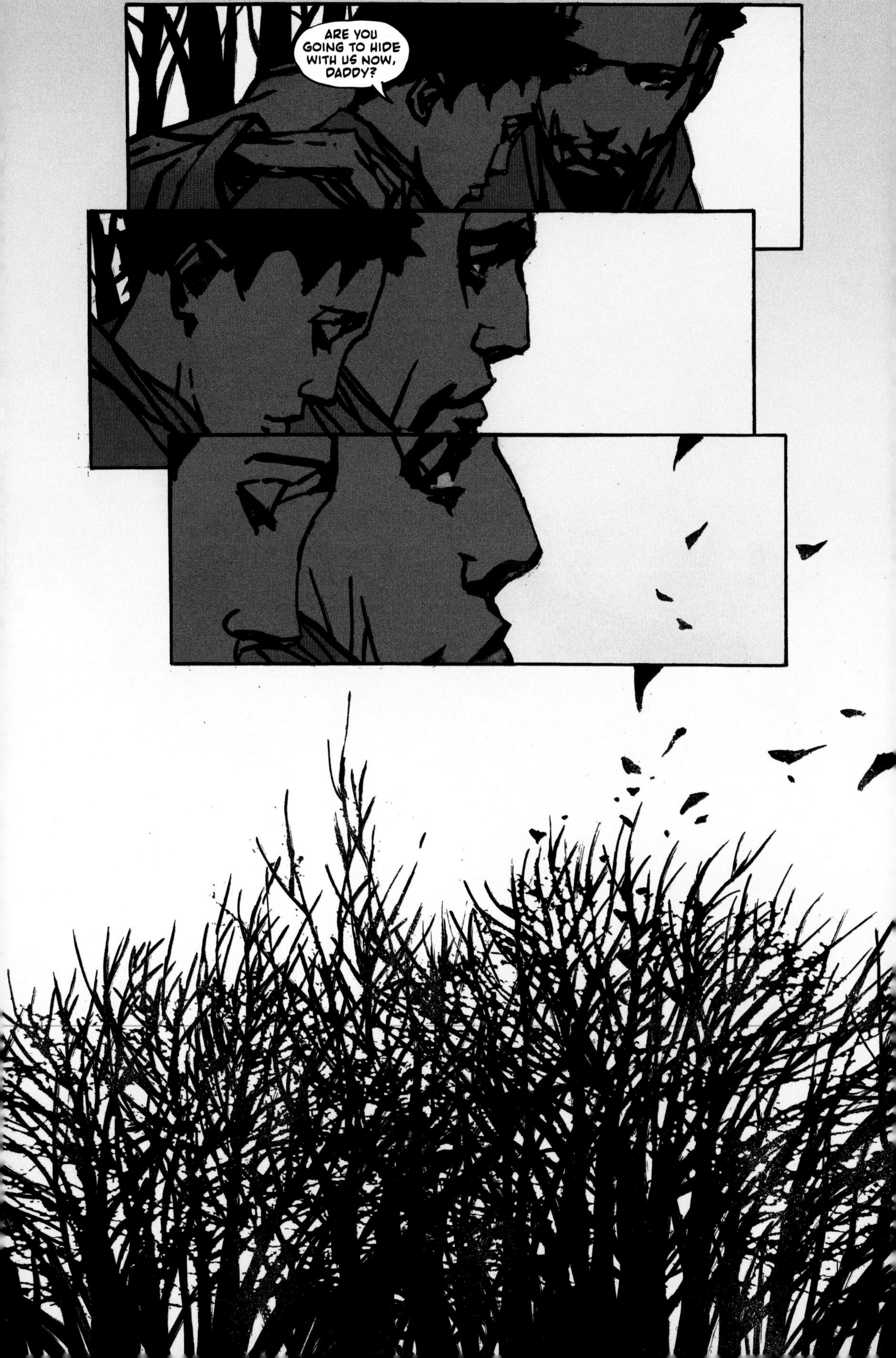
ARE YOU GOING TO HIDE WITH US NOW, DADDY?

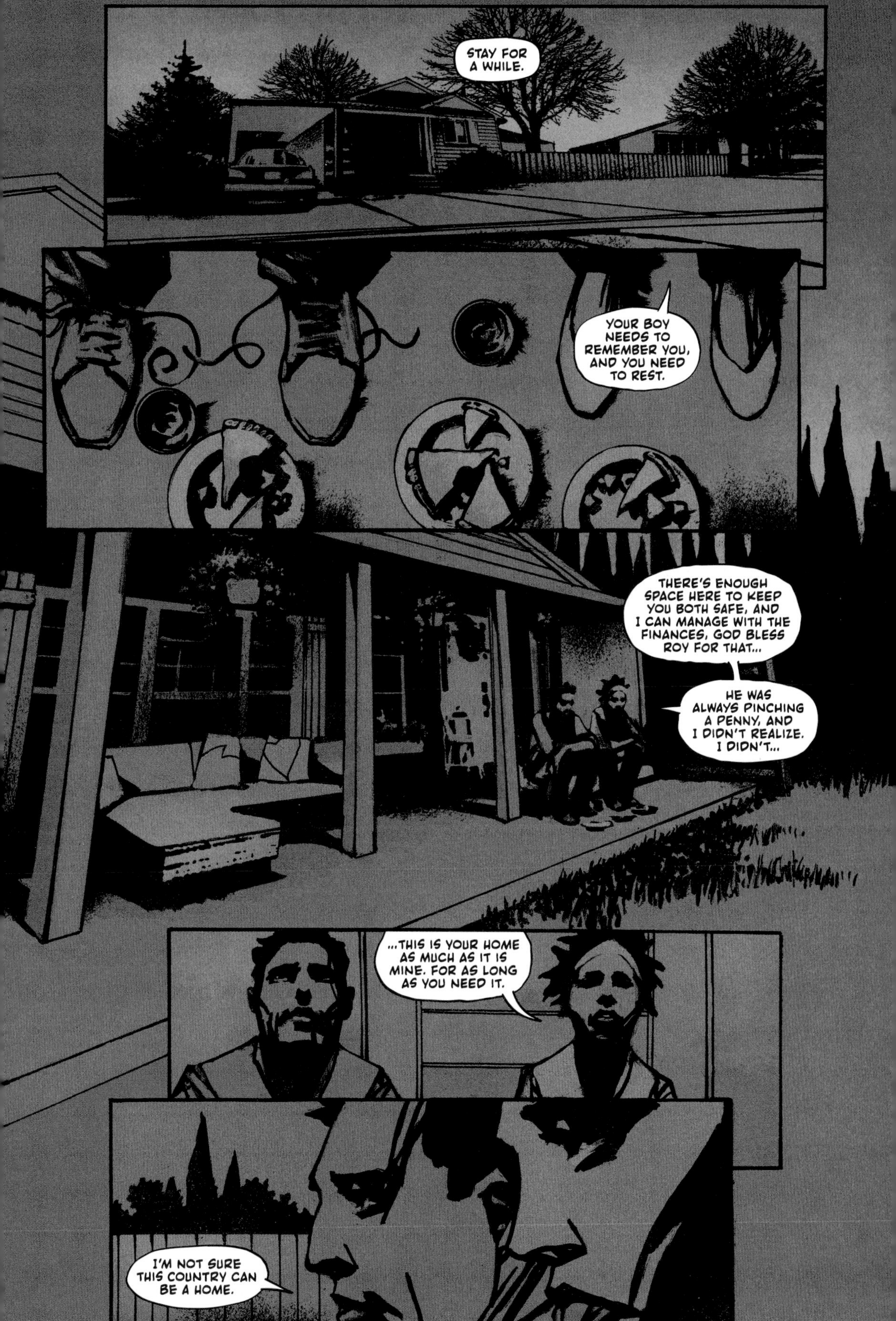
STAY FOR A WHILE.
YOUR BOY NEEDS TO REMEMBER YOU, AND YOU NEED TO REST.
THERE'S ENOUGH SPACE HERE TO KEEP YOU BOTH SAFE, AND I CAN MANAGE WITH THE FINANCES, GOD BLESS ROY FOR THAT...
HE WAS ALWAYS PINCHING A PENNY, AND I DIDN'T REALIZE. I DIDN'T...
...THIS IS YOUR HOME AS MUCH AS IT IS MINE. FOR AS LONG AS YOU NEED IT.
I'M NOT SURE THIS COUNTRY CAN BE A HOME.

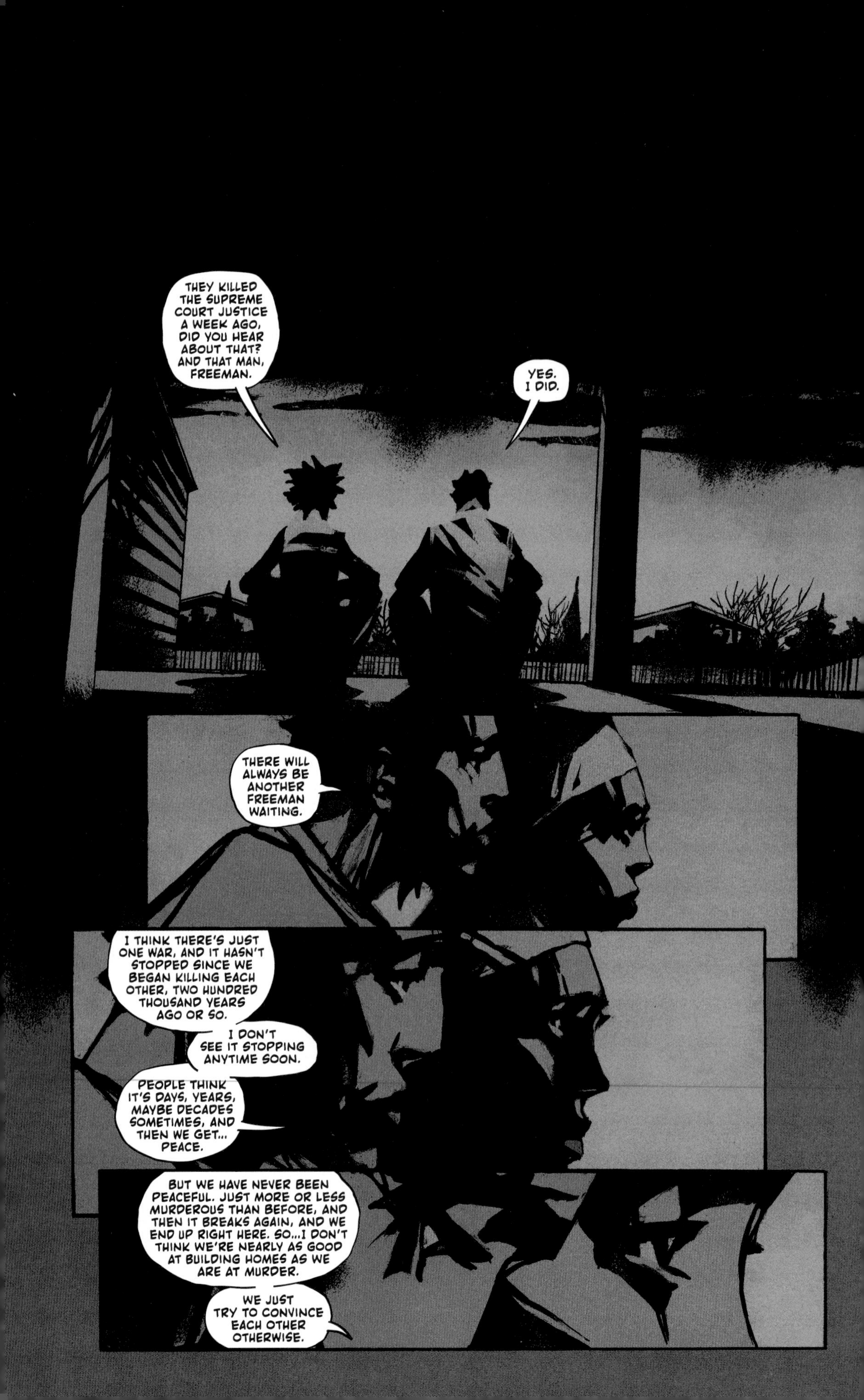
THEY KILLED THE SUPREME COURT JUSTICE A WEEK AGO, DID YOU HEAR ABOUT THAT? AND THAT MAN, FREEMAN.
YES. I DID.
THERE WILL ALWAYS BE ANOTHER FREEMAN WAITING.
I THINK THERE'S JUST ONE WAR, AND IT HASN'T STOPPED SINCE WE BEGAN KILLING EACH OTHER, TWO HUNDRED THOUSAND YEARS AGO OR SO.
I DON'T SEE IT STOPPING ANYTIME SOON.
PEOPLE THINK IT'S DAYS, YEARS, MAYBE DECADES SOMETIMES, AND THEN WE GET... PEACE.
BUT WE HAVE NEVER BEEN PEACEFUL. JUST MORE OR LESS MURDEROUS THAN BEFORE, AND THEN IT BREAKS AGAIN, AND WE END UP RIGHT HERE. SO...I DON'T THINK WE'RE NEARLY AS GOOD AT BUILDING HOMES AS WE ARE AT MURDER.
WE JUST TRY TO CONVINCE EACH OTHER OTHERWISE.

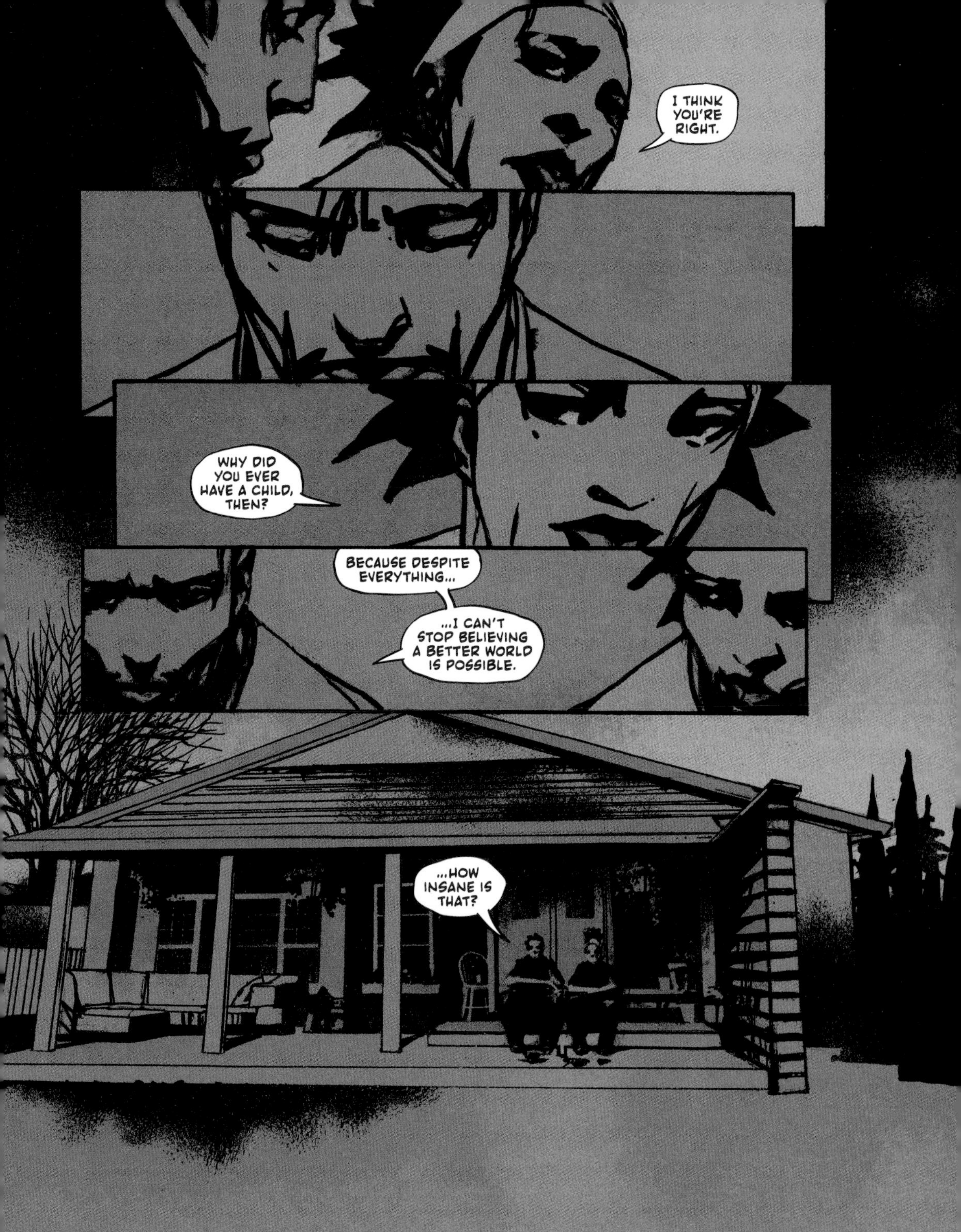
I THINK YOU'RE RIGHT.
WHY DID YOU EVER HAVE A CHILD, THEN?
BECAUSE DESPITE EVERYTHING...
...I CAN'T STOP BELIEVING A BETTER WORLD IS POSSIBLE.
...HOW INSANE IS THAT?

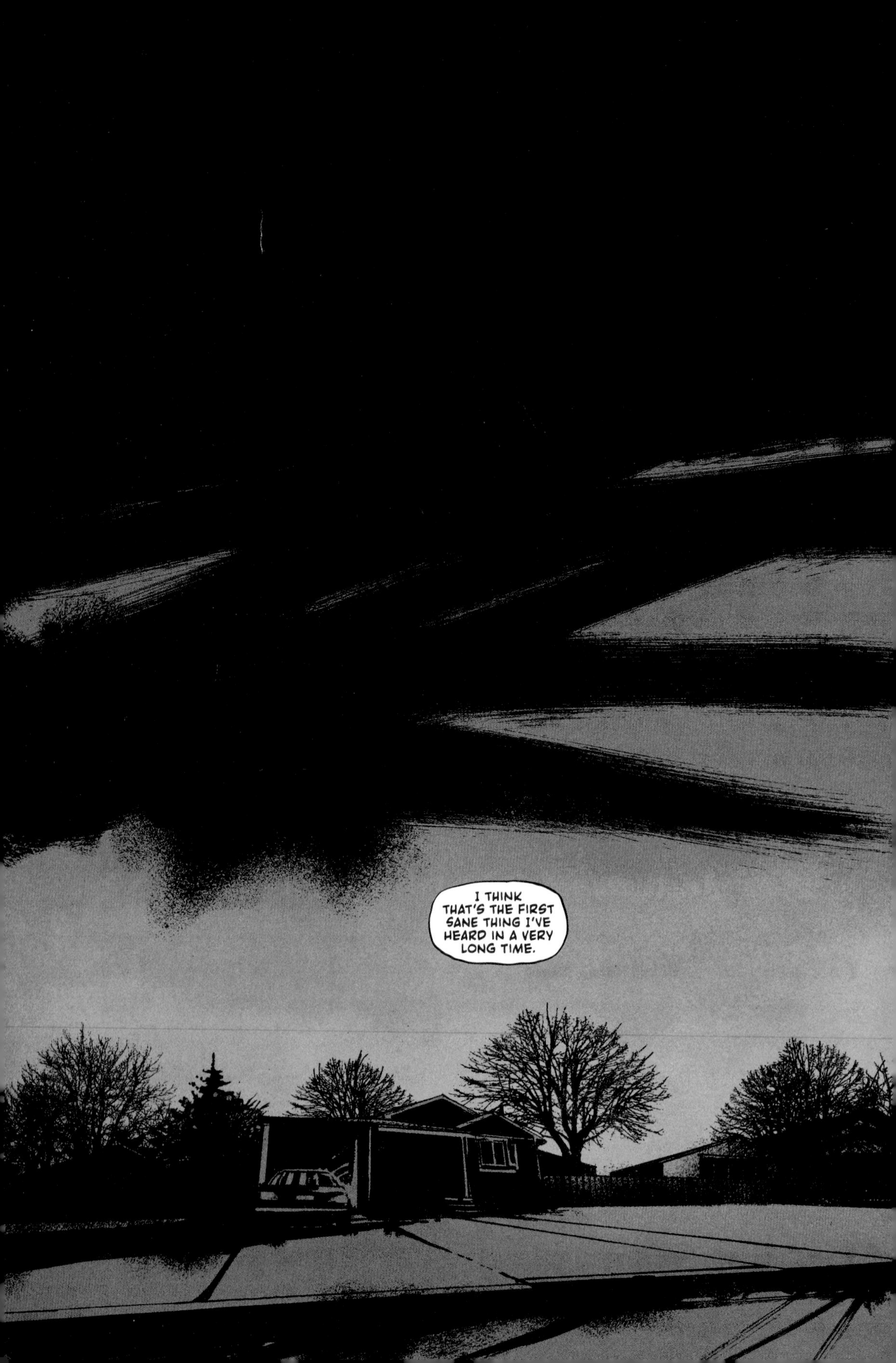
I THINK THAT'S THE FIRST SANE THING I'VE HEARD IN A VERY LONG TIME.

DEDICATED TO THE LOST,
AND TO THOSE WHO
WILL SURVIVE.

RECOMMENDED MEDIA:

Kier-La Janisse
HOUSE OF PSYCHOTIC WOMEN

Roberto Bolaño
DISTANT STAR

J.G. Ballard
HIGH-RISE

Grouper
DRAGGING A DEAD DEER UP A HILL

Hanif Abdurraqib
THEY CAN'T KILL US UNTIL THEY KILL US

Sarah Kendizior
THE VIEW FROM FLYOVER COUNTRY: DISPATCHES FROM THE FORGOTTEN AMERICA

Andy Stott
FAITH IN STRANGERS

Anne Carson
IF NOT, WINTER: FRAGMENTS OF SAPPHO